WHISPERS OF BLACKWELL HOUSE

AMÉLIA COGNET

ALSO BY AMÉLIA COGNET

To my mother-in-law Cecile, who has been cheering me on from the start even if my books kinda scare her.

PROLOGUE

They'll know. And they'll catch me.

The thought hounds me as I stumble blindly through the woods, my blood pumping in my ears. Dead leaves crunch under my shoes, and tree trunks creak around me, their spindly branches snagging at my clothes. Even in such darkness, I can find my way. I've spent enough time in this godforsaken place to know the layout by heart.

Branches groan behind me, making me stop. I listen, my mind racing, my heart pounding in my chest. No one knows I'm here. They *can't* know.

"Hello?" a voice says behind me.

My stomach drops. I can't let anyone stop me. I can't let them catch me when I'm so close to freedom.

The person hiding in the dark behind me speaks again, the words snatched away by the unforgiving wind. I don't listen or answer as I bolt forward, trying to put as much distance between us.

The sound of the angry waves crashing against the rocks reaches my ears. The icy wind slaps my face as I break through the tree line, panting. Though I can't see a thing, I know the ocean is a deep black under the dark sky, the razor-sharp rocks waiting below. The edge of the cliff, just a few feet ahead, is daring me to come closer and look down. I feel the pull of the drop before me. Goosebumps cover my legs, and a cold sweat breaks down my back.

In such darkness, at least I don't have to look down. I only need to take a few steps forward and let gravity do me in. And if by some miracle my broken body doesn't die, the ocean will pull me into its cold embrace and finish the work, slamming me against the base of the cliff and dragging me under. No man can escape these frothing waves. No soul can escape this place. I certainly never could.

I need to hurry, or they'll catch me. My feet feel like bricks as I step to the edge. The whistling wind and the roaring ocean fill my head, and my skin prickles the further I walk. Three, four, five steps. I stop, listening to the thundering waves directly below me. One more step. That's all I need. One more, and I'll never feel pain again.

Taking a deep breath and flexing my numb fingers, I let myself fall forward. That's when I hear the voice behind me. A piercing scream that sets my teeth on edge and sends my heart to my throat. But it's too late. I feel the sickening rush through my stomach as my body drops. It's cut off harshly as my bones shatter against the sharp edges of the cliff.

CHAPTER ONE

River climbed the four floors to her small apartment. Tiles broke under her shoes, and she didn't dare touch the banister for fear that it would collapse or give her splinters. Her feet ached from her workday at the coffee shop, and her neck felt tight. Wild, curly ginger hair obscured her vision, reminding her to straighten herself back up.

Zach's laugh seeped through the front door and made her stop. At least *he* was happy, as though their breakup had breathed new life into him. After squaring her shoulders, River unlocked the door and stepped inside, intending to go straight to her room after making herself a TV dinner. Instead, she froze, listening.

"Yeah, don't worry, she'll move out soon," Zach said. He was standing in the tiny living room, his back to her as he looked through the window, completely oblivious to her presence. The afternoon sun outlined his fit frame and tousled, brown hair. "I can't exactly throw her out. I'll talk to her about it again."

A female voice answered him, though River couldn't hear what she was saying. She just stood there, numbed by exhaustion, sadness and anger making her teeth clench. No matter what she said or which questions she asked, he would deny it—no, of course he hadn't left her because he'd met someone else. He had left her because after three years together, she wasn't good enough anymore. Too curvy, clothes that weren't sexy, hair too thick, too curly, or too many freckles on her face that she could have the decency to at least *try* hiding with makeup.

"I don't know, honestly," Zach said. "She was always a bit weird. I mean, all that voodoo crap?" He burst into laughter. "I hope she's not gonna curse me or some shit."

The words stung her heart. Although her habits had become a pet peeve of his, he had never insulted her like this. Not in front of her anyway. The crystals she carried everywhere in a navy-blue velvet bag, the glass jars full of herbs she placed in the apartment, lighting a candle and drinking rosemary tea every morning, all of that was once seen as quirky and cute. Now, it was judged as weird and annoying and often made him roll his eyes.

River stepped the rest of the way over the threshold and slammed the door.

Zach whirled around, his eyes widening. "I gotta go," he said into the phone. "I'll talk to you later." He hung up, then cleared his throat. "Hey."

There were so many things she wanted to tell him. To *scream* at him. But the words failed her, stuck in her throat. It wasn't as if anything she'd say would change their situation. When Zach had broken up with her two weeks ago, she had just sat there, eyes burning while he told her how she had changed and he just wasn't attracted to her anymore. She hadn't said a word then, and she wasn't going to start now. She headed to the tiny kitchen and opened the freezer to grab a box of frozen lasagna.

"Hey, um…" Zach said, as he joined her, scratching at his head. "Any luck with finding an apartment?"

River put the tray in the microwave and waited. "I was at work all day, so no. And it's hard to find something I can afford. I'll keep looking."

"Maybe you should look for another job?"

She turned. "I know you want me out."

"It's not that, River. It's just that… this situation is as unpleasant for you as it is for me."

"I'm doing my best, okay?"

He sighed, nodding. "I know."

She turned her back to him, waiting for the crappy meal to finish heating up. Her grandma would roll over in her grave if she saw it. She had loved to cook, and she had gifted River her recipe book for her twenty-third birthday, the last birthday they spent together before her grandma died only a few months ago. The thought of it tightened her throat.

Having lost her parents at a young age, River had been raised by her grandma, Willow. She'd loved the woman more than anyone, and her absence had carved a deep hole in River's heart. She used to cook for Zach and herself, but since their breakup, this kitchen, the whole apartment, didn't feel like hers anymore. She was just an unwanted guest.

Zach couldn't wait for her to leave, but she was lucky he was letting her stay until she could find her own place. She had nowhere else to go, no one to ask for help. And with her salary as a barista, it was nearly impossible to find even a studio in New York within her budget. The only reason her and Zach could afford this one-bedroom apartment was because they shared the rent.

At least you have the bedroom while you still live here.

"These aren't good for you," he said, as the microwave beeped.

"The food I'm eating is none of your concern anymore."

He shrugged. "Doesn't mean I don't care about your health. You've let yourself go recently."

A heavy sigh escaped River's mouth. "My grandma died, okay?"

"That was *months* ago."

She turned to him, staring, a million words swirling in her mind but dying on her tongue. Finally, she asked the question she had been wanting to ask this whole time. "Is that why we broke up? Because I'm sad?"

He scratched his head again, a clear sign that he was uncomfortable. She hoped he would backtrack. Just say something nice. But that wasn't Zach's style. If he had an opinion, he couldn't keep it to himself. "Not because you're sad, but... you *did* gain a little weight. It's not good for you."

"You mean for *you.*"

They stared at each other for a moment. Her anger was progressively stifled by the sight of him, his mesmerizing green eyes and his tousled hair. A lump swelled in her throat. She should walk away and lock herself in the room. Cut short this conversation that was only meant to torture her. Against her better judgement, she decided to hurt herself further. "Is *she* healthy? The girl you met?"

He sighed, rolling his eyes. "I haven't met anyone."

"Don't lie to me. I might be naïve, but I'm not stupid. I know she was the one you were talking to earlier. Is she prettier than me? Is she thin and athletic? Is that why you're leaving me?"

"I'm leaving you because I don't love you, is it really that hard to understand? I was bored, all right? We fell into a routine. We lost our spark. You stopped caring about your appearance, you eat like crap, you can't even bother to wear some makeup to look pretty. I didn't sign up for this, okay? I didn't break up with you because of her, but because of *you.*"

River dropped her gaze to the floor, now uncomfortable in her own skin under his stare. So many things she wanted to say. So many slaps she wished she could give him. But her mind went blank. She took her plate and left the room on numb legs. Tears flowed freely down her cheeks by the time she closed the bedroom door.

She dropped onto the bed, burying her face in her hands to silence her sobs. How pathetic. Of course, it was her fault. She wasn't good enough, was she? She reached inside her jeans pocket and took out the little blue bag, dropping the crystals into her palm. A rough purple amethyst and a rose quartz for healing. A smooth, long white selenite and an oval purple lepidolite for peace. A black tourmaline, irregular and streaked with white, for protection. The last one, River's favorite, was the black obsidian she was wearing as a necklace, fixed to a silver chain. It was perfectly round and smooth and shiny, a rune engraved on each side. Runes her grandma had carved herself. *Oak* and *Aspen.*

"For protection, strength, and healing," Willow had said, pointing to *Oak,* as she handed a twelve-year-old River her birthday gift. "And this," she turned the obsidian around, "is for *Aspen.* The sacred Celtic whispering tree."

"Why did they call it the whispering tree?" River asked.

"It's associated with language and communication. They believed it had the power to communicate with the next world."

River had run her thumb over the smooth stone, feeling the rune under her skin, then looked up at her grandma. "The next world?"

Willow nodded.

"Can you communicate with the next world, Grandma?"

"I can. So will you one day."

River chuckled, shaking her head. "I'm not magic like you."

"We all have a little bit of magic inside of us, sweetie. But you… you have a lot. I can tell. And when the time comes, don't turn your back on your gift. Embrace it fully and trust yourself."

Willow had smiled, making her eyelids crease around her deep blue eyes. Despite the wrinkles on her skin and the long, flowy white hair, those eyes were bright and young. Even at the end of her life, with a frail body and shaking hands, her eyes had always sparkled, especially when teaching River about Celtic symbols and history.

River was proud to have inherited those eyes, although the 'magic' she was supposed to possess was nowhere to be seen. Zach liked to make fun of her because as much as she had loved the stories when she was a kid, River had never practiced and didn't really believe any of it. The history and symbols, yes, but not the magical properties that her grandma said the crystals or the tea or the glass jars had. She had only started doing certain rituals since her grandmother had passed away as a way to honor her memory, or maybe as a way of coping and finding comfort. The candle she lit every morning while drinking rosemary tea was for Willow. Rosemary had always been her favorite and the mug was hers as well. Chipped on the side, covered with intricate vines and pink and purple flowers. The type that could only be found in an antique shop. And if any of those things truly provided protection or healing or peace, then River would take as much as she could get.

Her appetite gone, River abandoned her plate on the nightstand and snatched her laptop, placing it on her lap as she rested back against the headboard. She needed a new place to live as soon as possible, but her search so far had been unsuccessful, making her a little more desperate each day.

She scrolled for a long time, the realization that she not only needed a new place but a new job as well sinking in. There was no way she could afford to live alone in Manhattan. She needed to go somewhere else, and depending on how far, she'd probably have to work somewhere else.

After looking for potential places to live, she looked at different job offers to get a feel of what was available. All the same low-paying, dead-end type of jobs began blending together after a while. She was about to close the window when an offer caught her eye.

Housemaid wanted. $500 per week. Housing included.
"Housing included... Feels shady."
It had to be fake. Or misleading. Still, River clicked and read the description.

Housemaid needed at the Blackwell House, Stormhedge, Maine.

The Blackwell family is in need of a new maid to be part of the cleaning staff.

Tasks include but are not limited to: cleaning the floors and dusting the furniture, washing the windows, doing laundry, changing the sheets, cleaning the bathrooms, and serving meals.

Housing included. $500 per week with one day off.

River read the offer again. There was no picture of the place. Was that even real? She had never heard of a town Stormhedge in

Maine. She wouldn't mind the pay, and it would solve the housing problem. But it wasn't in New York.

Frowning, River opened a new tab and typed the words *Stormhedge, Maine.* The map zoomed in on the place, showing her what looked like a tiny village with colorful roofs close to a harbor. It was way up north, as close to Canada as it got. The place was surrounded by the ocean on one side and kilometers of forest on the other. Upon further research, Stormhedge seemed to be a quiet place with a coffee shop, a mini mart, a florist, an inn, and a library. Outside of the main street, little houses stood apart from each other, becoming more and more sparse the further they were from the village.

Who the hell needs a live-in maid out there? They mentioned a staff, so that means there are several people working there.

She read the details again. The Blackwell family. River looked it up, but nothing came up. Not only did these people offer good pay, but they had more than one person working for them. It seemed quite bizarre in a place like that, small and quiet and nearly invisible on the map.

River stared at the screen for what could have been a minute or an hour, her fingers brushing the runes carved in the obsidian.

"What should I do, Grandma?"

Willow had never been fond of the city. She used to live in Upstate New York, in a little house surrounded by trees. River had loved it. It was always quiet, and the birds sang in the morning during spring. Maybe moving to a similar place would help her heal. Find her roots again, surrounded by the nature her grandmother had loved so much, though according to her stories, no prairie or forest or hill would ever be as lush and green as the plains of Ireland.

River's fingers moved before she could think. She hit *reply* and submitted for the job.

CHAPTER TWO

F ive days and still nothing. It wasn't surprising, really. She
didn't have any experience in housekeeping. Still, a surprising
feeling of disappointment weighed her down as the days passed.
In just a short while, she had grown fond of the idea of leaving
New York. Of starting fresh where Zach couldn't hurt her and
make her feel less than. Of living a simple life in a small village
where hopefully no one ever ordered a venti iced coffee with
twelve pumps of sugar-free vanilla sirup, ten pumps of sugar-free
hazelnut sirup, ten pumps of sugar-free caramel, six pumps of
skinny mocha, a splash of soy, coconut flakes, and whipped cream.

"Venti iced coffee for Jan," River called out, as she settled the
drink onto the counter.

She turned away, brushing back a thick, ginger strand of hair springing free from the giant hair clip that apparently still wasn't big enough to conceal even the top half of her mane.

"You forgot the whipped cream," a voice called behind her.

River looked at the girl named Jan. She held the cup in one hand, still holding her phone with the other, her eyebrows raised, and her perfect lips opened a fraction in bewilderment.

River glanced at the cup filled to the brim with whipped cream. "Um, I did put the whipped cream."

"I said *extra* whipped cream. Do it again."

"Oh… My apologies. I'll add some extra for you," she said, taking the cup.

"It's too late. It's ruined now. Make a new one." She gaped at River, blinking her fake eyelashes impatiently.

"Adding the cream now will taste the same as if I had added it a minute ago."

"Don't you know the customer is always right? I want you to make it again, or I'm not coming back here."

Oh no, what a loss.

Heat burned River's cheeks. She had always been a pushover, and even at her job, she had to keep quiet and let herself be bullied by entitled customers.

Stephen, her manager, stepped up and took over. "We apologize for the inconvenience. She's going to redo it right away."

He raised his eyebrows at her, giving her the stink eye, while the girl stared at River with a smirk on her face. River nodded and quickly remade this insanely complicated iced coffee, with extra whipped cream this time. If she'd had some guts like some of her coworkers, she would have spit in it given the opportunity, but that wasn't like her. Just the thought of it brought some comfort, though.

"Here you go," she tried to say as nicely as possible, straining to offer some kind of a smile.

The girl huffed and snatched the cup out of her hand before spinning around and leaving the coffee shop.

River hurried to make the other orders waiting for her when Stephen lightly tapped on her shoulder.

"Come see me during your break."

Already tired of this day, River took a deep breath, holding the black stone of her necklace to center herself, then set out to work again. She went fast, catching up on the orders she should have made instead of redoing a stupid iced latte.

This job wasn't bad though. She liked it, even. Making frappes and macchiatos and lattes was fine, and she got along with her coworkers well enough. It just wasn't what she had envisioned for herself, and certainly not what her grandma would have wanted.

River dreamed of owning her own coffee shop and bakery. An Irish coffee shop. A place that would be warm and cozy with a space dedicated to board games like the ones Willow had gone to when she lived in Ireland. She would make and sell sweet Irish soda bread and Barmbrack and apple crumble cake. Irish tea cakes and scones as well.

The dream seemed attainable while she lived in Upstate New York. When her grandma was there to fuel it. But then, she had met Zach and had moved with him to Manhattan. She had tried to convince herself that she could make it here, but the competition was tough in such a big city, and she had put her dream on hold to try to save money.

During her lunch break, River sat at one of the small tables with the stocky manager. He sighed, crossing his arms and looking at her in a way he probably hoped was diplomatic.

"What's going on?" he asked.

River shrugged. "Nothing."

"You've been distracted lately."

"I haven't. I never make mistakes. Usually—"

"Well, you did this morning."

She flexed and unflexed her fingers over her lap. "It won't happen again, I promise."

"It's not just what happened this morning. Something's been up with you lately. You're… I don't know, moody. You need to smile more. Pamper yourself. Look at Claire." He gestured toward her coworker, a sweet girl who smiled easily and was naturally pretty. "She's outgoing, she takes care of herself, she's extra nice with men—"

"What does that even mean?"

"Don't scare our customers away is what it means. Have a makeover or something. And just *smile.*"

She opened her mouth, but only a stunned little sigh came out. She had been working there for two years. In those two years, she had never missed a day of work, had never been late, had never gotten into trouble, and now, her recent mood was apparently a good reason to tell her she wasn't good enough.

"I just… I went through a breakup a few weeks ago…" she said. "It's been hard."

"Well, pull yourself together. You need to leave your feelings at the door when you're coming in. And wear some makeup, seriously. You look pale as hell."

River nodded, looking down at the table to avoid the looks she was getting from her coworkers, her cheeks burning, which probably made her freckles sparkle like a disco ball. Stephen was an ass, and his comments about her appearance were out of line for a manager, but the sad truth was that River wasn't brave enough to stand up to him, or anyone else for that matter. After losing her grandmother, being dumped, and having to move out, she couldn't afford to lose her job too.

Stephen walked away after making extra sure she apologized and looked like she meant it. River ate her lunch, a breakfast sandwich with a latte, while browsing Instagram on her phone.

A picture caught her attention. Zach's handsome face stared at her, a brilliant smile lighting his features and green eyes. An ache grew in River's heart. Of course he smiled. Why wouldn't he, when he was posing next to the gorgeous blonde with the shiniest hair, his hand tightly clamped around her firm waist?

The caption read: *Had such a nice time with you, as usual.*

And it was followed by three kissing emojis.

Not one, not two, but three.

And of course, she had commented. Bella. Their comments went back and forth, something about an amazing evening with champagne and how she'd make sure to show him her gratitude for inviting her next time.

The coffee turned sour in River's stomach. She already knew he had met someone; she shouldn't be surprised. And yet the shock made her dizzy, and a new wave of sadness sliced through her chest. She clicked on Zach's profile and unfollowed him, her fingers shaking. Her lunch break was up. She needed to get up and go back to work, but her legs refused to move.

Not even a minute later, Stephen called out to her from the other side of the room. "Time's up, River."

Tears pricked her eyes. She took a deep breath.

Keep it together or you'll get fired.

Her phone beeped, showing her the notification for a new email on the screen. A response for the live-in maid. Her heart flipped inside her ribcage.

"River, back to work. *Now.*"

She met Stephen's eyes. His arms were crossed over his chest as he glared at her. Against her better judgement, River unlocked her phone and opened the email, vaguely hearing the manager mumble, "Are you kidding me?"

She quickly scanned the content of the email, heart pounding. The message was short, curt, and almost rude, but she didn't care.

Miss Devin,

When can you start?

Edith Roberts

Seeing Stephen walking toward her out of the corner of her eye, she hit the reply button, her thumbs flying over the keyboard.

Dear Miss Roberts,

I can start as soon as necessary. I just need to plan a day to make the trip to Stormhedge, as I'll be driving there from New York.

I am looking forward to your response.

River Devin

She sprung off her chair and found herself facing her manager.

"Are you *trying* to get fired?" he said loudly, making sure everyone around heard him.

Warmth rose to her cheeks. "I just... I had a really important email to answer to. Family matters..."

The lie made her blush even more, the heat spreading down her back. She hated to lie; it wasn't how her grandmother had raised her. But something told her that if she didn't get this job now, someone would steal it from her. This was her best shot at a fresh start, away from Zach and his gorgeous new girlfriend.

"You'll stay longer at the end of your shift to make up for the lost time."

"Yes. Of course." She was only a minute late, but okay. Whatever kept him sane.

"Hurry up," he said, turning away.

River gathered her trash, ready to put the phone in her pocket when it beeped again, making her freeze.

Stephen stared at her, a scowl on his face. "Go back to work. I mean it."

A quick glance to the screen told her it was a response from Miss Roberts, the woman posting the listing.

"All right, give me your phone," Stephen said.

What was this, high school? River reached for her phone, hesitated, then quickly unlocked it.

"River, give me your phone *now*. You don't want to cross me."

Defying authority wasn't something she was used to doing, but at this moment, for the first time, River didn't care. She couldn't keep the smile from stretching her lips as she read the email.

Miss Devin,

Consider yourself employed by the Blackwell family, starting on Tuesday, September 20th. I attached your contract to this email. Please print it, sign it, and bring it back with you on your first day. Also bring a copy of your ID.

We will see you in two days.

It was without a doubt the weirdest way River had ever been employed. Everything about it was odd. No interview. No phone call. No questions asked or background check. Miss Roberts didn't even want to wait for River to send the signed contract back before hiring her. But she didn't care. She had found a way out. The fresh start she had wanted was being handed to her. She would finally be able to save money for the Irish coffee shop she wanted so much, and she didn't have to worry about finding a new place to live.

Stephen got right up close, anger dancing in his eyes. "I don't want to have to fire you right now, but I'll do it if you don't do as I say."

Feeling light and hopeful for the first time in months, River looked up at him, biting back on a smile. "No need to fire me, *Steve.* I quit."

River considered the open suitcase on her bed. Her whole life fit in it, which was a bit pathetic. Most of the space was filled with clothes, not because she owned a lot, but because a few fluffy sweaters took more space than she had thought. The rest was for the toiletries, the lavender scented lotion and shampoo, the glass jars full of herbs she had made, the tea, and the recipe notebook her grandma had given her.

For the first time since moving into this apartment, River was grateful to own a Kindle instead of books. Zach didn't want her to buy books. He said they were taking unnecessary space, so she had bought a Kindle. Once she saved enough money to open her coffee shop and have her own place, she would splurge on the biggest shelves she could find and fill them with hundreds of books.

This place had always been Zach's. She barely owned anything and had barely been able to make any additions to the apartment, except maybe for kitchen utensils. It was in his interest, after all, that she cooked for him.

New start, new you. You need to learn to stand up for yourself.

The contract she had printed lay on the bed. She hadn't read or signed it yet, too eager to start packing. River sat down and scanned it. It was only one page long, with barely anything written on it. It was just a reminder of her pay and duties. Nothing more, nothing less.

Except there *was* one more thing as River reached the bottom of the page. A disclaimer written in small letters.

"By signing this contract, you agree to not disclose the location of the Blackwell House and keep their family matters private for the entirety of your working period. Failing to do so will result in a lawsuit."

"Geez, okay." She grabbed the pen from the nightstand and signed the paper. "That seems a little excessive, but I guess they just want their privacy."

The sound of the front door opening stole her attention. She stood, a knot tying her stomach as Zach walked in. He glanced in her direction, frowning as he eyed the suitcase on the bed.

"Going somewhere?" he asked, standing in the bedroom door-way.

"Yes, actually. I'm moving out."

His eyebrows shot up. "You are? Like, now?"

"Tomorrow morning."

"Well…" He smiled. "You found a place after all. Where is it? Brooklyn? I told you it'd be more affordable there—"

"I'm going to Maine."

Zach's mouth hung open for a moment, his smile gone. *"Maine?"*

Anxiety squeezed her chest. She had thought she'd be happy to tell him that. But she wasn't, and she couldn't help but twist her fingers together as though afraid she was going to be scolded. "Yeah, uh… I found a job there."

"Doing what?" There was an edge in his voice.

Suddenly, saying *housemaid* sounded incredibly dumb. Something he would clearly make fun of. "Housekeeper. For a rich family. The pay is really good, and housing is included. I start the day after tomorrow."

Zach registered the info, saying nothing.

"I thought you'd be happy for me," she said, offering a shy smile. "And we'll both finally be able to move on, right?"

"Yeah, but… Maine? I didn't think you'd leave that fast or go that far, and I guess I…"

"What?"

He scratched his hair, disheveling it a little more, and River was dying to run her fingers through it like she used to. "I guess I sort of thought I'd still see you around. I'm gonna miss you."

It felt like a dagger piercing her heart.

Then, tell me to stay. Tell me you still love me. I'll make it work. I'll be better.

24

She stared at him, her throat tight, hoping he would beg her to take him back, hoping he'd realize he would lose her for good if he didn't do anything.

Eventually, he shrugged. "But sure, I'm happy for you. Congrats. Don't forget to give me your key back."

CHAPTER THREE

I t took almost ten hours to reach Stormhedge by car, twelve if she counted the breaks she took to eat and stretch her legs. River had left at five in the morning, hoping to avoid most of the traffic on her way out of New York. The rest of the drive had been uneventful, peaceful even. She took this opportunity to listen to an audiobook and enjoy her favorite Celtic music, which Zach didn't like, once again reminding her that they didn't have much in common. She'd thought they did, probably because she had tried to be like him, to meet his expectations. In the beginning, her quirks and flaws were seen as cute and original. After a while, they were perceived as annoying and weird, so it had been better not to be herself too much.

The sky turned dark by the time she entered the small village. She slowed, searching left and right for a clue about where to go.

The GPS couldn't find the Blackwell House, so River had only put Stormhedge. Now that she was there, she had no idea where to go. The contract didn't give much information.

The main street looked dark and dead like a ghost town. In the night, it didn't fit the colorful picture River had seen on the internet. She could hear the ocean raging somewhere to her left while a sharp wind slammed against the car, rocking it. Ahead, a single building seemed to have its lights on. They shone weakly through dusty windows. River parked along the sidewalk, squinting to read the name above the front door.

Storm Inn.

Glancing around herself and seeing nothing but an empty road, River killed the engine and exited the car. The icy air slapped her face, slicing through the fabric of her sweater. She tasted salt on her lips. She snatched her coat from the passenger seat and put it on, shuddering as her hands turned numb, then hurried inside.

Dimmed lights and a smell of potpourri greeted her. A carpeted hallway stretched in front of her. The reception desk stood to her right, where a man with white hair and large glasses blinked at her.

"May I help you?" His voice, though a bit croaky, was warm and welcoming.

River approached the reception desk. "Hi. I'm looking for a house, but I'm afraid I don't have the exact address."

"That'll be hard to find it then," he said, the corners of his mouth quirking up.

She let out a small chuckle. "My thoughts exactly. Would you happen to know where the Blackwell family lives?"

His smile vanished, and his eyes hardened behind his glasses. "You're a new employee, aren't you?"

That made River pause for a second. "Yes… Do you know where they live?"

"Everyone does. It's not hard to find. Just keep following the main street until you're out of the village, then you'll see a path through the forest with a sign. Follow it."

"Through the… forest?"

"Drive slowly, the road is bad. You wouldn't want to burst a tire and get stuck there. The closest mechanic is a dozen miles away."

"Thank you so much. I'll be careful."

River edged toward the door, stopping when the man said, "You can still turn back."

The words sent a chill running down her spine. They sounded sad and ominous, as though all the luck in the world wouldn't be enough to protect her. She considered him for a moment, unable to find an appropriate response. "Why would I turn back?"

The man pushed his glasses up his nose and flattened his white hair. When he looked back up, he had fixed a brand new, plastic smile on his face. "Good luck on your new job."

"Um… thanks."

She hurried outside, uneasiness spreading through her, and jumped back into her car. Chilled to the bone, she cranked up the heat and drove slowly between the closed shops, the encounter playing on a loop in her mind. As she exited the town, River found herself in the darkness. No more streetlights flanked the road. Her eyes scanned her surroundings, frantically searching for a sign that would tell her where to go. The trees thickened on all sides, the car's headlights struggling to pierce through the dark and the mist that was rolling in.

The road took a sharp turn to the right, and River wondered if she had missed the path the inn keeper had been talking about. She stopped in the middle of the bend, making sure no one came the opposite way, and made a U-turn. The front tires left the cement and sank into the soft dirt. Before she could back up, a worn down, wooden sign caught her eye.

Blackwell House.

River hesitated, her gaze trained on the shadowed path before her, a path swallowed by darkness and mist and crooked branches. A deep sigh escaped her mouth as she wrapped her fingers around the necklace underneath her coat.

"It looks like a horror movie… I'm in a horror movie." She put the car in drive and inched forward, shaken by the thick roots and rocks under her tires. "I don't have main character vibes, so I'll probably die soon. Well," she chuckled, trying to reassure herself with the sound of her own voice, "I'm not blonde, so maybe not *too* soon."

The trees closed in as she went, their branches scratching the roof of the car as though trying to consume her. Her heart refused to slow down, and her palms had turned clammy as she gripped the steering-wheel. Her muscles were sore and numb from the long drive, and the thought of the warm little apartment in Manhattan made her feel homesick. She missed the movie nights in Zach's arms, the two of them huddled under a blanket and eating take-out.

What was she thinking, quitting her job like that and moving hundreds of miles away to a village she had never heard of? Was she that desperate?

The answer was crystal clear as she made her way into the threatening woods. Yes, she was. It was a mistake to think she could have stayed in Manhattan. If her grandma hadn't sold her house, River would have gone there, to Upstate New York. In her childhood home, close to the small town she had grown up in. Not to Murder Forest.

Tendrils of fog curled around the trees. The movement reminded River of people hiding behind the trunks, peeking out from behind them to watch her. She kept her eyes trained on what was before her, worrying that the path would never end, that the forest closing in would soon trap her car and never let it go. But after what felt like hours, the trees cleared, and she was in the open. The mist danced in front of the headlights, but she knew she was still close to the ocean, the sound of the roaring waves heard even from inside the car.

No house was anywhere to be seen, and it suddenly occurred to her that she had blindly trusted that weird ad for that weird job that paid way too well. She hadn't questioned it for one second, too desperate for a fresh start. She might have fallen for a trap, and now someone was hiding behind a tree with an ax, waiting for her to get out of her car.

You're being stupid, stop it!

A dark silhouette emerged from the fog in front of the car, immobile, its stare fixed on her. River gasped and slammed the brakes. The shape before her didn't move. With a new wave of mist rolling in, it disappeared. River's breath caught in her throat as she looked around, but she couldn't see anything.

A sharp knock at her window made her cry out. A bony face stared at her from the other side—a woman in her sixties with gray hair tied into a tight bun.

Swallowing around the lump in her throat, River rolled the window down, the cold air instantly biting at her skin.

"Miss Devin?" the woman asked, and River now knew who she was talking to.

"Yes. Miss Roberts?"

"It's about time." Miss Roberts straightened up and pointed to a wide, open shed. "You can park your car there."

Her mouth dry and her voice almost gone from shock, River simply nodded. She zipped her coat all the way up and put the thick, wool beanie over her wild hair. Miss Roberts stood straight with her fingers laced together, seemingly unbothered by the cold, as River pulled her suitcase from the trunk.

"Did you bring the contract back?" she asked.

"Um, yes." She fumbled with her purse to find the two folded sheets and handed them over to Miss Roberts. "With the copy of my ID."

She took them, made sure the contract was signed, then slipped everything inside the pocket of her gray coat. "This had better not be too heavy," she said, pointing at the suitcase. "It's a bit of a walk to the staff's quarters."

With that, she turned away and walked through the fog like a ghost. River did her best to keep up, as she pulled her luggage over spongy, uneven ground.

"I'm sorry for getting here this late," River said, already out of breath. "I wanted to call you to let you know, but there wasn't any phone number on the contract."

"I don't own a phone. And even if I did, it would be useless here. There's no signal. No internet as well."

"Oh…"

Miss Roberts stopped walking and turned to look at her, eyebrows raised, though the rest of her face was stoic and expressionless. "Will that be a problem?"

"No. Of course not." It wasn't like she had anyone to call.

Miss Roberts whirled around and kept walking, her motion stiff.

"Wait, if you don't have the internet here, how did you post the job offer and answer my email?"

"The local library has old computers we can use."

"Do you often go downtown?"

"Once a week during my day off. Stormhedge is the only place where we can buy our food."

That explained why it had taken five days for Miss Roberts to answer River's inquiry.

River almost tripped on a root, still fighting to keep her suitcase upright. "I suppose you could drive further, but it *is* pretty isolated here."

"I don't own a car."

"You don't?"

"No. We walk to Stormhedge. Cars tend to break down easily here. I suspect because of the salt and humidity. The path is treacherous and will damage your car if you drive it too often. Walking will be a better option for you too."

As someone who had lived a few years in New York, some walking didn't scare her. But the thought of crossing those creepy woods alone and on foot wasn't exactly exciting.

"Where is the house exactly?" River asked. "I can't see anything."

"It's directly to our right, but the fog is thick tonight."

River glanced right, squinting. A few yellow, blurred lights barely shone through the mist. Although she could discern neither the walls nor the roof, those lights seemed to rise high above the ground. "How big is the Blackwell House exactly?"

"Big."

The ground, squishy under River's feet, seemed to go downhill a little. Despite the thick coat and hat, the moisture drenching the air seeped through her clothes, chilling her to the bone. Her breath misted out of her mouth, and humidity clung to her face. Her hair, already curly and thick, was probably a frizzy mess right now. She wondered how long they would keep going like this when Miss Roberts stopped abruptly, and the sound of a door squeaking open made River look up. They had reached a doorway leading into a long hallway. She couldn't even make up the building around the door, the fog saturating the space around them.

"Hold the door, please," Miss Roberts said, looking for something inside her coat pocket.

River reached for the long, thick handle attached to the heavy door and wrapped her fingers around it. A sharp point sunk into the soft skin of her index. River gasped, pulling her hand off the handle. Miss Roberts snapped her head in her direction, looking faintly annoyed, and caught the door before it slammed shut.

River inspected her finger in the dark. A bead of blood formed in the middle of it. "Sorry. I cut myself."

Her lips tightening into a thin line, Miss Roberts fished a tissue from her pocket and handed it to River without a word before stepping inside the hallway. River pressed the tissue against her finger and hurried after the woman, grateful to get out of the freezing cold.

Miss Roberts shed her coat, and in the low light, River realized that she was wearing a uniform—a straight, long-sleeve black button-down dress that reached her knees, black tights, and a white apron covering her chest and thighs. She headed to an old armoire standing halfway down the hallway and opened it.

"What size do you wear?"

Really? A uniform? That's gotta be a joke.

But Miss Roberts's stoic face told her that it was anything but a joke.

"Um, fourteen."

The older woman rummaged for a moment before taking out two dresses, two aprons, and two pairs of tights. "Shoe size?"

Really, the shoes too?

She looked down at Miss Roberts's feet, biting down on her bottom lip to keep herself from wincing. The black, shiny dress shoes were not only ugly but seemed uncomfortable as well.

"Miss Devin. Your shoe size, please."

"Nine."

Miss Roberts pulled out a pair of shoes and dropped them onto the pile of clothes she was holding. "Follow me."

River obeyed and followed the woman. She stopped next to an open doorway, and River peeked inside. The kitchen was modest but pretty with bricks encrusted into the walls. A rectangular, heavy table stood in the middle surrounded by six chairs. It was fully equipped with a stove, a fridge, and a microwave.

"This is our kitchen. The shared food goes inside this pantry." She pointed to a door on the left-hand side of the room. "You can use one basket on the shelf for your personal food. If you put something in the fridge that is yours only, write your name on it. You won't have your first paycheck until a week from now so feel free to eat the shared food. Keep in mind that you'll have to replace it."

On the back wall stood long shelves with individual baskets stored on them. Some of them had name tags, and a few were blank.

Miss Roberts nodded to the right side of the room. "Here's the trashcan for your tissue if you need it."

River quickly tossed the stained tissue before following Miss Roberts down the hallway to the right. On the left side, she discovered a large bathroom. To her surprise, four stalls were lined against the right-hand side of the room. A row of sinks with old mirrors above them faced her, and a beat-up armoire loomed to the left.

"Are these... shared?"

"Yes. Towels are in the armoire."

Miss Roberts kept going, and River had to hurry up to keep up with her. That woman waited for no one.

A shared bathroom? Really? She hadn't imagined that when she had read that housing was included. It made her wonder what the bedroom would look like.

She didn't wonder for long. The room before her wasn't like anything she had imagined. It wasn't a bedroom, it was a dormitory. Beds were aligned under the windows against the opposite wall and on each side of the doorway River was standing in. Each of them had a wooden trunk at its feet.

The quiet conversation of the people in the room ceased, and all eyes turned to her, making her feel hot.

"Everyone," Miss Roberts said in her usual dry tone, "this is River. She's replacing Simon."

A few of them said hi, others just stared. They were all women, some as young as River and others older. Miss Roberts stepped inside, and River followed her to the right-hand side of the room, where a young man lay on the bed against the wall, reading a book.

"Thomas," Miss Roberts said.

He put the book down, his eyebrows raised into a question. He was about River's age, probably his mid-twenties, with light brown hair.

"This is your new partner," she said. "From now on, you're in charge of her orientation."

Thomas sat up. "I'm not sure I'm qualified to—"

"It has always been this way, Thomas. If you get a new partner, you're in charge of explaining the rules to them. If I had to do it every time, I would have had to do it hundreds of times."

"Okay… I suppose we're on the same schedule?"

"Yes." She turned to River, dropping the clothes and shoes in her hands. "Thomas will explain to you everything you need to know about your schedule and the way we do things. But before I leave, a few things. You'll get your paycheck weekly. You are responsible for the cleanliness of your bedding area, your cubby in the kitchen, and you must clean up after yourself every time you use the shower. You must wear your uniform at all times in the Blackwell House and always make sure your clothes are clean. You are forbidden to speak to any member of the Blackwell family unless you are directly being spoken to. Do not stare. Make yourself invisible, be quiet, and stand to attention if one of them walks in a room while you're cleaning. If you ever have any question, ask me, not them." Miss Roberts turned to leave but glanced back before walking out, wincing slightly. "And please do something about that hair of yours."

She left without looking back, and for a second, River didn't know what to do with herself.

"She's delightful, isn't she?"

River turned to Thomas, who was smiling at her. "A peach."

"Well, *I* like your hair. And those freckles?" He kissed the tips of his fingers. *"Chef's kiss."*

That got a smile out of her. "I've always hated them."

"I bet everyone at school called you Freckles."

"They opted for Carrot."

Thomas laughed, and his positive energy felt like a soothing balm after such a long and exhausting day. "Don't pay attention to old Roberts. She looks like she hates everyone, but really, when you get to know her, you realize that she actually really *does* hate everyone."

River laughed, something she hadn't done in a while.

"I heard she's been working here for decades. I guess that's how she earned her own bedroom."

River sat on her bed, facing Thomas and putting her uniform aside. "I admit it's not what I imagined when the offer said, 'housing included.'"

"None of us did. It's weird for sure, but for most of us, it's just temporary. And look at the bright side, it could have been *bunkbeds.*"

"When you put it that way..." River chuckled.

"Get some rest, you look tired. You and I are the evening crew. We work from eleven in the morning to eight in the evening. That'll give me some time to explain to you how things work tomorrow morning. Oh, and our day off is Tuesdays."

"Got it. Thanks."

He lay back down and slipped under the covers, picking up his book. "I'm glad they finally found someone. I've been doing my shift alone for two weeks, and I'm exhausted."

After shedding her coat and beanie, River opened her suitcase and rummaged through it to find her warmest night clothes. The room, although heated by an old woodstove, was still chilly. It came from a draught in the window above her bed, she realized.

She raised her head and met a few eyes. She should probably go and introduce herself, but her awkwardness got the best of her. She counted six other maids. This room held fourteen beds, so despite having Thomas directly to her left, the bed to her right seemed to be empty. "Eight people is a lot for just one house."

"It's actually not enough."

"Not enough? For real?"

"You haven't seen the house yet, but trust me, it's *huge*. A freaking castle. And there's not just us, either. There's Roberts, of course, the head chef and his assistant, and in a separate cottage, there's the landscaper's crew."

"They have a *chef*? How rich are these people?"

"Insanely so. Oh, and there's Dorian's personal helper too. That's Simon now. He was my partner, but the last aide left, so Simon was asked by Roberts to replace him."

"Who's Dorian?"

"The son."

"Why does he need a personal aide?"

"He's blind."

"Oh. Well, at least money gets him the help he needs." She rose, holding her pajamas and toiletries in her arms. "Gonna change up."

River headed to the shared bathroom, the chill still clinging to her bones. She would take a warm shower tomorrow. There would be less people, surely, if they were already working. Tonight, she just wanted to change and go to bed.

In the bathroom, the same type of shelf as in the kitchen stood on the wall next to the row of sinks. There were also cubbies in there with names on them. River found an empty one after brushing her teeth and put her stuff inside. She stood there for a moment, wondering if she should get into a shower stall to undress, when a dark-haired girl entered the room, a white towel wrapped around her body.

"Trust me, new girl, no one cares if you're naked. Simon has his own private cottage now, and Thomas is gay, so…" She leaned into a shower stall and turned on the faucet. "I'm Shelly, by the way."

"River. Nice to meet you."

"River?" She chuckled, dropping her towel to the floor. "Weird name."

River quickly changed while Shelly showered, the short encounter enough to make her grateful to work with Thomas and not her. When she went back to the dormitory, the lights were off, the room only lit by the stove heater. The small flames sent shadows dancing across the walls. River discarded her clothes in the trunk at the foot of her bed, planning on taking stuff out of her suitcase when she had some time the day after.

She checked her phone, but just like Miss Roberts had said, there was no signal. She probably lost it as soon as she entered the path leading to this place. Exhausted but uneasy, River slipped into bed, tucking the bag of crystals under her pillow as always. She felt homesick. Homesick and angry at Zach for putting her in this situation. It wasn't like he had intended for things to go this way, and it wasn't like anyone had forced her to take this job, but logic didn't play a role in her swirling emotions.

I miss you, Grandma. If only you were here.

Her eyes burned despite her efforts to keep her feelings to herself. River rolled onto her side, keeping the rest of the room at her back.

"It'll be okay, Freckles," Thomas said, whispering in the dark.

River cleared her throat. "How do you know I'm sad?"

"Because when I first got here, I also thought it sucked balls."

A small chuckle slipped out of her mouth. "Thanks. I needed to hear that."

Someone softly closed the door, and sheets ruffled as the last of them got ready for bed. The room got quieter and quieter, soon filled with the sound of the stormy ocean outside, soothing River's nerves and helping her sleep.

CHAPTER FOUR

W hispers woke River up. It took her a moment to remember where she was, blinking at the wall illuminated only by a struggling ray of moonlight. In the darkness, she recognized the bed next to hers with Thomas in it. At her back, a maid was talking to another, though River couldn't make out the words. They were slurred. She tried to ignore them and shut her eyes, wondering why they were talking in the middle of the night. Or maybe it wasn't that late, and she hadn't been sleeping for long.

The chilly air seeped through her covers. She rolled over, adjusting them, and frowned. The subdued, orange light from the heat stove shone shyly through the dark room. Everyone was asleep. River strained to listen but only caught the whistling wind and the roaring ocean. No one was whispering. Her sleepy brain must have been dreaming.

She laid her head harder on the pillow and forced her eyes shut. She didn't want to be exhausted on her first day of work. She had to sleep.

A whisper rose in the darkness. Her eyes shot open, her gaze scanning the room. It stopped on the bedroom doorway. The door was wide open, and someone stood on the threshold.

River stared at them, her heartbeat picking up. They didn't move. The stove heater's weak light outlined their shape, but River couldn't tell if they were facing the room or not. They just stood, unmoving.

Their head turned. Though the face remained painfully dark, the icy certainty that they were looking right at River spread through her. She gripped the cover tighter and opened her mouth to speak, but the person turned away, slowly, and slipped in the dark hallway.

One of the maids probably needed to go to the bathroom or something. But then why did they stand immobile for so long? And how could they be so quiet? Not even the shuffle of their feet against the floor could be heard. And why didn't they turn the light on?

For reasons she couldn't explain, River threw the covers aside and tiptoed to the doorway. Her rapid heartbeat sent blood rushing to her ears as she leaned to peek into the hallway. The maid entered the kitchen. She seemed weirdly hunched over, as though the weight of her own body was too much to carry.

She might just be thirsty. Leave her alone.

River turned back, ready to ignore the icy chills pooling at the base of her spine and go back to bed. She could see the other maids sleeping peacefully, their bodies a series of bumps the weak light struggled to outline. There were four in the beds under the windows, Thomas included, and three in the beds against the opposite wall.

River stopped halfway to her bed. Four on one side, three on the other. With her, that made eight. The pit in her stomach deepened, and she slowly turned, staring at the dark doorway. None of them was missing, so who was that?

She should wake up Thomas. Someone. Anyone. But before she could realize it, her feet carried her to the hallway. There was nothing to fear. It was probably just Miss Roberts. But the knot in her stomach refused to loosen as she approached the kitchen doorway.

A rasping sound made her freeze. It sounded like labored panting. River swallowed and forced herself to step forward. She peeked into the kitchen.

The person was inside, their back to River. They were hunched over, grunting and swaying back and forth.

"H-hello?" River said, her voice barely audible.

The woman—she thought it was a woman—let out a long, painful groan in response.

River took a step forward, the chill biting at the skin of her face and hands. "Do you need help?"

The woman stopped swaying. She turned her head and pivoted her body to face River. She took a wobbly step forward, another shaky grunt escaping her. Instinctively, River stepped back, irrational fear squeezing her throat. The woman stepped again, then stumbled, a hand raised.

The sudden movement made River scramble back, her heart in her throat. The woman fell to her knees and crawled in River's direction, her labored breathing filling the space.

The light came on, harsh and blinding. River blinked at it for a moment before recovering her vision, her ears pulsing. The kitchen was empty except for her.

"Are you looking for something?"

River whirled around. One of the maids stood in the doorway, her hand still on the light switch. She was in her fifties, light blonde hair peppered with gray.

"Are you okay? You look pale," she said.

River swallowed around the lump in her throat and glanced over her shoulder, making sure the kitchen really was empty. "I'm okay. I wanted some water. I didn't want to turn on the light and wake everyone up. I got turned around. Sorry for disturbing you."

She waited for a judgmental side-eye or an irritated sigh but got a compassionate tilt of the head instead. "Don't worry about it, sweetie. We all have to get up in the middle of the night sometimes. Next time, just turn on the light, or you'll end up hurting yourself." She shuffled to the sink and grabbed two glasses of water from the cupboard above. "I was thirsty too. I'm Annie by the way."

"River. Nice to meet you."

"You'll get used to this old house, don't worry," Annie said, handing River a glass of water. "I know it's intimidating at first."

River drank, the cold water making her shiver a little more. Maybe it would clear her head from any remnants of sleep clouding her brain. She had to have been half-sleeping until now, the anxiety of this new job, this new place, fueling her mind with nightmares. "How long have you been working here?"

"Oh, almost five years now."

River bit back on a wince. She hoped she wouldn't have to stay here for more than a few months, a year max, just enough time to get back on her feet.

"Thomas is a good lad. You'll like working with him, you'll see." Annie rinsed her glass in the sink and left it out to dry. "Don't forget to turn off the light, okay?"

"Sure."

"Goodnight."

Somehow, River doubted it would be a good night.

CHAPTER FIVE

T he next morning was almost entirely spent with Thomas explaining to River how things worked in the staff's quarters,
which was a much needed distraction from the weird nightmare
and restless night she'd had. She was responsible for washing her
clothes and sheets, cleaning after herself in the bathroom and the
kitchen, and doing her own dishes. He showed her the schedule
that told them whose turn it was to clean the floors.

After taking a shower that left her shivering, the water just about
lukewarm, River tried on her uniform for the first time. She looked
at herself in the mirror, wincing at the way the fabric hugged
her curves. It fit well, but she was used to wearing loose clothes.
The white apron around her waist accentuated the effect, and she
regretted not asking Miss Roberts for a size larger. Maybe she'd

have time to rummage through that closet before her shift started. For now, she had to tame her hair.

It was still damp from the shower, and River brushed it the best she could before attempting to make a bun. Even her largest hair tie or scrunchie didn't fit around that gingery mess.

"Braid it," Thomas said, as he entered the bathroom, also wearing a black uniform. He, at least, was spared the obligation of wearing a white apron. "When you're done, I want to show you something before we start."

"What is it?" she answered, trying to make a decent braid, but the strands around her face kept getting loose, and she had to start over.

Thomas stood behind her and swatted her hands away before taking over. "The staff's quarters are an extension of the house. They made it so that we have direct access. Not for our personal comfort but so, you know, they can call a maid at any time. If we go straight to work, you'll only see the inside of the house. I thought we could first go outside so you'd see the giant monstrosity you're about to start cleaning."

River let out a laugh. "Okay, I'd like that."

After brushing her hair thoroughly, Thomas quickly made a perfect braid. It brushed the middle of her back, and when River moved her head, the strands framing her face stayed safely tucked in. "Impressive."

He shrugged. "I have sisters."

They put on their coats and boots and exited through the door that led outside. While thick fog had clouded the view earlier that morning, the day was now bright. The crisp, cold air greeted them as they stepped out. Their breaths plumed. River smiled at the sun, scanning their surroundings. She hadn't been able to see anything the night before.

They faced the woods, thick with red and orange leaves. The sound of the ocean was still there, a constant background noise. When River looked the other way, she gasped at the immensity of the house attached to the staff's quarters.

"That's the back," Thomas said. "Come on, I'll show you around."

She followed him around the building, their shoes squelching in the mud. The forest surrounded the place, but as they rounded the house, the dark blue ocean peeked over the horizon through the tree line. Not far down the slope, a small but cute cottage stood alone.

"What's that?" she asked.

"That's the private cottage for Dorian's helpers. That's where Simon lives now. Lucky bastard. He didn't even invite me."

"Wow, they get their own place?"

"Yes, unlike us peasants."

River laughed.

"I'm serious," he said, though a smirk lifted one corner of his lips. "They call us *'servants.'* If you're not like old Roberts or the chef, you're replaceable. They don't care about making us happy."

River kept glancing at the house, now to their left. Finally, they stopped and faced it.

"Woah," River breathed out.

"I know, right? I don't know why they didn't call it Blackwell motherfucking Castle."

It was gigantic and imposing. Also incredibly beautiful. It stood tall above them. There had to be thirty or forty windows on this side alone between the first and third floor. The high roof was

AMÉLIA COGNET

slanted, and bright green ivy snaked up the gray brick walls, in-
filtrating every crack. It was breathtaking, but the realization that
River would have to clean this thing dampened her admiration.

"Holy hell… I understand why they need so many housemaids.
You were right, it doesn't even look like there's enough of us."

"By the time we're done cleaning, it's time to start over. I'll
show you the schedule. There are three floors and three teams.
This week, we're cleaning the second floor. Next week, the third,
and the next, the first. We all rotate like that."

"Why not just assign a floor to each team?"

"I asked Simon the same thing, and he said he had also asked
before. Roberts decided to make it this way because people were
complaining it wasn't fair. The maids cleaning the upper floors
said it was more work because of all the sheets to change and the
bathrooms to clean. The teams working on the first floor thought
they were at a disadvantage because the rooms are *huge*. Like,
there's a freaking *ballroom*. And a gigantic library that's a pain to
clean with all the shelves. So, Roberts made it so that everyone had
to clean everything. No more complaints."

"I suppose that's fair." River gazed up at the house again, mesmerized by its beauty. "What are they like? The Blackwell family?"

Thomas shrugged. "I hear there used to be a lot of them once.
Not now. Barely a few members. They don't care about us, and
they don't talk to us if they can avoid it. Except Mrs. Blackwell's
brother, Richard. I heard a few things."

"What things?"

"Um…" He hesitated for a moment before continuing. "I heard
he can get inappropriate with some of the maids."

"Oh… Ew."

"Yeah. I didn't mean to scare you, though. I shouldn't have said anything."

"That's okay. I know how to make myself invisible. I'm not pretty, so I'll be fine."

Thomas scowled at her, an eyebrow cocked. "What are you talking about? You're so pretty!" Then, he chuckled and threw an arm around her shoulders, steering her back to their quarters. "But for your sake, I do hope he's allergic to freckles."

A surge of gratitude filled River. Everything about this new job was overwhelming and intimidating. The few maids she had seen that morning had barely talked to her, except Annie, the sweet lady she had met the night before. The others were already working. Shelly, the dark-haired girl, always seemed to internally judge her. But at least River had Thomas. His energy and devilish smile made everything better. As long as she worked with him, she would be okay.

Once inside, they traded their muddy boots for their clean, black working shoes and shed their coats.

"Question," River said, as she followed Thomas through the hallway that led to the house. "If each team cleans a floor, why does it matter that we start earlier or later?"

"Because the morning team serves the Blackwell family breakfast. The day team serves them lunch, and we serve dinner."

"I thought they had a chef?"

"The chef cooks, but we do the service." He stopped in front of a heavy wooden door and turned to River. "Uniform check. I don't have mud or anything, do I?"

River scanned the button-down black shirt and pants, especially at the hem to make sure it hadn't been stained while they were outside. "All good."

Thomas quickly looked River over from head to toe, wrinkled his nose, then tucked a small strand of her hair behind her ear. "Don't want you to get in trouble with Roberts. Ready?"

She nodded, even though the stress of starting a new job gave her a stomachache, and he pushed the heavy door open. A cold, stone hallway stretched before them, the tiny lamps overhead barely strong enough to cut through the dark, and ended with a short set of stairs where another door waited to be opened.

River's heart pounded as they approached it. The exterior of the house had intimidated her, and she had no doubt the interior would as well. Mostly, she was anxious to meet the family.

The door opened onto a larger hallway. Rich, dark wood covered the floor, and several paintings and mirrors covered the high walls, almost up to the ceiling. Tall side tables held white sculptures held together by little wires, their abstract and modern look a big contrast from the rest of the house. Light streamed from a doorway ahead, to the right side of the hallway. Melancholic piano notes floated into the air.

"This right here is the ballroom," Thomas whispered. "You won't see it today because we'll be on the second floor." He pointed to their right, showing her a spiraling, stone staircase just outside the door they had just come out. "That's the stairs we're supposed to use, not the main ones at the front of the house."

"Too bad. This looks all so beautiful."

Shelly and Annie walked in their direction, one of them pushing a cart with cleaning supplies.

Thomas hesitated, then his lips lifted into a grin, and his eyes sparkled. "I think they're gonna clean this room, maybe we can just peek. Don't tell Roberts."

"I'm not insane."

He gestured at her to follow him, and they reached the door at the same time as the others. A young man about River's age with dark hair stood next to the doorframe, waiting. He glanced at them as they approached and gave them a small smile of acknowledgment.

"This is River," Thomas whispered behind her shoulder. "Your replacement."

"Simon," he whispered back. "Hi."

Annie knocked loudly on the open door. The piano stopped. "We're just here to clean the room, Mr. Blackwell," she announced, letting herself in.

River leaned in to peek through the doorway, Thomas leaning behind her, while Shelly looked at them amused.

The room was enormous. The floor was dark and shiny, and the walls were cream-colored. A huge armchair sat against the back wall, resembling a throne overlooking the room. Its wood was carved with intricate markings. Light streamed through the tall windows, making the massive, black piano in the middle of the room glisten.

A man wearing a black suit was sitting at it, his long fingers resting on the keys. His jet-black hair, tucked behind his ears, almost reached his jawline. His gray eyes stared straight ahead at the sound of the maid's voice. "I told you to call me Dorian, Annie. I hope you don't mind me and Simon being here."

"Not at all."

River's jaw dropped. *"That's* Dorian?" she whispered.

"Yep," Thomas said.

"When you mentioned him, I sort of imagined a kid. I didn't think he was—"

"Drop-dead gorgeous?" Shelly said.

"Insanely fucking hot?" Thomas added.

"I was gonna say an adult, but… sure."

Shelly sighed, gazing at him. "I nearly begged Roberts to be his personal aide. But the old hag refused." She smirked. "Shame. I would have done anything he'd asked of me."

Simon winced. "You guys are gross. I promise you he's not that fun."

"Probably 'cause you're not his type," Shelly teased.

"Pretty sure he doesn't care about your looks."

"He can care as long as he has hands."

She winked and entered the room. Thomas pulled on River's arm, and she glanced at Dorian briefly as he started playing the piano again, the music bouncing against the walls of the room.

"You said the family didn't care about the maids," River said, as she followed Thomas up the stairs to the second floor. "But Dorian knows Annie's name."

"Yeah, I suppose he's the only one who makes the effort of learning the staff's names. And he insists we call him by his first name. Though, we're not supposed to even talk to him at all."

A blood red carpet ran the length of the endless hallway stretching before them. Several closed doors stood between huge paintings featuring people in elegant clothing and extravagant jewelry.

"Every person you see on these paintings was part of the Blackwell family, down to their ancestors," Thomas said, opening a large closet next to the staircase and grabbing a cart full of cleaning supplies and stacks of clean sheets.

High windows to the left side of the wall showed them the view out of the back of the house, overlooking the trees and the ocean beyond, deep blue peeking through sharp red. Thomas turned into another hallway, which led to the front of the building. The scent of their cleaning supplies followed them as they went, subtle yet permeating the air.

For a moment, River heard nothing but their muffled steps on the carpet. The space didn't feel as luminous as the piano room, and she was almost eager to start cleaning so she could warm herself up.

A small tap to her left stopped her in her tracks. She stared at the human-size painting of a tall man with black hair, who seemed to stare right back at her. A floorboard creaked close to her, the wood shifting under her feet even though she stood completely still. River frowned, unsure about what she had just felt, and glanced over her shoulder. Thomas wasn't close to her, so it couldn't have been him.

Another muffled tap startled her, and she took a step back, her eyes darting over the portrait.

"Freckles?"

She turned to the voice.

Thomas stood in front of an open door down the hall and looked at her with raised eyebrows. "You alright?"

"Yeah…" She glanced at the painting again, then hurried forward. "I thought I heard something. As if someone was walking just next to me." She let out an embarrassed chuckle. "Don't pay attention to me, I'm tired. Had nightmares last night."

"It's an old house, it happens. I hear creaking and stuff too. Sort of freaked me out when I worked alone. I always feel like someone's watching me."

The opulent bedroom made River pause, her mouth agape. The enormous bed stood to the right, facing antique chairs huddled in front of a big chimney surrounded by bricks.

"Maybe it's haunted," she said, smiling as she helped Thomas tear the sheets from the bed to put new ones.

He huffed. "I'd be surprised if it weren't."

CHAPTER SIX

R iver felt sore by the time dinner came. Despite two ten-minute breaks and thirty minutes to eat lunch, she and Thomas had cleaned non-stop. Sheets had been changed, and old ones had been washed, dried, and folded. Expensive, antique furniture had been dusted and waxed, floors had been cleaned, bathrooms had been scrubbed from top to bottom. And that was just a part of the floor. They would have to do it all over again the next day, and the days after that. River felt somehow grateful that they would rotate with the other floors. At least, each week there would be a change of scenery.

River followed Thomas back to the first floor. This time, he led her to the front of the house where the main stairs were divided into two staircases, each one descending into a gigantic foyer. An opulent chandelier hung from the high ceiling, its many white crystals shining. Two ivory structures flanked both sides of the double doors, spindly and crooked into indescribable shapes. At the back of the foyer, a door opened onto the largest kitchen River had ever seen.

A big guy with a bald head and a short, white-speckled, brown beard was busy at the stove while a blonde woman chopped vegetables. Miss Roberts was there, stacking glasses full of white wine onto a tray.

The big guy turned to River as she entered with Thomas, a skillet in his hand. "Hi there. You new?"

"Yes. I'm River."

"Mack. Welcome aboard." He offered his big hand, and River shook it.

"Thanks. It's nice to meet you."

"Hi, I'm Cassie," the woman said. "The sous-chef."

"Hi."

"No time for small talk," Miss Roberts snapped. "It's about time you got here."

"Relax, Edith," Mack said, delicately placing the contents of the skillet on small plates. It smelled divine. "It'll be fine, as usual."

Miss Roberts rolled her eyes at him. "Hurry up, they just sat down."

Stress twisted River's guts. "What should I do?"

"You're gonna help me carry the appetizers," Thomas said. "Just put the plates in front of them and leave the room. Easy."

"And don't utter a single word to anyone. Don't even look at them," Edith said with her usual dry tone. She exited through another door that seemed to directly reach the dining room. It bounced behind her and closed before River could peek at the family inside.

Thomas grabbed two plates, nodding at River to pick up the last one.

Three? That's it? Only three people live in this gigantic house?

"Be careful with that," Mack said. "The last maid who dropped a plate was fired on the spot. Edith doesn't mess around with that stuff."

River nodded. She grabbed the plate, her hands clammy with stress. It seemed ridiculous to need two waiters to serve three plates, but River supposed Edith wanted to make sure everyone was served at the same time and that nobody had to juggle with three plates.

The delicious smell of the expertly grilled scallops filled the space, making her mouth water. She followed Thomas to the dining room, her heart beating too fast. She had arrived almost twenty-four hours ago and still hadn't seen who she was working for.

Thomas nudged the door open with his shoulder. River followed him, discovering the dining room. A dozen paintings stood out against the dark wooden walls. More sculptures were scattered here and there, bright white against dark brown. A chandelier hung above the long, sturdy table, a table way too long for only three people. The Blackwell family huddled on one side. As much as River tried to avert her eyes, she couldn't stop herself from quickly scanning the faces. At the head of the table sat a woman in her mid or late fifties. Her jet-black hair was tied into a perfectly tight ponytail, the long, straight hair falling gracefully behind her back. A golden rose glistened at the top of her head, tucked inside the ponytail. Black eyeliner and eye shadow darkened the brown of her iris. Thick, heavy, golden earrings swayed as she moved her head. She wore a silky red blouse that matched her red lipstick perfectly. Her deep voice filled the room as she talked, ignoring the three maids buzzing around her.

"The invites have been delivered. I have a good feeling about this year's celebration." She glanced at her son briefly, her expression turning a bit sour. "Unless *someone* decides to act up again, but I trust that will not happen."

Dorian tightened his lips but didn't answer.

"We need to impress those ladies. Quite a few are very pretty," she added, swirling the wine inside her glass.

To her left sat a man with thick gray hair and a mustache. One of those mustaches that curled at the end. His brown eyes turned to River as she entered the room, a smirk lifting his lips.

The uncle, I suppose.

River looked down. Thomas rounded the table to serve him and the black-haired woman, so River walked up to Dorian, who sat to his mother's right. Feeling the burning gaze of the mustached man on her, River kept her eyes on the plate and set it as delicately as she could in front of Dorian.

He straightened up slightly, tilting his head in her direction, just an inch, though his gray eyes didn't move. "Thank you," he said, unlike anyone else at the table.

Mrs. Blackwell was still talking, and while Edith had told River not to talk to anyone, it felt rude not to answer.

"You're welcome," she murmured against her better judgement.

The room fell silent. River left his side, heading back to the kitchen, head bowed down.

"You. Stop," Mrs. Blackwell said behind her.

River froze, unsure.

"Yes, you. The redhead. Turn around."

Thomas glanced at her with worry, then went back inside the kitchen. She slowly turned, her hands shaking slightly. She should have shut her mouth. As she looked at Mrs. Blackwell, she caught a glimpse of Edith's glare.

Mrs. Blackwell considered River for a moment, pursing her lips. "Miss Roberts, who is this?"

"It's the new maid, ma'am."

"When did she get here?"

"Yesterday evening, ma'am. She started today."

Mrs. Blackwell's eye twitched ever so slightly. "I didn't know she was here. And I *always* know what goes on around here."

All eyes were trained on her, making her feel hot. Except for Dorian's, of course, but even *his* body language had changed. Before, he seemed completely disconnected from the rest of them. Now, his dark eyebrows were knitted in a subtle frown, his shoulders tense.

"My apologies, ma'am," Miss Roberts said.

The uncle spoke up. "You have been awfully busy lately, Selene. Planning the party and everything."

"This is no mere party, *Richard.*"

"My point exactly."

Mrs. Blackwell, Selene, kept staring for a moment, then swatted them both away. "Out now."

She didn't have to tell River twice. She swiveled around and hurried inside the kitchen, followed by her superior.

"Why did you talk?" she snapped. "I *specifically* told you not to talk. I have fired people for less than that."

"Well, he talked to me… I'm so sorry…"

Thomas stayed frozen, his eyes darting between them. Even Mack and Cassie had stopped what they were doing, looking at them with raised eyebrows.

"One more misstep, and you're fired. I have been working here for a very long time, River, and I will not have my job jeopardized by a stupid little girl who can't follow simple directions."

Frustration rose in River's chest. She had left behind a jerk of a manager and had replaced him with a tyrant. But as much as she wanted to defend herself, or at least attempt to, she wasn't about to risk losing this job. She would find herself homeless.

She bit back on her frustration and nodded. "It won't happen again."

"It better not."

Miss Roberts grabbed the bottle of white wine she had left on the counter and hurried back to the dining room. River exhaled, burying her face in her hands to gather herself and hide her cheeks, hot with embarrassment.

"Hey." Thomas stood next to her, patting her shoulder. "That was really unfair. Mrs. Blackwell was mad at her, not you."

River dropped her hands. "It doesn't matter who she was mad at. If Roberts wants to fire me, she will."

"Bitter old woman," Mack said, now busy again searing what looked like filet mignon. "I'm glad she has no power over me."

Edith stormed back inside the kitchen after a minute. She stood straight, her fingers laced together as she looked at Thomas. "You're doing the dishes tonight. River will be serving."

Thomas frowned. "Cassie does the dishes usually—"

"I want to make sure River can handle it." She set her eyes on her. "This is your chance to prove to me that you are fit for this job. Make one mistake tonight, and you are done. Understood?"

A warm rush came over River. "Understood."

The rest of the dinner dragged for what felt like hours. After the appetizers came the entrees, this time paired with red wine. Then, she cleaned the table and prepared it for dessert. She served more red wine. Edith mostly stood by, watching River more than she helped.

Although River had learned her lesson and kept her mouth shut, she noticed the looks she got from Selene and Richard each time she entered the room. She had to bite her tongue every time Dorian thanked her, pondering how lonely it must feel not being able to see and have people ignoring you when you talked to them.

Dinner finally ended. Selene stood gracefully on high heels, ready to leave the room, as Richard sipped the last of his wine. River didn't waste a second cleaning the table, gathering plates and glasses onto her tray. She had made it. She had served everyone efficiently and hadn't talked to anyone. She hadn't even looked them in the eyes. Her job was safe for now.

She lifted her tray, feeling Richard's burning gaze on her. She ignored it and turned away, relieved to escape the room, when she felt his hand slip under her dress, brush her thigh, and squeeze her ass. She gasped, startled. The tray slipped from her hands. It crashed onto the floor, the sound of the dishes shattering deafening and echoing through the room.

Selene whirled around, gazed at the mess, and rolled her eyes. "For Christ's sake, Miss Roberts, choose your employees better." She turned and walked out of the room, and River felt somewhat relieved that she didn't care that much.

Edith did. Her murderous glare was set on River. "Don't just stand there, pick it up!" She stormed into the kitchen.

Richard stood, and River froze as she felt his breath behind her neck. "Don't worry, pet. You'll get used to it."

A shiver crawled down her spine. Her body stayed numb for a moment, rooted to the floor. She listened to his footsteps fading away as he walked out of the room. Her eyes burning, she kneeled and started gathering the broken dishes with shaky hands. Nausea strangled her throat as the feeling of Richard's disgusting touch lingered on her thigh. She would get used to it? What the hell did that mean? A sob escaped her mouth. There was nothing to get used to. She was about to lose her job.

She suspended her movement as she noticed the black shoes attached to the long legs in front of her. She slowly looked up at the slender man standing over her. Dorian put one knee down, his hands searching for the shards on the floor. He gathered broken pieces and felt for the tray to lay them down.

River wiped her eyes, ashamed of her tears even though he couldn't see them. "You… you're gonna cut yourself. I can do it."

"This isn't right," he said in a low voice, still picking up the shattered dishes. "The way they treat the staff." He raised his blind gaze toward her, and River realized that his eyes weren't gray, not really. It looked like a white veil had settled over his iris, making them *look* gray. "Are you okay?"

At first, she couldn't make a sound, mesmerized by the man in front of her. Drop-dead gorgeous, Shelly had said, and that wasn't an exaggeration. Strands of his black hair hung in front of his face, a face that looked like it was carved into stone. "I… I'm all right. Thank you…"

His mouth twitched slightly, and he dropped a piece of plate. Blood trickled from his finger, the drops landing on the dishes below.

"Sir," River said, grabbing his hand without thinking and wrapping the hem of her white apron around it, applying pressure.

Dorian let her do it, the ghost of a smile lifting the corner of his lips. "What's your name?"

"Um... River."

"River," he repeated. "That's a beautiful name. Please, call me Dorian."

Edith stormed back inside the room, armed with cleaning supplies, a mop, and a bucket. She did a double take as she saw them, and River quickly cleaned up Dorian's finger before letting go of his hand, her apron now stained with blood.

"I apologize for this maid's behavior, Dorian," Edith said. "I promise this will not happen again, as she will be leaving us tonight."

River's stomach dropped. That was it. She was already done.

Dorian stood slowly, and River took in his height. He towered above her.

"She will not leave, Miss Roberts," he said.

"But, Dorian—"

"I am sure you know that River is not to blame for this incident. I can't see, and even *I* know that much. You are not blind, are you?"

Edith's jaw clenched, tightening her features. River followed their exchange, immobile and still kneeling on the floor.

"She is simply not fit for—"

"I suggest you leave River alone if you want to keep your job. And it's Mr. Blackwell to you."

Her bony face turned red, and her hands balled into fists. "I have known you since you were a little boy."

"And I am still your boss, *Edith.*"

"If your mother knew—"

"There is nothing my mother can do that could scare me."

Edith's eyes darkened, but she finally stopped arguing.

"River," Dorian said, his voice now gentle again.

She snapped her head up, surprised. "Y-yes."

"You are done for the night. You may go back to your quarters and rest. Edith will clean this up for you." He turned his head toward Edith, his jaw working. "Won't you, Edith?"

Bitterness spread over her face and tightened her lips. "Yes, sir."

River gingerly stood and exited the dining room, avoiding eye contact with Edith. She pushed the door and almost cried out, startled by the three people spying that were huddled behind it. They jumped back as she entered.

"Have you guys been listening?"

Thomas scoffed. "I mean, *yeah*. That was *wild*."

"I guess you're in Dorian's good graces now," Cassie said.

River looked at them, her mind still reeling from what had just happened. "I guess that's a good thing, right? I still have my job at least."

Although Thomas looked overjoyed by the situation, most likely for how Dorian had handled Edith, Mack's face looked deadly serious, worried even.

"Mack?" she said, his expression worrying her.

"Just be careful. With Dorian, you never really know what to expect. Being in his good graces may not be as good a thing as you think it is."

Thomas huffed, more dramatic this time. "It's not good to be the hot guy's favorite, who happens to be the boss and can keep you from being fired? Give me a break. Freckles," he turned to her and squeezed her shoulder, "I'm not saying I'm jealous, but I hate you a little bit."

This got a smile out of her.

"I'm just saying," Mack said. "I've known these people for a long time. I know Dorian seems all nice and polite, but you don't want to get too close, or you'll regret it."

"What does that mean?" River asked, her smile gone. "Regret it how?"

Mack considered the question. "He's had a lot of personal helpers over the years. *A lot.* They've all left running. That alone should tell you that he's someone you don't want to get close to."

CHAPTER SEVEN

R iver sat on her bed, cross-legged, her back resting against the wall. The hot cup of rosemary tea on the nightstand sent steam billowing into the air. The lit candle next to it smelled of pine. She hadn't had the time to sit down for her morning ritual that day, and if she was being honest, she had been a little self-conscious to do it with other people around. She had missed it, and after such a busy and crazy day full of emotions, she needed to gather herself.

Thomas was still in the common room with most of the staff, rambling about what had happened during dinner. He started talking about it as soon as they had come back, and River didn't want to deal with people's looks, so she decided to have dinner in her bed. She discarded the plate on the night table and laid the tarot cards in front of her, mentally asking them if this job really was worth the emotional strain. So far, it didn't inform her of anything she didn't already know.

"It's useless, you know."

The voice made River look up. Shelly stood in the doorway before walking nonchalantly toward her and dropping onto her bed.

"What are you talking about?" River asked.

"Dorian. Whatever you think you're doing, it's not gonna work. The guy can't even see, so he won't care about you either way. Trust me, I've tried." Her sneering tone reeked of jealousy.

"I'm not doing anything."

Shelly rolled her eyes. "Right. So, that little incident of yours wasn't an act to gain sympathy?"

"That incident could have cost me my job. I *never* would have done that on purpose. It's that… *pervert* who made me lose my composure."

Shelly considered this, and her face softened slightly. "Richard?"

"Yes. He grabbed my ass."

"Well, there's not much we can do about him. I've already told Roberts, and she doesn't care. All she cares about is her job."

River tilted her head. "That happened to you before?"

"That old fuck can't keep his hands to himself. Roberts told me that if I couldn't handle it, I was free to quit. My advice? Until you're ready to leave this place, just give him what he wants and don't think about it too much."

Thomas appeared in the doorway. "That is *terrible* advice." He made his way to his bed and sat on it. "As long as we work together, I'll keep serving him, so you don't have to get close. I can't do much, but I can do that."

Shelly cocked an eyebrow. "That'll only frustrate him more, and one day, he'll corner her in one of the rooms."

Nausea rose in River's throat. She looked down at her cards, trying to hide the discomfort spreading through her.

Thomas noticed it anyway and turned back to Shelly. "Don't you have somewhere to be? Someone else to annoy?"

Shelly threw her hands up, standing up. "Fine, don't listen to me. But don't come complaining later."

She left, and River breathed out, realizing she'd been clenching her tarot cards. She quickly laid them down on the bed, smoothing them out the best she could. She still used the tarot cards her grandmother had bought for her sixteenth birthday. She'd said that a deck should be offered to someone, but she still wanted River to choose the one she wanted, the one she felt connected to. So, she took River to a shop that smelled of incense and was filled with crystals and tarot cards and pretty candles. River browsed the aisles, somehow uninterested in all the classic decks on display.

And then she saw it. The one she wanted. The drawings were gorgeous, colorful, and each card was represented by an animal.

"This one," she'd told Willow, who nodded in approval.

"It suits you. Nature and animals. Your element is earth after all."

And green was her color. That's what her grandma had always said, and River naturally gravitated toward green clothes.

"Don't pay attention to her," Thomas said. "She's just jealous Dorian talked to you more on your first day than to her in eighteen months."

"That's okay."

He tilted his head at the cards. "What's that?"

"Tarot."

He gasped. *"Do me."*

She offered a lopsided grin. "Do you?"

"You know what I mean." He sat cross-legged on her bed, facing her. "And don't tell me something super ominous. Lie to me if you have to."

River grabbed the cards and put them back inside the deck, then handed it over to him. "Shuffle them. And be careful with them."

Thomas shuffled the cards thoroughly and gave them back to River. She settled the deck in front of her, drank a long sip of warm tea, then took a deep breath to relax as much as possible before drawing the first card. Her grandma always told her how important it was to clear her mind before a reading as to not taint the cards with negative energies.

"The first card is your past, the middle one is your present, the third is your future. I'm just doing a simple reading for tonight, okay?"

"Sure."

River drew the first card and laid it between them. "Five of Pentacles. You wanted to grow, but a higher authority was keeping you from that. You experienced difficulties and lacked the resources you needed to thrive. It left you feeling like an outcast, like you weren't accepted. You lost something, whether it's a job or someone or the ability to take care of your mental health, and it was hard to find your way back to the right path. This card also means that like everything, this too shall pass."

"Well, I guess it passed when I left my house."

She peered at him. "Do you wanna talk about it? If it's any consolation, I had that exact card in my own reading earlier."

A weak smile lifted his lips. "I went back to live with my parents because my mom had early onset dementia. I wanted to be close to her and my sisters. But my dad, the asshole that he is, couldn't stop belittling me the whole time, not even for my mom's sake. After she died, I stayed longer for my sisters. They're young, you know. Twelve and fifteen."

"I'm so sorry about your mom."

"Thanks."

"What are your sisters' names?"

"Audrey and Emma. We're really close. I was the one taking them to school when they were little."

River smiled. "That's sweet."

"Yeah… But my dad was driving me crazy, and my mental health took a hit. As well as my confidence. I saw this weird-ass job offer, and I applied. I don't like it that much, and I miss talking to my sisters every day, but you know what? The ocean air is doing wonders for my mind."

They chuckled.

"What's your story?" he asked.

River told him about her grandma, trying not to ramble even though she always loved to talk about her and could spend hours telling stories. She told him about Zach and the events leading to their breakup. "I guess I wasn't the person I needed to be for him anymore, and he found better."

"The person you needed to be for him? Are you kidding me? This guy sounds like a prick."

"He's not, he's just—"

"A dick. Making you feel bad about yourself, your appearance, and fucking *grieving* the death of your grandma? Come on, Freckles. He did you a solid by breaking up, let me tell you."

"Let's just keep going," she said, dismissing his comment. Zach might not be perfect, but she believed both parties had some responsibility in the way things had turned. He couldn't be blamed for everything.

She reached for the second card and drew the Six of Swords. "Nothing exciting happening now. Think of this card as being a boring, gray Sunday afternoon. Nothing bad, though. Life is moving on, and it's not horrible."

"You brilliantly described our lives here."

"Well, you may not be super enthusiastic about this job or this place, but you *are* moving in the right direction. You need to feel at peace at a slower pace and protect yourself from negative self-talk or outside influences."

Thomas pursed his lips, considering this. "I wanted to do this for fun, but it's all a bit too… *accurate.* I hate it."

"Sorry…"

"Tell me my future now. Something like, 'you'll meet a beautiful, rich man, who'll take you to live in his mega mansion in California."

She wrinkled her nose. "It doesn't work like that."

"Lie to me."

River drew the third card. At the sight of it, she tightened her lips a little, glancing up at Thomas.

"Death?" he said, widening his eyes. "Where's my rich millionaire?"

People tended to get nervous around that card, and she'd been hoping it wouldn't come up. "Death doesn't necessarily mean death. A lot of people hate it, but trust me, it rarely means you're about to die. It announces an imminent change in your life. It'll soon be time to close a chapter and open a new one. Who knows, maybe you'll find a better job than this one."

"*Or* a rich, sexy boyfriend. I'll take the sexy boyfriend even if he isn't rich."

"Yes, I definitely see a beautiful man in your close future."

He gave a brilliant smile. "See? That wasn't so hard, was it?"

"Maybe your rich, gorgeous man is Dorian."

He gasped, a hand on his chest. "*Maybe.* Well, actually, you know what? No. He *is* attractive, but—how can I say it? He lives here, his family is obviously insane, and I want to leave this place eventually."

"Maybe he wants to go to California."

"Doubt it. Isn't he older than us? If he wanted to leave, he would have done so already."

River thought about it. Upon seeing Dorian up close, she estimated his age to be somewhere between his late twenties and early thirties. "Yeah… And his mother was talking to him about a woman. Or women. I think she wants to play matchmaker. What was that about by the way? That party thing?"

Thomas shrugged, shifting position. "I don't know. I think it's something they do every year, but I only started working here two months ago."

"It's a celebration of sorts," Annie said, as she entered the room. Both Thomas and River turned to her. "They don't celebrate Christmas, but the winter solstice. The whole town is invited. They come wearing beautiful suits and gowns and have a ball."

A huff fell out of River's mouth. "*A ball?* Do people still have balls?"

"The Blackwell family certainly does."

"That sounds endearing," Thomas said.

Annie dropped onto her bed, looking tired and sore from her day as she stretched her shoulder. "Endearing for them, maybe.

That day is literal hell for all of us. We all have to be there, no exceptions. We carry trays of food and drink all evening without a break until they kick us out."

River frowned. "Kick us out?"

"Yes. Sometime before the sun goes down, the staff has to leave the room, and they shut the door. I think that's when they truly celebrate, kind of like a midnight mass. Then, everyone leaves, and we have to clean up the mess."

Thomas pulled a face. "Fun…"

Annie shrugged and shed her purple robe. She was only wearing a thin nightgown underneath, and River wondered how she could sleep like that. It felt like all the woolen socks and flannel pants and long sleeve-shirts she had to sleep with weren't enough to keep her warm.

"It is what it is," Annie said. "You'll get used to it if you work here as long as I have. The only weird thing is the way they behave a few days after their ball."

"What do you mean?" River asked.

"Mrs. Blackwell and Richard always look giddy. Dorian looks even more depressed than he usually is. It's quite bizarre." She put herself to bed, throwing the covers on top of her. "But nothing that concerns us. Life just goes on the way it was. Goodnight now."

Thomas and River mumbled goodnight in return. After he went to bed, River stayed awake for a while, nursing her lukewarm cup of tea and watching the candle waste away. She couldn't get the dinner out of her head. How Richard had grabbed her, and how Edith must absolutely hate her.

Most of all, she couldn't stop thinking about those washed-out yet intense gray eyes boring into her without seeing her. It hadn't occurred to River that Dorian's demeanor the whole evening betrayed a depressive state of mind. What could he possibly be depressed about? He came from an insanely rich family and lived in a huge mansion with staff that was there to serve him. Mack had told her to stay away from him, but he had seemed so kind when he'd helped her and saved her job.

Exhaustion getting the best of her, River blew out the candle and fell into a disturbed sleep filled with images of the tall, dark-haired man living within these halls.

CHAPTER EIGHT

The whistling wind made the windows rattle in their frames, jolting River out of sleep. The dormitory was pitch-black, except for the soft orange light of the heater against the opposite wall. River quickly glanced at the doorway, making sure the door was closed and that no one was standing there, watching her. She shuddered at the memory of the nightmare, at how real it had seemed.

The air was cold, so she tightened the covers around her shoulders. No one seemed bothered by the screaming wind, sleeping peacefully as if already used to every sound surrounding the mansion. The stormy ocean had been nice to hear on her first night, but the gale frightened her as it rammed into the windows.

Another gust shook them. River scrambled to her knees and looked at the window above her bed to see if there wasn't a way to steady it, to be sure it stopped making such an annoying noise. But she couldn't see how to fix it. She'd have to learn to live with it.

Just when she was ready to get back under the covers, movement caught her eye outside, and she leaned closer, her breath misting over the glass.

A figure moved through the shadows. It went downhill and headed toward the woods at the edge of the cliff. She couldn't make out who it was. The darkness swallowed any identifiable feature. What was someone doing out there in the middle of the freezing night? And with no light?

They weren't just walking, either. They were running. As though someone, or something, was chasing them.

Should I call for help? Wake up Miss Roberts?

Edith would probably tell her off, especially after what happened after dinner.

The night before, River could have sworn someone was here with them, but they had vanished as soon as Annie had turned on the light. Could she be dreaming again?

Someone's out there. I know what I saw.

River shuffled out of bed, grabbed her phone, and sneaked out of the room. The air in the hallway felt ten times colder, and she hurried to the foyer to get her coat and boots.

The icy wind was as sharp as razor blades on her face, but at least there was no mist tonight. Hugging herself with one arm and brandishing the phone's flashlight with the other hand, River strode to the tree line. Through the sounds of the frothing ocean and the branches creaking above her, she couldn't hear any footsteps. She stopped, squinting into the darkness beyond her light and regretting her decision to come here.

Movement between trees caught her eye.

"Hello?" she called, her voice barely rising above the screaming wind. "Are you alright? Do you need help?"

The figure froze for a second, enough for her to catch a glimpse of dark hair, then it darted away.

"Wait!"

She sprinted through the trees.

Stop! You're crazy! You'll get murdered!

But her grandma had taught her to pay attention to signs in nature. To listen. To trust that nothing happened by luck. She would probably argue that if River had woken up at this exact moment, there was a reason for it.

The cold air rushed in and out of her lungs as she ran, drying her throat. The stormy ocean below grew louder, and River could taste salt on her tongue. The closer she got to it, the stronger the gale rammed into her.

The trees parted. She squinted against the wind and searched for the figure.

It was right there, straight ahead, standing on the edge of the cliff. The night was impossibly dark, but River gasped at the sight of the tall, slim silhouette. Black hair, black clothes.

She took a step forward and opened her mouth, but before she could call out to him, his body plunged into the darkness below, disappearing from her view.

A scream escaped her mouth, and she bolted to the edge of the cliff. She skidded to a stop and fell to her knees, heart in throat, before gingerly peeking over the edge.

"Oh my God…"

The menacing, deafening sound of the ocean stifled the sound of her voice. River shone her flashlight, but it couldn't reach more than a few feet. The drop seemed painfully high, and a few sharp, gray rocks protruded from the black sea below. No one could survive a fall like that.

She had to alert someone. Anyone. Sick to her stomach, she scrambled back to her feet and whirled around. Someone stood in front of her, making her yelp in surprise.

She raised the flashlight, panting. "Shelly? What are you doing here?"

Shelly blinked at the light. "Me? I followed you. What are *you* doing?"

"Someone just killed themselves." The words rushed out of her dry mouth.

"What?"

"I saw someone, and I followed them, and they just... *he* just jumped!"

"Who?"

"We need to go get help!"

Shelly closed the distance between them and grabbed River's shoulders, steadying her. "Who was it?"

"I think..." She bit her trembling lip. "It was Dorian."

River held the throw blanket tightly around her shoulders, unable to stop shivering despite sitting in front of the fire in the common room. She must look insane with her wild hair frizzier and more tangled than ever after the wind had messed it up. The first rays of light peeked through the windows, and the hushed chatters of the staff buzzed in the background as they waited for Edith to come back.

Thomas sat next to her, placing a cup of tea on the coffee table. "That'll warm you up."

"Thanks," she said, her voice nothing but a whisper, though she didn't reach for the cup.

The door at the back of the staff's quarters that led to the Blackwell House opened and shut with a heavy creak. Footsteps approached, and all the voices quieted as Edith entered the room, her back straight and her hands laced together in front of her.

River stood, tightening the blanket around her. "So?"

Edith shot her a condescending look. "I just talked to Dorian. He's fine."

A sigh of relief rushed out of her. The rest of the maids seemed to relax at the news.

"Thank God," Shelly said, a smile playing at the corners of her lips. "Dorian is literally the only thing that makes working here worth it. Who am I gonna stare at if he's not here?" She cackled, getting a few smiles from the others.

Edith squared her shoulders. Unlike the other people in the room, her expression only seemed to darken even more. "Show some respect to your superiors, Shelly."

Shelly rolled her eyes.

"Then, who was it?" one of the maids River didn't know asked.

"I'm afraid Miss Devin was sleepwalking and had some kind of dream, then felt the need to bother everyone about it," Edith said, glaring daggers at River.

"I didn't dream it. If it wasn't Dorian, then it was someone else. Did you see the whole family? Did you talk to the rest of the staff and—"

"Everyone is present and alive and well, River. No one is missing. You were mistaken. You should feel glad about it."

Her mind still reeled from seeing that body drop into the darkness. Surely, she couldn't have dreamed something like that.

Well, you did see something that wasn't there the other night.

But it had never happened to her before coming here. Edith was right, though. She should feel happy that no one was hurt.

"I don't want more trouble from you now," Edith said through gritted teeth. "I know what Dorian said, but I *will* fire you if I feel like this is the right decision for the Blackwell family. I expect you to make yourself invisible to me and to them. And stay in your room at night. Is that clear?"

River nodded, feeling embarrassed, and Edith left the room. The quiet conversations resumed. River sat down on the couch, finally taking the cup of tea Thomas had made for her.

"Emma sleepwalks too," he said, his tone soft. "It used to freak me out. Then, I became used to it and would just steer her back to bed when it happened."

River offered a small smile, but it vanished in an instant. She had never sleepwalked in her entire life. Could stress do this to her? Would working in a new environment cause her to have real-life nightmares? If it was the case, she could only hope something like this wouldn't happen again. Her job depended on it.

CHAPTER NINE

R iver and Thomas made progress cleaning the second floor. It was just as tiring as the day before. Her arms ached, and her back hurt. Thomas made everything better, though. The two of them talked and joked as they worked, making time go by faster.

River removed her shoes and perched onto a chair. The cold of the room instantly curled around her toes, but she didn't have a choice. The high windows needed to be cleaned, and she couldn't risk damaging the antique chair. Despite the aches in her arms and neck, it wasn't the worst chore. That spot offered a wide view of the backyard. It looked like a maze. Steppingstones snaked between dead plants and dry trees. In some corners, high gray statues loomed above stone benches. It made sense for most plants to look a little shriveled with such harsh weather, but the many rosebushes seemed to thrive, their flowers as red as blood and their thorns clinging to the benches and statues.

To the right side was a greenhouse. River could make out carrots, potatoes, lettuce, zucchini, tomatoes, and butternut squash.

"It makes sense for them to grow their own vegetables," she said, spraying and wiping the glass.

"It's one less thing for Mack and Cassie to get downtown," Thomas answered, as he applied bee wax onto the furniture. "Though I must say that for a town that is in the middle of nowhere, they've got everything we need."

Four landscapers were working hard, trimming and cutting and cleaning. Beyond the backyard, the bright red trees shielded them from the ocean wind. But from here, River could get a glimpse of dark, cold blue. Despite only being on the second floor, the view was dizzying and sent chills up her legs.

After the second window, the spraying bottle spurted out. River climbed down from the chair and put her shoes back on. "I need more. It's all in the same closet next to the staircase, right?"

"Yep."

Bottle in hand, she left the room and walked down the long, carpeted floor. That ever-present smell of harsh cleaning supplies floated about the air, even if they hadn't cleaned that hallway recently. It was everywhere, all the time, permeating the carpets and the curtains.

The paintings seemed to watch her as she went, the dozen pairs of eyes burning River's back. One of them moved. River caught their movement at the edge of her vision and whirled around. She stared at the picture, expecting it to move again, but it stayed still. The subject, though, seemed to stare right at her, his dark eyes piercing through her.

River gazed up at the huge painting. A man sat on a chair, his suit matching his black hair and short beard. Behind him stood a young man, his hand resting on the man's shoulder. River recognized him instantly.

Dorian's eyes looked different. In place of the pale gray was a deep, dark brown. The same as the man in the chair.

"My late husband."

The voice made River jump. She turned, a rush of heat spiking through her.

Selene Blackwell stood at the end of the hallway. Once again, her black hair was tied into a stark ponytail, the golden rose tucked inside it and glistening in the soft light. Her dark purple fitted dress matched the color of her lipstick. Her high heels made almost no sound as she walked onto the carpet toward River.

"Mrs. Blackwell," River whispered, bowing her head. She hoped with all her heart that the woman wouldn't think she was slacking on work.

Selene stood next to River and gazed up at the painting. "Benjamin. He killed himself eight years ago. Jumped out a window on the third floor. Most of our ancestors died a tragic death."

"My condolences…"

"This was painted before Dorian's accident. He wasn't born blind, you see."

River dared look up, at the woman first, then at the painting. Her lips burned, wanting to ask what had happened, but her mistake the night before had been enough for her to learn to stay quiet.

Selene answered River's question without being prompted. "Well, it wasn't really an accident. More like an assault. Benjamin did that. Blunt force trauma on the face. He was not a really good man. Can't say I cried when he died."

River swallowed a gasp, staring at the man in the painting. He seemed to stare back. She had no idea that someone could be hit in the face so hard they could lose sight.

"If only blindness had been the sole result of the impact, it would have been easier, but… it did something to his head too. Dorian was never the same after that."

"That's terrible," River said in a small voice.

Selene tilted her head in River's direction and smiled. "Are you carrying something?"

River looked at her. With those heels, Selene was much taller than her, intimidating despite her gracious smile. "I, um…" She looked at the spray bottle in her hand, confused.

Selene swatted her away. "Not this. Are you carrying any jewelry? Anything?"

River's heartbeat kicked up a notch. She wasn't supposed to have jewelry on her, but she couldn't separate herself from her necklace, tucked inside her shirt, nor the little bag of crystals that she had stuffed in her pocket, conveniently hidden under her apron.

"Nothing, no."

She forced herself not to grip the spray bottle too tight and to keep her shoulders relaxed, but the lie nearly made her wobbly. What was she thinking? Selene wasn't nearly as scary as Edith, maybe River would have been better off telling the truth.

Selene squinted and stared at her for a moment, then her lips quirked. "Do not talk to him if you can avoid it."

River frowned, taken aback by the comment. "Who—"

"My son. He may not see, but he notices things, and he seems to have noticed you. That is the consequence of you talking to him when you weren't supposed to. You opened your door to him, and now, he will try to latch onto you like a leech. So, I am telling you: stay away from him. For your own good. And because losing another servant would be quite inconvenient."

She turned and walked away, her movements graceful and elegant.

River watched her go, deliriously relieved that Selene didn't inquire further about her jewelry, but also unsettled by the warning. All she had said was "you're welcome," and it was treated as though it was the worst thing in the world.

The smallest movement caught River's eye. She faced the painting again and stared at Benjamin, putting some distance between her and the portrait. Something was wrong with this painting, with his eyes. They seemed alive. They seemed to see her.

After another tiring evening serving the Blackwells and avoiding stepping too close to Richard, River was relieved to have made herself invisible. Despite Selene shooting her a curious glance once or twice, River had kept her eyes low and hadn't opened her mouth one single time. After the service, she insisted on staying in the kitchen to help Mack and Cassie clean up, but they kicked her out.

"You're sweet, but your day's over, River," Cassie said, smiling. "Go and rest."

"Thomas didn't need to be told twice." Mack chuckled. "We'll see you tomorrow, love."

"Okay, then. See you tomorrow."

She exited the kitchen, returning to the large foyer. Behind the doorway on the far right was the hallway that would lead her back to the staff's quarters, but River gazed at the large and heavy double doors leading to the front of the house. After looking through the windows almost all afternoon, she wanted to take a walk outside and see the garden. It would be dark and cold, but her blood was still running hot from all the trips she'd made between the kitchen and the dining room that evening. If she walked fast and didn't stay outside for too long, her body wouldn't have time to become too cold. She stepped to the main entrance and quickly glanced around her to make sure no one saw her.

River pulled the heavy door open, surprised at how swiftly it moved, and slipped outside. She gasped at the sharp cold, regretting going outside wearing only her flimsy uniform. There was no wind at least, but a fresh fog was rolling in, making it even harder to see. It felt like walking through a gray cotton ball.

She climbed the few steps down and turned left, walking briskly and hugging herself. She strode alongside the brick wall swallowed by ivy, the house towering above her. The windows on the first floor seemed to be taller and more numerous than the second floor. She wasn't looking forward to cleaning them.

She rounded the house. The mist wasn't too thick here yet, and River could see glimpses of trees and rosebushes and statues thanks to the wrought iron lampposts spread around the backyard, shining on the path of steppingstones. The statues loomed high above her head, frozen in place. She looked at them for a moment, trying to decide if she liked them or not. The sculptor had obviously been

WHISPERS OF BLACKWELL HOUSE

very talented. The faces seemed alive, and the clothes looked like real, flowy texture. But at the same time, they looked like dozens of ghosts lurking in the night. River had found them beautiful when looking at them in the daytime from the window. But right now, alone in the dark with them, she felt like she was being watched.

Tightening her arms against her chest, she resumed walking but froze on the spot as she looked ahead. A gasp caught in her throat. A figure seemed out of place, as though it had stepped off its pedestal. The fog blurred it, but River could tell it was only a few yards away. She took a few careful steps, squinting.

"Who's there?" a voice said.

River startled to a stop and opened her mouth, but no sound came out. What if it was Richard? Had she really been so stupid that she had managed to find herself alone in the dark with him? Was he going to come closer and corner her?

He didn't. Instead, he simply sat down on the stone bench behind him. "I know someone's there."

Her body shaking, as the cold quickly made its way through the fabric of her uniform, River approached and sighed in relief. It was Dorian. Though that didn't mean she wouldn't get in trouble for being here. "It's just River, sir... um, Dorian."

"I'm sorry I frightened you."

"That's all right." She paused, not knowing what to do or say. Normally, she wasn't even supposed to talk to the Blackwell family at all. "How did you know I was frightened?"

Dorian turned his head toward her a fraction. "You gasped. And you froze when I talked to you." The lamppost nearby allowed her to see the tiniest ghost of a smile lifting his lips, though it looked sad. "I have developed very good hearing."

"I see."

"I don't."

Her mouth went dry. "I didn't mean—I'm so sorry—"

He laughed, a soft, quiet sound that seemed to make the cold night one degree warmer. "My apologies, I thought it was funny. But maybe I don't have the greatest sense of humor."

River walked closer until she stood next to the bench. "It *was* funny. It's just that—"

"Miss Roberts has told you that talking to us is a sin. I promise you have nothing to fear from me. I appreciate some conversation. And the occasional joke."

Her heart went out to him. Despite trying to smile, he looked unbelievably sad, even more so than the day before. His slumped posture betrayed the way he truly felt. What Selene had said about him earlier flashed through her mind.

'It did something to his head too.'

It was hard to imagine what could possibly be so wrong about this polite and well-spoken man.

"What are you doing outside in the dark and the cold?" he asked.

"What are *you* doing outside in the dark and the cold?

A dry chuckle escaped his mouth. "Touché. I don't mind the dark, though."

The freezing cold clawed at her hands and face and neck, but River found herself sitting down on the stone bench, feeling bad for him being ignored by the staff. "I just needed some air. And I wanted to see the garden up close."

"I see."

Before she could bite her tongue, she said, "Do you?" She cringed at her own words. Was she insane? Because he had made a joke didn't mean she could.

Surprisingly, Dorian's smile widened, and he let out a small laugh.

"I'm sorry if I crossed a line," River said anyway, feeling mortified.

"It's a harmless joke, River. My life wouldn't be so morose if everyone else relaxed a little around me. If I could get to truly know the people living with us. But my mother wouldn't allow it." He turned to face her. Strands of black, dampened hair fell in front of his gray eyes, which almost seemed to look at her. "I know what she says to the staff about me. That it is better to steer clear of me."

Selene *had* told River to keep her distance, and here she was, making conversation. A shudder shook her body, and she couldn't tell if it was from the cold or from the memory of Selene's warning. She would freeze to death in a few minutes if she stayed outside without moving, though. That much was obvious.

"Are you cold?" he asked.

"Did you hear me shudder?"

"Yes."

"I don't have a coat. I better go inside."

He stood up when she did. He had looked tall when she'd been kneeling on the dining room floor after dropping her tray, but now, as she faced him, she realized he was a solid head taller than her.

"Take this." Dorian shed his long, black coat and handed it to her.

"Oh, thank you, but I couldn't."

"Please. I feel bad for keeping you out."

River's mind scrambled for a way to tell him nicely that it was a bad idea, the worst idea even. She wouldn't know how to explain that coat to Edith or Selene if they saw it. Which meant that she would have to hide it if she didn't want to get in trouble, and then she wouldn't know how to bring it back to him without being caught.

Before she could voice any of her thoughts, Dorian stepped closer and felt for her shoulder. He found it, and the way his hand grazed her sent a little shiver through her body. He reached around her to drape the coat behind her back, and the heavy, thick fabric instantly warmed her.

"Do you know the way to the ballroom?" he said, stepping back.

"Uh, yes. It's just next to the door leading to the staff's quarters."

"Yes. Just leave the coat on the piano bench tomorrow. That way no one will see you walk around the house with it, and you won't get in trouble."

She smiled and tightened the warm coat around her shoulders. "Thank you. You've read my mind."

He bowed his head slightly. "Goodnight. Thank you for the conversation."

"You're welcome," she said in a barely audible whisper.

River sidestepped him and began walking toward her quarters, expecting Dorian to be on his way too. But when she glanced behind her, she saw that he had sat back down. Any trace of a smile had vanished from his features. He just sat, his fingers laced together, and his gaze lost. Something about him saddened her.

"I have ginger hair," she blurted out.

Dorian raised his head in her direction.

"I have long, *very* thick, ginger hair. Kids in middle and high school used to call me Carrot. With the humidity, I'm lucky I have a braid right now because I would look like a lunatic otherwise."

She wrenched her hands together, feeling stupid and wondering if someone more awkward than her had ever existed. "Just letting you know in case you wanna take a swing at me next time. As revenge for the bad joke I made earlier."

A new smile warmed his handsome features. "I don't know what I could possibly make fun of. That sounds rather charming."

An unwelcome swarm of butterflies filled her stomach.

"Go now," he said. "We will not be able to have another conversation and make fun of each other if you freeze to death."

River walked away on numb legs. A smile crept over her face, one she couldn't shake off. Dorian, a devastatingly attractive man, had enjoyed his conversation with her, an awkward, shy maid. Not only that, but he was looking forward to talking to her again.

Despite Edith's severe rules, River was looking forward to that as well.

CHAPTER TEN

A few days later, River and Thomas left for downtown Stormhedge during their day off. It was cold but sunny, and the taste of salt permeated the air, swirling in the wind. It wasn't even nine in the morning. Thomas had insisted it was better to leave early, since it started getting dark before four in the afternoon. That way they'd have time to hang out at the coffee shop and charge their phones to check their emails and other social media. After lunch, they'd go to the mini mart to buy some groceries. With only one day off per week, Thomas had no desire to stay at the Blackwell House if he could avoid it.

River glanced at the house, standing tall and sturdy and magnificent at the top of the hill, before they entered the woods and walked the main path. It looked so different than when she had driven there on the night of her arrival. The forest had been pitch-black. But now, the sun glistened through the branches shedding their bright red and orange leaves.

While she had felt like this road would never end by car, it was fairly easy to walk it during the day. About twenty minutes at a brisk pace, which was good for warming up. At least River was wearing her own, warm clothes instead of that flimsy uniform. She had left her long hair down, enjoying the freedom.

As they exited the forest, River barely recognized the town. It had been so dark and foggy the last time she had seen it. Now, the sun shone on the shops' windows and highlighted their colors. To the right stood the Storm Inn, a cute little building made of bricks. Facing it was a flower shop made out of the same bright red bricks. A young blonde woman was placing colorful bouquets behind the windows, arranging them so they looked fluffy and full. River noticed an antique shop with a big window to showcase their objects, a mini mart, and a liquor store. Further ahead, they walked past a butcher shop next to a fishmonger shop. People were buzzing in and out of the stores, waving at each other or striking small conversations as though they all knew each other. No one talked to Thomas and River, though. They noticed them but looked away almost instantly, and every time River attempted a polite smile when meeting someone's eyes, they didn't return it, instead busying themselves on their task.

"You were right. There's everything you'd need here. I see where Mack gets his fish and meat." She lowered her voice. "Why is everyone ignoring us, though?"

Thomas shrugged. "Probably the kind of small town where people don't like strangers much. Not everyone is like that, though. You'll see."

Further to the right, on the bend of the road, waited the coffee shop. The sight of it brought her an unexpected wave of joy. In there, she would forget about the cold halls of the Blackwell House and relax in the familiarity and warmth of the shop with a latte in front of her.

"Literally my favorite place in this town," Thomas said, as though reading her mind.

As they approached, River read the name—the Black Bean. Thomas opened the door, and the delicious, warm smell of coffee instantly lifted her spirits. The barista, a young man with auburn hair, offered them a bright smile as they came up to the counter, a nice contrast from the people they'd seen outside.

"Hey, Thomas," he said, then gestured at River. "New partner?"

"That's right, my new partner in crime, River. Freckles, this is Luke."

"It's nice to meet you," she said.

"Likewise. Welcome to Stormhedge."

Thomas chatted with him for a moment. Clearly, Luke was used to seeing Thomas here every week. After he handed them their order—a giant lavender latte paired with a steamy, still warm banana bread for River, and a caramel macchiato with a cream cheese Danish for Thomas—the two of them settled at the table near the large window. The sun warmed River's back, melting all her troubles away.

She took her phone out and plugged it in. "Nice place."

"The best," Thomas said, glancing at Luke before turning on his phone. "And these are the best cream cheese Danishes I've ever had."

"I know why this is your favorite place," she said, grinning.

A smile tugged at Thomas's lips, but he kept his eyes on the phone.

"Luke's cute. I think he's into you."

He put the phone down and leaned forward. *"I know."*

"Then, what are you doing? Ask him out or something."

"Have you met us and our insane schedule? When would I have time to date that guy? During his lunch break every Tuesday?"

Her shoulders slumped. "Yeah… True."

"I'll keep flirting. It's good enough for me." He looked at his phone again for a moment, then peered at her. "What did Mrs. Blackwell really tell you the other day?"

"I already told you." It was partly true. She had kept to herself the part when Selene had warned her against Dorian. Why, she didn't really know. Maybe because it made Dorian look bad, and she didn't like that.

"Really, though? That's it?"

"Why?"

"Because she never talks to any of us. *Ever.* Except for Roberts. But you say she just… came up to you and talked to you. It's not even like you ran into each other by accident."

River hesitated a moment, wanting to tell him the truth. She decided against it for now, curious to know what he made out of it. "All right, Sherlock. What do you think that means?"

"Well, if you *must* know, my dear Watson, I have a theory. Two, actually. One that I wish were true, and one that I think is true."

"The suspense is killing me."

Thomas leaned forward, a twinkle in his eye. "Theory I wish were true: she likes you. She pities you a little bit for Richard's misplaced gesture, or she just wants to get a feel of the new employee."

"You wish she pitied me?"

"Better than the alternative."

River made a sound at the back of her throat. "Which is?"

"She *hates* your guts."

"Great."

"And the reason for that is because Dorian came to your rescue and made sure you kept your job, and she's afraid he likes you."

Heat spread through her cheeks. "Likes me? No. He can't even see me." She chuckled, oddly destabilized by the thought. "Nuh-uh. No chance."

A smirk lifted his lips. "You'd like that, wouldn't you?"

"Shut up… Your theory's all wrong. Mrs. Blackwell wasn't in the room when that happened."

"But she has a little pet who I bet tells her everything—Roberts."

"Why would she care, though? Dorian's an adult."

"Haven't you heard them talk about their little party? About these women she's trying to push on him? That's why."

River considered all this. Could that be the real reason Selene wanted River to stay away? Because she was afraid her son would fall for a 'servant,' as she called them?

The idea of Dorian liking her felt ridiculous again as she heard the words in her mind.

"You like gossip, don't you?" she said.

"I live for drama."

They laughed, though River quickly steered the conversation away from that subject. Dorian could never like someone like her. He had been quite nice that night when she saw him outside, but she hadn't talked to him since. The day after their conversation, she had put his coat on the piano bench like he had told her. Edith hadn't caught her, which was a relief.

One little thing had changed, though. She hadn't talked to him, but he had talked to her. Every evening, when she served him or took his plate away, he always said, "Thank you, River." He seemed to know the difference between her and Thomas as well, God knew how.

After chatting for a moment, the both of them spent some time on their phones. River felt stupid for having missed it. It didn't bring her any type of joy, but the lack of connection to the outside world for days had felt isolating.

Thomas showed her pictures of his little sisters, and the smile it brought on his face warmed River's heart.

"I'm gonna call them if that's okay," he said.

"Of course."

River scrolled aimlessly on her own phone while Thomas had an animated conversation with his sisters. She had no one to call. She had secretly hoped that Zach had texted her. Asked how things were going. She'd hoped he had been a little worried not to hear from her for days. But there were no text messages, no emails, nothing.

River opened Instagram and typed his username in the search bar. Her heart sank. More pictures of him and his gorgeous girlfriend had been posted. The two of them in a bar or in Central Park, either smiling at the camera or kissing.

The final blow was the selfie of them in a familiar place. The cream-colored wall behind the dark brown couch. That girl was sitting on the couch River had sat on so many times. In the apartment she had lived in for three years. Kissing her boyfriend. She stared at the picture, her throat tight, and her hand shaking.

Thomas snatched her phone away. "Why do you do this to yourself?"

She looked up, meeting his brown eyes. She must have been staring at those pictures for way too long and hadn't noticed him hanging up. "I know. I'm being stupid… He moved on. He truly doesn't care that I'm gone."

Thomas's shoulders slumped, and he put the phone down. "He's an asshole, and he doesn't deserve you, trust me."

"Yeah… That doesn't make me feel better."

A mischievous smile stretched his lips. "Do you know what would make you feel better? Show him you moved on too."

"He wouldn't care even if I had."

"You've been *way* too nice to him. You need to do something petty. And you're in luck, 'cause petty is my middle name. He'll react. You'll see."

River thought about it and smiled cautiously. "What do you suggest?"

"Take half a dozen pics with your 'new boyfriend' and post them on Instagram. Does he still follow you?"

"I doubt it. I don't follow him anymore." She checked, and to her surprise, Zach hadn't unfollowed her. It didn't mean anything. He might just not have thought about it at all. "And I suppose you're my pretend boyfriend?"

He wriggled his eyebrows as a response, making her laugh. The next twenty minutes were dedicated to taking pictures, some inside, some outside with another background, and some generously taken by Luke, who seemed to find this petty game amusing. To her surprise, River felt a little jolt of satisfaction as she posted the pictures, especially the one where Thomas kissed her on the cheek, and they *did* look like a couple.

"Gimme," Thomas said, asking for her phone. "I'll write a killer description."

"Don't overdo it, or he won't believe it."

"He will because I'll shout my consuming, burning love to you in the comment section."

River switched chairs and looked over his shoulder to read the description. She couldn't hold a giggle.

Love you @Thomas_Brooks. I've felt happier these past few days than I've been the last few years. #loveatfirstsight #Iloveyou #inlove

"Wow, you know how to hit where it hurts."

Thomas posted the pictures and gave River her phone back. "And that's how it's done. He may have moved on, but I just gave him a big, fat complex of inferiority."

As they commented on her post and responded to each other with ridiculous love declarations that no one would ever make after dating for five days, River realized that she hadn't had this much fun and hadn't laughed like that in a long time. Well before her grandma had passed. It might even have been before she'd started dating Zach, which was both sad and eye-opening.

"You were right," she said. "Doing something petty and childish made my day."

"When in doubt, do something petty."

While she would have loved to wait to see if Zach saw the post, time flew by quickly, and it was almost time to head back.

Luke waved at Thomas, a brilliant smile on his face. "See you next week."

"You bet," Thomas answered, smiling back.

The cold humidity slapped their faces as they exited the Black Bean. The fog was rolling in, clouding the street. River followed Thomas to the mini mart, excited to buy her own food. She stocked up on cereals for breakfast, bread and cheese and ham for lunch, and decided to buy the necessary ingredients to make the

Irish Stew her grandma used to make. It would be for her and Thomas, to thank him for being such a good friend.

As they walked back through the woods to reach the Blackwell House, River didn't feel so nervous anymore. She was safe as long as they stuck together.

CHAPTER ELEVEN

"**I**'ll do the bathroom," River said, as they entered another suite. The last they would clean that day.

"Thanks. I can't scrub another bathtub today. My skin will fall off."

"Sure." She grabbed the bucket with the cleaning supplies she needed and headed to the bathroom. "I'll help you with the sheets when I'm done."

She started cleaning the two sinks, gently rinsing and wiping the detergent away with the cloth. Thomas was being dramatic when he said he had been scrubbing. Edith would fire them on the spot if they aggressively scrubbed the marble bathtubs. This expensive material needed to be taken care of. Talking about Edith, River hadn't seen her that day.

"Do you know where Roberts is?" she said loud enough for Thomas to hear her from the other room.

"No. Not that I care. Why?"

"I don't know. She's usually buzzing around our quarters every morning, but she wasn't there today."

"Oh, *that's* why my breakfast felt so quiet and peaceful. I couldn't put my finger on it."

River laughed.

"It's not the first time," Thomas said. "Sometimes, Mrs. Blackwell calls for her at odd hours."

"Really? How do you know that?"

"Because Shelly's an insomniac who goes out herself at odd hours to smoke, and she said she once saw Roberts go into the house late at night. Sometimes it's early in the morning before the sun's up. So, don't worry if you didn't see her yet today."

"Okay."

After finishing the sink, River kneeled in front of the clawfoot bathtub and began cleaning it. As she turned the faucet on and used the warm water to rinse it, a noise gave her pause. Shuffling. She turned the water off, listening. The shuffling returned, more insistent. Was that Thomas? It couldn't be. It sounded too close, as though it was behind the wall next to the bathtub. As though someone was on the other side.

An icy cold breeze grazed her ear, making her gasp. She whirled around but saw nothing out of the ordinary. The space felt abnormally cold. Thomas must have opened a window in the bedroom.

River resumed cleaning, going a little faster, but stopped again when the light above her head flickered.

"Do they have spare light bulbs somewhere?" she asked, looking up as uneasiness seeped in her chest.

"What?" Thomas said, his voice far away.

River stood. "The light isn't working properly."

Before she could reach the doorway, the door slammed shut in front of her, making her yelp.

"What the…" She reached for the doorknob and shook it. The door didn't budge. "Thomas?"

The light flickered faster and brighter. River's ears whistled, her vision clouding at the edges.

"River?" Thomas's voice felt impossibly far, almost inaudible.

A sinking feeling had burrowed into the pit of her stomach, something heavy and suffocating that she couldn't explain. River shook the door harder, her fingers growing increasingly cold.

The light failed, plunging her into darkness. She let out another cry. Despite the blood pumping in her ears and her heart pounding in her chest, silence fell over her like a heavy blanket.

"Thomas?" she said, her voice nothing but a raw whisper.

He didn't respond. In his place, a raw, croaking breath wheezed through the silence. Her muscles tightened and froze.

She slowly turned, pressing her back against the door and mindlessly clutching the crystal on her chest. "H–hello?"

A ragged breath answered.

River's legs turned numb, and she had to force herself not to drop to the floor. Someone was standing just a few feet from her, their loud breathing the only sound in the room.

"I–is someone here?"

Shoes clicked on the tiles, coming closer. Fear shot through her spine. She turned back to the door and clutched at the doorknob, turning it frantically. The door stayed shut. Another step was taken behind her, and the icy air clawed at her skin some more.

River pounded at the door. "Thomas!"

The ragged breath grazed her ear, and she froze, her forehead pressed to the door. It chilled her to the bone. Feeling once again for the stone on her chest, she forced herself to breathe and tame her panic.

"They did this," a raspy voice whispered. "It wasn't me."

The light buzzed back to life. River looked around, blinking at the sudden brightness. She was alone, and the room wasn't silent anymore.

On the other side of the door came a frantic knock. "Freckles? What's happening?"

"It wasn't me…" the ragged voice said, coming from behind River.

Every muscle in her body tensed, aching. She slowly turned, her breath coming out in short spurts. She let out a choked gasp at the sight of her reflection.

It wasn't her. A blonde woman stood in her place, looking back. Her eyes were wide with fear, her mouth agape.

Thomas knocked on the door again, which still refused to open.

The woman lifted her hand. A knife shone in it. She pointed it toward her midsection and sank the blade inside her stomach, staring at River.

River screamed and pressed her back against the door, a hand clasped against her mouth. Thomas was still calling out to her, but the sound of his voice faded into the background. Her focus was on the bright, red blood pouring out of the woman's stomach, soaking her clothes. She stabbed herself relentlessly, her face frozen, frightened.

"They did this to me."

River choked on a sob as the woman brought the knife to her own throat and pressed the blade to her skin.

"They did this," she said, then slit her throat in one sharp move.

River saw the blood gush out of the wound, but only for a second, as the light flickered the apparition away.

The door opened behind her, and she stumbled, deprived of her support, but Thomas caught her. She fell into his arms, clinging to him.

"Are you okay?" he said, his voice strained. He pulled away, trying to catch her gaze. "What the hell happened?"

Her mouth had gone dry. "I…" She turned to look at the bathroom, certain for a second that she would see *her* again, but the mirror only showed her frightened reflection. "I-I don't know. The door got stuck, and the light went out, and…" She looked at Thomas again, swallowing around the lump in her throat. "I don't know."

"Hey, it's gonna be okay. There's nothing in there." He offered a humorous smile. "Didn't I tell you this house must be haunted?"

A sob caught in her throat.

Thomas's face fell. "I'm *kidding!*" He pulled her into a hug again. "I didn't mean to freak you out. I'm an idiot."

She closed her eyes, willing her heart to slow down. "A little bit, yeah."

He pulled away, his hands still on her shoulders. "You good?"

She opened her mouth, but the words stuck in her throat at the sight of the blonde woman standing behind Thomas. Blood covered every inch of her white shirt and poured through the open wound in her stomach. Above the neckline, the clean slit ran across her throat, dark red blood gushing out. River's gaze travelled to the face. Her blonde hair hid most of it, but she could make out one bloodshot eye through them. It stared right at her.

Cassie's dry lips parted as she whispered in a ragged voice, "They did this."

River bolted out of the room and down the hallway, ignoring the paintings. Their eyes seemed to follow her as she rushed by, nearly sprinting down the stairs.

"River, what the hell!" Thomas shouted, but she couldn't slow down.

She had to know. She had to see for herself that it had been nothing but a hallucination. An incredibly real one. The vision had disappeared as soon as she screamed, leaving no trace of its passage. If Cassie had been there, there would have been a puddle of blood in the middle of the room and footprints everywhere.

River reached the foyer and headed to the door at the back. In a second, she would see Mack and Cassie, and all would be well. She would laugh at herself for being a little crazy, then go back upstairs to help Thomas clean the last room before they served dinner to the Blackwells.

She pushed the kitchen door open and burst in. Mack snapped his head up at the sound. He had already started cooking, making some kind of dough.

"Hey," he said. "Why are you here so early? Did Edith send you?"

River searched the kitchen for Cassie. "What? No... Where's Cassie?"

"Um, Cassie's gone."

Her stomach dropped. "Gone? What do you mean, gone?"

Mack shrugged, working on his dough. "She quit. I thought maybe Edith had sent you to help me, but apparently, I'm gonna have to run this kitchen by myself tonight. At least Annie helped me earlier."

River stared at him, her mouth ajar, none of his words registering after *she quit.* "Why did Cassie quit?"

"I don't know, love. I didn't see her leave. She was already gone when I got up this morning. Had packed all her shit. Edith told me she left." He huffed, shaking his head. "I mean, isn't that weird? We've been working together for more than a year, and she couldn't even find two minutes to come and say goodbye."

River stopped listening. The picture of the woman stabbing herself was embedded in River's mind. Cassie. The way she'd slit her own throat. Completely shredded her abdomen. The blood pooling around her feet.

River could have believed she had dreamed everything. That stress had put a number on her. But now, Cassie was gone, truly gone.

"They did this to me."

Who had she been talking about? Had someone murdered her, and Cassie had shown River how?

You're insane. Truly insane.

Insane or not, Cassie was gone, mysteriously leaving without telling anyone goodbye.

115

River climbed the spiraling staircase on wobbly legs, her mind racing and her heart hammering her chest as she tried to convince herself that she must have had some kind of hallucination, like her first two nights here.

Her grandma often said she felt connected to the other side. The way she would talk about it, it sounded magical, pleasant even. But this… this was wrong. Horrible and nauseating. It made her want to crawl into bed and cry herself to sleep. But no matter what the state of her emotional health was, she had to go back to work.

She looked down at her shaking hands and realized she had pulled the bag of crystals out of her pocket, squeezing its velvet fabric and feeling the rocks inside. It was soothing and helped her stay grounded.

As she reached the second floor, voices floated in the hallway, making River freeze. Clenching the little bag in her hand, she peeked around the wall. Selene stood with her back to River. Facing her was Dorian, once again wearing that heart-wrenching, depressed expression on his face. It seemed to be getting worse as time went on.

"You need to stop what you're doing *immediately*," Selene said, her voice as cold as a glacier. "What on earth were you thinking?"

"Then, give me what I want, Mother."

"Stop trying to manipulate me and everyone around you. We'll lose all our servants at this rate—"

"And we wouldn't want that, would we?"

"It is your own fault you are losing all your aides. How many have you had now?" She sighed heavily when he didn't respond. "Don't you understand? I only have your best interest at heart."

A strained, cynical laugh tumbled out of Dorian's mouth. "Right, of course. That is really the impression I got from your speech last night."

"Enough. All of it. I will give you what you want, but in exchange, you had better be on your best behavior from now on and during the celebration. Don't make a fool of yourself like you did last year. You need to believe me when I say that the consequences of your actions are far worse than you think they are."

"I do not believe a single word coming out of your mouth."

Selene cocked her head. "If you do as I say, I will give you what you desire most. And then you will believe me."

She walked past him, away from River, in the direction of the main stairs.

"I think you are mistaken on what it is that I desire most," Dorian said without turning to her.

Selene paused for a second, then disappeared behind the bend of the hallway.

River pressed her back against the wall, taking a deep breath to calm her nerves. If they knew she had heard part of their conversation, they'd be furious. Still squeezing the bag, she gathered her courage to get out of her hiding place and go back to work. No matter what she had seen or heard today, she still had a job to do.

River stepped into the hallway and gasped as she collided with Dorian. The bag escaped her hand and fell. A few of the crystals spilled out of it, rolling onto the carpet. She quickly shuffled away and dropped to her knees to gather them.

"I'm s-so sorry," she stammered, hoping he would think she apologized for running into him and not because she had heard him and his mother talk. She picked up the rose quartz and the amethyst. When she looked inside the bag, she only counted four crystals. The selenite was missing. Her gaze swept the floor around her until the shiny white rock caught her eye. It had stopped against Dorian's black shoe, and River held her breath as he kneeled to pick it up.

His gray eyes stared into nothingness as he rolled the crystal in his hand. "What is this, River?"

"Just a crystal... I know I'm not supposed to carry any personal items."

She stared at him, trying to decipher the expression on his face. His eyebrows were knitted together slightly. He didn't seem angry, just sort of puzzled, as though something wasn't right. Eventually, he handed the crystal back to her. As River reached for it, her shaky fingers slightly grazed his, and she realized that the two of them kneeled close together, enough for her to see each detail of his handsome face.

"Don't let my mother see it," he said. "Or Miss Roberts."

"Yes. Thank you."

"Don't tell anyone you have these and never take them out again."

River looked at him, taken aback.

Dorian's face was hard. "The walls have ears here. Sometimes, eyes too."

Benjamin's portrait jumped back at her, sending a chill crawling down her spine. "O-okay. I'll keep that in mind." She winced at how unsteady her voice was. This day couldn't end fast enough.

Dorian cocked his head, his features softening. "Are you alright?"

"Yes. Yes, I'm fine." She scrambled back to her feet.

He rose too, a lot more gracefully than she had. "Have a good rest of your day, then."

He walked away, and just as he was about to turn the corridor, River called out to him. "How did you know it was me?"

He stopped, tilting his head in her direction the way he always did when talking to her. "You smell of lavender. I knew you were behind that wall long before I ran into you." A hint of a smile lifted his lips as he said that, as though to say, *I may be blind, but you can't hide from me.*

Warmth rose to River's cheeks. He knew she'd eavesdropped on their conversation, then. He didn't seem mad about it, though. She shoved the bag in her uniform pocket. "May I ask you something?"

"Of course."

"Do you know anything about Cassie leaving?"

She gauged his reaction, watching for any signs that he might know something, especially following his conversation with his mother. But his face only showed surprise.

"Cassie? Did she leave?"

"So I've been told."

He opened his mouth a fraction but froze. A shadow fleeted over his features, narrowing his eyes slightly. "Pardon me, there is something I need to do." He walked away, his fingers trailing against the wall, either to keep himself steady or find his way back, River didn't know.

119

The only thing she did know was that mentioning Cassie had provoked something in him, only intensifying the dread gnawing at River's guts.

CHAPTER TWELVE

C assie had packed her stuff and left a note for Edith saying she quit. At least, that was what Edith had told them when everyone asked. She had been gone for a few days now, and River hadn't seen another apparition since. It had begun to blur in her mind, and she was seriously questioning whether she had really seen it or not.

She blew onto the rosemary tea she made for herself and took a sip of the steaming beverage. The temperature inside the kitchen was so cold it was almost painful, and all the layers of flannel pants and fluffy sweaters and woolen socks couldn't make River truly warm. The chill always managed to get to her somehow.

A candle was burning, and the crystals were arranged in a semi-circle around it. That wouldn't really charge them, but the sight of them soothed River.

The quarters quieted as everyone left to start their shift, and she enjoyed that time alone. What she would enjoy even more was her day off. That week at work had taken a toll on her. The constant creaks and cracks of the house. The paintings that always seemed to move at the edge of her vision, then stilled when she looked at them. The smell in each room and corridor that burned her nose. The memory of Cassie stabbing herself in the mirror, giving River nightmares. Mirrors had started to make her anxious. She often avoided looking into them when working, afraid to see a face that wasn't her own.

What Dorian had said also played on repeat in her mind.

"The walls have ears here. Sometimes, eyes too."

She wished he hadn't said that because she couldn't stop thinking about it when she was inside the house, always glancing around to make sure she wasn't being watched.

Thomas entered the kitchen, dragging his feet on the stone floor and ruffling his brown hair. "Morning."

"Slept in today, did you?"

"My only reason to get up early is if it's my day off and I can get the fuck away from this place."

River grinned. "And see Luke."

"That too, yes."

He poured himself some coffee left in the pot and sat opposite her. "Are you gonna be okay today?"

"Of course. Why?"

"You've been jittery since your freak out."

"I'm okay," she said too fast, drinking more tea to warm her insides.

"Why don't you tell me the truth? You've been dodging the subject all week."

She sighed, not knowing what to say.

"I won't judge, you know," he said. "I have two little sisters. I'm a good listener."

"I know. I'm just scared you're gonna think I'm crazy."

"I pretty much know what happened already."

"Really? I don't think you do."

"You saw a ghost."

She frowned and opened her mouth a fraction. "Well—"

"I *knew* it. I knew this place *had* to be haunted. I've heard Annie talk about how people died tragic deaths in here, so it can't *not* be haunted. It always makes weird noises, and it's always so cold everywhere—"

"Well, this *is* Maine."

"And that door *was* stuck. When you were in the bathroom, I thought you were playing a prank on me for a moment, but no one can act that good." He paused, looking at her expectantly. "So?"

"Listen. I thought I saw a ghost. Now, I'm not so sure."

"Considering your reaction, I'd say you did. Who was it? A member of the Blackwell family? Anyone we'd recognize by looking at the paintings?"

River hesitated, tapping her fingers on her mug. Should she tell him? He believed in ghosts, that was something. But if she told him about Cassie, it would only scare him.

"I don't know who it was. I didn't see the face properly."

He nodded, taking this in. "Next time you see one, talk to them."

"I really hope I won't see another one. Maybe *you* will."

"I'll make sure to really look at them and tell you what they look like, unlike you."

River chuckled. "Do you *really* believe in that stuff?"

"Don't you? You're the one who saw a motherfreakin' ghost." His eyes fell onto the candle and the crystals. He grabbed the rose quartz, looking it over. "What are you, a witch?"

She gave him a tight smile. "No."

"Maybe that's why ghosts talk to you. Maybe you're conjuring them without even knowing it."

River grabbed the washcloth used to clean the table and threw it in his face, making him laugh.

The door leading to the house opened and shut. Heels on stone clicked their way to the kitchen, and Edith appeared in the doorway.

"Thomas. Pack your bags and come with me."

He did a double take. "Am I fired?"

"Simon quit. You are Dorian's new helper."

"What?" Thomas and River said at the same time.

"The cottage is yours," Edith replied, unphased as usual.

Thomas glanced at River, his mouth slightly ajar. "When did he quit? Why didn't he say goodbye?"

"When members of the staff quit, they are asked to leave the premises immediately."

A sinking feeling settled inside River's stomach. Cassie had apparently 'quit,' too.

"Did you see him leave?" she asked.

Edith turned her cold, blue eyes on her. "Excuse me?"

River hesitated, then swallowed. "Did you see him drive away?"

"What kind of question is that? Of course I did. I always escort people to make sure they *do* leave."

"Did you escort Cassie too?"

Edith glared daggers at her, and River was certain she had seen the tiniest twitch of an eye. "I did. Now if you are done interrogating me, I would like to escort Thomas to his new quarters."

"But what about River?" he asked.

"She'll have to work on her own. Just like you had to before her."

"I…" He glanced at River again. "No, thanks."

Edith's face fell. "Excuse me?"

"I wanna keep working with River."

Warmth and gratitude filled River, but that idiot didn't know what was good for him. "Thomas…"

"I mean it."

"Dude. No more cleaning for you. And you'll get your own cottage instead of sharing a room with seven other people!"

"That is correct," Edith said, for once not too unpleased with River's intervention. "It's also an extra five hundred dollars a month."

Thomas's jaw dropped open. "For real?"

River leaned over the table and reached for his hand. *"Five hundred dollars extra.* You'd be stupid not to do it. I will kick your butt if you say no again."

"But what about you? I feel bad for leaving you alone." He tried to smile. "With the ghosts and all."

River returned the smile. "I'll be fine. They'll hire someone else to take your place. Plus, I wanna see that cottage, so you better invite me for dinner."

He squeezed her hand in return. "You got it."

Edith sighed loudly behind them. "If you don't hurry up, I will ask Shelly to—"

"And let that bitch take my extra money? Uh, no thank you. I'm coming."

River laughed as Thomas headed to the doorway.

He turned before walking out. "Good luck today. I'll see you later, okay?"

"Yeah, okay. Good luck on your new job."

He left, and River's smile vanished. She was happy for him, but he had become a true friend to her these past weeks, and the perspective of working without him saddened her. No more chatting and joking while cleaning. She would wander through the cold halls of the Blackwell House alone.

Or maybe not completely alone, and that scared her even more.

CHAPTER THIRTEEN

R iver's body ached from cleaning windows, scrubbing bathtubs, changing sheets, washing floors, all of that faster than
she usually did so she could be on time to serve dinner. She rushed
down the main stairs, a minute away from being late. Her feet
throbbed in her shoes, and the thought of having to stand for
another hour made her nauseous.

She burst through the kitchen door. "I'm here!"

"You're fine, love," Mack said, attempting a smile, though he
looked just as cranky as the other nights since Cassie had left.
Without her, Edith had to step up to help him in the kitchen, and
the two of them barely tolerated each other. In Mack's defense,

not a lot of people could tolerate Edith, and Edith most definitely hated everyone.

She glared daggers at River, her wrinkles more pronounced as she frowned. "Hurry up, and serve them the appetizer."

River made sure she wasn't too disheveled and tucked the strands of curly hair that had sprung free from her braid behind her ears. She rounded the counter and frowned at the two plates. "Two?"

"Dorian's not here," Mack said.

River's heart sank. The only thing that made serving dinner bearable was Dorian saying thank you to her, always calling her by her name because he could apparently smell either the lavender lotion or the lavender shampoo she used.

"Is he sick or something?"

Edith shoved the two plates in River's hands. "It's none of your concern. Go now."

River pushed the door to the dining room with her shoulder and slipped inside.

"I can't believe you still gave him what he wants," Richard said to Selene. "He's manipulating you."

"He is my son, Richard. And I think it will be different this time." Selene picked up her glass as River put the plate in front of her, the wine swirling inside as red as her lips. "I didn't want him to be affected by the truth, but he figured it out on his own. It is hard to accept for him now, but he'll be happier for it in the end."

River rounded the table.

"I wish you would have told him earlier." Richard winced, tugging at the collar of his dress shirt. "I didn't think he would be capable of something like that. Your son is damaged, Selene."

River served Richard, trying as best she could not to look at him, even though his gaze had followed her since she had entered the room.

Before she could turn and leave, his fingers grazed the back of her thigh just below her dress. "Thank you, little pet."

River clenched her teeth and balled her fists, trying to hide the shiver of disgust that ran through her. She left his side, though she couldn't help listening to their conversation as she walked to the door.

"He has had a lot of hardship."

"You should still punish him for what he did."

The wine glass clinked loudly as Selene put it back onto the table. "Do *not* tell me what I should or shouldn't do with my son. You don't know him like I do."

River entered the kitchen, wondering despite herself what the hell Selene was talking about. For someone who claimed her son wasn't right in his head, she sure seemed a bit odd herself. Dorian always looked the most depressed when his mother talked to him. Whatever had happened, Dorian had apparently decided that his mother's presence was too much to take tonight. Maybe Thomas knew something. Good thing she would have dinner with him later.

The sharp wind tried to knock River over as she crossed the property to reach the small cottage on the other side. Darkness surrounded her, and her phone's flashlight struggled to pierce through it. It was almost out of battery, even if she had only turned it on a few times to use its light that week. She suspected the cold drained it quicker. After the day she'd had, walking that distance felt like a true workout.

Soft yellow light glistened through the two windows facing her. She hurried, longing for some warmth, and knocked on the wooden door. It opened in an instant, and Thomas greeted her with the biggest smile on his face. He grabbed her hand and pulled her inside.

"Look at this place!"

Warmth swallowed her. She looked around the place and gasped. *"Shut up."*

"I *know.*"

"This is amazing!"

"I know!"

The place wasn't big, but it was far warmer and cozier than the staff's quarters. To the left was a fireplace. The flames sent shadows dancing across the walls, illuminating the cottage with a welcoming light. Against the wall opposite the entrance was a queen-sized bed. Then, to the right-hand side was a kitchen area and a solid, square table.

"The bathroom's this way," Thomas said, leading River to the right.

The shower looked brand new, enclosed within glass walls and a glass door that almost went up to the ceiling. The white tiles on the floor and above the sink sparkled.

"I'm not jealous, but I hate you a little bit," River said, wrinkling her nose at him.

Thomas laughed and led her back to the kitchen area. "Guess what, there's wine in there. Want some?"

"I'm offended that you're even asking."

"Fair enough."

River shed her coat and scarf and sat down, admiring the small but cozy space. Dorian sure treated his staff well.

"So, how was your day?" she asked when Thomas settled across from her.

"Well, I'm not completely exhausted for the first time in months."

"I bet. How is it working for Dorian?"

"The man is definitely a little odd, but he's not bad at all. He's a lot nicer than his family, but we already knew that."

River smiled. For a reason she couldn't explain, she didn't want to think he'd be like his family. She wanted to hold on to the few times he had talked to her, how kind he had been each time. "What's the job like? What do you have to do?"

"Not gonna lie, I was a bit anxious before starting. Simon and I got along fine, but once he became an aide, he didn't really feel the need to talk to me anymore, so I never got to know what it was that he did. I thought maybe Dorian needed help with, I don't know, stuff. But he doesn't. Except for shaving, that's it."

"Then, why does he need an aide?"

Thomas offered a small smile and shrugged. "You know, I think he's really lonely. He just… wants to make conversation."

River's heart broke a little. Why would Dorian stay here if he wasn't happy? Why didn't he have friends? Why couldn't he get a job or something instead of living in this castle alone?

"He asked a lot about me, my life, my sisters. He really took the time to get to know me." Thomas paused, as though thinking. "I read to him for the better part of the afternoon, and then we took a walk outside to get some air. He sent me on my way at five."

"Wow."

"Yeah."

"That makes me a bit sad."

"Me too. He likes to go downtown a few times a week, so we're going tomorrow. He definitely needs help with that."

River sipped on the wine, lost in thought for a moment. "Did he talk about himself?"

The twinkle in Thomas's eyes returned. "Why, Freckles? Are you interested?"

"Hey, you're the one who called him 'insanely fucking hot.'"

"And I stand by it."

River laughed, but it soon died down. "He wasn't at dinner tonight. Do you know why?"

"Oh? I don't know. I mean, he seemed really depressed."

"He always does look sad."

"I know, but somehow, it felt worse." He paused, thinking. "Or maybe not. Maybe it's just because I got to really talk to him."

"Maybe he's bummed out about Simon leaving."

"That's possible. But don't worry, Freckles. I'll make sure to entertain him. I know I said this place sucked, but between the cottage and the extra money, it's really not bad. And Dorian's nice. I think I'll keep working here a while longer."

"Nicer than Richard for sure." River winced and drank some wine.

Thomas frowned. "Aw, I'm sorry I wasn't there to—"

"It's okay, don't worry about it. I didn't mean to make you feel bad."

"Hey, you can come hang out here anytime you want, okay? You can even use my shower if you want some privacy."

"Thanks, I appreciate it."

The two of them cooked something easy with what was already in the cupboards, and the rest of the evening was spent chatting, laughing, and drinking the rest of the wine. Not working with Thomas sucked, but having a place to discuss and relax without anyone around was quite nice.

"All right, time to go for me," River said when it was almost eleven. She didn't start early in the morning, but her body begged for some sleep.

Thomas rose and followed her to the door. "Do you want me to walk you back?"

"I'm fine." She put her dark green coat on and wrapped the scarf around her neck. When she opened the door and turned back to Thomas to say goodbye, he seemed lost in thought. "What is it?"

"Hm? Nothing, I was just thinking about something."

"Well, now I wanna know."

He chewed on his lip for a second. "I didn't want to talk about it, but I guess I can tell you. Dorian is nice and all, but he *did* make an odd demand."

River's curiosity flared. "What did he ask?"

"Roberts brought me to his room, and as soon as she left, he asked me to look around and tell him if I saw any paintings or mirrors. If I did, I was supposed to throw them out the window. Literally."

"Oh… Why do I find this creepy?"

"Because it is."

"Did you find any?"

Thomas shook his head. "No. But why does he care if there are paintings or mirrors in his room? It's not like he can see them."

Maybe they can see him.

The intrusive thought sent a chill crawling down her spine. Maybe Dorian hated those paintings as much as she did. Maybe when he could still see, he used to feel like they watched him, like River felt every day as she walked past them. What about the mirrors, though?

"I tried to make a joke about the windows," Thomas said. "I asked if I should remove them because they can be like mirrors sometimes. You know what he told me? 'No one can hide behind a window.' What the fuck does that mean? And he wasn't joking, either. The guy was dead serious."

"That's odd for sure… On that note, thanks for giving me the creeps before I leave."

"You're very welcome."

River said goodbye and stepped outside. No fog blurred her vision that night, and the moon shone brightly in the black sky. She could see pretty well without the phone's light. As she walked back to her quarters, the Blackwell House loomed at the top of the hill. All the windows on that side were dark, and everything was still.

Except for one window on the last floor.

The shape of a person stood behind it, and River froze, staring. They stayed immobile, and she knew in her gut that they were looking at her. Then, they stepped back and disappeared into the shadows. River released her breath and resumed walking.

She hadn't taken two steps when the sound of broken glass startled her to a stop. The window on the last floor shattered as a man flew through it, his scream splitting the night air as he fell. The sound his body made when it crashed to the ground froze her insides. She broke into a sprint. Her throat burned and her legs ached as she ran uphill, but she didn't slow down. Whoever had fallen, they had to be dead. No one could survive a fall like that. Bile rose in River's throat at the thought that she was about to stumble upon a corpse.

She skidded to a stop, her breathing erratic. "What…"

No one was there. No dead body lying in the mud. She looked up. The window that had shattered into a million pieces only a minute ago was now intact.

CHAPTER FOURTEEN

"Talk to me."

River stared at the painting, willing Benjamin to come to life. His eyes, once so animated, were dead and cold.

"I know you reached out to me like Cassie did. I saw you fall from that window. You wanted to show me something, didn't you?"

Silence. A cold breeze enveloped her, clawing at her exposed skin.

"You didn't jump like Selene said. You were pushed."

Benjamin's face turned an inch, the skin straining over the canvas. River gasped. Whispers trickled down the hallway. They intensified as they passed by her, murmuring in her ears and grazing the small hairs at the back of her neck, then faded into the distance.

River swallowed, balling her fists to control the shaking. "Who did it? Was it—" She stop mid-sentence, looking up at the teenager standing next to his father in the painting. Could it be? According to Selene, Benjamin had been violent and had caused Dorian to lose his sight. That was reason enough to want revenge.

She swallowed at her own thoughts. She couldn't picture Dorian doing something like that, but still... It could have been an accident.

"Did something happen to Simon?" she asked instead.

Something knocked against a wall. The painting slightly shifted. Muffled footsteps resonated through the house, making River's heart pick up the pace. Before she could react, a voice made her jump.

"What are you doing here?"

River whirled around, her stomach dropping as she saw Edith.

"You're supposed to be on the ground floor this week."

River nodded. "My apologies. I got mixed up. I'll go right away."

She dropped her head and headed to the stairs, but Edith grabbed her arm before she could leave.

"The only reason I haven't fired you is because Dorian took a liking to you, and now because we are understaffed. But make no mistake, Miss Devin. As soon as I find a replacement for Thomas, you're gone. I'll simply tell Dorian you quit."

River's stomach churned. "Miss Roberts, I haven't done anything wrong, I swear."

"No? I just found you on the wrong floor, and I don't believe you got 'mixed up.' I also see how Dorian always calls you by your name at dinner, which makes me think that you disobeyed my rules and have been talking to him more than you should have been."

"I haven't—"

Edith's bony fingers tightened around River's arm. "Don't lie."

"I..." Her mind scrambled to find the right words to say, but she wasn't doing well under the pressure of a superior. "I only talked to him when he talked to me. You said I couldn't talk to them unless I was being talked to. I didn't break any rule."

The fingers released her. "In any case, I suggest you start looking for a new job and a new place to live. You'll be gone soon."

"But—"

"Go to work. *Now.*"

Her throat tight, River hurried down the stairs. The old woman was serious. She had hated River from the start, and for reasons she had no control over.

She gathered her cleaning supplies and headed to the library. Thomas had drawn her a little map so she would find her way. The third floor had been fairly easy. The layout was similar to the second floor, and no one ever seemed to be up there, so she didn't bother anyone by cleaning the different rooms. But on the ground floor, there was more life. She couldn't risk stumbling into a room where one of the Blackwell family members was. She had a schedule and needed to respect it. Right now, the schedule told her to clean the library.

She was curious to know what these people did all day. The cleaning and the food were taken care of for them. Did they have hobbies? Did they ever leave this place to go downtown or somewhere else? Did they spend their time here having tea parties, walking in their garden, and staring at their creepy paintings? She rarely saw them, but from what Thomas had told her, Dorian wasn't going anywhere, except downtown a few times a week.

She crossed the foyer, past the dining room and what looked like a sitting room. The library was at the far end of the hallway. The imposing double doors were wide open, giving her a glimpse of the inside. It looked enormous. Rows and rows of shelves filled with books. It was beautiful and intimidating at the same time. She had to clean those shelves all on her own, and the task was daunting. At least they weren't so high that she would need a ladder, something small to be grateful for.

Before she could reach the room, a figure emerged from another hallway to the right. River's legs stopped working. Richard seemed taken aback by her presence, but a smirk quickly lifted his gray mustache. "Oh. Hello, pet."

River looked at the floor, letting her gaze get lost in the intricate patterns of the carpet.

Richard closed the distance between them. He pressed a knuckle under her chin, forcing her to look up. "I said hello. It's just the two of us. You can speak."

River swallowed around the lump in her throat. His dark eyes bored into hers, chilling her to her core. "H-hello, sir." Her voice was so low that even he couldn't have possibly heard it.

He leaned over, and River gave her all not to flinch. "That's more like it."

He looked at her from head to toe, his gaze lingering over her chest. River gritted her teeth, her shoulders tense, cursing herself for not asking Edith for a larger uniform for fear of annoying the woman.

After staring at her for what felt like a literal minute, Richard whispered, "When you go back to the higher floors, we'll have more intimacy."

He sauntered past her, and she hurried to the library, her stomach in knots. Her heartbeat quickened, and her eyes burned. Maybe it was a good thing that Edith wanted her gone. On her next day off, River would start looking and applying for jobs. The ghosts were bad enough, but Richard was far more frightening.

River took a deep breath, trying to calm her raw nerves, and looked around the room. It was bigger than she had anticipated. To the left-hand side, a large sitting area with comfy couches and armchairs surrounded a huge fireplace. The fire was roaring, and through the tall windows on each side, River could see the gray sky and the red forest surrounding the property.

The rows of shelves created a labyrinth of books in which River could get lost cleaning. These were heavy, shiny, the wood carved with an intricate pattern of roses and stems and thorns. She started dusting the best she could. She worked quickly and maybe not so thoroughly, overwhelmed by the thought that the floors also needed to be washed in this gigantic room.

Gray clouds darkened the sky as she made progress. The soft yellow lights of the room and the fire were barely enough to see correctly. River finished one row of shelves, which ran along the back wall, and turned to the last one. It made a sharp angle and spread all the way to the middle of the room, efficiently putting an end to this maze of books.

Movement caught River's eye. She turned, staring at the small gap between the shelves. Where the angle was, a thin, black line filled the space. And in that space, an eye stared at River.

A scream caught in her throat, and she dropped her rag, stumbling backward. Her back hit something. Not a bookshelf, but something that moved behind her and clamped her shoulders, and she let out another cry.

"What's happening? Are you alright?"

Heart in throat, River looked up at the man steadying her, but her throat was too tight to speak. Dorian looked vaguely in her direction, genuine concern painting his features.

"River?"

She looked back at the gap between the shelves. Only blackness remained. She took a steadying breath, forcing herself to relax her shoulders a little, and realized that Dorian was still holding her, his hands gentle but firm on her arms. "I thought I saw—I don't know, like a… It's stupid…"

"What was it?"

"There's just…" She bit her lower lip, already feeling dumb for saying that to him. "There's a gap between the shelves in the corner, and I thought someone was behind it." She laughed nervously. "It's nothing, never mind. I think I scared myself… And you startled me. How did you get in here so silently? Were you a cat in a past life, or…"

"My apologies. It seems I have a bad habit of frightening you or running into you."

She let out a tight chuckle, her heart still hammering her chest, this time also because he was standing close to her. The thoughts she'd had before seemed ridiculous now. He couldn't have hurt his father. The simple sight of him melted the doubts away.

"I can see you knew it was me once again," she said. "Does that lotion smell that bad? Maybe it's the shampoo."

He let go of her arms, dropping his hands slowly as though to make sure she was steady. "I never said it smelled bad. On the contrary."

Warmth rose to her cheeks.

"Are you sure you're okay?"

"Yes. It's just…" She shrugged. "This house."

A smile stretched his lips, and he bowed his head lower, as though wanting to share a secret. "I hate it. Hated it when I was a child, still do, even if I can't see it anymore. Don't tell anyone."

"Your secret's safe with me." She glanced back at the gap. The sight of it prickled at her skin. "Would you believe me if I told you I think I keep seeing ghosts in this place?" The words escaped her mouth before she could stop them. She forced out a nervous laugh, trying to make it sound like she was kidding.

Dorian didn't laugh. "I would."

River peered at him for a moment. "I can't tell if you're joking."

"I only am if you are." He took a step back. "I initially did not come here to bother you. I need to find a book."

She picked up her rag. "I can help with that. Or is Thomas with you?"

"I sent him on his lunch break. But I know where to find the book, thank you."

He sidestepped her and turned after the bend, walking by the gap. Before following him, River stared at it, making sure she wouldn't see that eye again.

Dorian moved swiftly through the rows, running his hand on the shelves to the right. He was muttering something, and River had to strain to listen to him.

He's counting.

143

He was using his hand to feel the separation of each shelf, counting them to get to where he needed. River watched him in fascination as he stopped in front of one of them, running long fingers along the top shelf, then the one underneath it. He started at the far right and counted books, grazing each of their spines. After the nineteenth, he grabbed a worn out, red book and pulled it off the shelf.

"That was just for show, admit it," River joked. "You have no idea what you just grabbed."

Dorian laughed. The sound of it was music to her ears, but it was nothing compared to that devastating smile. "I have organized my favorite books in a certain way so I could always find them. It's easier than trying to explain to Thomas how to find them or make him search for half an hour."

"Fair. What book is it?"

He tucked the book under his arm. "You probably wouldn't know it. It was published in the year eighteen-seventeen."

River pressed her lips together.

"I can almost hear you smile," Dorian said.

"Not at all."

"Go ahead, make fun of me."

"I would *never.*"

His smile widened, making her blush. Good thing he couldn't see her. "You think I'm a snob."

"No, no… *But.*"

He raised an eyebrow expectantly.

"I have a Kindle with hundreds of *modern* books on it. All sorts of genres. I can give it to Thomas if you want. If not for you, do it for him. Poor guy."

This stole a laugh out of him, and she chuckled too. She didn't want to tease him to the point of offending him—he was her boss after all—but Dorian didn't seem to mind. He looked like he enjoyed it, even.

"I'll talk to him about it. Thank you for the offer. And the conversation."

"Of course."

He turned away and walked down the aisle of books. "Don't worry about the ghosts. They're harmless."

The oddity of that sentence left River stunned for a minute, but she didn't have time to waste. She finished cleaning as fast as she could, forcing herself not to look inside any dark gaps between bookshelves.

CHAPTER FIFTEEN

G oing to Stormhedge alone wasn't nearly as fun as going with Thomas. The walk there seemed twice as long, and while River enjoyed her lavender latte and banana bread each time, the few hours at the coffee shop quickly became boring.

Thomas had been working for Dorian for nearly two weeks now. He seemed to enjoy it, and he even got regular visits from Mack, who liked to give him the leftovers the Blackwell family hadn't touched. He could go downtown more often than River and had taken the time to add cheesy comments on the pictures they'd posted on Instagram. River checked them as her phone charged. Zach hadn't taken the bait. His own pictures with Bella only multiplied, and he hadn't reached out to her. River had to admit that if one good thing had come from working at the Blackwell House, it was that she hadn't had too much time to think about him, and she began to wonder if she still cared about him. She was too busy looking over her shoulder and jumping at every creak and whisper.

Because the house whispered to her, or at least, some ghosts did.

There was no point in arguing with herself about it. Her grandma would explain to her that if spirits didn't move on, it meant they had unfinished business, or something was keeping them from leaving. The reasons for that were varied and could be difficult to pinpoint. The sad truth, Willow had said, was that unlike what was portrayed in the movies, finding a way to make a spirit cross over was much harder in real life. The living had very few ways of doing that, even if they could communicate with the afterlife. Ghosts had different ways of expressing themselves, and River had experienced it first-hand.

After spending a couple of hours at the coffee shop looking for another job and applying to different places without much hope, River waved Luke goodbye and headed to the mini mart. Aside from the basic groceries River needed, she stocked up on herbs to make new protection vials. She had always liked to make those, mostly because her grandma used to and because they looked pretty, but this time she truly felt the need for them. If not for the ghosts, maybe they would help against the old man lurking in the hallways. He hadn't made another move on her despite his usual staring and ass-grabbing at dinner. One time during the week when she was cleaning the upper floors, she heard him coming up the stairs. Without thinking about it, she opened one of the oversized wardrobes and hid inside, only coming out several minutes later, when she was sure he had left.

River grabbed some rosemary, as always, then sage and mint. At the register, she bought the smallest rose bouquet—she would use those petals as well.

She headed back to the Blackwell House, the sharp wind still trying to infiltrate her green coat, the taste of salt on her tongue. On her way, she did something she had never done while living with Zach and hoped no one would see her. Something she hadn't done since she was a child. Drinking tea while lighting a candle was one thing, making pretty vials with dried herbs and carrying shiny crystals was another, but this... this was worth getting the stink eye.

And yet, it reminded her of her childhood, of the hours spent walking in the woods with her grandma. River found a long stick, about three feet long, and gathered smaller ones, the thinner the better. She took her time, enjoying spending time in the woods, weaving between tall trees, the scent of moss floating about the air. Despite the cold, she felt at ease in nature, focused on her task. Once her spare plastic bag was full of sticks, she returned to her quarters, her boots crunching on the falling leaves along the way.

The rest of the afternoon was spent making a makeshift broom-stick while the herbs and the rose petals were drying in the kitchen oven. Air drying was preferable, but it would take days, and River wanted to make those vials now. She tied the thin sticks around the branch using pieces of ivy she had torn off the wall outside. The task was difficult, and the branches dug into her fingertips, but a sense of childlike joy took hold of her upon finishing. The broomstick was crooked and looked like the ones she used to make as a little girl, meaning it didn't look great, but it was the intention that mattered.

Once the herbs were as dry as she could make them, she grossly crunched them. She grabbed two bags of the chamomile tea and tore them open to add to her mix, then filled up her glass vials. It smelled like sweet childhood memories, like her grandma.

Night had settled over Stormhedge by the time she was done. It was after five, which meant that Thomas was probably done working. River grabbed two vials and the broom, then braved the cold outside, her scarf wrapped around her hair and the lower half of her face.

The windows in the cottage were lit with a warm glow. She strode to the small structure, craving the warmth inside. Thomas would undoubtedly tease her for bringing him such weird gifts, but she would feel better if he had them. She would have made a broomstick for herself as well, but everyone would make fun of her. She shouldn't care so much about what people thought, but she did.

As River reached the front door, voices rose from the cottage. Did he have company in there? She hesitated a second, not wanting to bother him. Maybe it was just Mack.

She knocked, and the voices fell quiet. She couldn't hear anything but the ocean, not even footsteps. It was like whoever was inside had turned into a statue, not wanting to open the door.

She knocked again. "Thomas? It's just me."

Another few beats of silence followed. Then, the sound of the footsteps she had been waiting for finally echoed, and the door opened a crack.

River smiled at Thomas, but it didn't stick to her face. He looked ghastly, his eyes a little too wide. He held the door open just enough to peek through the gap as though hiding something at his back.

"Hi," he said, though he didn't smile.

"Hi."

She peered at him. He only stared back.

"Are you okay?" she said eventually.

He nodded a little too eagerly. "Yes, of course. I'm fine."

She almost asked if she could come in but didn't. Every time she visited him, he greeted her with a wide smile and opened the door for her to come in. This time it was clear he didn't want her to be there.

"Are you with someone?" she asked.

"Nope. No."

"I thought I heard voices."

"It was just an audiobook."

She studied him a little longer. "Are you sure everything's all right?"

The neutral expression he was trying to wear faltered for a second, and River could swear she saw fear in his eyes.

"I'm okay," he said. "I just have a cold. I wouldn't want to give it to you."

"Oh, okay." She reached for the vials in her pocket and handed them to him. "I just wanted to give you this. For protection. And healing too, so maybe it'll help with the cold."

Thomas took the vials and looked them over, his features softening. "Witchy stuff. *Great.*"

"Here's a broomstick." She untucked the broomstick nestled under her arm and raised it for him to take, ignoring his teasing.

A chuckle escaped his mouth, and he shook his head. "Am I supposed to fly on it? Where's my pointy hat?"

"You have to put it next to your door."

"Okay, weirdo."

"If it falls, it means it has protected you against a bad spell."

She expected more laughter, but it didn't come. Thomas looked at her with a puzzled expression, as though wondering if maybe she had a concussion.

"This place gives me the creeps, so just humor me and take the witchy stuff."

A small smile lifted the corner of his lips, and he looked the broom over. "Did a five-year-old make it?"

"Hey."

"I'm kidding. Thank you."

"All right. Well, take care, okay?"

"I will."

River started walking away when Thomas called out to her.

"Freckles."

"Yeah?"

He looked like he wanted to say something important, his eyes once again filled with what looked like fear or worry. Maybe even the beginning of tears. "I may have to leave."

"Leave? When? Why?"

"Just… family emergency."

"Are your sisters okay?"

He glanced behind him briefly. "Yeah, it's hard to explain, but… I just wanted to tell you…" His eyes found hers. "You're a good friend. And I'm happy I got to know you."

Her stomach sank all the way to the ground. Why did this feel like goodbye forever?

"Thomas—"

She didn't have time to finish before he shut the door.

CHAPTER SIXTEEN

"Thomas left."

River's jaw dropped, and no words would come out of her mouth. Edith stood in the common bedroom's doorway, her back straight and her lips as pinched as usual.

"Another one who left?" Annie said, who apparently could talk while River still felt like her mouth was glued shut.

"I'm afraid so," Edith answered.

River's head spun. So, he *had* left, then. He had told her he might, but it still felt strange. Why leave overnight? Why did his goodbye feel so ominous? Against her will, her mind wandered to Cassie and her alleged departure, making her breath catch in her throat.

Thomas had not acted like his usual silly, solar self. He seemed scared, and he was definitely hiding something—or someone—behind that door. River had heard voices, and that was no audiobook. Did whoever was there threaten or hurt him? As if having a will on its own, her hand reached into her uniform's pocket and held the crystals tight. She had been *right there*. She should have done more, asked more questions, tried to help him.

"Not it," Shelly said, jarring River out of her thoughts.

Everyone turned to her.

She shrugged. "I don't want to be Dorian's aide. Just telling you before you ask. I'd rather run into creepy old Richard."

River stared at her, still at a loss for words. A few weeks ago, Shelly would have begged to work for Dorian. Now, she looked at the floor, her arms crossed against her chest and her eyebrows knitted together. None of this was right.

"Actually, Dorian has chosen his aide himself." Edith turned her stone-cold glare to River. "He specifically asked for you."

"M-me?" Her dry tongue could barely form coherent words.

"Pack your bags and follow me. You have five minutes."

River opened her mouth to answer, but Edith left the room before she could.

"Great," one of the maids said. "That'll mess up our schedules. *Again.* What the hell does he put his aides through that they all run away so fast?"

Annie sighed. "He's a sweet boy."

Shelly huffed, leaving the room. "You know, I really don't think he is."

River took a moment to gather herself and take a few breaths. Thomas was gone suddenly, and Shelly's opinion of Dorian had completely flipped. Had something happened between them? Did she know something River didn't? Dorian always seemed so polite and genuine each time River talked to him, but could he be hiding something?

Selene had implied that the hit he took on the head did something to him, aside from making him blind. On the other hand, Thomas had told River Dorian was a decent man.

Nausea roiled in her stomach. She didn't even have time to ponder any of this, she had to get ready and leave. She was already wearing her uniform, which was now useless, but her hair was undone, curly and wild and falling down her back. She didn't have time to change or put her hair up, she had to pack as fast as possible.

Edith came back exactly five minutes later, just as River was closing her suitcase. She looked at River's hair with unmatched disdain but didn't say anything about it. Instead, she turned and walked down the hallway, and River hurried after her.

"Carry that suitcase. God forbid you wreck those floors with the wheels," Edith said, not turning around.

River didn't argue, walking awkwardly through the mansion as she strained to carry her suitcase, making sure it didn't touch the floor.

"Do you know why Thomas left?" she dared ask, hoping Edith would have more information.

"No. I don't care *why* he left. I care that he did without telling me."

"So, you didn't escort him out like you did with Simon?"

She sighed loudly to make sure River heard how irritating her questions were.

River powered through. "I'm worried about him. He's my friend."

"This isn't the first time one of Dorian's aides leaves without saying anything. I found out this morning from Dorian himself."

She followed Edith down a hallway that stretched to the left of the house. They headed to a section River had never stepped foot in, a section only Edith was allowed to clean. There, she stopped in front of a closed door and knocked.

Dorian's voice floated from behind. "Come in."

She opened the door but didn't enter, instead waiting for River to step inside. As soon as River did, Edith shut the door.

River took in the room before her. It wasn't a normal bedroom. This was a giant suite, far bigger than her apartment in New York, with dark wood everywhere. To her left was a bed, a wardrobe, and a door leading to a bathroom, and to her right, a large sitting area with a beautiful sofa, two armchairs, a long, rectangular coffee table, the whole thing complete with a decadent fireplace. On the opposite wall stood three sets of French doors leading to the garden outside.

"Hello, River."

River startled a little at Dorian's voice. He was sitting on the sofa facing the fireplace, his back to her.

She put the suitcase down as delicately as she could and waited. She didn't know what to do or say. She didn't know what to think about this man anymore, but she swallowed around the lump in her throat and managed a small, "Hello."

"Before you sit down, I need you to look around the room and see if you find any mirrors or pictures. Look under the bed, inside the wardrobe, and open all the drawers."

Thomas had told her about this odd demand, something he had to do every morning. Despite this, he hadn't complained about working for Dorian. He'd even seemed to enjoy it.

"If you find anything let me know," Dorian added.

River did as she was told, rummaging through the unfamiliar space. Now that she paid attention to it, this room was at odds with the rest of the house. Aside from the French doors, the walls were empty, devoid of any paintings. She searched the wardrobe, the drawers, looked under the bed and inside the nightstands, then went into the bathroom. The bare wall above the sink made her pause. She looked inside the cupboards, which were empty except for a few towels. At last, she walked over to where Dorian was sitting and looked at the mantlepiece, the small shelf in the corner, and finally headed to the desk against the wall, opening its drawers.

"I didn't find anything," she said.

"Thank you. Please, sit."

River sank into the chair next to the sofa facing the French doors and peered at Dorian. He was wearing only black, as usual, this time not a suit but a more casual sweater. Despite having brushed his dark hair back, a few strands fell in front of his eyes, brushing his smooth jaw.

Something was different, though. The dark circles under his eyes. He looked like someone who hadn't gotten any sleep the night before. An emptiness painted his features, darkening his gray eyes. He slightly raised his head but didn't tilt it in her direction. "I'm aware you were friends with Thomas."

River clenched her teeth. "What happened?"

Out of all the questions she should have asked—why did he quit, did he tell you anything—she chose this one. Because something *had* happened. Because she couldn't shake Cassie out of her head.

"He's alright, if that's what you're asking."

"Is he?"

"Yes. And he asked me to make sure I tell you that."

"Why did he leave so suddenly?"

"We went into town yesterday afternoon. He got a message from one of his sisters. A family emergency, I don't know much more. We returned here so he could pack his bags and leave."

River let that sink in, her mind scrambling. If he'd been in town in the afternoon, then she would have missed him by little, since she had decided to come back early. Thomas had mentioned an emergency, and he'd looked so disturbed that it was believable, but why not explain anything to her? Why hide what was inside the cottage? He'd looked frightened by something.

"Are you sure he's okay?" she asked, unconvinced.

"He was the last time I saw him."

"When was that?" Dorian was her boss, and she was pestering him, but she couldn't help it.

"We came back to the house around four. I let him go early so he could leave. We said goodbye to each other then."

She stared at his face, trying to detect a potential lie, but didn't see anything except sadness. "So, you don't actually know if he left the property safely."

His eyebrows knitted together slightly, and he waited a beat before answering. "No. I suppose I don't."

She was probably reading too much into this. Even if Thomas was dodgy about his story, he did let River know he might leave. It was nothing like Cassie or Simon. And talking about Simon, she had never seen his ghost. Dorian's aides may have had a habit of leaving, but that didn't mean much. River took a slow breath, convincing herself that she was being too dramatic. "I don't mean to be annoying. I'm sure he's fine."

Dorian thought for a moment. "Maybe the next time you go downtown, you can reach out to him. Or maybe he will have already sent you a message. I would also be happy to hear from him."

Hope grew in her chest. He was right. Maybe Thomas had been in a hurry to leave, and that was why he didn't have time to talk to her or invite her in. But once he reached his house and settled for a little bit, he would reach out to River. "Maybe. I hope so."

"We can go today if you like. If you think it would make you feel better."

A little surge of gratitude filled her chest. "It would. If you don't mind going again."

"I don't. I enjoy Luke's lattes."

A smile tugged at River's lips. "Thank you for doing this."

Dorian nodded once. "We can leave in about half an hour. It's too early now."

River looked down at her clothes, remembering that she was wearing the stupid uniform and that her suitcase was waiting for her by the door. "Do you think I could change first? I'm wearing my uniform. I didn't have time to change when Miss Roberts came to fetch me. I didn't even brush my hair." She touched her hair self-consciously.

"Didn't she move you to the cottage?"

"No."

Dorian stood up. "Could you get my coat, please?"

River rose from the chair, looking around, then spotted the coat thrown over the other armchair. She took it and handed it to him. "Here."

He took it, his fingers grazing hers, sending a small jolt through her stomach. "Do you have yours?"

"In my suitcase."

Dorian surprised her by wrapping his coat around her shoulders. "Wear it for now. Where is your suitcase?"

"By the door, but I'll get it—"

She didn't finish her sentence before he walked to the door and groped for the suitcase, then dragged it back. She thought he was going to hand it to her, but he walked past her and opened the French doors.

"I can carry my suitcase," she said. "And I can wear my own coat."

He briefly turned to her, a smile hanging on his lips. "But if you do, then my coat won't smell like lavender."

River pinched her lips, internally cursing the warmth rising to her cheeks again, probably making her freckles pop out even more. She followed Dorian outside and through the garden, passing the bench he had been sitting on the first time they'd had a true conversation. Watching him move so easily while carrying her suitcase baffled her. The man was completely blind, but he seemed to know exactly where he was going.

"Have you always lived in this house?" she asked.

"Yes."

"Aren't you scared to trip over something?"

He chuckled. "I know every inch of this place, and the landscapers do a good job at keeping this path cleared. I will need your help to get downtown, though. The woods are treacherous."

They rounded the house, walking on unpaved earth. Although Dorian walked with confidence, River feared he would slip on uneven, muddy ground, especially as he carried her suitcase. She pressed her steps to walk next to him and threaded her arm around his. Butterflies swarmed her stomach, but she pushed through. Her new job was to assist him after all. When she glanced up at him, she saw the ghost of a smile lifting the corner of his lips.

"I promise you I have walked these ground hundreds of times without hurting myself."

"I'm doing it to ease my own anxiety."

"Are you afraid *you* are going to fall?"

"I'm very clumsy, so you never know."

A small laugh escaped him. "Hang on to me, then."

They walked side by side, as River kept her eyes trained on the ground. Being so close to him felt strange. After working at the Blackwell House for weeks and only running into him occasionally, now she would spend every day with him. She felt both anxious and excited. In some ways, Dorian's expressions made him almost transparent, as though he couldn't hide his feelings, but in other ways, he was the most enigmatic person River had ever met.

Edith exited the cottage just as they reached it, holding something familiar in her hands.

River's heart skipped a beat, and she left Dorian's side to trot in Edith's direction. "Where did you find this?"

Edith's gaze pierced her, as usual. "Inside, where do you think?"

"Did you break it?"

Her eyes crinkled. "Excuse me?"

Dorian stopped next to River. "What is it?"

"Just a silly thing that is none of River's business," Edith said.

River stared at the broken object in Edith's hands. "I made that broomstick and gave it to Thomas. It was a gift."

She waited for Dorian to laugh, but he didn't. "May River have it back, please, Miss Roberts?"

Edith stared at River for a moment, a new hardness set in her features. *"You* made this?"

"Yes."

Something happened then. River couldn't tell what, but there was a spark in Edith's eyes, something that resembled realization. She took a few steps forward and handed the broken broomstick to River, along with a golden key. "The mirror will need replacing, but you'll have to keep it for a while." She walked back up the hill toward the staff's quarters, carrying her cleaning supplies.

Uneasiness churning River's stomach, she stared at the pieces of wood. That stick was pretty thick—someone would have had to use some force to break it in half like this.

"Is everything all right?" Dorian asked.

River threaded her arm with his again, steering him toward the cottage. "Yes. Fine." She unlocked the door and stepped inside.

Dorian put the suitcase in the doorway but stayed on the threshold. "Is the cottage to your liking?"

She looked around a space that seemed all too empty now that Thomas was gone. "Yes, it's very nice."

"Good. I'll wait for you outside. Take your time." Dorian shut the door, giving her some space.

River set the broken broomstick down on the table, still puzzled about how it could have snapped in half like that and rummaged inside her suitcase to retrieve a pair of jeans, a fluffy sweater, and her coat. Dorian would need his coat back too. She hoped he wasn't too cold while he was waiting for her. She quickly changed and hurried to the bathroom to check her hair.

She paused in the doorway. The oval mirror hanging on the wall was shattered, its cracks and pieces showing River hundreds of tiny reflections. When Edith had told her it was broken, she had imagined a fissure or two, but it looked like someone had deliberately smashed it. Did Thomas do that? Was there a specific reason, other than being a little eccentric, for Dorian to hate mirrors?

And if so, what convinced Thomas that they were to be feared?

CHAPTER SEVENTEEN

U neasy and unnerved, River went back into the main room, grabbed her coat and her scarf along with Dorian's coat, and left the cottage. She locked the door behind herself and looked for Dorian. Her heart made a painful flip in her chest when she found him. The cottage was on the side of the hill, a lot closer to the cliff than the house or the staff's quarters. Dorian had walked to it and now stood, immobile, dangerously close to the edge.

The memory of seeing him—even though it hadn't been him—jump off the cliff in the middle of the night surged in her mind. She sprinted to him. "Dorian!"

He turned, his expression telling her she had wrenched him out of his thoughts. "Are you okay?"

She skidded to a stop next to him, panting. Her breath caught in her throat at the sight of the angry ocean underneath, its waves crashing onto sharp rocks. Her legs wobbly, she clasped his arm and dragged him away. "Are *you?* What insane person stands so close to the freaking edge of a cliff? You could have fallen!"

"Are you mad? You sound mad."

"You scared me, you—" She bit her tongue before finishing her sentence. "And put your coat on, it's cold."

Dorian did as he was told, smiling. "You were about to call me an idiot."

"No." *Yes.* "But you would have deserved it. What the hell were you doing?"

He shrugged. "I like listening to the ocean. Feel the breeze on my face."

River threaded her arm in his and steered him toward the forest, to the path they needed to take to go downtown. "You call that a breeze? That's no breeze. More like a glacial, freezing gale from hell."

"My apologies, River. I did not mean to scare you."

"And yet you keep doing it."

That made him chuckle.

River started breathing more easily once the trees sheltered them from the wind.

"Where are you from?" Dorian asked. "I take it you're not fond of the cold."

"New York. It gets cold there too, but it's definitely worse here."

"What made you come here?"

"I'm not sure you'll find it interesting."

He tilted his head. "Of course I will. I like to get to know the people who work with me."

She noticed how he had said 'with' and not 'for,' now for the second time. As though he was somehow embarrassed to have someone at his service and would prefer to have a partner instead. Or a friend.

They made their way slowly through the woods, the leaves covering the ground crunching under their feet. "I came here after my boyfriend and I broke up. I couldn't find another place to live on my salary alone and decided I needed a fresh start. So, I quit my job and came here."

"Do you ever regret it?"

She thought for a moment before answering. "I do sometimes. But then I remember the situation I was in before, and I'm glad I made the move."

"Even if there are ghosts?" he said with a smile.

"Any of us would choose the ghosts over your uncle."

"I don't blame you. You don't have to worry about him anymore."

"I might still run into him."

"If you prefer it, you can reach my room from outside and knock on the French doors. The same path we took earlier. No need to go through the house and risk running into him."

Gratitude warmed her again. "Thank you, I appreciate that."

They walked in silence for a while, though it didn't feel awkward. River kept her eyes trained on the ground, making sure to guide Dorian and keep him from tripping over something.

"What was the job you quit?" he asked.

"Barista. I actually liked it. I'd like to open my own coffee shop someday. An Irish coffee shop." She bit her tongue, cringing at her words. She was going to bore him to death.

"That sounds nice. What made you want to do it?"

She glanced up at him. He looked like he meant it, like he wanted to know more. "My grandma. When she lived in Ireland, she used to go to a coffee shop to hang out with her friends. She said it was her favorite place in the world. She loved the ambiance, the library corner, and the board games table they had. That's where she met my grandpa. She took me there when I was a kid, and I just loved it."

"You seem very fond of her. Does she live in New York?"

"No. She passed a few months ago."

"I'm very sorry to hear that," he said, and it sounded like he meant it.

"Thank you. I miss her a lot."

"What about your parents?"

"They died when I was a child. I moved in with my grandparents, but my grandpa died about a year after. My grandmother basically raised me."

Dorian stayed quiet for a moment, registering this. "You went through a lot."

"I don't remember much from that time. It was harder for her than it was for me. My mom was her daughter."

A soft grin stretched his lips. "Do you get your ginger hair from your Irish origins, then?"

She chuckled. "Yes. My grandma was a redhead before turning white, and my mom was a redhead too."

"Did they have freckles too?"

"Yes." The smile fell off her lips, and she frowned. "Wait, I didn't tell you I had freckles."

"Um…" He hesitated a second. "Thomas referred to you as Freckles once. I assumed."

"He was nice enough not to call me Carrot. My middle school years were rough."

"Ah, well, at least you got to go to school."

She looked up at him briefly. "Didn't you?"

"No. I was homeschooled and bored to death."

"Oh." It made her a little sad, reinforcing the feeling that he was lonely. "Who taught you to play the piano?"

"Miss Roberts."

River snapped her head up. "No way."

"Edith wasn't always as bitter as she is now. She has been working for our family for a very long time. I was a child when she first started as my tutor. Then, as time went by, she became the staff manager."

"When you say she wasn't always bitter, do you mean she used to be nice? Because I'm having a hard time imagining *that*."

"Well…" A shadow fleeted over his features, bringing that sadness again. "She was. At first. I liked her. I liked being able to talk to someone new. I thought I could be more genuine with her, tell her things. But ultimately, she was always loyal to my mother, and I quickly understood I couldn't trust her as much as I thought I could."

River nibbled on her lips, wanting to ask more questions, wanting to know everything about him, but Dorian looked depressed now, and it felt like crossing a line. "What about your family?" she asked instead. "Do you have anyone else?"

"I used to. Other uncles and aunts and cousins. They're all gone now."

A brick settled in the pit of her stomach. She had no idea if that meant they had moved away or if they had died, and she chose not to ask.

The trees cleared ahead. River didn't wait and took her phone out, turning it on. To her disappointment, no message from Thomas popped up on her screen, and she sighed.

"Nothing?" Dorian asked.

"No… He might have been too busy. I'll send him a message once we sit down."

As they walked through the main street, River noticed the glances they got from the people that were out and about. The blonde woman in the flower shop briefly pointed at them, and the older woman she was talking to turned around to look. People coming in and out of the butcher shop or fish market whispered in each other's ears. The man walking to the antique shop stopped in the middle of the street to watch them pass by. Everyone seemed to gawk, making River pull Dorian a little faster to the Black Bean.

She quickly pushed the coffee shop's door open, eager to hide. But there were a few people inside, and they all turned to them, falling quiet. If there was one thing she hated above all, it was to draw attention to herself, which had always been a challenge with such bright, ginger hair, but usually, people didn't care about her. Today, their stare made her feel itchy in her own skin, and she averted her eyes, guiding Dorian to the table at the far corner.

"How about you sit here while I order?" she said, helping him out of his coat before he sat down.

"You sound nervous."

"I'm fine."

"They're staring, aren't they?"

River glanced around. "Yes. More than they usually do. Why?"

"All of my aides so far have been men. I suppose you being with me gives them a new reason to gawk."

"Oh." That didn't make her feel better one bit. She cleared her throat. "What do you want to drink?"

"Lavender latte, please."

"It's delicious, isn't it?"

He smiled, handing her a small wallet. "I figured you would like it to."

She pushed down on the wallet. "Don't worry. My treat."

"Please. This is for scaring you."

She chuckled. "All right, then. Do you want something to eat?"

"Anything sweet will do."

"Okay, I'll be right back." She brushed his shoulder as she said that, then walked past him and instantly felt weird for doing it. Dorian wasn't a child that she needed to reassure.

At the counter, Luke gave her a modest 'hi,' as though seeing her with Dorian had suddenly made her unsympathetic.

"Hey. Two lavender lattes and two slices of banana bread, please."

He nodded and got to work. River waited, feeling awkward, until he brought her order and she could pay.

"Hey, um, did you see Thomas yesterday?" she asked.

His expression softened at the sound of the name. "Yeah. He was here yesterday afternoon. With Dorian."

"What about after? In the evening?"

"No, why?" He glanced over at Dorian.

Poor guy, he didn't even know. "Well, he had to leave because of a family emergency. It was just very sudden. You don't happen to have his phone number by any chance?"

"No. I wish I did."

"Okay. Instagram will do, I guess." She grabbed the cup holder along with the paper bag holding the slices of banana bread. "Thanks anyway."

He gave her half a smile in response.

Right after she sat down and gave Dorian his order, taking the banana bread out of the bag for him, she sent a quick message to Thomas on Instagram. She told him she hoped he and his family were okay and asked him to message her back when he had a moment.

Dorian's face lit up like nothing she had ever seen as he sipped the coffee. He bit a huge chunk off the banana bread in a not-so classy manner that made River laugh.

"Wow, someone has a sweet tooth, huh?"

"Don't you?"

"I do. But I don't eat fancy, five course meals every day."

He took another bite, clearly enjoying himself. "Mack's cooking is incredible, but I was never allowed sugar or treats or desserts as a child."

River smiled as she watched him. He looked different somehow. As though the weight that seemed to crush his shoulders each and every day was temporarily lifted. The constant sadness painting his features was gone too. His smile took years off his face.

"How old are you?" she asked.

"Twenty-nine," he said, his mouth full, which was funny coming from someone like him, who was always so formal. "What about you?"

"Twenty-three." River's phone beeped on the table, making her jump. She snatched it, anxious to see a message from Thomas. Her heart sank.

"Is it Thomas?" Dorian asked.

"No. It's, um… my ex."

To think that she had initially been longing to hear from Zach, hoping that he was missing her. Hoping that he regretted breaking up with her. But then, she had begun to stop caring, too preoccupied by the man now sitting in front of her. She felt nothing as she read the text. She had expected a spark. The butterflies swarming her stomach. But her guts felt as empty as a dry well.

Hey River. I hope you're doing good. I saw the pics with your new boyfriend. It's weird to see you with someone else, but I hope he treats you right. Call me when you get the chance.

Then, a separate text said: *I miss you.*

"What does it say?" Dorian said after taking a long sip of coffee. "If I may ask."

She exhaled, trying to form a response. "He says he misses me."

He paused, putting the banana bread down, as though it didn't appeal to him anymore. "Do you miss him too?"

"I did for a while. Thomas and I did this stupid thing where we took pictures together to pretend he was my boyfriend, then we put them on Instagram to make Zach jealous."

Dorian's eyebrows knitted together. "Instagram?"

"Yeah, you know, it's an app where you can put pictures, and people can like them and follow you and…" She trailed off. Her explanation did nothing to undo the puzzlement on his face. The guy lived in a secluded mansion. During all those weeks she had cleaned that house, it only now occurred to her that she had never seen a computer. "Do you know what the internet is?"

He dropped his head, as though not wanting to look in her direction even though he couldn't see her. "A little. All the things I know about the outside world, I know them because my aides were nice enough to tell me about them."

"But…" She put her phone down, having completely forgotten about Zach. "Dorian, have you ever travelled outside of Stormhedge? Did you ever go on vacation or studied somewhere?"

"No, I'm afraid not," he said, his voice low. "I was never allowed. And then my accident happened."

She fought the urge to reach for his hand. How sad. "You know, a lot of blind people live alone. With maybe someone who could check on you or help you around the house, I'm sure you could—"

"It isn't as easy, River. I know I look like I have money, but I don't. It is my mother's money. I used to want to leave and go far away from this place. I would have taken any job and lived anywhere else." He paused, and that invisible weight settled on his shoulders once more. "But I cannot do that."

The sorrow on his face broke River's heart.

"What are you going to do about your ex?" Dorian said, changing the subject.

"Uh… I don't know. It's gonna sound childish, but I like the idea of him being jealous. I think that's the petty part of me that wants to get back at him."

"He hurt you." It wasn't even a question.

"Yes… He made me feel like I wasn't enough. Like it was my fault that he started talking to that girl. And you know, I know I'm a bit weird. I was raised by a woman who believed in magic and had all sorts of rituals. Someone who believed in the power of intentions and homemade broomsticks." Shy, warm anger rose in her chest. "He said I wasn't fun anymore because I was grieving my grandmother. How messed up is that? And you know what the worst is? I said *nothing*. It was like my words were stuck in my throat, and I never found the courage to tell him to go f—" River paused, exhaling and feeling embarrassed. "I'll stop babbling. You don't care about any of that."

Dorian made no reply for a moment, then took a small inhale. "I know how you can tell him to go fuck himself without actually telling him."

River snickered, clasping a hand over her mouth. "Dorian, I didn't know you could cuss."

He smiled. "I'm only saying out loud what you were thinking."

"Okay, I'm all ears."

"Don't answer him but take another picture of you with someone else. And then put it on your internet thing."

"That's some Thomas-level of pettiness right there."

"Well." He leaned forward, resting his forearm onto the table. "He should have treated you better. You deserve to be loved for who you are."

There came the swarm of butterflies tickling her stomach. They only came when Dorian was around now. River swallowed, forcing herself not to stare so hard at his face, the black strands of hair brushing his jaw, the lips that showed a devastating smile.

When her own mouth couldn't form words, Dorian spoke. "Maybe Luke will accept to play the part."

She looked up, feeling weird about asking Luke. Her gaze settled back on Dorian. "What about you? Would I cross a line if I asked you? I don't know Luke that well."

"I wouldn't mind, but I'm not what you would call photogenic." He briefly pointed at his eyes as he said that, and River ached to tell him that the gray veil that covered his eyes did nothing at altering his handsomeness.

"Nonsense."

She dragged her chair around the table to place it next to him. Her heartbeat raced uncomfortably inside her chest as she sat down. Never mind getting back at Zach or posting the picture on Instagram. It wasn't like she cared anymore. Sitting close to Dorian made her both nervous and thrilled. She raised the phone in front of them, noticing the color that had risen to her cheeks.

"Okay, ready?"

Dorian slipped his arm over the back of her chair, sending another jolt through her as it brushed her back. Instead of looking straight, he turned his face to her. "I'll pretend I'm looking at you. I wouldn't know where to look otherwise."

His cheek grazed her hair. She could hear his breath and smell his shampoo. As she took the picture, she could swear he took a slightly deeper inhale, as though smelling her. She dropped her hand and faced him. Dorian seemed to sense it, slightly raising his gaze, but he didn't move. Warmth emanated from his body, and River had to refrain from reaching out and feel that warmth, to trace a finger against his smooth jaw or brush a strand of black hair away from his face.

Cutlery clattered in the coffee shop, breaking the spell. River almost shot out of her seat. She dragged it back to the side of the table, hot with embarrassment. What was she thinking? Dorian couldn't even see her, so she needed to stop imagining that he was somewhat interested in her. He probably didn't realize that they were this close and that she was staring at him.

"Thank you," she said, sipping her coffee.

She hesitated for a moment, looking at the picture. They looked good. The way he was turning his head, it *did* look like he was looking at her, almost in the same way a man would look at his lover.

"Is it a good picture?" Dorian said.

"Yes. You're more photogenic than you think."

That made him smile slightly.

Without thinking too much, River opened Instagram and posted the picture, forgetting about the cheesy hashtags.

A minute later, a new text from Zach popped up.

Really? A new guy?

The petty satisfaction it brought her was unmatched. "He texted again."

"Did you want to stay longer to talk to him?" Dorian asked.

Grinning, River turned her phone off and put it back inside her coat pocket. "No, I'm good."

CHAPTER EIGHTEEN

R iver craved the warmth Dorian's suite would offer and was
disappointed as they stepped inside. "Boy, it's freezing in
here. Would you like me to make a fire? Not sure I know how,
but I'm willing to try.

"After lunch. I have to join my family in the dining room."

"Okay, I'll escort you."

His handsome smile made her weak. "I need help to walk
outside, not inside. But thank you."

"I don't mind. And I wanna say hi to Mack."

"Very well."

River didn't take his arm this time, and Dorian didn't request it.
They walked side by side in the large hallway, surrounded by the

paintings. River tried to ignore them, as usual. As they reached the back of the foyer, Dorian stopped in front of the dining room door.

"When should I come back?" she asked.

"In about an hour is fine. Don't worry if you are not exactly on time."

"Should I meet you here or in your room?"

"My room. I will wait for you there."

"Okay."

Dorian opened the door and stepped in. Before it bounced shut, River got a glimpse of Selene's dark eyes, alive with fury.

"Where the *hell* were you?"

"I am surprised you don't know," Dorian answered. "Did you forget to track my every move this morning?"

River's curiosity ate at her, but she shouldn't stand there and listen, so she walked to the back of the foyer and opened the door to the kitchen. What was Selene's deal? Dorian went downtown several times a week. Surely, it wasn't news to her.

"Hi, Mack."

"Hey, love. I see you got a new job."

"Yeah. I'm not complaining."

"You're in luck. I might have some leftovers for you tonight."

"That sounds great, thanks. Hey, did you happen to see Thomas yesterday?"

"No, I'm sorry. I heard he left. *Another* one gone. That sucks."

"Yeah…"

Mack nodded toward the door. "How's he treating you?"

"Good. I don't know what all the fuss is about. He's really nice."

Mack focused on placing the food on each plate, almost in an artistic way. "Right. Nice man, nice hours, nice cottage, and better pay. Then, why do all his aides keep quitting?"

"Well, Thomas had a family emergency."

"Did they all have a family emergency?"

"What's your point?"

He sighed. "My point is, something doesn't quite add up, so protect yourself. Look out for red flags."

That whole house was a giant red flag, lit up by thousands of tiny, blinking red flags. "I'll keep that in mind."

Shelly and Annie entered the room, ready to serve the Blackwell family. River didn't stick around, afraid to be in their way. Instead, she headed back to Dorian's room to retrieve her coat and decided to walk through the gardens like they had that morning to reach the cottage.

The gardens looked colder and more shriveled, thanks to the temperature dropping more each day. The trees' branches were twisted and spindly, their bark darkened by moisture. The thinner branches might be good for a new broomstick, though, and River decided to go and check them out. The broken broomstick she had given Thomas was still on her mind.

She walked through the thicker parts of the garden, the bushes and the roots clinging to her, the tall statues towering above. When she reached the tree line, she began hunting for sticks, hoping none of the maids would see her from the windows. She could have gone back to the forest, but it was farther away, and she wouldn't have time for lunch if she did that. Later this afternoon, once her workday was over, she would sit down and assemble the broomstick, then scatter the glass bottles full of herbs around the cottage.

A freezing breeze brushed against her neck. River paused, listening. The wind carried voices. They whispered to her. She strained to listen, her fingers clasped on the sticks she had picked up.

"They did this to me."

She whirled around, but no one was there. Heart pounding at her throat, she scanned the area around her, expecting to see Cassie. But the voice hadn't been feminine.

A low creaking noise made her look up. A tree, bare of leaves, stood in front of her, its multitude of branches splayed around it. Those branches were round and thick and smooth. Except for one. River squinted. A long line like a scar ran down the branch, as though something had been tied up there.

When she was a child, River used to have one of those makeshift swings. A huge tire hanging off a tree, tied with thick rope. But from what she knew, Dorian didn't seem to have had the kind of childhood where his parents would make him something like that.

The whispers grew louder, and River's hair stood on end. She recognized that feeling all too well, but Cassie's ghost was nowhere to be seen. Benjamin's, either. She took a deep breath, closing her eyes and reaching for the pendant around her neck. The cold sharpened.

"Is anyone here?" River said, opening her eyes. "Show yourself to me."

Footsteps behind her made her spin around and drop the sticks. A man wearing working boots and khakis walked in her direction, carrying rope and a stepladder. She let out a sigh of relief, her breath misting in front of her face. He was one of the landscapers she had seen through the window while cleaning one of the upstairs rooms.

"Hi. I didn't see you there."

The man made no reply. He walked past her as though she wasn't even there and unfolded the stepladder, placing it in front of the tree.

"I was just picking up some sticks. I hope that's okay," River said, feeling a bit awkward. "I won't be in your way."

The man stepped onto the ladder and threw the rope around the branch. It covered the scar perfectly as he tied it. Grabbing the end of the rope, he made a noose.

River's mouth fell open. "Sir? W-what are you doing?"

He slipped the noose around his neck.

"Wait, stop!"

She ran to him, but he kicked the ladder away before she could. A scream fell out of her mouth. His body swayed from side to side as he struggled. River tried to grab his legs, but her arms went through him as though his body was mist. She froze, panting, and looked up at him, realization sinking in.

His body fell suddenly motionless. His arms were limp at his sides, and his wide eyes were locked on her. His colorless lips moved. "They did this to me."

River took a step back, breathless, and tripped over a root. The world spun as she fell back, the impact punching the air out of her. When she opened her eyes, the hanged man had disappeared, leaving behind the scar the rope had cinched into the tree when he had died.

She was being paranoid. The broomstick, the jars of herbs, the crystals, and the lit candle weren't going to protect her against the ghosts because the ghosts didn't want her any harm. They were incredibly unsettling, of course they were. But Dorian had been right when he had said they were harmless, whether he truly believed in them or had just said that to humor her. They were trying to tell her something.

Sitting at the table and fidgeting with her pendant, River mentally reviewed what she had seen. Two suicides from the staff. Cassie had stabbed herself, and the landscaper had hanged himself.

After lunch that day, River had asked Dorian if he knew anything about a missing landscaper. What she got was conflicting information. His face had darkened, but he'd said he didn't. Even if Dorian didn't know, the rest of the Blackwell family had tried to cover it, and Edith had helped. She said Cassie had left a note saying she quit, which was obviously a lie.

River's heart skipped a beat.

Cassie wasn't the first ghost you saw.

"Oh my God…"

The lady in the dormitory. River had tried so hard to pretend this encounter had been a dream that she had almost forgotten about her. Who could that have been? Another housemaid? She hadn't seen her face. Replaying the memory in her head, she now realized that when the woman stumbled forward in the kitchen, it hadn't been to grab or scare River. Whatever her cause of death had been, *that's* what had made her fall to the ground.

And that other night. Maybe you saw a ghost too.

The man she had followed outside on her second night. She had thought it was Dorian because of his dark hair and clothes, but Simon had dark hair too. A few days after that incident, Edith had announced that he was gone. Had River seen him that night? Him, or his ghost replaying his death?

River shot out of her chair and gathered her crystals. She threw her coat on and stepped outside, striding to the spot she had seen the man that night. He would come if she opened her mind to him, she was sure of it. He would show himself like the others had.

Facing the staff's quarters and staying at a safe distance in the darkness, River took deep breaths and took hold of the crystal around her neck again. It was possible she didn't need it at all, but it felt reassuring and helped her stay grounded.

She shut her eyes. "Whoever was here that night and jumped, please show yourself. Talk to me. I want to help."

The cold air turned to ice on her skin. Her eyes flew open, and she clenched her teeth at the sight of the figure striding toward her. She didn't move, squinting to make out his features.

"Simon..." she breathed out.

The ghost walked past her and headed to the trees and the ferocious ocean below the cliff. She followed him, her throat dry and her blood pulsing in her ears. Simon disappeared behind the tree line, River at his heels. She wove between the trees like she had that night, and nausea squeezed her insides. She could have saved him, but she'd been too slow, and he had jumped.

The trees cleared. Simon stood at the edge of the cliff. River skidded to a stop, afraid to come closer. The ocean roared underneath, the wind blowing through her hair.

Simon glanced over his shoulder. "They did this to me." He turned his back to her and stepped forward.

CHAPTER NINETEEN

River had said she wanted to help, and she meant it, but how was she supposed to do that exactly? It had been days since seeing Simon, and she still couldn't quite come up with any kind of plan. It wasn't like the movies where they just stumbled upon a dead body by chance and buried it to free the spirit. She had seen *five* ghosts. While the landscaper, Cassie, and the unknown housemaid's bodies could be buried somewhere on the property, Simon's body would have disappeared long ago into the dark ocean. Dorian's father surely had a proper grave.

Dorian's father. Benjamin. He didn't fit into that story. He hadn't died recently, but years ago. He had been killed instead of committing suicide. And he obviously hadn't been part of the staff.

What link could he possibly have with the others? Maybe there was no link. Maybe those ghosts just relived their deaths because that was what ghosts did. And the housemaid? Her death hadn't looked like a suicide like the others. Nothing made sense.

"Do you need to take a break?"

Dorian's voice snapped her out of her thoughts. She was still sitting on the armchair close to the fire, the Kindle in her hands while the heavy rain battered against the French doors. Dorian was sitting on the far end of the sofa, which put him almost next to her.

"I got distracted for a minute. I can keep reading."

"It is quite all right. Take a break."

She turned the Kindle off, wanting to preserve its battery. "Do you like the book so far? What does it feel like to read stories written by authors who are still alive?"

He laughed. "It would not be as great if you weren't the one reading it."

"Stop it," she said, her cheeks growing warm. Dorian had a way of making her blush way too often.

They had settled on a science fiction novel this time. During the previous days, she had read him a fantasy one. Dorian didn't like the horror genre because living in his house was already like a horror book—his words—and he didn't want anything too suspenseful, for the same reasons probably. In the end, he wanted something that made him travel far away from this place, if only in his mind. River couldn't blame him.

"That book was actually adapted into a movie. It was pretty good. Not as good as the book, but I liked it. Did you used to watch movies before?"

"Have you seen a TV around here?"

"No."

"There's your answer."

Her mouth fell open. "Dorian, you *have* to have seen a movie in your life, though, right?"

While his face had been turned to her before, he now tilted it away. "I'm afraid not."

"Never?"

"There are a lot of things I didn't get to do because I have been stuck here my whole life."

"That must be hard." His life seemed so sad it broke her heart. "Can I ask you something?"

"Always."

"What does your family do all day? They're not cooking or cleaning or gardening, and they don't have a TV."

"That is an excellent question. My uncle's favorite hobby is harassing the staff. I think he drinks quite a lot too. As for my mother, she has a wide range of activities she likes to choose from, including spying on everyone and trying to find new ways she can make my life harder." He paused, his fingers becoming a little restless on his lap, crossing and uncrossing. "She also paints. And sculpts."

"Wait, she's the one who made all those paintings and sculptures?"

He nodded.

"Wow… And, uh…" She shouldn't ask. She most definitely shouldn't. "She… *spies* on people?"

"She always seems to know where everyone is and what they're doing at all times. Especially me."

River didn't know what to make of that. Was it his imagination, or was there some truth to that? After all, Selene hadn't even known it when River had started working for her, and the other day when she and Dorian had come back from town, his mother had sounded furious not to know where he had been.

Seconds passed, the heavy rain and the crackling of the fire competing to chase the silence away.

River gazed at Dorian, his features so full of sorrow it physically hurt her. "I would help you if you wanted to leave this house."

He raised his face, his gray, unseeing eyes turned in her direction. "Pardon me?"

"If it's the financial aspect that scares you, I could help with that. Once I've saved enough money and can rent my own apartment, you could come and stay with me. I'd help you."

"River…"

"I'm sure there are jobs out there that you could do. You don't have to stay stuck here just because your mother won't support you. You're an adult, no one can keep you here if—"

"*River.*"

She paused, swallowing. "I just… You look so sad. And you seem to have missed out on so many things. I hate it."

Dorian let out a drawn-out exhale. "I truly appreciate what you are trying to do. But unfortunately, I cannot leave."

"But why?"

"It's complicated."

"I'm sure it's nothing I can't understand—"

"I do *not* wish to speak about it," he said, his tone sharp.

River made no reply, taken aback by the sudden shift in his mood. It was her fault; she shouldn't have pushed him.

"My apologies," Dorian said eventually, his voice low.

"No, no. It wasn't my place to say those things."

His gaze was cast down while he crossed and uncrossed his fingers. "I will tell you one thing, and then we cannot speak about this again."

Her stomach twisted into knots. She nodded, unable to speak, but then remembered he couldn't see her. "Okay."

"My mother wants me to inherit this house. She wants me to marry and have children. I am the only one left in this place, and if I don't do it, the Blackwell name will die along with all the traditions my mother would like to pass on."

Imagining him with another woman sent an unwelcome spike of jealousy burning through her chest. "Is that what you want?"

"What I want is irrelevant." He paused, seemingly composing himself before continuing. "I am lonely. That much is true. And the only reason I am not completely mad today is because I am allowed to have people working with me. That wasn't always the case, but eventually, this is one thing I was granted. And it helps. To talk to someone who isn't from here." He turned to her. "Asking too many questions will cost you your job, River, like it cost the job of all my other aides. I was sad to lose them. But you... I... Please, believe me when I say that I would *hate* for you to leave."

Although she had considered leaving this place many times, the thought of not seeing him every day dug a hole in her chest. It was stupid, she still barely knew him. But she enjoyed the conversations, the reading, the walks with him. She liked the expressions he made when listening to her, as though what she was saying was the most interesting thing in the world, even when it wasn't. Without thinking about it, she said, "I'd hate to leave you too."

A cautious smile stretched his lips.

River opened the Kindle once again. "Would you like me to keep reading? I really need to know what happens next."

"I would like that. I think a few members of the crew are going to die."

"Hey. I don't need that kind of negativity in my life."

Dorian laughed, and it lit up his whole face, making River smile.

She read for the rest of the afternoon, taking a few breaks so they could share their thoughts on the story. It was a pleasant afternoon, although what he had said earlier was nagging her. How would asking questions make her lose her job? How come *all* of Dorian's aides had left?

Not all of them. Simon killed himself. And Thomas still hasn't answered me.

When the clock struck five, Dorian shifted in his seat. "Thank you, River. I will see you tomorrow."

"I can stay longer if you want. I don't mind." She had wondered what the hell his family was doing all day, but also often wondered what Dorian was doing when he was alone with no one to talk to and nowhere to go because of the rain.

"Go back to the cottage and rest. I wouldn't want you to become sick of me."

I don't see that ever happening.

"Well, what are you going to do now?" she asked.

"Don't worry about me."

"I guess I do worry a little."

"I might play the piano for a while."

The thought somewhat reassured her. Dorian wasn't a child; he knew how to busy himself. She needed to stop worrying for nothing. She stood up and put her coat on, stuffing her Kindle into her pocket. As she braced herself to walk into the pounding rain, Dorian rose from the sofa.

"River."

She turned, raising her eyebrows. "Yes?"

"I would like to ask you something. But before I say anything, I want you to know that it is something I have asked all my aides."

"Um, okay. What is it?"

"You don't have to agree. I wouldn't want to do anything that makes you feel uncomfortable."

She chuckled. "Got it. Shoot."

"I... When I spend time with someone, I like to know what they look like." He cleared his throat. "I would like to see what your face looks like."

"Oh."

"And I need to use my hands for that."

Never mind the butterflies, fireworks shot through her stomach just at the idea of Dorian touching her face. "Yeah—okay. Sure."

"Are you certain?"

She tried to make her voice sound more stable. "Of course."

Dorian took a hesitant step forward, and River did the same.

"I'm right here," she said, chuckling nervously and feeling stupid for doing so. It truly was no big deal.

He raised his hands slowly, as though afraid to hurt her or be too abrupt. River took them, holding them lightly, and guided them to her cheeks. A small shiver shook her as Dorian trailed his fingertips up her face to her temples and her forehead. His thumbs brushed over her eyebrows, then her nose. His hands lingered for a moment on the lower half of her face, light fingers tracing her jawline. It was dizzying to have him lean over her this way, looking down at her even though he couldn't see her. River closed her eyes, not wanting this moment to ever end.

Her breath hitched when a thumb grazed her lips while his other hand had settled under her jaw. She opened her eyes. He seemed closer than before, his thumb lingering on her bottom lip. She wanted to kiss that thumb. She wanted to kiss him. The desire to do so burned through her limbs, making them weak.

But Dorian's hands left her face. He ran gentle fingers through her hair, down to the ends, following the pattern of her curls.

"You didn't lie," he said, his voice low. "That is a lot of hair."

Words had deserted her.

"It's beautiful," Dorian added with that same, low voice that made her wobbly and ran his fingers over one of the curls framing her face. "You are beautiful."

Lightning split the sky open. Its thunder shook the windows a few seconds later, making her jump a little.

Dorian straightened up and dropped his hands. "You should go now before the weather gets worse. Thank you for allowing me to get a mental picture of your face. And hair."

"You're welcome… I'll see you tomorrow."

She opened the French doors and stepped into the rain. Its icy drops did wonders at refreshing her flushed cheeks. She'd be soaked to the bone long before reaching the cottage.

"Goodnight," Dorian said before closing the door behind her.

River hurried along the garden path, her boots splashing in the puddles. Soon, she would take a nice, hot shower and eat something warm and comforting.

"Don't get your hopes high, little girl."

The voice startled her to a stop. She whirled around, searching for its source. Down another path and next to a statue, Selene

Blackwell stood underneath a black umbrella. She slowly walked to River, the high heels of her leather boots clicking against the stone. She wore a black, long-sleeved velvet dress that hugged her slender figure. She came to a stop a few feet away.

"I don't blame you. I am very well aware of my son's good looks," Selene said. "Who do you think he takes after?"

"I-I don't know what you're talking about—"

Selene swatted her away. "Now, now. None of that with me. I am not mad, I simply want to warn you. Again. Don't get attached. He will take that soft little heart of yours and smash it to pieces. Trust me. You wouldn't be the first. Why do you think I always give him a man as an aide? I am tired of him playing with these poor young women. I do hope he will be more respectful of his future wife."

River's throat tightened. Dorian had been nothing but polite and decent with her, but no one would know him better than his own mother. Her body started trembling, her coat now soaked with cold rain and her curls sticking to her temples. "I'm not expecting anything."

Selene, on the other hand, didn't seem bothered by the temperature. She closed the remaining distance between them. "Good. And if you ever did, remember that I know everything that goes on around here." Her gaze slid down and stopped at River's neck. "You *are* wearing something."

Hot flashes spread down River's back. She briefly looked down. The chain around her neck was showing, but the obsidian was still safely tucked inside her coat. She couldn't lie like she had the first time Selene had asked her if she was carrying something. She wasn't a housemaid anymore, though, so why did it matter?

"What is it?" Selene asked, cocking her head. Although her voice was gentle, River could detect the tiniest hint of warning.

"Just a silly thing I got for cheap in a store," she lied, not really knowing why. "Dorian said it was okay," she quickly added, another lie that turned her hands clammy.

Selene's dark eyes slightly creased, as though she was trying to see through the coat. Her gaze fixed on River's face, and River could almost feel the air around them hardening, the density changing into something heavy and oppressive, a vice trying to crush her.

Selene's blood red smile stretched her lips again. "Go on now. Before you catch your death. I do hope we have the chance to speak again."

She walked away, following a path that weaved through thick rose bushes. The air felt lighter again, but a slight pressure remained at the base of River's skull. She turned away and hurried back to her cottage, holding none of Selene's grace. She trampled through the water, her fingers so cold they throbbed and her toes turning numb in her boots.

Had Selene told the truth? Had Dorian been disrespectful to women? Or was Selene's perception biased? It was entirely possible that Dorian had been with other women before. In fact, it was unthinkable that he hadn't been. Almost any girl would fall for him. Dorian had admitted he was lonely. It seemed logical for him to want to be close to someone, even if it meant nothing. He was only human after all.

"Stop trying to manipulate me and everyone around you."

The thought jumped to River's mind as she strode downhill to the cottage. Selene had said this to Dorian when River had heard them talk. Could Dorian really be manipulative and River was just another prey? Another casualty?

The problem was, even if Dorian was sincere, even if he somehow felt something for River, it wouldn't lead anywhere. Because he was supposed to marry someone else.

In both cases, River's heart would be the casualty. Because no matter what Dorian's intentions were, she was falling hard for him despite all the mystery that surrounded him.

And if he had asked her if he could feel what her body looked like, she would have said yes.

CHAPTER TWENTY

I t took a solid fifteen minutes under the hot water to bring her
extremities back to life. Now with warm pajamas on and a fire
going, River rifled through the cupboards to look for some food.
Her eyes fell onto an opened pasta box that was already there when
she'd moved in. Thomas had probably bought it. She grabbed it
and put it on the counter, then found a saucepan and filled it with
water.

Music. That's what was missing in this place. She had a few
albums on her computer, but she hadn't used it in so long that the
batteries were drained. Next time she went downtown, she would
take it with her and charge it. For now, she would have to make
do with the sound of the rain, now reduced to subdued tapping.

River turned down the flames under the saucepan as the water
started boiling and grabbed a wooden spoon. Thunder split the

sky and made the cottage shake. River jumped out of her skin, the spoon slipping from her hand and clattering to the floor. It skidded under the fridge to her left.

She steadied her breath. They were so high on that cliff that the thunder seemed to strike right next to her cottage. Dropping to her knees, she tried to peek under the fridge. The shape of the spoon lay a little bit further, and River slipped her hand under the tight gap. Her fingers brushed the handle a few times before she managed to slide it closer and drag it out.

As her hand brushed the floor, something sharp stung her wrist, making her gasp. She straightened up, holding her hand up and squinting at a tiny cut and the drop of blood that pearled from it. River stared at it, then at the shiny piece of glass lying next to the spoon. She picked it up and looked at the familiar object. One side was round, another was flat but dented.

She scrambled to her feet and reached for one of the glass jars she had aligned onto a tiny shelf initially made for spices. She turned the bottle over. The bottom was flat in the middle and dented on the side, just like the piece she was holding. Her mind raced for a moment, trying to understand. Did that piece belong to one of the jars she had given Thomas? It sure looked like it. A sinking feeling rose in her stomach. Her grandma always said that if a jar broke, it meant someone was trying to harm you, and the jar had protected you.

Or he dropped it. As simple as that. Stop being crazy.

Shaking the thoughts away, she tossed the piece of glass in the trash can and grabbed the pasta box. Nothing had happened to Thomas. He was with his family, safe and sound. Even if he hadn't responded to her messages.

An unpleasant thought had been forcing its way into her mind for the last few days. Maybe Thomas simply didn't care about her that much. The only reason they'd been close was because they had to work together and this place felt lonely. But once back in the real world with his friends and family, River probably wasn't that important to him. It hurt to think about, but it was still better than anything happening to him.

River opened the box, ready to pour its content into the boiling water, and froze. A piece of white paper was wedged between the cardboard and the dry pasta. She pulled the crumpled paper out and smoothed it. Words were scribbled onto the page, as though the person writing them had been in a hurry, and the single sentence nearly knocked her off her feet.

Freckles, find Dorian's favorite book.

"What the hell is this?" River whispered, her heartbeat racing.

She read those few words close to twenty times, trying to make sense of them. Thomas had wanted her to find this note. She looked at how crumpled it was and how difficult it was to read the quickly written words, and pictured Thomas writing them hastily, then harshly stuffing the note into the pasta box. Why? What had prompted him to leave this to her? And why couldn't he write more information?

He was out of time, and then he left.

Or worse.

The unwelcome thought churned her stomach. Her hands shook, clutching the note. A sickening dread seeped through her skin. Thomas wasn't okay. He hadn't just left. Like Cassie, Simon, and the landscaper hadn't suddenly left. She needed to know what had happened to him. She would find Dorian's favorite book, and then hopefully, everything would make sense. Luckily for her, she had been there with him that day at the library and remembered exactly where that book was.

A flicker of light caught River's attention outside, and it wasn't the lightning this time. It moved through the trees, along the cliff. She walked to the window, squinting, but couldn't see anything. Someone was outside, though, she was sure of it.

After stuffing Thomas's letter inside the pasta box again and turning the stove off, she grabbed her coat and boots. Any warmth that had built inside her body since showering instantly left her as she stepped outside. She rounded the cottage, her arms wrapped around her chest, and headed toward the patch of trees where she had seen the moving light. Through the soft rain, small branches cracking could be heard. River headed that way, trying to stay quiet. It was pitch black around her, and she regretted not taking her phone.

Her boot snapped a branch in half, making her halt. Silence stretched for a few seconds until a white light flickered through the trees.

"Is anyone there?" a voice called out.

The voice slowly registered in River's mind. "Shelly?" She moved toward the light.

Shelly stood under an umbrella, her phone in her other hand. She sighed and rolled her eyes at the same time. "Ugh, it's just you. I thought old Roberts had caught me."

"Didn't mean to startle you. I saw your flashlight from my window and wondered who was out here." She frowned. "Wait, caught you doing what?"

"Don't tell anyone, okay?" Shelly slid her phone under her fingers holding the umbrella and took out a cigarette pack. Using her lips, she pulled a cigarette out. "At least don't tell Roberts. She'll kill me."

"Does she even care?"

"Uh, *yes*. On my first day here, I asked where I could smoke, and she told me she better not catch me smoking or I would be fired. That old hag needs to loosen up a little."

They stood there for a moment while Shelly lit her cigarette.

"That night when I thought I saw someone jump, were you here? Is that why you followed me?"

"Yeah."

A question burned River's lips. It would sound stupid, but she had to ask, especially after finding that note. "Have you seen anything weird lately?"

Shelly took a drag, her gaze falling to the ground. "What do you mean?"

"Well... We're pretty close to the cottage. I saw you walk by from the window, so I guess you could see inside from where you were too."

"I wasn't spying on you if that's where you're going."

"No, not at all. I was just..." She licked her lips. "Did you notice anything strange when Thomas was here? Were you here the night he left?"

Shelly briefly glanced up before turning away.

"Shelly? Did you see something?" River asked, taking a step forward.

"I don't know what I saw."

"Well, what was it?"

She took another long drag, as though trying to find the courage to talk. "I saw you."

River shook her head, not understanding. "What do you mean?"

"I saw you walking to the cottage that night. To visit Thomas."
River's heart skipped a beat. "Was he with someone?"

"Yes. The curtains were closed, so I didn't see who it was at first."

"At first?" Her blood pumped faster in her veins.

Shelly pursed her lips, staring at River. "Listen, I'm not sure about what happened in there, okay? I just know that Thomas didn't leave because of an emergency. Unless you've heard from him?"

"No… I haven't." She didn't want to tell her about the note, or its contents.

"Thought so."

"Please, tell me what you saw."

"I… I heard stuff."

"What stuff?" River pressed, her voice a little louder.

"Struggling. Stuff breaking. It started only two minutes after you left. I was just finishing my cigarette."

"Struggling? He was in trouble?" *I could have been there when it happened. I could have helped him.* "Did you go and check on him?"
Shelly looked down again. "No."

"Seriously? You knew he was in trouble, and you didn't do anything to help him?"

"I was scared, okay?" Shelly shouted. "If someone was hurting Thomas, who is a *man,* what the hell was I supposed to do?"

"Tell someone about it!"

"Who, Carrot? Who should I tell that Dorian Blackwell is a *murderer?* His mother?"

River's jaw fell open. Shelly's words had felt like a slap in the face. "What are you talking about?"

"I *saw* him. After all the noise and the struggling and the shouting, I saw him drag Thomas out of the cottage." Her voice caught in her throat. "And Thomas was still struggling and begging…"

"No… No, that can't have been—"

"It *was* him. I've had a crush on him since I started working here months ago. I stared at him long enough to recognize him. I'm even starting to wonder if he's truly blind or if that's not just a ruse to get close to his aides so he can hurt them."

River kept shaking her head, unable to believe she could have been such a bad judge of character. "We don't know that—"

"Do you know how many people have worked for Dorian, River? *Dozens.* All mysteriously gone. If I were you, I'd pack a bag and leave before he could hurt me."

"Have you told Miss Roberts?"

"Of course I did. And you know what I think? I think she knows. And she's covering for him."

"That's just insane…" River said, massaging a headache out of her forehead.

"Is it? Do you hear Mrs. Blackwell talk about her son? How good-looking and wonderful he is? She's fucking clueless. But my guess is that old Roberts isn't just here to serve her, but to cover for Dorian. *She's* the one who 'escorts' the aides off the property. *She's* the one who cleans up the cottage after them. And *she's* the one who chooses who works for Dorian." Shelly glared at River. "Well, until now. I guess he has a thing for you. That alone should convince you to run away."

Shelly took another cigarette out, hands shaking so much she struggled to light it.

"Why do you still work here if you're so sure he's a psychopath?" River asked.

"Why do any of us work here, Carrot? I need the money. I almost saved enough. I'll leave soon."

Shivers coursing through her, River thought about the note. The broken broomstick, and the piece of glass that was once part of a jar. Shelly's theory almost made sense, but where did Cassie, and the landscaper fit into all this? They weren't working for Dorian.

They don't fit. Like Benjamin and the other housemaid don't fit. Because I'm missing some crucial information. And Thomas might have pointed me toward that.

"I'm sorry, okay?" Shelly said. Her voice had lost all its strength. "I can't stop thinking about it... I wish I'd helped him. I froze."

Warm tears filled River's eyes just imagining what Thomas might have gone through, but she blinked them away. "What makes you think Edith knows? What did she say when you told her?"

A bitter laugh escaped Shelly's mouth. "She asked me what the hell I was doing here. Reminded me that if she caught me smoking or saying 'silly stuff' about the Blackwells, she would fire me on the spot. Don't you think that's weird?"

It was. It also meant Edith knew about Cassie's death and lied about it. River had thought it was to protect everyone else, but maybe Shelly was right. But... Dorian? She couldn't think of him as a murderer.

His mother said he had changed since his accident. She called him manipulative. She warned you about him. Maybe it's time you open your eyes.

That was the one thing Shelly was wrong about. Selene wasn't clueless. She was protecting her son.

"Watch out for yourself, River," Shelly said. "Don't let him charm you into thinking he's a good man." She crushed the cigarette under her shoe and turned away, leaving River in the dark as she walked back up the hill.

River walked to the cottage on numb legs, her mind reeling. She had to get her hands on that book as soon as she could, but she couldn't risk going to the library at the wrong time. She would also have a word with Dorian. He might not answer her, but she knew just how to get some truth out of him.

CHAPTER TWENTY-ONE

R iver hurried up the hill toward the Blackwell House, the object she was carrying heavy in her pocket. Her stomach twisted the closer she was to seeing Dorian. She still couldn't believe she had been so wrong about him, though that shouldn't be such a surprise. She had dated Zach for three years without even realizing how much of a jerk he could be to her. There was always a good excuse for his behavior, a little voice in the back of her head telling her she was at fault. She had always been naïve like that.

And now she had fallen for someone who probably was far worse than a harmless jerk. After what Shelly told her the night before played on repeat in her mind, River had come to accept it.

There just wasn't a good explanation for what Shelly had seen. Dorian had done something, and even if it was hard to imagine, Thomas's scared expression didn't lie that night when River visited him.

She rounded the house and squared her shoulders, her teeth clenched so hard they ached. Shelly was right, leaving this place was better, but River had a visceral need to find out exactly what had happened to Thomas.

Standing behind the French doors, she knocked on the glass. Dorian stood on the other side. He looked taller and more intimidating than the day before, River's new perception of him having been altered. The French doors opened.

"Good morning, River."

"Morning." Her dry tone made her wince. Dorian might be blind, but if there was one thing he was good at, it was listening. The change in her tone wasn't lost on him. River could tell by the way his smile faded away and how his eyebrows knitted together ever so slightly.

"Please, come in," he said, moving out of the way.

Despite itching to get on with what she wanted to do, River knew the drill: look for mirrors and paintings. Dorian wouldn't talk to her unless she did that first. She shed her coat and started rummaging through the room. Dorian stood there a little awkwardly for a moment, seemingly feeling the drop in her mood, then decided to leave her be and sat down at his usual spot on the sofa.

River went through the same routine. The wardrobe, the bed, the nightstand, then the bathroom, and back to where Dorian was sitting. As usual, there were no mirrors anywhere.

Until she opened the last drawer of the dresser and something rattled inside. River leaned to the side, looking at the back of the drawer. A small, square mirror lay inside. It hadn't been there the day before.

She grabbed it and turned to Dorian. "There's a mirror."

He snapped his head in her direction. "Throw it away."

"In... the trash can?"

"Outside. Make sure to break it first."

The small object in her hand made her shudder, as though bad vibes came from it. It was only her imagination, but she couldn't wait to get rid of it. Dorian's fear of it creeped her out. She opened the French doors and smashed the mirror against the wall outside. A small weight lifted off her chest. River threw the broken thing as far away as she could, breathing easier. Back inside, she reached for what was in the pocket of her coat.

"Would you like to keep reading?" Dorian asked, though his voice was still clipped, because of her or the mirror, she wasn't sure.

"Actually, I had something else in mind for now." She pulled the tarot deck out and put it onto the coffee table. "How about tarot reading?"

He cocked an eyebrow. "Tarot?"

"Yeah. I'll read your fortune."

"I'm not sure that is a good idea." He shifted on the sofa.

"Don't worry, it's just for fun. And the same card can have a very different meaning depending on the situation." Her voice caught in her throat. She had read Thomas's fortune. He had freaked out when she'd pulled out the death card for his future. She'd given him the nice speech about how the death card often meant a big change in one's life, but in his case, it might have truly meant death. Shaking the thought away, she opened the box and took the cards out. "I can start with a simple reading. Three cards. Your past, present, and future."

"I already know what the future holds for me."

"We'll see about that. Do you think you could shuffle the cards?"

He exhaled, giving up. "Sure."

River stood and pushed the deck into his hands. Watching him, a tiny voice at the back of her head screamed at her that he was innocent and this was all a big misunderstanding. She banished that voice.

When Dorian gave the cards back, River retrieved her seat on the armchair. She took a few deep breaths and picked three cards, placing them face down on the coffee table.

She turned the first one. "Past. The Hanged Man."

"That doesn't sound good."

"The Hanged Man represents inaction or stagnation at some-one's hands or a situation that is out of your control. You are, or were, stuck."

"I am."

She looked at him, expecting to see a small grin on his face, but he was dead serious.

"Well, the Hanged Man can teach you that sometimes the offensive isn't the right way to go. Fighting will work against you. Instead, lay low and show patience."

"Interesting."

"Let's see your present, then." River pulled out the Death card. "Death."

"If only."

"Death can mean change is coming. A chapter in your life has run its course and is ending. Change can be uncomfortable but inevitable, and you have to choose whether to stay in a situation that doesn't serve you anymore and makes you miserable or to have the strength to rise and walk away from what's holding you down."

Dorian made no reply. He seemed to let that sink in for a while before he finally said, "What about the future?"

River reached for the last card when an icy breeze brushed the back of her neck. She gasped and whirled around, but no one was behind her. No one could even reach underneath that mass of ginger hair anyway. But still, goosebumps ran over her arms and down her back. That strange feeling, the vibrations she had felt before seeing the spirits, came back with a vengeance, almost choking her.

"River? Is everything okay?"

Dorian's voice was drowned by the rising whispers around her. Shapes of people blinked in and out of life. The tarot cards flew off the table and scattered on the floor as though knocked by an invisible hand. River jumped out of her seat, her heart in her throat. Painted faces stared up at her from the cards, a multitude of eyes open wide, rolling in their sockets. They looked like the hundred faces that hung in the Blackwell halls.

"What the…"

Their skin began to melt, blurring their features. Dark bubbles erupted from the cards. Blood. Blood was everywhere, pooling onto the coffee table and soaking the carpet.

River let out a shrill cry and stumbled away until her back met the wall. Dorian sprung out of his seat and hurried toward her, feeling for her until he found her, gripping her shoulders.

"What is happening? Are you alright?"

Ghosts stood motionless, scattered around the room, some of them staring at River. She recognized Cassie. Simon. Benjamin. The landscaper, whose name she still didn't know. But there were more. Maybe a dozen, half of them wearing the familiar black and white uniform. Some bleeding, others with broken limbs or twisted necks.

And in the corner, a young man with light brown hair faced away from her, blood dripping down his neck, his shoulders shaking.

"Thomas…" A sob escaped her, and she clamped her hand over her mouth. "Oh God…"

"Do you see them?"

She could barely hear Dorian over the sound of her sobbing.

He shook her slightly, bringing her focus back on him. "Can you see them, River?"

She looked at him through her tears, her lips parted, but unable to speak.

"I can always feel them staring at me."

River forced air into her lungs. Dorian's fingers were still clamped on her arms, grounding her. She would have sunk to the floor without them.

They were alone. There were no ghosts, no blood bubbling from the tarot cards. No dark stain soaking the carpet. No portraits glaring at her from the cards. If the tarot deck hadn't still been scattered through the room, River would have thought she had dreamed everything.

"Are they gone?" Dorian asked, worry edged in his features.

River focused on him, her vision blurred with tears. "What did you do to him?"

He did a slight double-take, confusion replacing worry. "Pardon me?"

"Thomas. He's dead."

"Thomas? Did you see—"

She wrenched herself from his grip and took her distance. "Did you hurt him?"

"No."

"Are you even blind!" she shouted, more as an accusation and less like a question.

He turned somewhat in her direction as she moved away from him, keeping close to the wall. "Could you please just explain to me what is going on? I haven't done anything to Thomas, I swear."

He looked so confused, and he clearly couldn't tell where she was. Guilt tugged at her guts, but she couldn't trust him. She couldn't trust anyone in this place. Not when he'd said Thomas was okay the last time he had seen him, even though Shelly had told a completely different story.

River wanted to leave this room, but she couldn't bring herself to leave her tarot behind. Dorian didn't try to come closer, which allowed her to shuffle on her knees and gather her cards.

"River, *please.* Tell me why you think I did something to Thomas." His voice had changed. It was tight, almost strangled. Could he have found out about Thomas's death just now?

"The spirits… They've been trying to tell me…" The box now closed, River scrambled back to her feet and stood close to the exit. "Were you with Thomas the night he left?"

"I already told you I was with him that day."

"What about later?"

Dorian pressed his lips together, his jaw working.

"Answer me."

His chest deflated. "Yes."

"You were hiding behind that door…"

"But I didn't do anything to him."

"Shelly heard you fighting. She saw you dragging him outside, and he was hurt. Stop lying to me."

Her throat dry, she held her breath, trying to decipher the range of expressions fleeting over his face. She had wanted to believe so hard that this was all a misunderstanding. That Shelly could have been wrong and confused him for someone else. In the dark, it was entirely possible. That night, when Simon had killed himself, River had also thought she'd seen Dorian.

But the fact that he wasn't answering told her everything she needed to know.

"Did you kill him?" She pressed her back to the door, trembling at the sound of her own question. She was alone with him. Who knew what he could do?

His face hardened. "If this is what you believe, then I suggest you leave."

"Is that your way of admitting it?" Her voice quivered, but she couldn't control it.

Dorian's hands balled into fists. "Go now. Before you get hurt too."

His voice, low and menacing, nailed her to the floor for a moment. River swallowed around the lump in her throat and forced herself to move. She wrenched the French doors open and burst outside, leaving her coat behind.

CHAPTER TWENTY-TWO

P uffy, red eyes looked back at her. Seeing Thomas's ghost that morning had torn a hole through her chest and ripped out her heart, and she had broken into sobs as soon as she'd stepped inside the cottage.

She put the mirror down. No mirrors. Dorian's fear of them had rubbed off on her. Even if he hated them, someone had still been stubborn enough to sneak one into his dresser for a reason that she couldn't understand.

"This is a madhouse," she whispered to herself. "All of them. Crazy."

But it was time to go back inside the Blackwell House. According to the time, they were starting lunch now, and no maid should be cleaning the library today.

River stepped outside, shivering just at the sight of the heavy, gray clouds. The cold curled around her neck and seeped through her sweater, making her walk faster up the hill. She couldn't go through the staff's quarters, some of them might be there. And if they weren't, Edith could be there. No, River would have to use the front door and hope everyone was safely tucked in the kitchen and dining room.

She took long strides, refusing to think about what would happen if someone saw her. Hopefully, Dorian hadn't told anyone yet that she was fired. And River *would* leave. She'd sleep in a hotel if she needed to. She'd beg Zach to let her sleep at the apartment for a few weeks. Anything. But she owed it to Thomas to follow the one instruction he'd left her before dying.

River stopped in front of the massive, wooden doors and caught her breath, gathering her courage. Slowly, she pushed the door open and peeked inside. The enormous foyer was dark and silent. Muffled sounds echoed from the kitchen, where Mack was busy cooking for the Blackwells.

River slipped inside and closed the door behind her as gently as she could manage. She hurried down the corridor to her left, the one that would take her to the library. A shiver coursed through her as the paintings watched her, reminding her of the faces that had appeared on her tarot deck. She'd never get used to them. She pressed her steps, her eyes trained on the door ahead.

Once inside the library, she hurried to the maze of books. She needed to find the place she and Dorian had run into each other that day, otherwise it would be impossible to remember where that damn book was. The rows of shelves made her dizzy. She searched for which aisle she had been in and stopped suddenly.

That dark gap between shelves made her flesh break out in goosebumps. That was exactly where she had been. When the eye had been staring at her through that gap.

It was probably just a spirit.

Funny how the idea comforted her. Because it was better than the alternative—an actual person spying on her.

Making sure no eye glared at her, River retraced Dorian's steps. Left, another left, then a right. Third shelf, starting from the top. She put a finger onto the book at the far right, then counted nineteen books, just like he had done, and pulled out a worn out, red book with golden lettering.

Her heart slammed against her chest. River glanced around, then opened the book. Nothing was there. Frowning, she turned the pages, but her hope of seeing anything out of the ordinary faded as she reached the middle of the book.

But when she turned to page 103, she let out a quiet gasp. A folded note was tucked inside. It was crumpled, as though it had been handled many times before.

Her fingers itched to open it, but she shut the book instead. She had to leave. Now.

River put the note inside her jeans pocket and replaced the book where it belonged. Her heartbeat matched her strides as she stalked down the hallway again, and her back was slick with sweat by the time she stepped outside despite the cold that greeted her.

She trotted back down the hill but didn't go to the cottage. People could interrupt her if she went there. They could knock and ask her to leave. Maybe Edith already knew River was fired and she would want to escort her off the property.

It was better to find a spot where no one could find her. River walked closer to the edge of the cliff and in the direction of the woods. The dark ocean raged underneath her, bringing her attention to a path not far below that would enable her to walk down the cliff. The rocks were sharp, and the path was steep, but no one would come and find her there.

A hand on the wall for support, River climbed down. The drop next to her seemed to want to pull her down, sending shivers down her legs and feet. Ahead, the path flattened. A small cavity in the wall came into view. It would be perfect. River hunched over and sat with her back against the wall. The view was breathtaking, and that tiny pocket in the rocks made her feel safe from the rest of the world. She crossed her legs, satisfied to see that not even her knees poked out of the small space, which meant that nobody could see her from the top of the cliff.

Inhaling the salty air, River pulled the piece of paper from her pocket and unfolded it. Neat writing filled it. A different writing than Thomas's note. This one was much longer too, as though the person writing the letter had taken their time.

River held the letter firmly in her hands, scared the wind would snatch it away from her, and began reading.

If you are reading this while sitting in my room with me, please don't say a word. Act as if everything were normal. Someone may be listening. You can either read it quietly or put it away and read it on your own time later. Tell me which page you are on, and that you need a break from reading. I will understand that you have just found this letter.

If you are holding it, it means I trust you enough to ask for your help. "Beg" would be a more appropriate term. Everything you read will sound insane. But it is all true, and I have a way of proving it.

I am a prisoner of this place. I cannot get out. They won't let me. All my attempts at fleeing have failed. You are probably wondering how it is possible, and the answer will undoubtedly surprise you. My mother is a witch. Plain and simple, as unbelievable as it is. And no, my 'accident' hasn't done anything to my head. There never was an accident in the first place.

While I have been taught the basics of witchcraft growing up, I do not possess my mother's vast knowledge on the subject, and I still don't fully understand the extent of her power. I could never find her weakness, no matter how many times I have tried. I am being watched. The more I try to get away, the more she takes from me.

She has taken my free will. My father. My sight. I can't possibly keep doing this, but maybe someone else can. If her focus is on me, you might be invisible to her, and you might be able to do what I could not.

You are probably very confused and most likely incredulous. I do not blame you. But there is a choice to be made here and now.

You can decide you want no part in any of this. If that is the case, put this letter back exactly where you found it. You will bring this book back to me and say that you quit. You will leave the property as soon as possible. Please understand that I am not expelling you. But if you cannot help me, I need to ask someone else, another aide that Miss Roberts will assign me.

If you decide to help me, or if your curiosity is enough to make you wonder what proof I can possibly give, then keep reading. You need to go into my old room, which is located on the third floor. At the top of the main stairs, you will take the left corridor, the one leading to the back of the house, and then turn right and walk to the last door, the one that opens into the blue room. Go when you are sure no one will see you, whether it is my family or a maid. Having been part of the staff, I trust you will choose the appropriate time.

Once you are inside, the no mirror rule still stands. You cannot break them, or they will know someone has been in there. Take them off the walls and put them face down. Find a cloth and cover them entirely. Do whatever it takes to make sure no inch of a mirror is visible to you. Your life depends on it.

You need to go inside the bathroom. Under the clawfoot bathtub, on the right side, there is a hollow cavity covered with a large piece of tape. Take it off. A key is hidden inside the hole. It opens the wardrobe. Once you have opened the wardrobe, look at the left upper corner. A piece of wood creates an angle. Press it against the back of the wardrobe and push it down. It should slide off. Inside is another key.

Head over to the bed. Here is the tricky part. This enormous bed needs to be moved, and it will make noise. Take the pillowcases off and slide them under the feet of the bed, the ones close to the wall. Then pull the bed away from the wall slowly. You need a space wide enough to stand between the headboard and the wall.

Lift the fabric covering the back of the headboard. If you look hard enough, you will see the fine lines where I cut into its wood. It is tricky, but you can remove this piece. There is another key inside, similar to the one from the wardrobe.

Last step. Head over to the bookshelf. You will need a chair to stand on. The books at the top hide a wooden box. The two keys you found will open it. Look inside. Look carefully. Then, make up your mind. Do you believe me? Is this proof enough to convince you that what I wrote in this letter is true? Only you know the answer, and I will not blame you if you decide to walk away.

Whatever you decide, put everything back EXACTLY the way you found it so the next person can follow these instructions should you decide to leave. Hide the box behind the books. Put the key back behind the headboard. Push the bed back against the wall and replace the pillowcases, making sure that the bed looks well-made. Hide the first key back into its corner and lock the wardrobe. Back inside the bathroom, you will find a roll of duct tape inside the bottom drawer. Cut a brand-new piece and replace the key inside the hollow cavity under the bathtub. Make sure the tape sticks well. Take the previous piece of tape with you. Don't leave it there. You can discard it in the cottage.

Replace or uncover the mirrors and leave as fast as you can.

If you do decide to help me, do not say anything to me inside the house. Wait for us to be outside, far away from it. On a walk, downtown, anywhere as long as you are sure no one can listen to us.

I will not lie to you. I am not a good person. I cannot be, even if I try. I have done things I am not proud of. And I don't know how far I can continue to be pushed before I succumb to madness and commit the irreparable.

The rest is now up to you. Am I worth saving? And are you willing to risk your own life to rescue me?

Dorian Blackwell

River's heart was in her throat. She hadn't really known what to imagine after reading Thomas's note. She had thought that maybe he had found a way to leave her another clue. She certainly hadn't imagined *that*.

But it all made some sort of twisted sense. Some blanks still needed to be filled, but after all the ghosts, and Thomas's note, and the things Dorian had said to her, she simply believed it. No proof was really needed, except maybe to make her understand a little more what was going on. Dorian had said he couldn't leave this house even if he wanted nothing more.

After being raised by a woman who believed in magic, in the power of intensions and crystals and rituals, River's mind was already opened to the idea of witchcraft. Although, if this letter were true, Selene's power was far greater and scarier than River had ever seen in her life. Had she really taken Dorian's sight? His father?

But it could also be Dorian being manipulative. Think about what Shelly saw.

How could Dorian have written such a long letter? Some of the things he'd said suggested that he was already blind when he wrote it. The part about saying which page the book was on. It was a subtle way of letting him know his helper had found the letter without saying it outright. If he could see, he wouldn't have written something like that. But no one could write that many words with neat writing without seeing anything.

The echo of a voice, faint and far away, reached her before being snatched away by the wind. River folded the letter, fingers shaking slightly, and peeked outside. She couldn't see past the edge of the cliff above her from here. She emerged from her hiding place and climbed back onto the dirt and the grass, then stopped.

Dorian stood in front of the cottage's door ahead. He knocked. "River?"

River's words caught in her throat. Her guts begged her to answer him, but her mind told her to shut the hell up. She needed to stop being so emotional, so naïve. She needed to stop thinking that she felt something for him, and him for her. She had to stop thinking about the way his fingers had trailed across her jaw, her lips.

It was time to be smart and *think*.

"I just want to talk," Dorian said, and he seemed so genuine that River took a step forward.

A twig snapped under her boot.

Dorian whirled around. River stared at him, her heart pounding, holding her breath, her body stiff. But his gray eyes couldn't find her, they didn't lie. He looked deeply uncomfortable. River would feel the same if she knew someone was watching her and she couldn't see them.

No one can fake that good.

His jaw working, Dorian turned back to the door, hanging his head. "I haven't told anyone about what happened this morning, so… feel free to stay here as long as you need. Even if you don't want to see me anymore." He stepped away from the door, his eyes a little red. "I wish you well."

Dorian walked back to the house, River's gaze following him as her heart tore a bit further. She'd accused him of something horrible, and there he was, telling her she could stay in the cottage, wishing her well.

River watched him until he disappeared around the house, his fingers trailing on the ivy-covered walls.

Yes, a lot of blanks needed to be filled. Talking to Dorian would be necessary at some point. But not yet. Some of the answers to her questions were already waiting for her in his old bedroom.

CHAPTER
TWENTY-THREE

L unchtime, the next day. The Blackwells would be busy, and no maid should be on the third floor at the moment, or at least not on this side of the corridor yet. It was now or never, despite the exhaustion making her feel like there was sand under her eyelids. She hadn't gotten any sleep the night before, too unsettled by the things she'd read and scared to do what she needed to.

River climbed the last steps of the spiraling staircase, her nerves already shot, and peeked left and right. The third floor was silent. She turned left, smelling the peculiar odor floating in the air. The paintings' texture seemed to ripple as she walked by, their faces stretching into horrified, howling expressions.

At the end of the corridor, River turned right. The windows lining the left wall illuminated the space with a gray light, alleviating some of the anxiety gnawing at her guts.

Her eyes fixed on the last door. She had been into that room to clean it before. She had dusted those shelves. Not once did she think something was hidden behind the books.

Glancing over her shoulder, River pushed the door open slowly, her blood pumping in her ears. Right away, the three mirrors caught her eye. One fixed on the wall above a desk, one on the nightstand, and another one between two windows. There would probably be one in the bathroom as well. Urgency making her legs move, River darted to the mirror above the desk and unhooked it from the wall. She laid it face down, then headed over to the nightstand and did the same thing. When she got to the mirror between the two windows, she lifted the closest curtain and managed to drape it over the mirror in a way that hid it completely. Next, she hurried to the bathroom and grabbed a towel inside the cupboard underneath the basin to cover the last mirror.

She glanced around, making sure she hadn't forgotten anything, then took a deep breath. Lying on her side next to the bathtub, River slid her arm underneath, her fingers feeling over the cold surface. A tiny part of her mind kept telling her that there was no way any of this was real. That was probably how Dorian had lost most of his aides. They knew that letter was crazy. They knew that *he* was crazy.

A shiver crawled up her arm as her fingertips brushed something rubbery.

No way.

She scratched at the tape, pulling it free. A small object clattered onto the floor, ringing in River's ears. She closed her fingers around it and raised her hand above her face, staring at the bronze key.

How was this even possible? Dorian had been blind for eight years, which meant he had done all of this before he was moved to the suite on the ground floor, probably to avoid the stairs. He didn't have any aides before, did he? Why create this treasure hunt?

It would be something to figure out on another day. River shuffled back to her feet and walked to the wardrobe. She opened the double doors and looked into its corners, half surprised to see the slanted pieces of wood over them. Exhaling slowly to calm her raw nerves, River went to the desk and carried the chair back before taking her shoes off and climbing on it.

She knocked slowly onto the slanted piece of wood. It sounded hollow. Following Dorian's instructions, she pressed her fingers onto its side and pushed it down. The piece slid free, lying inside her palm. A small metal key rested inside. The wood didn't used to be hollow. It wasn't neat and clean. The inside had been carved out, leaving a small, bumpy hole just big enough to fit the key.

River climbed down the chair and hurried to the bed. The next step took the most strength. Lifting the bed just an inch above the floor while sliding the pillowcases underneath its feet nearly broke her back. That thing was heavy. No wonder Dorian had hidden something behind it. No one would ever move this enormous piece of furniture to clean behind it. At least the other aides had been men. They were all probably stronger than River.

She crouched down, hooked her hands under the bed, and lifted it while pulling, her jaw clenched and her shoulders straining. The bed slid away from the wall, not without noise, but it would have been much louder without the pillowcases.

It took more effort to put the bed down than lifting it. River didn't want to drop it and alarm everyone of her presence. Flexing her raw fingers to help the blood flow again, she squeezed herself between the bed and the wall. She kneeled and lifted the fabric covering the headboard. Her gaze travelled over the intricate patterns that snaked across the wood in a hypnotizing way, and she almost missed the fine lines scarring the headboard at the bottom on the right side.

"Okay... Here we go."

She bent over, her head tilted to the side, and wedged her fingernails into the cracks. The piece shifted, but it took a bit more digging for it to fall off. Just like inside the wardrobe, the wood inside had been roughly carved. The space was big enough for the second metal key and not big enough to completely pierce through the thick headboard.

Keys in hand, River turned to the bookshelves. She should have checked those first. What would she do if she looked but couldn't find the box Dorian was talking about?

There was no going back now anyway. She climbed onto the chair a second time and ran her hand over the books. Each time she pulled a book, anxiety squeezed her stomach a little harder. They were all books. Real books. Nothing was hidden behind them.

But when she pulled a new book, four large books came out with it. Her heart skipped a beat. If the books fell, it would make noise. She reached out to catch them, but none of them budged.

"Oh..."

The five books were glued together. When River pulled them completely out, she realized that in addition to sticking together, they had been cut in half to create an empty space behind them. And in that empty space sat a wooden box.

River sat on the floor, her legs crossed, staring at the box in front of her. It was a rectangular little thing with sharp edges and a rough surface. It looked homemade. Had Dorian made this? Two locks kept it shut, one slightly bigger than the other. River peered at the two keys in her palm. They looked similar at first glance, but they weren't exactly the same.

She inserted the bigger key in the lock to the right, and her heartbeat quickened as it clicked. The smaller key went into the lock on the left, which clicked just as easily as the first. The top popped open. River lifted it, almost scared to discover the contents of the box. Her eyebrows knitted together at the sight of an old leather journal. But that wasn't all.

As she lifted it, little things underneath rattled. A scalpel, an old bottle of hydrogen peroxide, a magnifying glass, and a broken piece of ivory that looked like the hundreds of sculptures scattered around the house.

Uneasiness tightening around her chest, River took the journal and opened it. It was filled with short, inconsistent entries. Although she knew she didn't have the time to read them all, she let her eyes sweep over some of the pages.

CHAPTER
TWENTY-FOUR

O 3/15/2013

    My aunt died. Another good member of the family who is gone. One day, I will be left with the bad ones. I don't know who is to blame for this, my mother or my uncle. Dad thinks it was an accident. I may be young, but I know my uncle as well as his inability to keep his hands to himself in presence of a pretty woman of the staff. I heard him argue with my aunt. I heard her scream. And then there was nothing but silence.

    03/19/2013

    Mother made a new painting. It smells strong, as usual. She says she puts a special chemical in the paint to make it last longer and that is why it smells like that. She always makes a new painting after someone dies. She wants to honor the dead. So, she paints them and hangs their portraits. I loved my aunt, but I hate this painting.

06/02/2014

I tried to leave. I got run over. I was so sure I died. It felt like dying. I heard my neck snap. But I woke up in my room. My mother was right after all. This place doesn't want to let me go.

06/09/2014

Another maid quit while I was gone. I never see them leave. They never say goodbye. My mother is very intent on having no one speak to me, except for Miss Roberts, but still, I talk to them when she isn't around. I say hello and thank you. I like to hear about the things they did before coming here. It helps me imagine a world beyond Stormhedge. It saddens me that none of them could say goodbye.

12/22/2014

I left yesterday during the celebration. I'm never allowed to stay the whole time, like the staff, so I thought I could sneak out after Miss Roberts escorted me back to my room. Mother was so busy that I didn't think she'd know, but somehow, she did. She always knows. She tried to teach me witchcraft. Love spells and control spells and telekinesis and talking to the dead and other things I want nothing to do with. But there is something else she can do, and that is spy on me. She always knows what I am up to. And I now realize that I did die that day when I got run over. This time, as soon as I was out of Stormhedge, I had a heart attack. A FUCKING heart attack. I am 20 FUCKING YEARS OLD. And after that, I woke up in my room again. And coincidentally, another maid had left while I was gone.

03/19/2015

She killed him. She killed my dad. He could never do anything against her power, but he tried to tell her I didn't want to be what she wants me to be. She said she pushed him out of the window because he *attacked her. Self-defense. That is what she goes around telling people of the town or our relatives when she sees them. That he had always been violent, especially with me. Lies. My father never laid a finger on any of us. He was better than her in every way, and thanks to the education she gave me, I am fairly certain the only reason he married her was because she forced him.*

No one could love that monster without a spell.

03/24/2015

There is a new painting. One with my dad. She even painted me with him. It smells. Now Mother is busy sculpting. Isn't she tired of making these atrocious things?

04/13/2015

I have finally learned my lesson. I tried to leave again, but I wanted to avoid Stormhedge, so I went around it, by the beach. It isn't very large, and the ocean is always angry, but it is still possible to walk a few miles.

Not for me. I don't think anyone would believe me if I told them that a huge wave came out of nowhere and swept me away. I got stuck between rocks. I drowned. I felt every second of it. And I woke up in my bed, panicking so much I punched myself in the face and gave myself a nosebleed. And that is when it hit me. The smell.

I was stupid to think I could flee. But I was even more stupid to miss the signs. Every time a member of my family has died, my mother has used their blood in her paintings.

I have no doubt she has used the remnants of the maids as well. None of them quit. I doubt they ever left this place at all.

05/25/2015

I told Luke about my suspicions. I hoped he wouldn't call me crazy after the things he'd seen. He didn't, and I realized what was so wrong with this town. I told him about the paintings, and he and I went to buy hydrogen peroxide. I am grateful to have a friend who has contacts with the outside world, unlike me. He looked things up on his computer. If there is blood in the paintings, it will fizz when we spray hydrogen peroxide on it. My mother may be a witch, but knowing a bit of science is serving me better right now.

Luke said it might not work if the blood is old, so I found the most recent painting my mother made. And it worked. I feel sick. Luke also gave me his magnifying glass. He read on his computer that bones are porous while ivory has lines. Before I even looked at the sculptures, I knew I would see pores everywhere.

07/14/2015

I hate her. I HATE her. I have never wanted any part of what she has been trying to teach me. I don't want that legacy. I don't want to marry and have kids just because she didn't get the daughter she has always wanted. I WANT TO LEAVE. I want to be normal. See the world. Luke keeps saying I should wait. That I will regret it if I try to leave again or if I stand up to her. He says the wellbeing of everyone in the village is at stake.

But I can't take it anymore. I have been a prisoner of this place my entire life. This ends now. She has already taken everything from me. I have nothing else to lose.

But he *did* have something else to lose. His sight. There was no entry after that one.

River put the journal down and grabbed the magnifying glass and piece of ivory. Thousands of little pores covered the white surface. Bones. Dorian wasn't insane or making things up. The piece she was holding between her fingers was a piece of bone.

There were *hundreds* of sculptures and paintings in this house. All of them made with the cadavers of Dorian's family members and the members of the staff. Was that what had happened to Thomas and the others? Had they been killed to serve as Selene's art supplies?

Nausea rose in River's throat, and the floor wavered under her.

She ached to read the whole thing to try to comprehend more of the things Dorian had gone through, but a muffled *thump* in the hallway made her jump back to her feet.

Her fingers shook as she locked the box, a key nearly slipping from her hand. The box was placed back onto the shelf behind the carved books in a record time. Pushing the bed back against the wall felt slightly easier, probably due to the adrenaline coursing through her. The pillowcases were back on their pillows in seconds. River smoothed the seat of the chair as soon as the first key was back in its hiding spot and the wardrobe was locked.

She put the chair back against the desk and darted to the bathroom. The previous piece of duct tape was already in her pocket, so she cut a new piece from the roll in the drawer to stick the wardrobe key back under the bathtub.

Footsteps filled the hallway.

The mirrors.

As quietly as she could, River replaced the mirrors on their hooks and uncovered the others.

The footsteps came closer.

"*Shit,*" she hissed silently.

Hide or pretend she had been sent here by Dorian? What could he have sent her here for? She would look suspicious, and she didn't want to end up as one of Selene's bone decorations.

Panic squeezing her insides and taking over, River dropped to her knees and shuffled under the bed. She had barely disappeared underneath when the door opened.

CHAPTER TWENTY-FIVE

The wooden floorboards creaked. Silence followed. Whoever had opened the door had stopped moving, no doubt peeking into the room. River couldn't even see their feet. While the sides of the bed were high enough to slip under, the bottom went all the way to the floor, obstructing the view of the door.

River listened, her heart pounding against the floor so hard she feared the other person would feel its vibrations. She kept her hand clamped over her mouth, slowly breathing through her nose.

Seconds stretched into eternity. What were they waiting for? Before reading what was in that journal, she would have been scared to be fired, but she wouldn't have hidden like that. It seemed that losing her job was the least of her worries.

The floor groaned again, sending a heat wave down her back. The door squeaked close a second later. River waited, listening to the muffled footsteps on the hallway's carpet.

She didn't move for what felt like hours. She had stayed here too long, and the Blackwells were probably done with their lunch already. If they caught her on the third floor, it would be bad, although not as bad as being caught in this room. She needed a good excuse.

What would she do, then? That was still a question she needed to answer. Dorian had written the letter so his aides could find what was in that box, so they would believe him. And by doing this, he hoped they could help him get out of this place. But how? If Dorian himself could never get away, if his mother was as powerful as he said she was, how could someone else break him free?

He knows the answer to that question. I need to get to him.

Hopefully, he would agree to talk to her after the horrible thing she had accused him of. He had come by the cottage, so all hope wasn't lost. If she could help him, she would. She might have been naïve and shy and a pushover all her life, but she wasn't a coward. Her grandmother had taught her to be brave and kind.

After what felt like an appropriate time to wait, River shuffled from under the bed and headed to the door. She opened it a crack, peeking into the empty hallway. Once she was sure the floor was silent, she shut the door behind her and tiptoed down the intricate hallways. She kept her gaze straight, refusing to look at the portraits, nearly holding her breath. That smell. It didn't come from the cleaning products. Repulsion made her take longer strides. The staff's spiraling staircase came into view, and River sighed in relief.

Her momentum was cut short as a door opened sharply, and Richard Blackwell walked out of it, standing in her way. A sick smirk lifted his mustache.

"I knew you weren't far, little mouse."

River swallowed around the lump in her throat, suddenly worried to hear nothing but silence on the whole floor. They were completely alone. "Mr. Blackwell, I was just—"

"Sneaking around? Maybe hoping to find something of value to steal? Whatever it was you were doing, I'm sure my sister wouldn't approve. You wouldn't want to be fired, would you?"

"No, I—"

"Don't worry." He closed the distance between them and raised a hand, grazing her jaw. "I am sure we can work something out. My silence can be bought." His finger trailed down her neck.

Repulsion and fear shook her. River took a step back, but Richard clamped his fingers around her hair before she could go further. A gasp escaped her. Richard tightened his grip, pushing her back inside the room he'd just opened. Hot pain blasted through the base of her skull as he pulled her, his nails digging into the back of her head.

River reached for his hand reflexively, scratching him. He let out a groan and released her, only to slap her face a second later. Her cry resonated in the room. Richard swung her around and slammed her against a desk, gripping her hair to keep her down.

"Please…" she said, her voice strained, as her cheek pressed against the wood.

"Don't worry, little pet. You will like it."

Her teeth clenched, River tried to get up, straining against the pressure behind her head. Richard pushed her back onto the desk. Pain shot through her cheek as it banged on the wood. Her scalp was on fire under his tight fingers. Tears filled her eyes when she felt his free hand curl around the waist of her jeans. She squeezed her eyes shut, fighting back the sobs rising in her throat.

"Uncle!"

Richard fell still behind her, and River opened her eyes. Dorian stood straight and tall in the doorway, anger edged into his features,

"Leave my aide alone," he growled.

Richard chuckled but stepped back. River tried to straighten up, but her legs turned to jelly, and she slumped on the floor.

"And what exactly are you going to do about it?" Richard sneered, walking slowly toward his nephew. *"Nothing.* You know it, and I know it. So, how about you give us some privacy?"

"Do not provoke me, old man."

"Or what?"

"Even blind, I can still hurt you," he said through gritted teeth. "You of all people should know that."

Richard paused. His back was to River, but she could see a slight change in his posture, as though he wasn't so sure of himself anymore. "Haven't you learned your lesson, Dorian?"

Dorian's eyes flashed with a murderous glint. "There are no words to describe the things I will do to you if you touch her one more time."

Richard took half a step back.

Dorian turned his head away from Richard and held out a hand. "River. Come with me."

His voice considerably softened as he spoke to her. Her legs still felt like lead, and silent tears kept springing free from her eyes. She wiped them with the sleeve of her sweater, refusing to cry in front of that pervert, refusing to show him how much he'd frightened her.

She pulled herself back onto weak feet, helping herself with the desk next to her, and crossed the room, avoiding looking at Richard. She slid her hand into Dorian's, and his long fingers gently curled around hers. He led her down the hallway, and River began breathing easier the further she walked from that room.

They didn't talk on their way down to the ground floor. They took the hallway that led to Dorian's suite, his hand still holding hers protectively, and River was grateful for his presence, so much so that emotion strangled her throat.

"What were you doing on the third floor?" she asked, her voice so small she wondered if he could even hear it.

"I am the one who should ask you that."

She made no reply, scared of the paintings and the mirrors they walked past.

"I was looking for you," he added finally. "I have been looking for you everywhere. I was worried."

After the things she had read in his journal, after so many people had died in this place, she didn't need to ask him why he was worried. They reached his suite. Dorian pulled her inside and closed the door behind them.

"Are you okay? Did he hurt you?"

"I-it's okay, I'm okay—"

"Your hands are shaking." He took her hands, holding them close to him, his thumbs softly grazing her skin. Concern painted his features. He looked almost in pain, a distress that reflected hers.

"I'll be fine, I swear, he just—" her voice caught in her throat as new tears blurred her vision. She clenched her teeth so hard it hurt, but already, her cheeks were wet.

Next thing she knew, Dorian pulled her against his chest, holding her tight. River melted into his arms, her face pressed against his sweater. Sobs poured out of her, but Dorian didn't let go until she was ready. One arm held her firmly, his other hand cupping the back of her head.

She pulled away suddenly. "Listen, I…" She cleared her throat, blinking her tears away. "I want to help you."

"What—"

"I read your favorite book."

His face darkened. "No…"

"Page 103."

"Please, stop talking."

"That's why I was on the third floor. I went into your room and—"

His gray eyes widened, and his fingers found her lips, pressing slightly against them. "River, I am *begging* you, stop talking." The volume of his voice dropped, and he spoke close to her, as though wanting to tell her a secret. "You are putting your own life at risk by saying these things."

"But—"

"Someone could be listening to us right now." He fastened his fingers around her hand again and led her outside through the French doors.

He was right. Of course, he was right. Dorian had even warned in his letter not to talk about anything unless they were far away from the house, and there she was, babbling about it. Clearly, both the exhaustion and shock had done a number on her, and she decided to keep silent until they reached the cottage.

As they stepped inside, Dorian said, "Get rid of the mirrors."

River headed to the bathroom, snatching the only mirror in the cottage, then opened the window and threw it as hard as she could. She slammed the window closed and went back to the main room. "Done. Now tell me why you're scared of them."

"It's complicated."

"Well, no shit!"

He did a double take, surprised by her tone.

River swallowed, taking a shaky breath, but it did nothing to calm her. "I wanna know exactly what's going on. I read your letter, I read parts of your journal, and I still can't completely piece it together."

"How did you know about the book?"

"Thomas left me a message. A note in the damn pasta box. *He* told me to find the book." She hated the way her voice sounded, uncertain and quavering.

"River..." Dorian stepped in her direction, searching for her, and when he did, his fingers curled around her wrist. "I am sorry you went through all that trouble, but you need to forget about all of this."

"Oh, is that all I need to do? You're right. I will forget about your mother the witch and her *bloody* paintings and bone sculptures. I'll forget about the ghosts too. Easy."

"It's the best thing to do."

"You can't even pick up on sarcasm, can you? You expect me to forget that you died *three* fucking times trying to get away? Should I forget about Thomas too?" She was shouting now.

His hands gripped her shoulders. "Easy."

He was steadying her, and River realized her breathing had gone out of control. She shut her eyes, exhaling slowly. Her body was begging for the sleep she had missed the night before, her mind a reprieve from it all.

"I'm so tired…" she said. "This is a lot to take. And then there's your uncle who…"

"Maybe you need to lie down for a moment."

Dorian pushed her gently in the general direction of the bed, and River corrected their trajectory. Sleeping now felt stupid. After the past hour, there was no way her reeling mind would let her sleep. There were too many things to think and talk about. Too many questions to ask.

But before she knew it, Dorian made her lie down, and she let him do it. The bed was unmade, and she covered her shivering body with the heavy blanket.

"I feel like I'm going mad," she murmured.

Dorian sat on the edge of the bed. "I know how you feel."

"I need to talk about all this, even if you want me to forget."

"Later."

"I don't want to sleep." Her eyelids slowly became heavy.

"Then, don't."

Sleep claimed her in seconds.

CHAPTER TWENTY-SIX

N ight had already settled by the time River woke up. The
cottage had grown darker, but not completely black. A
soft orange light cast dancing shadows across the walls. Had she
made a fire before going to sleep? She barely had any memories
of walking from the Blackwell House to her cottage.

She was facing the wall next to the bed, away from the front
door. She couldn't hear anything besides the crackling fire. Dorian had left, then. Sadness filled her chest, not only because she was
scared Richard would come find her here, but because she simply
wanted Dorian to be with her. The past forty-eight hours had
been emotionally exhausting, and while River had briefly thought
Dorian wasn't to be trusted, she now already missed spending

time with him, either reading to him or talking or walking in the woods. She craved his presence acutely, so much that it ached.

She rolled over, and her heart skipped a beat. Dorian lay on his back next to her, his breathing so soft she could barely hear it. He had fallen asleep too, his handsome face relaxed. He had stayed on top of the blanket, and River wished she could feel the warmth of his body.

She laid her head on the pillow, looking at him.

He shifted, cracking his eyes open. "Are you awake?"

"Yes. Did you make the fire?"

"I did."

"How did you manage that?"

A warm smile stretched his lips. "It took me a few tries, one burn, and a lot of cussing to finally make it stick."

She laughed.

"How are you feeling?"

"Better, I think. Calmer."

"Good."

She peered at him, a thousand questions burning her lips. "Please, tell me what happened to Thomas."

Dorian sighed and turned his face to her. "I understand how what Shelly saw made it look like I was hurting Thomas. But I swear, I didn't. I was trying to save him. I thought I did, but I was wrong."

River steeled herself. "What happened?"

"Are you sure there are no mirrors here? Are you *absolutely* sure?"

"Yes. There was only the one in the bathroom."

"Do you have your crystals on you?"

"I do. And you're gonna have to tell me why you're obsessed with them."

He paused, seemingly searching for his words. "I didn't hurt Thomas, but still, what happened to him was my fault."

River held her breath and stayed immobile.

"Once I got to know him a little better, I asked for his help, like I did with the others. I made him read that book so he would find the letter. I have lost a lot of aides, River, but it isn't because they all ended up hurt. Most of them quit right then and there, sometimes leaving without saying anything, sometimes calling me insane and *then* leaving. Only about half decided to go into my old room, and out of those, a small handful tried to help me. Thomas was one of them."

River smiled, but it quickly vanished. Thomas had been brave. He'd tried to do something scary to help someone he didn't know that well.

"I shouldn't have asked this of him," Dorian continued. "Him or anyone else. It has never ended well."

"What did he do to help you?"

Silence stretched for a few seconds. Dorian opened his mouth, hesitating. "It doesn't matter. It didn't work. And that night, when you came by, I *was* there. I was scared. I knew my mother was suspicious, and I told Thomas he needed to leave. I know he was trying to help me, but I got mad because he didn't listen to me. He insisted we could find a way. I was grateful that someone wanted to do this for me, but he didn't truly understand my mother's power, and that is what cost him his life. We were talking—or arguing—and then he…"

River's throat closed up. "He what?"

"He started… making these noises. Like he was choking. I went to him, and I felt blood. It was on me and my hands, and I realized it was coming out of his mouth."

River pressed her hand against her lips, sick to her stomach.

"I could tell he was in pain. He was begging me to help him. At least, when he could catch his breath to talk… I dragged him out of here. I thought that maybe if I could get him away from the property, my mother's spell wouldn't reach him anymore. I thought I was successful at saving him. But evidently, I was wrong."

"That's horrible…"

"I shouldn't have told you."

"I needed to know. It's just so awful."

"It is. I hate myself for it. After that, I finally accepted that none of this was worth it. My life isn't worth the lives of others. I am done. I have accepted my fate. If I stop fighting back, she will make my life easier, eventually. I was never going to ask you to read that book to me. It pains me that you found it and went into that room."

River frowned. "But… why did you request to have me as your aide, then?"

"Is it not obvious?" One corner of his lips lifted slightly, though it looked sad. "I wanted to spend time with you. Those brief moments when we ran into each other were not enough. I wanted more."

After hearing about Thomas, River had no energy to feel awkward or shy. If anything, she wanted to get closer to him, but remained immobile. "Why did you ask about my crystals?"

"I have a theory that they keep you hidden from my mother."

"How do you figure?"

"On your first day, my mother didn't know you were here. You caught her by surprise. Do you remember what she said? 'I know everything that goes on around here.' And she does. But somehow, you stayed under her radar. And when we ran into each other in the hallway, she had no clue you were close, or she would have stopped talking. On the day we went downtown together, your crystals kept us both hidden, which is why she was so furious when I came back."

River had had no idea her crystals would have such an effect. Well, not all of them, but one in particular. She fingered the pendant around her neck and peered at the black stone. "I have a black obsidian around my neck. My grandma gave it to me. She said it was for protection from evil. I didn't think she meant that literally."

"I am grateful she gave you that."

River rolled onto her back, staring at the ceiling. What had happened to Thomas was awful. She didn't want to end up like that. But at the same time... He had wanted her to help Dorian. And after reading those things in Dorian's journal, she understood why. He had led a terrible life full of torment. "I didn't know you were close to Luke. You guys barely speak to each other at the coffee shop."

"Luke grew up in this town, like I did. He was the only boy the same age as me, so we were best friends. I think I've asked too much of him over the years. He became sick of me and took his distance. I don't blame him. His parents were never too fond of us being friends. I suppose their fear of my family rubbed off on him."

"That's so sad." A million questions swirled in River's head, making her dizzy. "The things you wrote in your letter implied you were already blind. How did you manage that?"

He sighed, his chest deflating. "That is the last thing Luke agreed to do for me."

"He wrote it for you?"

"Yes. I told him what to say. And he hates me for it. He knew I would achieve nothing but put people in danger, and he was right. I wish I had listened to him."

"There are still so many things I don't understand. Does Miss Roberts know about all this? Why are you so scared of mirrors? And what about all the—"

"No more questions, River."

She looked at him, hoping he would feel her burning glare. "Well, tough. Because I still have about a hundred of them."

He turned to her, his blind eyes piercing through her. His black hair fell onto the pillow, making her want to touch it. "That's one of the things I like about you. You are not afraid to speak your mind. Everyone walks on eggshells around me. Not you. I will miss that, and you as well."

River pushed herself up and rested on her elbow, looking down at him. "What are you talking about?"

"If you recall, I fired you yesterday."

"You can't be serious."

"I am. When Thomas died, I thought I couldn't possibly hate myself more, but it turns out I can. You found the letter, and you got hurt. As hard as it is to believe, my mother is far worse than my uncle. If you stayed, you could *die,* and I will not take that risk."

"But... I want to help."

"There is no helping me."

"I can't just leave you—"

"That is exactly what you are going to do. Spend the night here. And tomorrow, pack your things and leave. No need to talk to anybody. I will tell them."

Emotions strangled her. She was scared beyond belief but leaving him to his fate dug a hole, a *crater,* inside her chest. She pressed her lips together, once again trying to bite back on those damn tears. "Dorian…"

He tried to smile. "It's all right. I promise. I will be happier knowing you are safe."

She sniffed, wanting to keep herself quiet, but the expression on his face told her he knew very well she was crying. "Is there anything I can do for you? Anything at all?"

Though his eyes misted over, his smile looked more genuine. "Lie with me."

River shuffled closer, and he opened his arm to her. She nestled against him, her forehead pressed inside the crook of his neck while he ran his fingers through her hair.

CHAPTER
TWENTY-SEVEN

D orian was gone by the time River woke up, leaving her feeling cold and lonely. Getting ready and gathering her stuff didn't take long, and soon, she was dragging her suitcase to her car, the mist clinging to her hair. She strained to lift it and drop it inside the trunk, then turned to gaze at the Blackwell House for a minute. The fog swirled around it, up to the first-floor windows.

She should be relieved to leave these haunted halls, this dangerous family. But what filled her heart was nothing that resembled relief. How could she move on with her life now? How could she start fresh somewhere and forget about Dorian?

She shook her head and climbed inside the car. "He told you to leave."

The inside felt colder than outside. River inserted the key in the ignition and started the car. It sputtered for a second, then purred as though it hadn't been stuck here in the freezing cold for weeks. A hint of disappointment made River sigh. She had half hoped the car wouldn't start.

It wasn't a movie. She wasn't in a situation where she had no other choice than to stay and fight. She could leave anytime. Free to go. No more threats of a dangerous witch or a pervert. No more having her heart broken by the gentle and handsome man who seemed to—ironically—truly see her.

The engine kept running, the heater blowing warm air onto her face, but River didn't move. She reached for the crystal hanging around her neck, holding it tightly, and closed her eyes.

"Tell me what to do, Grandma. Please, help me."

Willow's face came to mind, the soft, shiny white hair and deep blue eyes. The rosy cheeks and clever smile.

"Can you communicate with the next world, Grandma?"

"I can. So will you one day."

"I'm not magic like you."

"We all have a little bit of magic inside of us, sweetie. But you… you have a lot. I can tell. And when the time comes, don't turn your back on your gift. Embrace it fully and trust yourself."

"Trust yourself…" she said to the empty car.

The air blasting through the vent turned cold, and the engine died. River opened her eyes, a shiver running through her. Frost spread over the windows, crinkling and killing any light coming from outside. Her breath misting in front of her face, she turned the key in the ignition, but the car refused to start.

A whisper rose from the mist. "River."

Then, another. "They did this to me."

And another. "Help us."

Twigs snapped outside. River squinted through the frosted window. The shape of a person stood on the other side. Movement caught River's eye in front of the car. Another silhouette was there, immobile. She gazed at her surroundings. New shapes kept appearing. She counted more than ten. They stood near or far from the car, staring at her.

A few weeks ago, River's body would have shaken from fear. Sweat would have covered her back. But not now. The sign was clear. She took the key out of the ignition and pushed the car door open hard enough to break the ice holding it shut. Outside, only the mist remained. The mist, and the array of footprints in the mud circling her car.

No, it wasn't like the movies. It wasn't like the books she liked to read, where the characters found themselves in an inescapable situation by the end of the first act. She had a choice.

But maybe she wasn't the main character of this story. The main character was stuck in this house, and he needed help. Him and dozens of other souls begging to be set free. River would never forgive herself if she turned her back on them now.

The French doors shook as her fist rapped against them. Nothing moved inside. The fireplace looked dead, and the rest of the room was bathed in darkness. River knocked again, harder. If Dorian didn't open, she would storm through that front door like she owned the place.

Well, maybe not own, but at least belonged. There was something about knowing that the spirits haunting the house were on her side. It gave her courage.

She moved along the wall, peering through each set of French doors, and stopped at the last one, the one overlooking the bed. The shape of a body lay under the covers, a mass of dark hair peeking out of it.

River rapped her fist on the window. "Dorian!"

He jerked his head up. He was usually up at that time in the morning, and it was odd to see him so tired.

Dorian rubbed his face, blinking sleep out of his eyes. "River?"

"Can you open the door?"

He threw the covers aside, and River's heart flipped as he stood and walked to her. He was only wearing sweatpants, and she couldn't keep her gaze from lingering over his athletic chest.

Dorian unlocked the French doors, his hair disheveled and dark circles under his eyes. "What are you still doing here?" Even his voice was hoarse.

The beginning of a stubble covering his jaw was also foreign to River. "Why are you still in bed?"

"I couldn't find a good reason to get up… and I indulged in a bit of wine last night."

She raised her eyebrows. "A bit?"

He rubbed his forehead. "I may have gotten lost in the cellar."

"I didn't think you ever got drunk."

"Is it not what a lot of depressed people do? Drown their sorrows in alcohol?"

"Oh, Dorian…"

"You should have already left."

"I'm not leaving."

"River, listen—"

"No, *you* listen. I'm done being a pushover. I'm done letting people bully me or scare me."

"My family are not mere bullies—"

"I'm not talking about your family," she cut off. "I'm talking about my ex. I'm talking about my shitty manager in that shitty coffee shop. I'm talking about the fake blonde who orders the most complicated, snobbiest latte in the world just to piss me off."

He opened his mouth a fraction. "I'm afraid I don't understand."

"My grandma taught me to trust myself. To look for signs the universe sent me. And when I decided I was done with all that crap, I came here. I finally trusted myself, and I ended up *here* of all places. It's a sign. I was supposed to be here, and I was supposed to meet you. Why else would all these spirits show themselves to me? There is something I have to do here. And I think that's you."

A grin tugged at his lips. "You have to do me?"

"That's not what I—okay, I heard it as soon as I said it. What I mean is that I came to Stormhedge for you. I didn't know it then, but I do now. So, fire me all you want, I'm not leaving. You're gonna have to put up with me a little longer. It's destiny that I'm here."

"You think our lives are already planned out by destiny?"

"No. I think destiny brings you somewhere until you have to make a choice. I made mine. Now go back inside before you catch your death." She pressed a hand against his chest, forcing him to back away until she was inside and could lock the doors. "You are going to wash up and get dressed, and then you and I are going downtown. I need groceries to make dinner tonight. You're invited."

Dorian remained silent for a moment, his gray eyes uncertain. "I need help shaving."

"I'll help you. That's my job, isn't it?"

Before River could walk away to get what she needed to shave him, Dorian grabbed her wrist and pulled her to his chest. "I'm glad you're here."

River allowed herself to hug him back, pressing her cheek against his bare, hot skin.

Dorian tightened his hold. "Thank you for not leaving me."

CHAPTER TWENTY-EIGHT

R iver had so many questions. All the questions she had wanted to ask the day before still swirled in her mind. But there would be a time to ask those, and that time would be after dinner.

"Are you sure there are no mirrors?" Dorian asked.

"Positive." She put the shepherd's pie in the oven and started preparing the Baileys chocolate cake. "The curtains are shut, and the music is on. No one can see or hear us."

"I know I'm annoying. It's hard not to know if I am completely alone or if someone is listening to me somewhere."

"I understand. We're safe right now, I promise." She grabbed a beer from the fridge, opened it, and put it on the table in front of him, guiding his hand to it. "Here. That will be a nice change from the expensive wine you're so used to."

"I knew you thought I was a snob," he said before taking a sip. He pulled a face, making River laugh.

"You've never had a beer before?"

"There are a lot of things I have never had."

A new song on River's computer came on. She had taken it with her when going downtown to charge it. She had taken the opportunity to buy new herbs for new protection jars and had picked up sticks to make more broomsticks. Dorian sat there with her the whole afternoon.

"Do you even know how to dance?" she asked.

"I know how to waltz."

River chortled. "Why did I even ask?"

A smile stretched his lips. "See? I'm an obnoxious snob. I am enjoying the music, though."

One of the reasons Dorian liked to sit at the coffee shop was to listen to music. River liked to see him enjoying himself. "Celtic music is not everyone's cup of tea, so let me know if you want something else."

"It's fine. I wish I could listen to all the music the world has to offer. I have missed so much just living here."

River mixed the ingredients in the bowl and glanced at him. "I know. It's not right."

Dorian took another sip of beer. He seemed to get used to it. "Don't worry. I am content to sit here and listen to the music you like."

River finished up on the chocolate cake, and the shepherd's pie was ready to take out of the oven by the time the cake went in.

"It smells divine," Dorian said, making her smile.

"It's a far cry from Mack's refined cuisine. A lot simpler."

"I am looking forward to eating it, then. I need more simple things in my life. I am tired of complicated and sophisticated."

River cut the pie and served him a piece. He smelled it, and that ever-present tense expression tightening his features evaporated to leave place for that same relaxed, youthful face he had every time he ate banana bread at the Black Bean. As Dorian took a bite, he looked his age, younger even. River was still blown away how eating or drinking or listening to something that was so different from the things he was used to completely changed his expression and mannerism. In these moments, she got a glimpse of the real Dorian, the man he would have been if he hadn't been through all those horrible things.

"This is delicious," he said.

"I'm glad you like it. Keep some space for dessert. I guarantee it'll knock your socks off."

That made him laugh, but not enough to keep him from eating. "Did your grandmother teach you how to cook too?"

"She did."

"She seems like an outstanding woman."

"She really was. I've missed cooking for myself. And for someone who actually appreciates it."

He frowned. "Your boyfriend didn't enjoy your cooking?"

"Not really. Too greasy, too rich, too heavy, not 'clean' enough, it would make me fat, I could go on. I really don't know how I ended up with him. He also didn't like my crystals, my jars, my tarot, all the things that made me the person I am. He called me crazy once or twice."

"Hm." Dorian paused to drink some beer. "We had already determined he was a fucking idiot."

River burst into laughter. "I can't get used to the F-word coming out of your mouth."

"Keep talking about him, and you will."

She laughed some more, deciding that there was no place for
Zach in this conversation after all. Instead, she told him more
about her grandmother, her childhood, and Dorian listened to
each of her words while cleaning his plate.

The Baileys chocolate cake was an even greater success, seemingly taking more years off Dorian's face as he ate it.

"I could eat this until I die," he said.

"Death by chocolate."

She gave him seconds at his request, enjoying seeing him so
happy, even if it was temporary.

"Would you like another beer?"

"I think I would. Thank you."

River grabbed one from the fridge, opened it, and handed it to
him while sitting down with her own. "Dorian?"

"Yes?"

"Why are you so scared of mirrors?"

He slowly put his bottle down but made no reply.

The curtains were still shut, and the computer still played music.
It was safe. No one could hear or see them. "Thomas seemed to
believe I had a shot at helping you, or he wouldn't have left a note,
but I need to know what I'm up against. I understand why you
hate the portraits. What about the mirrors?"

He let out a drawn-out sigh. "The things she can do... Sometimes I regret rebelling against her so young. I regret not learning
all the things she wanted to teach me. If I had, maybe I could
have fought her." He paused, slowly spinning the bottle on the
table. "She travels through the mirrors. They are like portals for

her mind, and because of them, she has access to each and every room of the house. She sees and hears through them, and I know she makes someone occasionally plant one in my room to spy on me."

River stared, her mouth open a fraction as she let that sink in. "Okay... I didn't see that coming. Wait, who cleans your room? Miss Roberts, right? Would she be the one planting the mirrors?"

"I believe so. Edith is far from innocent in all of this."

"I see. Do you think your mother saw me coming into your old room? Before I could cover the mirrors? Is that why Richard came to check?"

Dorian thought for a moment. "I doubt it. If she had seen you, or if she knew about it, I believe you would already be dead."

River's stomach churned. "That's a reassuring thought."

"I told you. You are putting yourself in danger by wanting to help me."

"And I told you I'm an adult who can decide things for herself. But to help you, I need to know *everything*. I need you to tell me what happened to the others. Why they died. And I need to know exactly what it is you think I should do to break you out of here."

His lips tightened into a line, his gray eyes full of torment once again. "I have tried everything, River. I have tried everything, and I have failed miserably each time."

CHAPTER TWENTY-NINE

DORIAN

I'd tried everything. Starting by fleeing this place, which caused my death three times. I didn't understand back then the consequences of my actions. I couldn't fathom the extent of my mother's power. I didn't know how everything worked. I should have known. I should have let her teach me, that way I wouldn't have made such terrible mistakes.

I was always too stubborn, but eventually, she knew how to stifle the fire I had in me. She took my sight, leaving me suddenly weak and helpless, which was exactly what she wanted. I pretended to have learned my lesson. I stopped fighting. I did what she expected of me long enough that she would grant me something I wanted. Someone to help me in my daily activities and keep me company.

I truly felt lonely, but more than anything, I needed someone other than the staff to come to my aid. When my first personal helper, Chad, started, I requested he accompany me downtown to the Black Bean. I hadn't been able to go there on my own since becoming blind. I needed to talk to Luke. I asked Chad to go buy something for me so I could sit down with Luke and ask him to write the letter. It would have been foolish to openly ask Chad to help me, to openly tell him about my twisted family. I never knew who was spying on me anymore. I felt exposed all the time. I needed a better plan than that, as well as a backup plan if my current aide decided I was insane and quit.

Luke almost didn't write the letter for me. He had been telling me for a while that I needed to stop resisting, that it wasn't worth it. The fact that I was now blind proved him right. But I didn't listen. I was too angry. Eventually, he agreed to do this one thing for me, for old times' sake. I told him exactly what to write.

In my letter, I directed my aides to my old bedroom. When I was a child and didn't have an inch on this giant property to myself alone, I decided to build a box. A box that would be mine alone, where I could keep my secrets. There were all the tools I needed in the shed to build something. My father helped me make it. It was rough around the edges, but it was mine. And to keep it secret, I made sure to hide the keys in different places throughout my room so no one could ever find them.

This must have been the best thing I had ever done, especially when it came to asking for help. In that box was the proof they needed to believe me. The problem was a lot of them didn't even go to my old room. They quit, and I couldn't blame them. Chad was the first of many. I kept trying despite my growing reputation of being so terrible that no one could be around me, or worse, the reputation that I physically hurt them.

But one day, one of them decided to help. Preston. He read the letter and went into my room. He didn't get caught. We talked in the cottage, and he agreed to do what I asked of him.

Preston never came back. I didn't know how he died. And still, I selfishly kept going. I kept asking them to read my favorite book so they'd find the letter. I kept trying to take more precautions to make sure they'd be safe, but nothing ever worked. My mother always beat me to it.

It occurred to me that Luke was right. I needed to stop. I couldn't keep asking people to risk their lives for a pathetic one like mine. And that's when I knew what I needed to do. What I *thought* I knew.

I almost changed my mind that day when I heard the soft voice of the new maid saying, "You're welcome" after I said, "Thank you." It made me smile. Miss Roberts always told the staff not to talk to us. It made my blood boil. I needed to talk to people instead of being ignored. And that night, River made me feel seen. Not only that, but her presence had completely gone under my mother's radar, and I thought, *Is this a sign? Could she be different?*

But I quickly shook the thought away. No one else would die because of me.

In the middle of the night, I left the house and walked through the woods toward the highest point of the cliff. If asking for help didn't work, if fleeing didn't work, maybe killing myself would. Maybe she wouldn't see it coming. I would finally be free.

But someone saw me. River. After only a short conversation with her after dinner, I recognized her voice. I became good at that. And she was there, following me. Although it broke my heart that she might see something she shouldn't, I kept going. And I jumped. My bones shattered as my body hit the rocks below. A glacial wave swept over me and took me away. I thought I had succeeded.

But like the other times. I woke up in the house. The sorrow I felt ripped through my chest, the pain so acute it could have killed me a second time. My mother was there, watching me as I screamed and cried like a child.

The next day, Simon was gone, and my mother decided to punish me, as though being alive wasn't enough of a punishment. She refused to give me a new aide. I suspected no one in the house knew about Simon's disappearance for days. Except maybe my uncle and Edith.

The thing was, I didn't ask for a new aide right away. I begged her for my freedom. I begged her to let me die. Or to kill me. Whichever suited her better. Of course, she refused. I was her only heir.

We were in the kitchen. She was drinking some wine. I knew it because I heard the bottle clinking after she opened the fridge.

"Your attempts at leaving are useless, my son," she said. "I have been too patient with you. You do not want to anger me, Dorian."

"What else could you possibly take from me that you did not take already?"

The glass clinked onto the marble counter. Her heels poked against the tiles as she walked to me. I clenched my teeth as her breath grazed my ear. "This is where you're wrong, child. I can take so much more away from you. I can take your hearing and your voice and legs if I want to. Could you imagine what your existence would be like? You think you're suffering, but you have seen nothing."

My fingers itched as they slid over the counter. I remembered there was a knife block there, unless they had moved it. My heart pounded at the back of my throat. Any sense of sanity I thought I still had seemed to disintegrate.

"Do not threaten me," she said in my ear, "or you will truly regret it."

Rage made my blood boil, and before truly understanding what I was doing, I grabbed a knife and jammed it in her stomach. She let out a choked gasp, her fingers scratching at my hand. I pulled the knife out and stabbed her again. And again. Warm blood gushed over my hand, making the knife handle slippery.

I swear I wasn't planning on killing her. All the rage that had built up over the years exploded, and I couldn't stop.

At last, I yanked the blade out, grabbed her hair, and slashed her throat.

A scream behind me made me drop the knife. Richard. His pounding footsteps darted toward me, and his body collided into mine. We fell to the floor, the impact knocking the wind out of me.

"What have you done?" he yelled. His fist dropped on my face, pain blasting through my jaw.

But he was too late. Mother was dead. If she weren't, she'd still be talking or screaming at me.

"You fucking little brat!" Richard screamed, punching me again.

I may be blind but I was stronger than him, and in that moment, my rage still controlled my mind and body. I reached up, and my fingers met with his tie. I didn't think for a second before I grabbed it and yanked on it in a way that I knew would tighten the noose.

His hand released me as they flew to his throat, giving me the opportunity to push him off. He tried to get away, but I dropped onto his back, reached around his throat, and grasped the tie's noose. His grunts turned to pained, choking sounds as I arched back, pulling on the tie and strangling him.

"You disgust me," I spat. "You don't deserve to have a good life, not after all the things you've done."

I tightened my hold, feeling increasingly sick and lightheaded. My rage was leaking out of my body, leaving me incredibly aware of my actions. Still, I couldn't stop, and I held on to that tie until Richard stopped shaking under me.

My labored breathing filled the silence until footsteps approached, and a scream split the air.

"Dorian… What have you done…" Edith said, her voice nothing but a raw whisper.

I didn't have time to answer before a blow to the back of my head knocked me out. I woke up with a pounding headache splitting my skull. A sign that I hadn't died but just passed out. I had no idea what time it was. As I moved on the bed, feeling the fabric with my hands, the bedspread was instantly familiar to me. I was in my room. But my skin and my clothes felt odd. The scent of copper filled my nostrils, and for a scary second, I thought someone had put one of those horrible paintings in my room. But then I flexed my fingers. Dried blood crusted them, and I remembered who it belonged to.

I needed to find Mother, knowing she wasn't dead but hoping that maybe I was wrong. I took a shower first. There was no need to frighten the staff and make them more scared of me than they already were.

After searching the ground floor, I went upstairs and opened each room. When I started to think she wasn't there, her voice stopped me from going to the third floor.

"Looking for me?" she said. It was like she had come out of nowhere. She wasn't there, then the next second, she was. You may think that it was because I was blind, but even before then, she was always able to sneak up on me.

I stopped, a small part of me disappointed that she was still here, not that it really was a surprise.

"I must say, son, I am very disappointed in you."

I squared my shoulders. "How do you do it?"

"If you had been obedient and accepted to learn what I have always wanted to teach you, you would know."

She wouldn't tell me anything, so instead, I changed the subject. "I want a new aide."

She let out a strangled laugh. "After what you did, you are in no position to make demands. You are lucky I didn't take more from you. Yet."

"I do not believe you would go as far as turning me into a vegetable. It would be no fun for you. I may not be able to kill you, but this must not have been pleasant for you. I could make it worse. Make it last *longer*."

She took a sharp step in my direction, her body heat radiating against my skin, and I forced myself not to flinch. "You need to stop what you're doing *immediately*. What on earth were you thinking?"

"Then, give me what I want, Mother."

"Stop trying to manipulate me and everyone around you. We'll lose all our servants at this rate—"

"We wouldn't want that, would we?"

"It is your own fault you are losing all your aides. How many have you had now?" She sighed. "Don't you understand? I only have your best interest at heart."

A cynical laugh fell out of me. "Right, of course. That is really the impression I got from your speech last night."

"Enough. All of it. I will give you what you want, but in exchange, you had better be on your best behavior from now on and during the celebration. You need to believe me when I say that the consequences of your actions are far worse than you think they are."

"I do not believe a single word coming out of your mouth."

"If you do as I say, I will give you what you desire most. And then you will believe me." She walked past me, and I allowed myself to breathe slightly easier.

"I think you are mistaken on what it is that I desire most," I said, but she made no reply and left.

I did not mean those things I said. I didn't think I could ever kill her again, and I had no doubt she would not hesitate to make things worse for me, should she feel the need to. But I couldn't show her I was scared. Somehow, it worked.

I headed in the direction opposite her, following that pleasant scent of lavender, and ran into River. She dropped things on the floor, and one of them hit my shoe. I kneeled, searching for it. It was smooth under my fingers.

"What is this, River?"

"Just a crystal…" she said in that soft voice I loved so much, and I was afraid she thought I was angry. I could never be angry at that voice. "I know I'm not supposed to carry any personal items."

Crystals. My mother did not use them much, but she briefly told me about them when teaching me some of the basics. I suddenly wondered if they were the reason River had been invisible to my mother. Before talking to me just a minute ago, she must have looked into each mirror of the floor. She would never risk having that kind of conversation if a maid was around. And yet, River had been behind that wall. I didn't know how much she heard, but she was there, again undetected.

"Don't let my mother see it," I said. "Or Miss Roberts."

"Yes. Thank you."

"Don't tell anyone you have these and never take them out again."

I hoped I didn't sound too harsh, but if she at least could escape my mother's ever watchful eyes, it was worth it. Before I left, River said something that made me pause.

"Do you know anything about Cassie leaving?"

"Cassie? Did she leave?"

"So I've been told."

My mouth opened a fraction, but no sound came out. It was as though something clicked suddenly, and I had never felt so stupid. How could I be so blind? Literally and figuratively.

"Excuse me. I need to go."

I walked on weak legs through the hallway, in the direction my mother had taken a minute earlier. I searched for her like before and found her in the sitting room. I closed the door behind me. My blood drummed in my ears as my mind swirled.

"What do you want now?" she said. "I will get you your new aide, no need to keep pestering me. After what you did yesterday, I think a little distance is much needed, don't you think?"

"You have been killing them."

Silence followed my statement.

My throat tightened, and I brushed my hair back with a shaky hand. "All those maids that left each time I tried to flee. Each time I died... Simon was gone the day after I jumped. And now Cassie. Who else?"

"I don't know what you are—"

"Who else?"

She sighed. "One of our landscapers."

I put one hand on the wall to steady myself, cold sweat breaking over my body. "How could you..."

"Me?" She cackled, sounding like the true witch she was.

"You have shamelessly exchanged my life for theirs." My voice was losing its intensity. My stomach roiled, and I felt like puking.

"But it is your fault, son. *You* murdered them. All of them." The sofa squeaked, and her heels stabbed the floorboards in my direction. "They all died the way you did. Let that sink in, Dorian. Each time you tried to leave, you killed someone. When you jumped off that cliff? Simon did the same."

My heart hammered in my chest so hard I was afraid it would burst out. I rested my back against the wall and let myself slide to the floor, too weak to stand.

"And this morning, our poor Miss Roberts had to deal with the sous-chef *and* the landscaper's suicides. One stabbed herself the way you stabbed me, the other hanged himself on a tree after you strangled your uncle."

I didn't only cost my aides to lose their jobs or disappear. I cost the lives of at least five other innocent people who had done nothing wrong. Tears rolled down my cheeks, and I pressed my palms against my eyes, wishing I could simply die and never come back.

"Let. That. Sink. In," she repeated, a smile in her voice. "I didn't want to tell you, but I suppose it is a good lesson. Now you finally understand that your actions have terrible consequences. That should teach you to obey."

I made no reply. I couldn't. My voice, my guts, my will—they had all deserted me.

Fingers brushed my hair. "There, there, my child. It is not too late to make amends. I will give you your new aide, as you have requested. You will prove to me that you have learned your lesson and that you will no longer resist your legacy. And eventually, you will have everything you need." She wrapped her arms around me, and despite repulsion twisting my guts, I couldn't find the strength to move away.

"You're a monster..." I sobbed, quite pathetically.

"Shh," she said, stroking my hair. "One day, you will see. Everything I do is for you."

CHAPTER THIRTY

DORIAN

I gave up. I should have done it so much earlier, but instead, I kept pushing my luck, not realizing I was playing with people's lives.

That wasn't entirely true. I had no idea about the people that died when I died or when I killed. But I knew the risks my aides were taking. Thomas could have been spared, but after swearing to myself I would never put anyone else in danger again, the nagging thought that maybe things would be different this time, that I could try one last time, swayed me.

After battling with the idea for days, I decided to go get my book. Thomas would read it, and he would find the letter. My body shook as I walked to the library, and the blood pumping in my ears made so much noise that I didn't even realize someone was there until I heard a scream, and River's body collided into mine.

As usual, the delicate scent of lavender floated about the air, and I instantly knew it was her. She asked me if I'd make fun of her if she said she had seen a ghost. Honestly, I wanted to make fun of anyone who hadn't. Even blind, I could always feel them around us. Cold spots filled the house. Whispers trickled down hallways. Icy air blew down my neck. The idea that spirits only haunted me had sprouted in my mind in the last few days. Their deaths were my fault after all.

But River had seen something, and that made me feel less lonely.

I still grabbed the book because I was already there, and I didn't want her to think that I was just walking around aimlessly, or worse, that I was following her, but her presence in the library had stirred something in me. As I walked back to my suite, the idea of asking Thomas for help began to crumble. They knew each other. He was her friend. What would she think of me if she knew what I was about to do?

I knew I was a terrible person. There would never be a way to redeem myself. But could I really ask Thomas to risk his life, knowing what I now knew?

No. I couldn't. As terrible a person as I had become, I changed my mind.

I would behave and follow whatever plan my mother had for me. If I did it long enough, she would one day give me my sight back. I would marry a woman I didn't love and have children. If my mother was lucky, I would have a girl that would carry on her legacy.

The pit in my stomach deepened and bile rose in my throat at the thought that this child of mine, not even born, would either suffer like I did or become a monster like my mother.

As Thomas entered my suite the next day, I let him look for mirrors before giving him a choice—leave or go back to being part of the staff. I would love for anyone living here to just flee this place, but I was aware some of them had nowhere to go and needed the money. Thomas was one of them. He had told me enough about his private life that it felt wrong to force him to leave.

But then something happened. A muffled thud on the carpet snapped me out of my thoughts.

"Oops, I dropped your book," Thomas said. I heard the soft sound of pages brushing against one another. "Is that the book you want me to read?"

I had left the book on the mantelpiece, like a fool. My heart flipped painfully in my chest, and I rose from the sofa. "No. Please, give it back to me."

"Oh, okay. I thought—" He paused suddenly. "What's that?"

The pulse in my throat nearly choked me. I wasn't sure if he had found the letter, but if he hadn't, I didn't want to mention it. "Give me the book, please." My voice had lost all traces of authority it may have had before.

Silence followed, leaving me to wait uncomfortably in the dark.

Then, Thomas cleared his throat. "I'm on page 103."

My body went numb.

After what felt like an eternity, Thomas said, "Would you like to go outside for a walk?"

He walked me to the woods without saying a single word, which was very unlike him. Thomas never seemed to be able to stop talking, or to *want* to, which I didn't mind. It helped fill the emptiness of my existence. This brand-new silence of his unsettled me. The arm looped around mine felt stiff.

I wanted to tell him that this letter was not relevant anymore. That he could leave if he wanted to, that I wasn't expecting anything from him. I opened my mouth, but he talked before I could.

"What's in your old room?"

"You should not have seen that letter. You need to forget about it."

An indignant huff fell out of his mouth. "How does one forget about something like that? You said you're being held captive, that you are *begging* for help, and then you went on about motherfucking witchcraft and how your mother took your eyesight and killed your father—"

"Mind your voice, please."

Thomas caught his breath and lowered his voice. "Call me crazy, but I'm willing to believe anything that's in that letter."

"You *are* crazy. No one ever believes it."

"But my instinct of preservation is pretty strong," he continued, ignoring me. "So, if I can avoid going to the third floor and follow these *insanely* complicated steps to open a fucking box, then I'd prefer it."

"If your instinct of preservation was that strong, you would leave this place or ask Miss Roberts to put you back on the cleaning crew."

Another indignant scoff escaped him, a sound I was becoming used to. "The cleaning crew—are you kidding me? Cleaning that damn *castle* is the hardest thing I've ever had to do. I like this job, thank you."

Words jumbled in my mind, leaving me unable to form a proper sentence. I wasn't used to that kind of reaction. I would have *wished* for that before, but that never happened. People either fled right away or found the box in my old room and fled after that. "Why are you believing me so easily?"

"Why are you asking useless questions?"

"Thomas."

He sighed. "Because I'd be stupid not to. First of all, your house is haunted, in case you're not aware. Second, I happen to know a witch myself—" He gasped. *"River."*

Just the mention of her name made my heartbeat quicken. "River?"

"Maybe she could help! Although I'm not sure how much of a dent her crystals and candles will make in... well, whatever it is that you need to be done."

I was right, then. "I think her crystals keep her hidden from my mother. She always keeps track of everyone, but River's presence always seems to take her aback."

"How do you know that?"

"I notice things."

A beat of silence followed, and I imagined Thomas's puzzled face. What I was saying didn't make sense to him. He didn't know about my mother's ability to have her conscience jump through mirrors to spy on everyone.

"Well..." he said. "Whatever that means, then I'm right to think that River could help us."

Nausea roiled in my stomach at the thought of asking her to help. "You will not tell River about this. I *will not* put anyone else in danger, do you understand me?"

"I don't. You'll have to explain it to me like I'm five. And then I'll make up my mind like a big boy."

I admit it, he wore me down. He made it so easy for me. He believed everything without asking for proof, telling me that you didn't need to be a genius to know that my family and my house were creepy. Still, after he heard about all the people that died, he was shocked, as anyone should be. But that didn't deter him.

Thomas allowed me to let hope creep back into my chest. For the first time in years, someone was listening. Someone was standing by my side, ready to do what I couldn't. I felt lighter after telling him everything.

And he *did* do something that no one had ever done before. Which was what got him killed.

I still couldn't believe he went through with it, or at least tried.

I knocked on the cottage door, and Thomas let me in. He was jumpy, and I was both excited and terrified. On the one hand, he was back. Safe and sound. On the other hand, his nervousness set my teeth on edge.

As soon as the door clicked closed, I said, "No mirrors?"

"No, *obviously*. I tossed it through the window. And the curtains are closed."

"What happened? Are you alright?"

A shaky breath escaped him. "I saw it. The secret passage you talked about. I *found* it. Right where you said it would be."

My stomach dropped. I hadn't been sure about that at all, but I had recently gotten a hint when running into River in the library. "And?"

Thomas swallowed. "I didn't go in. Miss Roberts walked in."

My breath caught in my throat, nearly strangling me. "She *saw* you had opened the door?"

"I don't think so? I don't know… I invented some bullshit about getting a book for you. I grabbed one and left."

I got that sick feeling in my stomach. My heart quickened its pace, slamming against my chest. "Thomas, she will tell my mother. You cannot trust her. Thank you for trying, but it's over. Pack your bags."

"No, listen. This is why we need River."

"Leave this place before something happens to you!" I was nearly shouting, but I couldn't help it. Panic shot through my spine and tightened my chest.

"I can *help* you," he said too loud. "And I know River would step up too. I wouldn't ask her to come with me, but she could give me something to protect me or—"

"Nothing can protect you. You have to go. *Now.*"

"What about you?"

I forced air inside my lungs. "I will be okay."

"No, you won't."

"Thomas, you don't seem to completely grasp the gravity of the situation you put yourself in."

"Oh, but I do." His voice quivered, and he took a few seconds. "I know what I'm risking, but I can't just flee like a coward. This isn't who I am."

A knock on the door nearly made me jump out of my skin. We both fell quiet, holding our breaths.

The person on the other side of the door knocked once more, and a soft voice I recognized floated through it. "Thomas? It's just me."

River.

"Thomas," I whispered as low as I could, my hands balled into fists. "I am begging you, don't tell her anything. She could die. Answer her, and then leave before you die too."

He made no reply. Instead, his hand wrapped around my arm as he gently pushed me further into the room. Then, the door creaked open next to me.

"Hi," he said, his voice tight.

"Hi," River answered.

I pressed my back against the wall, praying that wherever Thomas had put me, River couldn't see me.

"Are you okay?" she said.

"Yes, of course. I'm fine."

Another beat of silence filled the space between them. If Thomas looked as scared as he sounded earlier, then she knew something was wrong.

I listened to their conversation, holding my breath, afraid River would hear me. Her presence now felt... I didn't know how to explain it. It was like she knew. Like she had sensed that Thomas needed her somehow.

I exhaled slowly as River began to leave. Then, Thomas called out for her again.

"Freckles."

"Yeah?"

Don't say anything. Please, don't involve her in this.

I clenched my teeth, waiting, hoping.

"I may have to leave," he finally said.

Thank you, Thomas.

Though it made me sad to hear the shock in River's voice, I was grateful that Thomas had decided to leave her out of it.

The door clicked shut.

I allowed my shoulders to relax. "You did the right thing."

"I wanted to tell her everything…" His footsteps moved from the door to the kitchen. "She brought me vials and a broomstick for protection. How much of a coincidence is that?"

"She must have a sixth sense," I admitted.

He sighed. "I guess I'll pack."

"It's better this way."

"Really? You could have had two people on your team, Dorian. We could have made a difference."

"My problems aren't your responsibility. I shouldn't have involved you in all this."

"Just—"

A sudden, snapping sound made me jump.

"What is this?"

"What the fuck?" Thomas said, sounding baffled. "The fucking broomstick just… *snapped* in half."

I pushed away from the wall, River's voice playing in my head.

"If it falls, it means it has protected you against a bad spell."

The fucking thing *snapped.*

"Thomas, you need to go."

Glass shattered, once again startling me.

"Fuck!" Thomas exclaimed.

I felt sick with dread. This couldn't be happening again. I couldn't have been so stupid, so naïve to think that I could get away with this. That *he* could get away with this. "She's onto you. My mother's onto you. Run! Leave everything behind!"

"Shit… Shit." His voice shook. He moved through the room, his feet pounding and shuffling around. I didn't understand what he was doing. I heard paper being ripped, then a cupboard opening and closing. I now knew what it was. He wrote that note and left it in the pasta box for River to find. Had I known, I would have begged him not to do it, but I was clueless, unable to see what was happening in front of me.

"I—" His sentence was cut short by a choking sound. Then, another followed by coughing.

"Thomas? What's happening?"

He kept coughing, making these horrible sounds. He couldn't answer me. My heart in my throat, I made my way to him, searching blindly. In my hurry, I slammed into the table but barely felt the impact against my leg. I felt for the chairs, moving forward, toward the gurgling sounds.

Finally, I reached him, or stumbled over him more like. He was down on his knees, hunched over. I wrapped my arms around his chest and pulled him upright. Thomas heaved, and warm liquid coated my hands. The smell of copper filled the air.

A small object hit my hand as Thomas coughed once again, but I couldn't tell what it was. I dragged him. In my panic, I struggled to find the door, and I thought for a moment I would never be able to get him outside. Eventually, I found it and burst through the door, Thomas still heaving in my arms. He could barely stand up.

"Dorian," he gasped. "Please…"

His legs wobbled under him once again, and more blood soaked my sleeves.

Holding on to him as hard as I could, I headed to what I *thought* was the woods with the path leading to town. Panting, my throat burning, I focused on the roaring ocean and the glacial wind coming from behind me to steer me in the right direction.

I was almost there. I could feel it. The wind lost some of its strength, which meant that the trees were shielding me. I could get him out of here.

He was becoming weak. Before, he'd been trying to stand despite failing. Now, his legs couldn't carry him anymore. His breathing sounded shaky and labored. It wheezed weakly in and out of him. His hand, though, still had some strength. As I kept pulling, I felt the cold jar he was clutching against his chest. It wasn't doing anything for him, but he kept it close to him, his last resort.

My body shook from the effort. I was completely in the woods now. The trees muffled the sound of the ocean, and the wind whistled in their branches. I was farther and farther from the house.

My foot snagged on a root, and I lost my balance. I held on to Thomas, trying to shield him from the impact as much as I could. My back slammed onto the earth, and the impact knocked the wind out of me. Thomas lay practically limp. He wasn't heaving and gasping anymore, but that glass jar was still tucked in his hand.

"Hang on, Thomas. *Please.*"

My arms and legs burned, and my hair stuck to the sweat on my forehead, but I refused to give up. Wincing, I wrapped my arms around Thomas's chest once again and lifted him with a grunt. The blood pumping in my ears and my erratic breathing filled my head, rendering me almost deaf to the sounds of footsteps coming from the woods.

Miss Roberts had to yell for me to hear her. "It's over, Dorian. You need to let him go."

"Go to hell," I hissed, still dragging Thomas's limp body through the dirt.

"Oh, Dorian…" The fake pity seeping out of her voice disgusted me. "Don't you see this is useless? Even if you had gotten him to town, her power would still have reached him."

My body failed me then, and I dropped to the ground, squeezing Thomas against my chest. A sob escaped me. She was right. All those times I had tried to flee, I had made it a lot further than this, and it didn't change anything.

I took a shaky breath, my eyes burning. "Is he dead?" I already knew the answer.

"I'm afraid so, my boy."

All those people had died because of me. But this, having someone die in my arms… it was the worst torture I had ever been through.

Something nestled in the crook of my arm cut into my skin. I felt for it and held it between my fingers. It was flat and slick with blood. Frowning, I made a mental picture of what I was holding, and as I turned it around, it sliced into my finger.

I swallowed. "Edith, is that a razor blade?" My voice had been reduced to a low croak.

Miss Roberts stayed silent, which was the answer I needed.

That had been my mother's choice of death for Thomas then—making him cough out razor blades.

"You saw him in the library," I said. "And you told my mother. How can you even live with yourself?"

"Dorian—"

"Why? Why are you so devoted to her? Is your life so miserable that you find pleasure in being at this monster's service? Does she make you feel important? Needed? You are *scum.* And if it didn't hurt anybody, I would kill you right now."

"Please, step away from the body and walk home now. I must take care of him and clean the cottage. Thanks to you."

"Get away from him. He had a family. Friends. He was a good person. He doesn't deserve to be turned into my mother's sick art!"

Miss Roberts let out a long exhale, as though I was boring her to death. "Do I need to get help for you to step aside? Please, boy, just let me do my job." A scraping sound in the dirt told me she was walking in our direction.

Then, I felt Thomas move. I sucked in a sharp breath, unsure if I had dreamed it. The next thing I knew, his body tensed and jerked, and Edith let out a cry of pain. I didn't know what he did exactly, but he was alive. I let go of him and pushed him away from me.

"Run!"

And he did. I heard him shuffling away before his unsteady footsteps pounded the dirt away from me. I turned back to where I thought Miss Roberts was standing and jumped to my feet before tackling her. She was right where I hoped she would be and let out a choked grunt as my body slammed against hers.

"No!" she cried out. "He can't leave!"

I couldn't tell if Thomas had made it, but I gave everything I had to restrain Miss Roberts for as long as I could. Despite not seeing anything, it wasn't that hard. She was old and frail, and she only struggled for a minute when I pinned her to the ground, an arm behind her neck, before she gave up, trying to catch her breath.

"Your mother will be furious with both you and me now," she hissed.

Despite all of it, I felt almost happy. My mother would punish Edith, and she deserved everything coming to her. I would also pay for the consequences of my actions, but at that exact moment, I could not care less. Thomas had made it out. He was alive.

At least, that was what I thought until River saw his ghost.

CHAPTER
THIRTY-ONE

R iver sat on the bed, her hands limp on her lap. She hadn't said a word the whole time Dorian had been talking, helping her fill the gaps in what had happened to Thomas.

"I was so sure he had left," he said, standing in front of the fire, a hand on the mantlepiece. The light cast dancing shadows over his features. "I know I lied about him having a family emergency, I couldn't tell you the truth, but I was genuine when I said he was fine. I was so sure... But then you saw him. You mentioned the blood..."

She swallowed. "Because of the razor blades..."

"Yes. I suppose the blood loss got him eventually, and Edith didn't feel the need to tell me."

River let her eyes sweep over the space, the kitchen table, the floor… "So, there was blood in here. And Miss Roberts cleaned it up."

"Yes."

She felt dizzy and sick. Edith was as much a monster as Selene, then. "I became your aide the next day. How? I thought Thomas was sort of your last chance."

"It's true. But it wasn't my mother who caught Thomas in the library. So, that night I stormed back into the house, and I must say, I have never lied so well. I gave quite the performance, still fueled by the adrenaline of what had happened to Thomas. I told her he had done nothing wrong, that he was simply getting a book for me, and Edith had gotten him killed. I said she hadn't held her end of the contract, and I threatened to keep killing myself until no one was left."

"Wow. Quite the tantrum."

"I wouldn't have done it, of course, but it worked. She believed Edith had made a mistake, and she believed it when I said I would behave, which was the truth. So, instead of punishing me, she tried to pacify me by allowing you to become my aide."

Every bit of information swirled in River's head.

The gap.

That gap in between two shelves in the library where she had seen an eye. "Maybe it wasn't a ghost in the library after all."

Dorian tilted his head in her direction. "Probably not."

"So, that's the secret passage you were talking about?"

"Yes. I have been suspecting there are secret rooms or passages for a long time now. My mother always seems to come out of nowhere. Being blind, I could never find them. Then, you said you

294

thought you saw someone behind a shelf, and I wondered if that could be one of the entrances. Thomas confirmed that theory."

"How many people know about it?"

"I don't know for certain. I was raised without knowing about them, and I don't know if my uncle knows, either. Maybe even my father wasn't aware of them."

"So, your mother and Miss Roberts at the very least. Otherwise, she wouldn't have ratted Thomas out."

"Most likely."

River let everything sink in, her body heavy and nailed to the bed. "Dorian, what are you hoping to find in these secret passages?"

He didn't answer for several, long seconds. The fire crackled while the rain began battering the windows again. "A way to break her hold on me. On all of us."

River stood on weak legs and took a few steps in his direction. "I'll go into the library. With my crystals."

Dorian turned to face her, trying to smile but failing at it. "Do you remember your first day here? Miss Roberts had just finished cleaning the cottage."

"Yeah."

"Your broomstick snapped in half. If what you said to Thomas is true, then it protected him against my mother's spell. She would have felt it. And you *did* tell Miss Roberts you made it."

"Oh... You mean—"

"That they have probably been watching you closely. Waiting to see what you were going to do." He took a step toward her and reached out. River took his hand. "Which means you will do nothing."

"I thought we were past that," she mumbled.

"I'm not."

"What if I said I'm not doing it for you?"

He cocked an eyebrow.

"Well," she continued, "not *just* you. I almost left once, and it became crystal clear that I am needed here. You're not the only prisoner of this place. All these people, these spirits, they're stuck here, and they asked for my help. I'm meant to be here, for better or worse."

"But if something happened to you, I'll—"

"You'll feel terrible, I know. Don't be so self-centered."

A scoff escaped him. "I'm self-centered now?"

"Think about how I would feel leaving you and everyone else behind. I wouldn't be able to live with myself." She straightened her shoulders and tilted her head up. "I'm staying, and there's nothing you can do about it. Don't worry, though. If I die and come back as a ghost, I'll still keep you company."

Dorian reached up, his fingers grazing her jaw and making her shiver. "I don't find that amusing."

"It was supposed to be reassuring."

"The idea of you dying is the opposite of reassuring." His thumb brushed her lip, and River let herself lean against his chest.

"Then, maybe you should make the most of our time together."

Dorian leaned forward and captured her lips between his. The kiss was intense, almost needy, the built-up desire finally finding release as he pulled her against his chest. River slid her hands behind his neck. She hadn't realized until now how much she craved his touch, how much she needed to feel the warmth of his body against hers.

She broke the kiss to pull her sweater off, and any clothing standing between her and the warm hands that eagerly explored her body. She helped Dorian do the same, and as he pressed her against his skin, his mouth trailing over her neck, River slowly pulled him toward the bed.

That feeling of being seen, more than she had ever been in her life, came back stronger than ever. Most men liked to watch, to admire. Deprived of his eyesight, Dorian sought out contact with her, craving her embrace and the affection he'd been denied all those years while showering her with passionate kisses as he made love to her with an intensity she had never experienced.

He ran his mouth over her chest, her shoulders, her clavicle, and her jaw. River could smell beer on his breath and taste chocolate on his tongue as he moved inside her and bit her bottom lip. She tightened her grip in his hair, her nails digging into his skin, and wrapped her legs around him to keep him close. She held him tight, knowing falling in love with him was a curse, not a blessing, but never wanting to leave this bed, never wanting time to tick by and force her to face the ugly reality that by helping him and the ghosts of Blackwell House, she might be rushing to her death.

CHAPTER
THIRTY-TWO

"Your best bet is to sneak into the library during dinnertime. It lasts longer than lunch. There will be no maid cleaning at this hour, and you won't risk running into my mother, my uncle, or Edith. I'll try to keep them talking to give you as much time as you need. Keep your crystals close. Whatever you see in there, whatever you find, be out in an hour's time."

Dorian's words played on a loop in River's mind as she moved in the dark, heading to the corner of the mansion where she knew the library was. A window was cracked open an inch, just like Dorian had said he would leave it. His suite was on the far right of the mansion, at the complete opposite of the library, so they decided it would be a lot easier and quicker if she sneaked in through the window.

The whistling wind tugged at her hair and clothes, but for once, she was grateful for the noise it made, as it muffled her footsteps. Standing on her toes, she pushed the window open, expecting it to squeak, but it stayed quiet. River clasped her hands on the windowsill, then lifted her foot, trying to find purchase in the ivy coating the outer wall. One of the branches felt strong enough to support her weight. She slowly pushed on it, pulling herself up at the same time, testing to see if it would hold. The leaves ruffled and the root shook, but it held long enough for River to climb onto the next one.

After what felt like ten minutes but wasn't even one, River threw her leg through the open window and eased herself inside the library, her arms burning a little.

I'm pathetically out of shape for something like this.

She gently closed the window behind her and stood there a moment, listening. The room was quiet. Not even a ghost in sight. River took the small flashlight she had bought that day out of her pocket and turned it on. She made sure her crystals were safely tucked in her other pocket and that her pendant still hung around her neck and rested on her chest.

She forced a deep breath into her lungs and marched toward the rows of shelves. She walked past several of them before turning left between two aisles. Ahead were the shelves lining the wall, and as she raised the flashlight, that dark line marking the gap appeared. Her heartbeat raced, and she shivered at the thought of an eye staring at her from behind.

Repulsion coursing through her, River slid her arm between the two shelves forming the angle and reached for the gap. She curled her fingers behind the bookshelf and pulled, but it stayed rooted to the floor. She tried again with the same result.

"Damn it."

A sigh escaped her as she pulled her arm free and looked the shelf over. If Thomas had found the entrance, surely, she could too.

The white light swept over the books as she looked at them, but nothing looked out of place or different, and so she did the only thing she could think of and started to pull on the books one by one, hoping it would be like in the movies and one of them would trigger a mechanism that would open the passage.

After pulling each book, the shelf stayed desperately fixed into place. River took a step back, anxiety eating away at her stomach. She was wasting precious time. If she couldn't find the way in soon, she would have to leave and come back the next day, or she would get caught. She looked at each shelf again, running her fingers over them, the small, white specks of dust dancing in her light.

Then, it hit her.

It can't be a book.

Dorian loved books. If the mechanism to open the secret door had been linked to a book, Dorian might have stumbled upon it by mistake in all the years he'd lived here. Selene wouldn't have allowed that. She was too smart. She also had to make sure no maid opened the passage by chance while cleaning.

River's gaze travelled upward and stopped on the intricate patterns running at the top of each bookshelf. A rose followed by spindly branches twisting around one another, followed by another rose. Repeat. While the branches and spikes were engraved in the wood, the roses protruded from it.

She reached out to one of them, ran her fingers over it, pushed it, but nothing happened. She took a step to the side and did the same thing with the next rose. A small gasp caught in her throat at the sight of the tiniest movement of the rose, something she never would have noticed while dusting the shelves. River fit her thumb in one of the petals and her index in another to get a better grip and turned clockwise.

The rose caved inward, and the shelf clicked before it opened a crack. River backed away and stared at the gap, her heart pounding. Her blood turned cold at the idea of exploring the passage, but there was no time to waste. She took a deep breath, gathering her courage.

"I hope you'll keep me company, Thomas," she whispered.

She pulled the shelf open and entered, sweeping the flashlight around and making sure she would find a way to get out. Fixed to the wall just inside was a small, simple lever, so she closed the door behind her as quietly as she could.

Flecks of dust surrounded her. The passage was narrow, barely large enough to contain her. The air smelled of humidity, the wooden walls soaked with the outside mist. The whistling wind infiltrated the cracks. River began walking down the tight corridor, trying to keep in mind the layout of the house.

At the end of the corridor, a flight of stairs full of crooked steps stood in front of her. They creaked under her boots but seemed solid enough. They stopped abruptly, leading to a new corridor that continued straight ahead. Normally, there would be many more steps to get to the second floor.

We're between two floors…

Which made sense, otherwise the passage would block the windows.

Scuttering and squeaking noises surrounded her as she moved, her imagination running wild and picturing giant rats scurrying in the dark as her light approached. She felt increasingly crummy. The humidity seeped into her clothes, and the cobwebs coating the walls kept brushing her face and sticking to her hair.

The corridor took a sharp turn to the right, and River found herself in front of a choice: keep going straight or go right.

"There are passages between the rooms…" she said to herself. "That's crazy…"

She tried to conjure the house's layout. She probably stood just above the hallway that led to the maid's quarters and passed by the ballroom, if she were right that is. Further down that way and to the left would be the kitchen and the dining room. If she went straight, she'd reach the back of the house.

River went straight. The other corridor would take her close to the dining room, where the Blackwells were currently eating, surrounded by the chef and the maids. She couldn't risk making noise and raising suspicions. If there was a secret room to be found, it wouldn't be stuck in the middle of a corridor anyways, and chances were, the passages led all around the house and connected to each other.

River kept walking, the sound of her footsteps muffled and contained within these walls. The floor felt spongy, as though several layers of carpet covered it. Only the sounds of her breathing and the little creatures scurrying in the dark disturbed the silence. It felt like walking underground.

The passage took a sharp turn to the right, and River let out a sigh of relief. She had finally reached the back of the house. She followed another endless corridor, praying her flashlight wouldn't fail her. She slowed down as she passed a door on the wall, a simple rectangle tall enough to let a person through, and she wondered which room it opened to but didn't stop to look. There was no time for that.

She stopped abruptly as she came upon another crossroad. She swept the light over the place, her mouth opened agape. "Crap…"

She had another choice to make, harder than the one before. The passage she was on could lead her straight, but another one stretched to her right, probably running right down the middle of the house. The tiniest, most crooked staircase ran upward along the wall, no doubt leading to the upper floor.

Her eyes darted from the stairs to the corridor ahead, then the one to the right, and back to the stairs. Where could a secret room be? The ground level? The third floor?

River let out a controlled breath and reached for the pendant around her neck, closing her eyes. "Thomas? Are you there? Anyone, really. Simon? Cassie? Please, someone tell me which way to go."

A whisper, something like a soft gasp, made River turn. Down the corridor to her right, a flash of white clothes soaked with red blood disappeared behind a wall.

"Cassie."

River darted in her direction, then stopped at the next intersection and looked around. She caught a glimpse of Cassie's dead eyes further down to the left. Heart pounding, River strode after her, one hand gripping the flashlight, and the other still fastened around the pendant as though she was afraid to lose contact.

She skidded to a stop at the next crossing. The flash of white hovered above the floor before vanishing. River cautiously walked to the spot Cassie had been, wondering where she could have gone. The darkness started to weigh on her. Her lungs itched for fresh air, but she couldn't leave this place until she found what she was looking for. She directed the light ahead, squinting. No one was waiting for her there.

She took another step, and the sound suddenly didn't sound muffled, but hollow, the floor squeaking under her. Her heart made a leap, and she stepped back, turning the light to the spot she had stepped on.

A trapdoor.

A small ring protruded from one side of the square. River crouched down, every fiber of herself expecting the door to resist. She hooked her finger in the ring and pulled. The trapdoor's side scraped against the floor surrounding it but opened without too much difficulty. River opened it all the way and took a few steps back, heart pounding. The black square on the floor seemed far darker than the corridor she was in. The soft sound of water drops echoed inside. Her insides shrunk. Chills multiplied at the base of her spine.

She had been scared in her life, especially since coming to the Blackwell House. But the dread that tightened her muscles and squeezed her throat was like nothing she had ever experienced. That square. That black square waiting for her to step inside, its lines jagged like rotten teeth. It woke up a primal, sweat-inducing fear.

River inhaled deeply and immediately regretted it. She coughed, covering her nose with her arm, and stumbled back. A smell of putrefaction wafted out of the hole, coating the roof of her mouth. She began shaking her head, her mind refusing to accept that she had to go in there. It wasn't just the rotting scent. Pure evil, something heavy and ferocious, emanated from below. It was like a claw reaching through her skin and twisting her guts.

She turned around and closed her eyes, steadying her breathing. Her eyes filled with tears, from the dread or the toxic smell, she didn't know.

"I don't think I can do it, Grandma…"

Nausea made her head spin and threatened to make her fall. She leaned a shoulder against the wall, almost feeling the black square pulse behind her, almost afraid that its darkness would turn into a clawed hand and drag her under.

"River…"

Her eyes shot open in the dark. Her name had been whispered so softly that she thought it might have been in her head. She turned to the mass of blackness behind her and stared at it. The voice had belonged to a man, at least she thought so. She couldn't know for sure, but her heart wanted this voice to belong to only one person.

"T-Thomas?"

She took an uncertain step forward and leaned to catch a glimpse of the room below. The shape of a man stood at the bottom of crooked stairs. It seemed to stare up at her, waiting, before its form crumbled on itself and evaporated into thin mist.

River forced a shaky breath into her lungs, squaring her shoulders and clenching her teeth. "Okay… Okay. I can do this. Thomas wanted me to do this."

Holding the flashlight as far from her as she could to ward off the smothering darkness, she began her descent into the bowels of the Blackwell House.

CHAPTER THIRTY-THREE

T he smell thickened. It burned her nose and her throat, but she didn't stop. The stairs ran between two walls, and River squinted to make out the details of the room she was descending into but couldn't see much from where she was.

Her feet touched the concrete below, and the putrid smell hit her full force. She turned away, gagging, and covered her nose and mouth with her scarf, though it did little to protect her. She would have to take a shower and scrub herself as soon as she was back at her cottage. She would burn her clothes if she had to.

After fighting to stay on her feet, she turned to look at the room. Her heart jumped out of her chest. People stood in front of the opposite wall. River almost lunged for the stairs, ready to escape, but none of them moved. None of them breathed. She raised a shaky hand, her fingers gripping the flashlight. Her legs turned numb. Two naked corpses were lined up against the opposite wall, hanging from thick chains fastened around their necks. Some of them had already been carved into. Another one lay on a table, stripped of its arms.

A thin, white cloth had been pulled over their heads, concealing their dead eyes. River was grateful for it. She had no desire to look at their faces, and apparently, neither did Selene.

Brown blood stuck to the concrete floor, and an array of white structures—bones—were scattered around the room. Dozens of white canvases leaned against the wall all the way to the right, waiting to be painted.

Selene, as distinguished and beautiful as she was, was a disgusting monster for doing what she did. So sick it made River dizzy, and it took all of her strength to stay on her feet. If she wanted to leave this place as fast as possible, she also needed to hurry up and find what she was looking for. Her eyes darted around the room, desperate to see something that could undo Selene's power, but all she could see were shelves and frames and canvases and corpses and a sculpting station.

Then, she steadied the light on the opposite wall. Just next to the bodies, a red door. River squared her shoulders and approached the door on wobbly legs, trying to ignore the cadaver on the table, trying to keep her eyes fixed on the door instead of looking at the corpses, afraid she might see through the white cloths and realize their dead eyes were following her every movement.

She paused in front of the door, her hand suspended mid-air. There was no doorknob, only a small keyhole. She swept her light over it and around it, searching for a button, a lever, a mechanism, *anything,* and even tried pushing against it, because she couldn't have done all this for nothing, all this to just turn around because the door was locked and, oh well, there was nothing she could do about it.

Footsteps pounded the floor above her head.

You left the trapdoor open.

Her guts turned to ice in the pit of her stomach, and she fumbled with her flashlight to turn it off. The footsteps ceased, and a beam of white light glided over the stairs. Just under them, River saw a tight space next to a rusty cabinet where she might be able to fit. It wasn't great, but no other spot offered her a place to hide. She sneaked to it, trying to be fast but quiet, and dropped to her knees. On all fours, she burrowed into the tight space.

The footsteps echoed on the steps above her. If the person entered the room completely, River would have to run. They would easily see her. If they decided to stay on the stairs, then she could remain hidden.

They descended lower. The beam of light danced over the room, highlighting every detail of it. River's heart pounded in her chest so hard she was afraid whoever was here with her would hear it.

Their shoes connected with the concrete. The light travelled through the room once again, taking more time, stopping to highlight the dark spaces between shelves.

River clasped a hand onto her mouth, willing her body to stop trembling and to keep her breathing under control.

They're gonna find you.

The person entered the room completely, and from her hiding nook, River could see their legs.

You need to run.

Her body tingled with fear and adrenaline. She wouldn't outrun them if they knew the layout of the passages, but she would get caught if she stayed here.

"I know someone's here."

She bit back on a cry as the voice broke the silence. She hadn't expected a deep voice like that. Richard. If it had been Edith, she might have had a chance to defend herself, but no way in hell could she take on Richard.

Take him by surprise, then run.

He slowly rotated one way, then the other.

Do it. Now!

"I don't know who you are or how you got in, but you need to come out now or you'll regret it."

Richard moved further into the room, his back to her, giving River an opening. Fear narrowed her vision and blurred her senses, but still, she sprung out of the nook and rammed into his back as hard as she could. His body lurched forward, his flashlight flying through the room. A sickening sound of a skull banging against the metal table shook River to her core. She stumbled and caught herself, looking at the body lying at her feet.

Richard groaned and shifted on the floor, sending a shot of adrenaline through River's body. She bolted toward the stairs. His flashlight lay at the bottom of them. She snatched it off the floor and ran, her legs heavy and numb. She didn't turn to see if Richard was on his feet or not. She raced up the stairs and closed the trapdoor. Hopefully, both the blow and the dark would slow him down.

Her feet pounded the thick carpet as she sprinted down a corridor. As soon as she took a turn, a bang—like a fist against wood—echoed behind her.

"Get the fuck back here!" the voice roared.

River's heart thudded in her chest as quickly as the beam of light bounced against the walls. At the next crossroad, she decided to take the stairs. She was disoriented and lost, but she needed to put some distance between her and Richard. But even without a light, he seemed to know his way well. His footsteps blasted up the staircase she had just taken.

River took another one, going upward, her throat burning. All the passages were interconnected. She crossed the length of the floor, then came back down. She dashed through the corridor, barely seeing where she was going. The next sharp turn made her lose her balance, and her shoulder crashed into a wall. The flashlight flew from her hand, its light dancing over the wall. Darkness swallowed her as it fell to the floor. A whimper escaped her. She searched for the other flashlight in her coat when a raw whisper stopped her.

"Where are you? Playing hide and seek?"

It didn't sound too close, but not that far, either. If she turned on the light, he would find her. Despite the wound on his head, he had caught up to her surprisingly fast. River resisted the urge to look for the flashlight she'd dropped and reluctantly moved forward, hoping he wouldn't find it.

A trembling hand on the wall, she walked in the dark, keeping her footing light and her breathing under control. Despite the cold air inside the passages, hair stuck to the perspiration on her face, and sweat soaked the back of her shirt.

Ragged breathing followed her, never too close but never far enough. Every time she thought she had lost him, she heard him backtracking his steps and take the corridor she had just been in. It almost felt like the horrible smell from the basement was clinging to every part of her, giving her away.

Richard began sprinting. The sound of his hasty footsteps slapping the floor surprised her so much, she only started running two seconds after him, trying not to crash into walls. She turned as her hand found an angle where a new corridor stretched to the right and pressed her back against the wall, holding her breath.

The pounding footsteps grew closer, passing just next to her, so close that she almost felt the air shifting, but kept going straight ahead. River went the other way, tiptoeing down the corridor.

A pair of glowing, unblinking eyes staring at her made her stop. She choked on a gasp, her feet rooted to the floor. She didn't dare speak or move, but Richard's footsteps, once far away, seemed to come back in her direction again.

The shining eyes didn't move an inch. River squinted at them, her blurry mind slowly realizing what they truly were. She slowly walked to them.

Holes.

Two holes perfectly spaced apart for someone to look through them. She had just found another entrance to the passages. With the flashlight before, she hadn't noticed those tiny holes anywhere else.

Her hands against the wall, she looked through them. The windows facing her and the chandeliers glowing with a soft light were more than familiar, and she instantly knew not only her position but what she was standing behind.

River touched the wall in front of her. Her fingers met with a small lever similar to the one she had seen behind the library wall. She pulled it down. The door shifted outward, creating a gap. River pushed it open, looked left and right, and squeezed out of it before gently closing the painting, already knowing who she would be looking at before laying eyes on it.

Benjamin's hollow eyes stared at her.

The ghosts might have been watching her at times, but people—made with flesh and bones—had been the ones observing her.

A muffled tap somewhere on the other side of the wall made her jump. Richard was still looking for her. River strode toward the staff's stairs, but stopped before climbing down, heart pounding. She couldn't risk seeing anyone, or they would know. She needed to find a way to go back to her cottage unseen and pretend she had never moved from it.

A shadow at the end of the hallway caught her eye. A tall figure stood there, wearing black.

"Benjamin," she whispered.

He turned and walked down the hallway, disappearing from her view. River chased after him. His misty silhouette strode to the end of the hallway and walked through the last door.

Dorian's old room.

A soft, scraping noise somewhere behind her made her press her steps and slip into the room. Benjamin was waiting for her, standing next to the window. He looked down.

"What's out there?" she whispered.

His foggy form evaporated. River hurried to the same spot, shivering at the icy remnants of mist he had left behind, and opened the window. The ivy clinging to the wall was thick all the way down.

"You don't want me to climb down, do you… I could hide in the armoire. He wouldn't have the key. I could just wait it out…"

She closed the window with a trembling hand when footsteps grew closer in the hallway.

Goosebumps ran over her arms, and her breath misted as a cold breeze flowed through her. The window clicked open as though beckoning her to come forth. River took a deep breath—which did nothing to appease the growing nausea squeezing her throat—and gritted her teeth before throwing one leg over the windowsill. Her hands instantly turned clammy as her leg dangled in the air before finding purchase in the snaking ivy branches. It took all her willpower to throw her second leg over the windowsill and start climbing down. The icy wind made her hair fly and shook the ivy. She gripped them, her knuckles completely white.

A soft click made her look up. The window was closed, and gratitude filled River. The dead were on her side.

She made her descent, caught between wanting to go fast so it would be over quickly and needing to be careful if she didn't want to kill herself. Her muscles shook and ached. Some of the ivy branches snapped out of the wall, making her guts liquify. The wood dug into her burning palms. She pictured a younger Dorian sneaking out of his room at night using the same technique, trying to get away from this place. If he had done it, she could too. Probably. Maybe.

It felt like an hour had passed when she finally reached the second-floor windows. A mix of relief and desperation fought for dominance in her mind. She was halfway there, *finally*. She was *only* halfway there. She could still fall and kill herself at that height. Or end up paralyzed.

An eternity later, her feet touched the ground, and River finally allowed herself to breathe, to truly breathe, as she ran back to the cottage, moving in the shadows.

CHAPTER
THIRTY-FOUR

N o one came after her. Nothing moved in the darkness outside. River kept staring through the gap between the curtains, the shivering of her body refusing to abate. She ached to rip her clothes off and take a shower, as though *that room* and the very air inside had poisoned her, as though her clothes and skin and hair would rot if she didn't clean them. The stench of the bodies still stuck to the roof of her mouth and coated the back of her throat. But she needed to be sure she hadn't been followed.

A tall figure moved toward her. River released her breath and hurried to the door, wrenching it open before Dorian could knock. She scanned the outside, not that she could see much, and pulled him inside. As soon as the door was locked, she let herself fall into his arms.

"Are you okay?" He sounded relieved to have her back, holding her tight.

"I'm not sure…"

Though his embrace felt warm and reassuring, it stiffened with worry. "Are you hurt?"

"No, just spooked." She looked up at him. "I found the passage. I went inside."

His gray eyes widened, his fingers clenching on her shoulders. "You did?"

Trying to keep her voice under control, River told him about the passages, the spirits, and the trap door on the floor. "It was her-her *craft* room. And there was a door at the back of it, but it was locked. I think what you were hoping to find is in that room, but I don't know how to get in. Any ideas where she could hide a key?"

Dorian sighed, letting it all sink in for a moment, the disappointment darkening his eyes. "Where would you hide an object that, if in the wrong hands, would bring your undoing?"

"I would… I guess I would keep it on myself at all times."

He nodded. "I would do the same thing. It cannot be hidden in any room. A maid could stumble upon it. I don't think she would leave it in the secret passages, either. She might trust Edith and Richard, but not to the point of risking them going into that room. She has too much to lose." His jaw worked. "I don't know what else I expected."

River swallowed around the lump in her throat. "Also… You won't be happy about this…"

He frowned.

"Richard came in after me."

"Richard?"

"He almost caught me, but I pushed him, and he hurt himself, and I ran. I don't think he knew it was me. But still, he knew *someone* was there."

Dorian tripped on his words, not able to get anything out. "W-wait—"

"And you know who helped me get out? Your dad! He showed me the way to your old room and hinted at the fact that I should climb down the ivy, which I did, and—"

"River."

The ominous tone in his voice made her stop talking. "What?"

"Richard was at dinner the whole time. Until just a few minutes ago."

Her stomach twisted. "Did he... Did he leave at all at some point?"

He shook his head. "What makes you think it was Richard?"

"He talked... I thought he was a man, but maybe—"

A knock on the door startled them, and they stayed immobile. Three raps shook the door after another handful of seconds, filling River with sickening dread. She led Dorian to the wall next to the door, hiding him from view, probably in the same spot Thomas had placed him before.

"Don't answer it," he whispered so low that she almost didn't hear him.

"I have to," she whispered back. She cleared her throat and opened the door a crack.

Mack stood outside, a plate in his hands. "Hey. Just wanted to bring you some leftovers."

"Oh." She stared at him, unable to move.

"Do you want it or…"

River forced herself to open the door wider and reach for the plate. "Yes, thank you. Appreciate it."

"Of course." He smiled. "Been doing anything interesting tonight?"

"Is there ever anything interesting to do here?"

Mack chuckled. "Touché. All right, have a boring evening, then. See ya."

"See you later. Thanks for the plate."

He turned around, the weak light of the cottage highlighting the swollen, bruised bump on the side of his head. Her fingers clenched the plate.

"What happened to your head?" she said.

Mack turned back, eyebrows raised. "Oh, this?" He pointed at his head. "Left a kitchen cupboard open. I bent over and hit my head on the way back up. It's really stupid."

River's mouth had gone dry. "Looks like it hurts."

He gave her a one-shouldered shrug. "Don't worry, I've got worse in my lifetime. Enjoy your meal."

He walked back up the hill in the direction of the house. Not his own quarters, despite the late hour. But to the house.

River locked the door and slammed the plate onto the table. "I'm gonna be sick."

"It was him, then," Dorian said, his jaw working. "I wouldn't have known if he had left during dinner."

"So, Miss Roberts isn't the only one. Mack is in on it too." Her voice quavered as she talked, trying to wrap her head around it. Edith was one thing. She had always been a little vile to River, so River had never felt close to her. But Mack… now *that* felt like a betrayal. He was always so nice to her, she never would have guessed.

Dorian crossed to her, a hand held outward as he looked for her and grabbed her hand. "You cannot stay."

"Dorian, let's not do this again—"

"This is different this time. He *saw* you."

"He saw *someone*. He doesn't know it was me."

"They will figure it out easily enough. Trust me."

"Can we…" She paused, her mind racing. "Can we take a moment to talk about all this? *Calmly*. I just need a moment to think… and to get out of these clothes. I smell like death. It's like the rot is sticking to me."

He sighed, as though knowing she was trying to buy some time, but his expression told her he wouldn't waver. As soon as she was done, he would make her pack her bag and leave this place. "Fine. But don't take too much time."

She gathered fresh clothes and hurried to the bathroom, refraining from telling him she would take as much time as she needed to scrub the stench off.

No amount of soap seemed to make her feel better, though. Despite the hot water fogging the glass walls and her nails digging into her scalp and rubbing her skin, that feeling of being stained remained.

Through the noise of the rushing water, something peeked through. River froze, trying to listen. "Dorian?"

The sound came again. She recognized it this time. One of the glass jars had exploded. A second later, a fist pounded on the door.

"River, you need to get out. *Now*."

She turned the faucets, but the pipe linking them to the wall shot out of the tiles, nearly hitting her. She let out a cry of surprise and watched in horror as water gashed out of the gaping hole. In seconds, it reached her ankles.

"River, open the door!" Dorian yelled, panic straining his voice.

I didn't lock the door…

She whirled around and pushed on the glass door. It felt like cement under her palms, hard and unyielding. River pressed her shoulder against it, applying more weight, but it didn't budge. The water reached above her knees. There was no plug, no way to keep the water from going down the drain, and yet it kept filling this glass prison she couldn't get out of.

Somehow, Mack must have known it was her in the passages, and Selene knew it too. Dorian had been right all along, but instead of leaving like he'd told her she should, she'd tried to buy some time.

She pounded on the glass as her lower body was completely submerged. "Dorian!"

A blow shook the door. Then, another. They came at regular intervals, telling her Dorian was trying to get in.

The water reached her chest. Panic choking her, River pressed her back against the wall and pushed the door with her feet, straining as much as she could. When that didn't do anything, she resorted to kicking it, hurting herself uselessly. That door wouldn't open for anything. It needed to be broken, but her weak legs couldn't get the task done.

Her feet lost touch with the floor, and realization started sinking in. She was going to drown in that shower. She tried to float to the surface, her breathing coming out in sharp bursts. The beating behind the door came on stronger and more frequently, Dorian's desperate grunts barely rising above the sound of the water gushing and bubbling.

Her cheek pressed against the glass ceiling, she called out for help one last time before the water filled the shower cabin and drowned her voice.

CHAPTER THIRTY-FIVE

Through the chaos of floating hair and bubbles clouding her vision, she saw the door blast open. Dorian stumbled inside, his features blurred by the water surrounding her. River banged on the glass, screaming. Fear widened his eyes, and he rushed to the shower cabin, desperately groping for a way to open it. When he couldn't, he bolted out of the room.

His absence seemed to last an eternity. River's lungs burned. Black dots creeped at the edge of her vision. But then Dorian returned, armed with one of the kitchen chairs. He lifted it and struck the glass door, making the whole structure shake. The second time he brought the chair down, fissures snaked out of the impact point.

"Move back!" he yelled.

Though River felt like she was about to pass out, empty of oxygen and her head spinning, she pushed against the door to move to the back of the cabin.

Dorian swung the chair. It crashed against the glass, shattering it completely. It exploded outward as water burst out and flooded the bathroom, pulling River with it like a rag doll and slamming her to the floor. Shards of glass dug into her arms and legs and body, but she didn't notice as she coughed and heaved.

"River!" Dorian kneeled next to her.

Pushing against the floor and broken glass, River straightened up, as he looped his arms around her and pulled her to her feet, his eyes wild with fear. "Breathe."

"I–I'm okay…"

"Come on."

He helped her out of the flooded bathroom, and River tried to avoid the broken glass on the floor. She gave the shower one last look before exiting. She'd been so stupid, and Dorian had been right. She should have left. But despite what had just happened, she couldn't flee. Give up. Abandon him here.

Before she could voice any of that, Dorian cupped her neck, his lips slightly trembling and his hair disheveled. "You need to get dressed and leave. *Now.*"

A sob rose in her throat. "I wish I could have done more…"

His eyes glistened, but he attempted a smile and leaned in for a tender kiss, a goodbye kiss. "Get ready."

River left her things behind, except for her crystals and her tarot cards. With Dorian pressing her, she couldn't pack anything. She had learned her lesson. For all she knew, she could start choking on razor blades anytime. Who knew what else Selene had in store for her.

They rushed through the night, the freezing wind blowing through her still wet hair and making her shiver. The Blackwell House windows glistened a sickly yellow glow as though mocking her. River turned away, keeping her eyes on her little car parked in the dirt not far away. Dorian's hand on her arm felt tight as he nearly dragged her.

She spun around as they reached the car. "Maybe this isn't over. Maybe I can still—"

"There's nothing left to do but leave. I *need* you to be safe. Please."

Her vision blurred. She wrapped her arms around him and buried her face in the crook of his neck. He held her tight in return.

"Thank you for fighting for me," he said, his voice charged with emotion.

River swallowed around the lump in her throat and raised her head, wanting to tell him she loved him despite having met him not that long ago, but the words died in her throat.

A tall figure loomed behind him. River didn't have time to scream before Mack brought the shovel down on Dorian's head, making him collapse.

"Going somewhere?" Mack said, a smirk stretching his lips.

A horrified cry fell out of River's mouth as he bashed Dorian's head with the shovel again. "You're gonna kill him!"

"You wanna know something funny? I didn't know it was you earlier in the passages."

River stayed rooted to the ground, watching Dorian twitch.

"And honestly, you look so…" He spun the shovel in his hand, searching for his words. "Innocent. Almost pure, it's crazy. I didn't even suspect you when I checked on you. But the thing with this place, River, is that you can't hide. There's always someone watching. Like Shelly, always smoking outside and seeing things she shouldn't."

Her insides seemed to liquefy, but she still couldn't move. Mack stood between her and her car, she had nowhere to go.

"And she told me the most interesting thing after I saw you at the cottage," Mack continued. "About an hour before I visited, she saw you leave the house. *Running.*"

"How can you do this?"

"This job has some nice perks. Plus, Selene and I, we're a thing if you know what I mean. And you just pissed her off real good. So, I'm sorry, River, but I can't let you leave. I like you a lot, but I don't make the rules. Didn't I tell you not to trust him? You wouldn't be in this situation without him."

Dorian opened his eyes. The blood from his wound trickled over his face. "Run…" he said, his voice nothing but a raw whisper that the wind snatched away.

Mack looked down at him, tightening his fingers around the shovel. "I wonder if your death will kill her. Would spare me the efforts of two kills."

He raised the shovel too fast for River to stop him and bashed Dorian's head until he stopped twitching. He looked back at her, studying her. "Do you feel an irrepressible urge to headbutt a tree?"

River made no reply but backed away, her eyes still locked on Dorian's dead body.

"No?" Mack sighed. "Wonder who'll die. Edith's gonna be pissed, but I'm just following orders here." He gave River a look that was almost friendly, almost compassionate. "I'm sorry, love. It's your turn."

As he stepped over Dorian's body, River bolted toward the trees. Queasiness made her see double. The sight of Dorian's dead body sickened her, and the only reason she wasn't screaming and crying was the man chasing her. Dorian would be okay. He would come back unharmed. If Mack got to her, she wouldn't.

She reached the tree line, sprinting despite feeling blind. Mack's heavy footsteps pounded the dirt behind her, gaining ground.

"It's pointless to run, love," he yelled behind her, barely out of breath, unlike her. "I know you think you'll be safe once you reach the village, but I guarantee you won't be. No one can leave this place."

His voice sounded closer. It felt like a nightmare. Her legs grew increasingly heavy, making her feel like she was running in slow motion. Her lungs burned and her heart banged against her chest, but adrenaline helped her keep her pace.

Her foot snagged against a rock, and she lost her balance, stumbling forward. She managed to straighten out before falling on her face, but as she darted forward again, strong fingers grabbed the collar of her coat and snatched her backward. In the dark, she made out his huge frame and the shape of the shovel rising above his head.

"By the way, what you did to me in the basement really hurt," he growled.

Fog rolled in out of nowhere. It curled around each tree, snaking through the branches. A stick snapped nearby, catching Mack's attention. He quickly glanced in the direction of the noise, giving River one precious second to bolt away from him. His fingers tightened over her collar, but she slipped out of the coat and sprinted away from him while the mist thickened around them in a record time. Through the fog, River caught glimpses of the spirits' shapes, her skin breaking into goosebumps each time she ran through one.

"You can't hide, River!" Mack shouted, and a hint of hope bloomed inside her chest. His voice sounded much further away than before.

Branches kept snapping around her, the loud cracks rising above the wind and attracting Mack's attention away from her pounding footsteps. Their whispers rose through the mist, plaintive and loud and almost inaudible at the same time, disembodied voices brushing the edge of her consciousness.

"Thank you," she murmured to the ghosts, panting. "Thank you, thank you."

She burst out of the forest, the sound of her boots suddenly different as they fell onto concrete instead of dirt. River glanced over her shoulder and gasped. The mist was choking each inch of the woods. The whispering spirits couldn't be heard from here, but River hoped they were still inside, confusing Mack and slowing him down.

River didn't linger. Despite her burning, dry throat, she resumed running toward the little shops, their windows dark except for one. The inn. She burst through the door, panting and sweating despite the temperature outside.

The old man she had seen on her arrival and on several occasions snapped his head up, looking a little scared. "Can I help you?"

River darted to the reception. "Someone's after me. I need you to call the police."

"The police? Who's after you?"

"It doesn't matter! He's dangerous, and he wants to kill me. *Please,* call the police."

The man didn't move. "I'm sure this is a misunderstanding. Maybe we can calmly talk to this gentleman. How about you sit down and rest for a minute?"

A mix of panic and anger constricted her chest. "How about calling the fucking police!" she yelled, slamming her hands on the counter.

"Miss—"

"Move over," she snapped, rounding the counter and reaching for the phone. "I'll do it myself."

She put the phone to her ear and pressed 911. An operator answered on the first ring.

"Nine-one-one, what's your—"

The line died. River stayed frozen for a moment, her mouth agape and her mind scrambling to understand what the hell was happening. "Hello? *Hello?*"

"I'm sorry, miss…"

River turned around, a pit in her stomach. The old man stood behind her, the cord of the unplugged phone in his hand.

"I can't let you leave."

Panic shot through her spine. The man reached for her, but River turned on her heels and shot through the lobby, almost crashing into the door. She stumbled outside and ran along the sidewalk. The door of the inn opened, ringing the little bell, but she refused to look back for fear to see both Mack and the hotel owner chase after her.

As she neared the coffee shop, a man stepped out of the shadows behind the wall. River staggered to a halt.

Luke stood there, a gun pointed at her face. "Stop running."

The hotel owner reached them, his breath wheezing in and out of his lungs. "Thank you, Luke. I'm too old for this."

"No worries," Luke said. "I'll take care of it."

"Thank you, boy. I appreciate it." He turned around and went back to the inn, mumbling under his breath. "The police... The police ain't never comin' here, sweetheart."

Luke took a step back and gestured with his gun. "Walk."

"So, you can put me down behind a building?"

"Don't make this harder than it has to be."

River forced her trembling legs to move. Luke kept his distance, not giving her the chance to attempt anything. They rounded the coffee shop. Behind it, an iron staircase led upward.

"Climb the stairs."

River obeyed with feet that felt like bricks. Why didn't he just shoot her?

Because he doesn't want to do it. As soon as he gets the chance, he'll call Mack or Edith or whoever from the house and hand me over.

"Why are you all doing this?"

"Open the door. It's unlocked," he said, ignoring her question.

She opened the door and stared inside. She didn't know what she had been expecting, but it sure wasn't a cozy apartment. She stepped into the kitchen area, which opened onto a small but comfy living room. The curtains were drawn, hiding the view of the street.

The door clicked close behind River, and she whirled around to look at Luke.

He turned the lock and sighed, dropping the gun onto the counter. "This is the part where you thank me for saving you."

"W-what..." Relief mixed with confusion, the adrenaline and the panic still pumping through her veins. "Why?"

He simply shrugged. "I'm not like them. I won't kill people just because some witch is keeping this town and its people alive. Though I'd rather not make a habit of hiding people here."

She opened her mouth, but no words came out, as a voice rose behind her back.

"Freckles?"

Her shoulders tensed, and her throat closed up. She had to be dreaming. River slowly turned, her jaw dropping to the floor at the sight of the young man standing just outside a small hallway. "Thomas…"

CHAPTER THIRTY-SIX

R iver ran to Thomas and jumped at his neck, breaking into
sobs. "I thought you were dead."

He hugged her back tightly. "I know. I feel awful."

She pulled away, almost choking. *"You* feel awful? Really? Think
about how *I* feel."

A sheepish smile stretched one corner of his mouth. "A little bit
happy to see me?"

"You idiot," she said, punching his shoulder before throwing
her arms around him again.

Thomas led her to the couch and made her sit down, throwing
Luke a grateful look. "He saw you running like mad outside. Well,
we didn't know it was you, but I convinced him to go take a look."

"Thank you," she told Luke, her voice still quavering from shock.

Luke offered an unbothered smile. "I'll make some tea."

River turned to Thomas as Luke left the room. "Have you been hiding here this whole time? I tried to reach you."

"I have. I couldn't contact you, though. It was too risky. Now, they need to think you're dead too."

"What happened to you? Dorian was sure you escaped, but then I found your note, and I thought I saw your ghost!"

"My *ghost?* No, that wasn't me."

She gave him a stern look. "I get that now."

"From what Luke told me, there have been *a lot* of people coming to the Blackwell House for work. Odds are one of them just resembles me."

"How did you survive?" She explained to him what Dorian had told her, hoping he would fill in the blanks.

"Well..." He shrugged, slowly shaking his head. "Dorian tried to put some distance between me and the house, but I don't think that made any difference. After I ran from crazy old Roberts, I made it to town and collapsed there. Luke found me and brought me here. He's been nursing me back to health." He glanced over at Luke in the kitchen, his eyes soft. But then he turned back to her, and his mouth twisted into disgust. "Even now I can still only eat soft food. Ugh."

River chuckled.

"But ultimately, it's you who saved my life, Freckles." He fished a familiar little jar full of dried herbs from his pocket and held it up. "I think that's why her spell didn't kill me in the end. I kept it close the entire time, and I'm scared to part with it now. Maybe it's helping me heal too."

She stared at the jar, then studied her friend. He looked healthy, not a scratch on him. "I'm glad I gave you that."

"I wanted to tell you everything that night when you came. But Dorian convinced me otherwise. I still thought I could handle things, but in the end, this curse, this house… it was just bigger than me."

"Not just you."

His eyes lit up slightly. "What happened to you? Did you say you found my note?"

River let out a drawn-out sigh. "Where to start…"

She tried to give him a condensed summary of the important things that had happened the past few weeks, and by the time she reached the moment where Mack chased after her to bash her head with a shovel, Luke had brought back the tea and they had drunk it. Slowly, River began to feel more human.

"Don't worry about Dorian," Luke said. "He'll be okay, as usual."

"I know… but someone else must have died…"

Thomas stayed silent for a minute, then glanced at her, a twinkle in his eye. "So, you guys are sleeping together now."

Her shoulders dropped. "Dude."

"For Christ's sake," Luke said, shaking his head.

"What? I'm just saying, you know, *score.*"

Luke scoffed. "Sure, if you're into dark hair, emotional baggages, and curses."

River turned to him. "What was that all about out there?" She looked back at Thomas. "And why are you still here? Why not leave and go back to your family?"

"Because no one leaves this place," Luke said, his tone flat and matter-of-fact. "And if we want to keep this town and its people alive, we have to do what Selene Blackwell wants."

"And what does she want?"

"Sacrifices. None of the staff has ever left. If Dorian thinks they quit or fled and went back home, he's gravely mistaken."

"But—" Her mind couldn't quite comprehend all of this. "Thomas, they *think* you're dead. You could flee!"

"Again, he can't," Luke answered. "If he stepped out of this town, she'd know. He's stained by her curse now, just like we all are."

"Are you saying everyone in this town is a prisoner?"

"Not exactly. We can leave. But those who did came back running when they realized that the stain left on them brought them nothing but the worst luck they could ever have. Some died from it. Here, they all have their health, cute houses, friends, shops where they can get all they need. The crops always grow. Cows are fed, and fish are found in abundance. In exchange, they agreed not to warn people coming to work at the house, as well as stopping them if they try to leave. They rarely reach town when they try to flee like you guys, but when that happens, Selene's wrath impacts us all."

Thomas stayed quiet. Evidently, he had heard that story before. River's jaw fell to the floor.

"And that doesn't bother you?"

"It is what it is. I can't fight against it. No one can. There's only one person who can't accept it, and that's Dorian."

Anger burned in the pit of River's stomach. "You have no idea what he's been through."

"*He* put himself through those things," he said, leaning forward suddenly. "His mother wants him to get married and have kids, there are worse fates than that. But no. Because he's stubborn as fuck, he died who knows how many fucking times and ended up blind!"

Luke let out a shuddering breath and leaned back in his seat. River saw it. That flicker of sadness, of worry. Despite his anger with Dorian, he still cared about him.

"So, you just gave up and accepted your fate?" she asked.

His lips tightened into a straight line. "No, I didn't *just* accept it. It's just…" He paused, looking away.

"You and Dorian were best friends, weren't you?" River said, and his eyes flickered back to her. "What happened?"

Luke took such a long time to answer that River wondered if he would say anything at all. Eventually, he inhaled, relaxing his fists. "Dorian and I, we wanted to leave together. We had those crazy dreams about travelling the world to see what was out there. But I quickly realized that this wasn't going to happen. My parents told me all the things I told you. Said Selene Blackwell was like a goddess, and we needed to obey her rules, or we would be punished. I didn't believe it, really. But then I saw what she could do with my own eyes."

There was a long pause. Thomas seemed to hold his breath, just like River was.

"Every time we tried to leave, he died. I saw him die *three times.* And then he was back the next day." He let out a small, humorless laugh.

"He didn't mention in his journal that you were with him," she said. "It must have been horrible."

"It was. And then there was all that shit about his mother painting with blood and making sculptures with bones. And I knew. My parents were right. There was no way out of this place for him. Not without dying."

"Why did you stop talking to Dorian altogether?" River asked. "You were both stuck here. You needed each other, didn't you? I don't know about you, but he could have used a friend."

He swallowed, looking down at his lap. "I know. I've just been trying to protect him, in my own, messed-up way, I guess. We always made these crazy plans to escape, thinking about what we would do once we got out. I liked to tease that he would be so pathetically clueless in the real world because of the way he was raised." He chuckled, but his smile vanished in a second. "I thought that maybe if I stopped talking to him, if I stopped enabling him, he would give up and stop hurting himself. It really fucks you up to see your best friend die, you know? Even if he comes back afterward. I didn't want that to happen again. And that's why I never left this town, either, even when I didn't know about the bad luck. But I knew that if Dorian heard from someone that I had left, he would want to leave too, and he'd do another stupid thing that would bring him nothing but misery."

"So, you stayed this whole time for his sake even though you guys weren't talking anymore," Thomas said.

Luke nodded. "Yes. And then I found out that I also actually couldn't leave."

"Dorian doesn't know about that. That you're all stuck here," River said.

Luke shook his head this time.

"So, what happens now? We just hide here forever? That's not gonna happen."

338

"I've been raking my brain since I got here," Thomas said. "I don't know what we can do."

River took a breath. "I wanna go back to the Blackwell House."

"That's either stupid or crazy," Luke said, deadpan.

"Maybe. But if we're doomed and can't leave Stormhedge at all, then I might as well give it a shot."

"What do you intend to do, exactly?"

"I got into those secret passages and found Selene's room. There's a door there that's locked, and I know the answer is behind it. I can go back. I'll find the key."

"Freckles…" Thomas put a hand on her arm. "You don't have anything to protect yourself with this time."

She had lost her crystals and tarot cards when slipping out of her coat before Mack could kill her. But she hadn't lost everything. She pulled the black obsidian stone from under her sweater. "This. This is the stone that kept me hidden. And it's not the only thing I have on my side."

Thomas raised his eyebrows.

"The ghosts, Thomas. There are so many of them, and they've been helping me. I *can do this.*"

A cautious smile tugged at his lips. "Not without me, you can't."

"I'm not asking you to come with me."

"I'm not asking for your permission. If we're stuck here forever, I might as well try to do something good before we die."

She squeezed his hand, grateful to have her friend back.

"You're not seriously going back there, Thomas, are you?" Luke said.

"Yes, I am."

"Are you insane? This is suicide." He rose from the armchair, pacing the floor and brushing his hand through his hair. "I mean, you do whatever you want, you know. I can't keep you here indefinitely, but it's just... I know we haven't known each other that long, but I care about you, okay? I've been stuck here my whole life, and then you came in and—" He paused, turning away, his head bowed.

Thomas rounded the coffee table and joined him, putting gentle hands on his neck, trying to catch his gaze. The soft smile on his face melted River's heart, but she didn't interrupt, already feeling like she shouldn't be in the room with them.

"Hey. I care about you too. I'm grateful for everything you did for me, and I'm happy to have met you. I haven't felt this good in years."

Luke looked back at him.

Thomas's expression saddened a notch. "I wish I could stay with you, but I can't hide here forever. We actually have a shot at breaking this curse and getting out of here. *All of us.* Isn't that worth the try?"

"Is it worth dying for?"

"I think so, yes. I have to go back with River."

Luke stayed immobile and silent for a while. He glanced at River, then back at Thomas. "You two don't stand a chance."

"Well," River said, "I might need to prepare some jars before we go."

"That won't be enough. Even with your magic jars and crystals, bursting back into that house will get you killed, and if it doesn't, you won't go far without that key you're looking for. How do you even intend to find it?"

The small spark of hope River had a moment ago withered like a flower.

"However," Luke said, his eyes glinting. "If you're patient enough to wait for the winter solstice on December twenty-first, we might be able to pull something off."

"The celebration," Thomas said, glancing at River, his eyes lighting up. "Annie told us about that, remember?"

Luke nodded. "The whole town's invited every year."

"For what, exactly?"

"The winter solstice is an important holiday for witches," River answered instead of Luke. "My grandma and I used to celebrate it."

Thomas smirked. "So, you *are* a witch. I knew it."

"I'm really not. I was just raised in the Celtic culture."

"Yeah, and ghosts talk to you."

"I got that from my grandma." She looked at Luke. "What happens during the celebration?"

"We celebrate the great year that passed. We eat, we dance… then go through the ritual."

"The ritual? What kind?"

"Oh, you know, the usual. We sit in a circle and allow her to draw our blood to strengthen and renew her power. It's also a good reminder to all of us that we need to keep obeying the rules."

Thomas pulled a face. "Lovely."

"What are the rules?" River asked.

"Don't leave unless you want so much bad luck you'll die from it. Keep taking care of the town. Act happy in front of the new staff coming. Kill them if you must, or she kills you."

River registered all that, thinking. "We'll go. We'll blend in."

"Not with that hair, Freckles."

"They will spot you in a heartbeat," Luke said. "Fortunately for you, there's a place in the next town where Amazon delivers. I go there every once in a while. We'll find you a wig or something."

Thomas scoffed. "You take the risk to die in a car accident or some shit because you want your Amazon packages?"

"Yeah."

"Unbelievable. Also kinda sexy."

"I like to go there. It's bigger. Where do you think I find those cream cheese Danishes you like so much? It's not like I make them myself."

"That's sweet." Thomas cocked his head and grabbed his hand. "How are we gonna get inside the house without being spotted, though? Even if Freckles wears a wig, they'll easily spot us. The Blackwells may not pay attention to us, but Edith and Mack will."

Luke smiled, a smile that told River he was about to tell them something good, something crucial that would play in their favor. "Something you have to know about Selene Blackwell is that she doesn't care to know us. She simply likes to make sure we worship her."

"So?" River said.

"Everyone has to wear a mask to hide their faces."

"You're kidding."

He shook his head. "The only ones not wearing a mask are the Blackwells themselves and the staff, but the people of the town have to. Dorian used to say it's because she doesn't see us as humans. We're nothing to her. Just a means to an end."

River's own lips stretched into a smile. They had a real shot. She would go back, and she would break that curse.

"Does that mean you're coming with us?" Thomas asked.

"I think it's about time I pay my best friend a visit. Plus, there's no way I'm leaving you two unsupervised."

Thomas grinned, wrapping an arm around him.

"The tricky part will be to find Selene's key and steal it without getting caught," Luke said. "Any ideas?"

Dorian believed that Selene always kept the key on her, which was what a smart person would do. No hiding place would ever be good enough for something that could destroy her power. However, River couldn't imagine where she would put that key. Selene always wore the tightest, most form-fitting dresses that didn't have any pockets. River pictured her, her clothes, her shoes, her decadent jewelry.

She gasped. "The rose."

Thomas raised his eyebrows. "The what?"

"The hair pin in her ponytail. That could be the key!"

He nodded, considering it.

"I've seen her wear that rose for as long as I remember," Luke said. "That's still a wild guess, though."

"We need to give it a shot," River said.

Thomas crossed his arms, blowing a big breath out of his mouth. "How? How do you intend to take a hair pin without her noticing? She'll strike you down and set you on fire in an instant."

He was right. Until now, River had had the ability to move through the house incognito thanks to her obsidian but getting close to Selene to steal that key—if it really *was* the key—would be far from easy. And what if they succeeded, but she realized it was gone only moments after? River stood, pacing the floor, her mind scrambling for a semi-reliable plan that wouldn't get them all killed.

"I think… I think maybe we can come up with something."

"You think?" Thomas said, smirking. "Good enough for me."

The winter solstice was two weeks away. It left them enough time to prepare. Her insides twisted at the thought that Dorian had to wait, that he'd think she was dead this whole time, but she had to be patient if she wanted to save him and everyone else.

Hold on, Dorian. I'm coming.

CHAPTER
THIRTY-SEVEN

The townspeople stayed disturbingly quiet as they walked
through the woods, as though they marched to their deaths.
The men wore black suits under dark coats. It was easy to distinguish the older women—all wearing black as well—from the
ones who were supposed to impress Selene. Those women wore
colorful dresses, a beautiful mix of purple velvet and pink lace and
blue silk.

Luke had explained to them that it didn't matter that Dorian
couldn't see them or that they had no desire to be part of the
Blackwell family. Not wearing their most beautiful dresses and
jewelry would cost them—or the whole town—to be severely
punished. So, they had to play the game each year, crossing their

345

fingers that Dorian would keep ignoring them or throw a fit like he had done the year before.

"What did he do?" River had asked.

"Basically flipped everyone off, told the whole town to go to hell because we're 'enabling Selene,' then he told his family to go fuck themselves and jump off the cliff." A discreet smile had tugged at Luke's lips as he told the story. "I know I said he should learn to shut up, but that made me a little happy."

River wondered now how Dorian would behave this time. Had he finally given up?

Luke, Thomas, and River stayed at the back of the crowd. Despite the brown-haired wig they had managed to stuff her hair into and the black velvet mask covering the upper part of her face, she didn't want to take the risk of being recognized.

People carried gifts. Flowers mostly, but also harvested foods, homemade recipes, or pretty things from the antique store. It wasn't like Selene needed any of that, but River guessed they tried to pacify her as much as possible.

Wind as sharp as razor blades enveloped them as they stepped out of the woods. A violent shiver shook River, her clear tights doing nothing to protect her legs against the cold. The house came into view, heavy and imposing, beckoning them to enter its bowels. River made sure the black obsidian was safe, tucked in the pocket of her emerald green, organza sundress under her new black coat.

She looked up, her heart thumping faster at the sight of Edith and Annie standing on both sides of the front doors. They helped each guest with their coat, hanging them in a large closet.

"They'll recognize us," Thomas said, his voice strained.

"They won't," she said, only half believing it.

Annie and Edith barely looked at the guests, too focused on their task. But still, River's stomach churned as she climbed the steps.

Thomas and River naturally veered to Annie's side. River turned away from her as she shed her coat, too afraid to look her in the eyes. It wasn't strange behavior, though. None of the townspeople dared look at the staff, their guilt oozing out of them.

River's heartbeat quickened a little at the sight of her own arms and chest. Her freckles would give her away. But Annie only hung the coat and took Thomas's and Luke's without batting an eye. The three of them followed everyone into the long hallway that would take them to the ballroom. As they progressed, melancholic piano notes floated in the space and reached them. River's throat tightened, but she kept her jaw clenched.

Thomas leaned to the side. "I'm regretting all my life decisions."

"We'll be fine. Just stick to the plan."

River slipped her hand in the dress's pocket, squeezing the black obsidian for courage, hoping the ghosts would be on her side tonight. In a place full of such darkness, all she was left with was the faith in her gift—her grandma's gift—and her ability to listen to the spirits reaching out to her from the other side.

The crowd entered the ballroom. A long table ran along the wall. Plates and dishes had been carefully arranged on it, the smell permeating the air. The black piano had been moved slightly to the side of the room. Dorian sat at it, his long fingers travelling over the keys. Sorrow was hedged into his features, the emptiness of his expression physically hurting River.

Against the back wall, the imposing, wooden chair engraved with intricate roses wasn't empty. Selene occupied it, Richard standing next to her. Selene rose from her seat as everyone gathered in the room, staying close together as though afraid to spread out. Gold earrings swayed under her ears. But what made River pause was the magnificent, blood red gown hugging Selene's body, the long sleeves fitted over her arms, the train spread over the floor around her feet. Her high ponytail was as tight as ever, the golden rose sparkling at the top of it.

"Welcome," she said. Her voice resonated and bounced against the walls.

The piano died, the last notes hanging in the air for several uncomfortable seconds.

Richard scanned the crowd, a smirk burrowing into his features as he looked at the young women. River looked down, afraid to make eye-contact with him.

"Thank you for coming," Selene said, crossing her fingers together, her pointy nails as red as her dress. She turned to her son. "Dorian."

Dorian tensed but made no reply. He rose from the piano and slowly crossed the room to his mother, knowing exactly how many steps he needed to take to reach her. He faced the crowd, his unseeing eyes turned to the floor.

She broke him.

"I think you all remember last year's... incident. My son would like to say something about that." She gave him a dark look, one he seemed to feel.

"I am very sorry," he said with no conviction at all. "It won't happen again."

Selene seemed satisfied, her red lips stretching over a perfect row of teeth. "No, it won't. Now please, enjoy the food and the music until the ritual begins. Ladies, come forward."

Classical music rose from the speakers scattered in the room's corners. A cautious chatter rose as people began moving, some gravitating to the table while others made a line in front of Selene, their gifts in hand. She sat down on her throne, amused by the attention she received. The younger women made small groups, whispering amongst each other as though deciding who should go first.

The staff entered the room, balancing trays full of champagne flutes they offered to the guests. River accepted one, avoiding eye-contact.

"Don't eat the meat," Luke whispered.

"Why not?" she said.

He took a sip of champagne and leaned in closer. "Dorian and I had a theory back then, and I still believe we were right, though I have no proof. Selene has been using blood and bones for her art. Maybe even skin. What did she do with the rest?"

Thomas shook his head, twisting his lips. "Nope. Nuh-uh. Don't wanna hear it."

"I'm just saying, that's a lot of people to feed every year."

"This is the moment you stop talking." Thomas turned to River. "All right, Freckles. When do we strike? I'd like it to be *before* anyone tries to take my blood."

"I want to talk to Dorian. We need his help."

"I'll give her the gifts," Luke said. "Try to butter her up a little."

A wave of nausea washed over River at the sight of the people eating, biting into the meat in their stew. She took a steadying breath and a long sip of champagne to calm her nerves before seeking out Dorian in the giant room.

One of the women, a blonde with a light blue dress, had made a move and was dancing with him. Despite her mask, River recognized her and her long, golden hair. The flower shop girl. She looked as tense as Dorian was, although she forced a smile on her face, sending unsure looks toward Selene, who watched the interaction from her chair closely.

River watched Luke approach the matriarch, then walked to the couple dancing. The heels on her feet felt like bricks. She stopped next to them, and the blonde glanced in her direction.

"May I?" River said. Though her voice was lost in the background noise, the woman seemed to have read her lips easily enough.

She made no effort to keep her place. She offered a curt, "Thank you, Mister Blackwell," and quickly walked away, avoiding the other people dancing awkwardly and pretending to have fun.

Dorian straightened up and held his hand somewhat in her direction, his face as cold as a stone. She took it and stepped close to him, sliding a hand behind his neck. His eyebrows twitched slightly, his hand on her back gripping her harder. He swallowed, his eyes now searching in front of him as though trying to recover his eyesight.

"Lavender," he said, his voice strained.

Not wanting to take too much from Luke, River had purchased her own beauty products, and she'd been hoping Dorian would recognize the smell. "Yes, Dorian. Lavender."

His gray eyes misted over. "River."

"Please, don't give me away. They don't know I'm here. Keep dancing."

Dorian gave her a short nod, his jaw clenching as he worked through the shock he tried to hide. "I thought you were dead."

"Luke helped me. He saved me."

"Luke?" Confusion filled his eyes before a hopeful smile stretched his lips. "Luke. I knew he would do the right thing if given the opportunity."

"He did the right thing for Thomas too."

A gasp caught in his throat. "You mean…"

"Thomas is okay. He's in this room right now."

A laugh of disbelief escaped him, but he quickly bit back on it. "Is she watching us?"

River waited for them to twirl enough to glance at Selene without looking too obvious. "Luke is keeping her attention for now. We're fine."

"River, why did you come back? You should have run away from this town while you had the chance."

"Because things aren't that simple. Thomas and I can't just leave. But I'll tell you whatever you need to know later. Right now, I need your help."

"Anything."

"We need the key to enter that room in the basement, and I think I know what it is. Her hair pin."

Dorian thought for a moment, furrowing his brow. "The rose?"

After another twirl, River glanced back over Dorian's shoulder. Selene laughed, cocking her head. The golden rose shone at the top of her ponytail.

Dorian nodded, as though letting that sink in. "She's been wearing that rose for decades. That might be it. But getting it won't be easy."

"I know. That's where you come in."

"What do you need me to do?"

"Luke says she never dances."

"She doesn't. She prefers watching me to make sure I engage with the women, as she likes to say."

"I need you to bring her a drink and dance with her."

His lips tightened, but he gave a curt nod. "She will know something is weird."

"Lie to her. Tell her you want peace or whatever. A truce. That you'll do what she wants. Or that you like the girl from the flower shop and want her approval. Make something up."

River glanced around, searching for Thomas. He stood on the far side of the room, half hidden by the piano so Selene wouldn't see him. He grabbed a brand-new glass of champagne from one of the maids, and as soon as she walked away, reached for the small vial River had made and tipped its content into the flute. He made his way through the crowd, snatching another glass on his way, and stopped next to River and Dorian.

Luke was still making conversation with Selene, but she looked like she was about done with him.

"Dorian," Thomas said, standing at his side.

Dorian stopped mid-twirl and, again, tried to keep the emotions from creeping onto his face. "Thomas. I am so glad you're okay."

Thomas smiled under his mask. "Turns out you don't have two but three friends on your team." He pushed the glasses inside Dorian's hands. "Give her the glass that's in your right hand. Keep the left for yourself."

River expected Dorian to ask questions, to flat out refuse because this would be too risky, but instead, he nodded and squared his shoulders. "Point me in the right direction, please."

She took his arm and led him as close to Selene as she would dare. "About ten more steps, and you'll be standing in front of her," she whispered in his ear.

She left his side as soon as Luke turned away from Selene. River took a steadying breath as Dorian's mother raised her eyebrows at him. They had to wait and see what would happen now. Would Selene take the bait? If she didn't at least sip from the glass, their plan would be ruined.

Luke glanced at Thomas, who glanced at River, who glanced back at Luke. River took some distance. Luke followed Dorian closely as Thomas hovered close to the food table, dropping some food he wasn't going to eat on his plate.

From that angle, River couldn't see Dorian's face. She could only try to guess what was happening by reading Selene's facial expressions. She looked unimpressed, almost suspicious, but her features softened a little after a moment, and she looked at the blonde woman for several seconds. Her blood red lips moved, forming words River couldn't understand, and quirked up. Her heart picked up the pace as Selene reached for the flute of champagne and raised it as though making a toast, then brought it to her mouth. She took a small sip before putting the glass aside on the arm of her chair and rising.

The crowd parted to let Dorian and his mother walk to the middle of the room. They all kept their distance, as though afraid of getting burned. Luke nodded in River's direction, motioning her to come dance with him. They needed to close in on Selene and be ready to act. If they just stood around doing nothing, they would look suspicious.

The sun hiding behind the clouds dipped over the tree line. Gloom filled the room, the chandeliers struggling to make the space cozy. Behind the melancholic music, the space was eerily quiet, as if the room was filled with nothing but dancing ghosts. Lightning lit the sky, and heavy rain began battering the windows.

River kept her eyes trained on Selene, looking for any signs of weakness. She didn't know what they would do if that didn't work.

Selene's head dropped an inch. She shut her eyes for a moment and blinked a few times.

River's heart flipped. "Now."

As soon as Selene faltered and Dorian caught her, Luke lunged in their direction.

"Mother? What's happening?" Dorian said, fake concern spreading over his face. "I need some help," he called to the room.

Not even a second later, Luke stood behind her and helped her stay upright.

"I feel dizzy," she said.

A quiet chatter traveled through the room. All their eyes were locked on the scene, making River nervous. A deafening crash startled everyone and made them turn to the other side of the room, where Thomas stood in front of a pile of broken plates.

"I'm *so sorry*," he said, and River caught him having to bite back on a smile.

In those two seconds of confusion where the staff rushed to clean up the space, River glanced back at Luke, seeing him pull the hair pin swiftly out of Selene's hair as he and Dorian helped her sit.

Edith crossed the room, a severe scowl on her face. She eyed the mess next to the table but didn't stop to help clean up, rushing to her mistress instead.

Hiding behind the people trying to get a glimpse of the drama, River snuck behind Luke's back, avoiding Edith's gaze, although the woman was way too busy to notice her. River gave Luke a gentle tap on the arm. Without turning around, he brought his arm behind his back, the golden flower resting in the palm of his hand. A rod protruded out of the delicate rose, thin but resembling a screw. River took it and edged toward the entrance to the room. Thomas was already there, waiting for her.

Selene started recovering, now shooing Edith away. She looked more annoyed than anything. Before anyone looked their way, Thomas and River ducked out of the ballroom, rushing into the hallway toward the staff's staircase, which was close. No maids would be working on the upper floors, so it was safer to go there. River began breathing easier as soon as they reached the second floor. The first part of the plan had worked, and she couldn't believe it, but she also knew that the hardest part was yet to come.

CHAPTER THIRTY-EIGHT

"Y ou think someone saw us?" Thomas asked, glancing over his shoulder.

"Let's not wait around to find out."

She strode to Benjamin's painting, Thomas at her heels, the lamps struggling to illuminate their path efficiently.

"Do you think it's the same mechanism as in the library?" Thomas said, as they reached the painting.

River's eyes wandered over the frame. "I was inside when I opened it. But I'd say probably, yeah." She looked up and ran her fingers at the top of the frame where her vision couldn't reach. "Right there."

She felt the engraved thorns and the rose protruding slightly. She pushed on it, and the satisfying click echoed behind the wall. The painting opened a crack. They glanced at each other. Thomas reached for the flashlight in his pocket and directed the beam inside the passage.

"Let's go," he said, sliding behind the large frame. "I do hope that all the Caspers and Slimers of this house are still on your side."

"Just hurry up."

A whisper caught River's attention to the left. A foggy figure looked back at her with wide eyes before disintegrating like mist. That's when River heard the footsteps. They were close, so close that she couldn't possibly hide. She reflexively pushed the painting close only half a second before Richard emerged from the hallway. He stopped, staring at her with surprise, and she took a step back from the portrait.

"What are you doing here?" he asked, squinting.

It hadn't occurred to River until now that she hadn't seen him downstairs in the ballroom in a while. He had been there in the beginning, then she had been so focused on Selene that she hadn't noticed he'd left. She suspected he wasn't really welcome there. Selene might not have wanted him to scare off Dorian's potential contenders.

River cleared her throat. "I–I was just looking for the bathroom."

"There are bathrooms downstairs."

He kept staring, unmoving. Her mouth went dry, and goosebumps ran down her back. She remembered too well what had happened the last time she'd found herself in a hallway with him. Her feet were rooted to the floor.

"Well? What are you waiting for?" There was a sneer in his voice, as though challenging her to move in his direction if she dared.

But she couldn't leave. It just wasn't an option. Her eyes darted to the white sculpture displayed on a wooden table tucked in the hallway's bend, right behind Richard. It looked like a crown, bones linked together by spindly wires, with an elongated and sharp piece protruding at the front. River forced her legs to move. The carpet under her felt squishy and unstable, her heels sinking into it. Her fingers tingled, and her jaw clenched the closer she got. She kept her gaze low, though she could still see him watching her every move from the corner of her eye. As she sidestepped him, his hand shot up, cold fingers circling her arm. She tensed, but he only tightened his grip.

"Please…" she said, her voice small.

"I know you."

River shook her head. "I'm from the town—"

Richard shook her, getting a yelp out of her. He towered over her, forcing her to back up against the wall, his hand a vice on her arm. "I'd recognize those freckles anywhere, little mouse."

With a forceful push, he slammed her against the wall. Before she could react, Richard yanked on her wig and threw it to the floor. River felt her unruly curls fall free over her shoulders and down the middle of her back. Richard ripped the black mask off her face, breaking the string. She ducked down, but he was quick to straighten her up, a hand around her throat.

"Not dead then, huh? I suppose we can have some fun before I kill you. And Dorian's not here to save you this time."

It could have been the hand strangling her throat or the warmth of his breath that made anger like acid spike through her chest, but in the end, it was those words that sent her over the edge. She was done being weak. She was done being a pushover. And she was done allowing him to terrify her.

River raised her foot and planted her high heel as hard as she could in his foot. He let out a cry, and although he didn't release her, his fingers loosened enough for River to duck and wrench herself from his grip. She lunged for the sculpture and seized it just as pain blasted through her skull. Richard tugged at her hair, giving her the momentum to crash back into him and smash the bone sculpture onto his head.

Pieces crumbled under her fingers. She suddenly realized that this wouldn't be enough, but then the long spike sliced through the skin on his forehead. His body slackened. Richard stumbled back, eyes open wide as shock spread over his features. He reached for his face, his fingertips sliding through the blood that now covered his skin and painted his moustache red. He swayed for a moment, trying to find purchase against the wall. His eyes rolled back, and he dropped to the floor.

River raised her gaze, shaking, and noticed Thomas standing a little further away, his expression probably reflecting the shock she was feeling.

"I was gonna help you... but I guess you don't need help..."

"Is he dead?" Her voice was back to mouse status, a shaky whisper.

"I don't know... I'm not checking."

"What do we do with him?"

"I don't know."

"We can't leave him here, can we?" she said, raising her voice.

"I don't know!" he whisper-yelled. "Stop panicking! You're making me panic!"

She forced a big gulp of air inside her lungs and sidestepped Richard, keeping close to the wall, afraid he would suddenly open his eyes and lunge at her. Thomas grabbed her hand and the both of them backed away from the body.

"Should we put him in a closet?" he said, wincing.

"I'm not touching him."

"Well, we can't leave him here."

"That's what I've been saying!"

"*Shhh!*" Thomas put gentle hands on her shoulders. "Let's calm down, okay? We need to get going, so we can't lose our shit now."

River nodded, though she suspected she still looked hysterical and unhinged. "Okay."

"Let's just leave him. We don't have time to clean up the blood and pick up *millions* of tiny bone pieces. If he wakes up, he'll come after us whether we move him or not. It's better to hurry before he does."

Thomas led her to the open painting and helped her inside the passage in a hurry. River glanced one last time at Richard, wondering how she would feel knowing she had killed him, which meant killing someone from the staff, but still hoping he wouldn't chase them through the dark corridors.

The frame clicked close behind them, and a white beam filled the passage.

"Where to?" Thomas asked.

"This way," River said, pointing to their left. She remembered hiding behind the wall the last time she had been there. She knew to take the next left, but what came after was a blur. She stopped at the next intersection, fishing the black obsidian from her pocket, and held it close to her heart. She breathed slowly and closed her eyes, willing her consciousness to connect with the spiritual realm.

Whispers rose in the hallway ahead. River followed their song, listening to how its intensity rose as she moved closer to her destination.

"Are you sure you know where you're going?" Thomas asked, but she made no reply.

She let the disembodied voices guide her, transport her through the darkness. Cold spots brushed her skin. Goosebumps travelled over her exposed arms to the base of her spine. Her breath plumed in front of her face, the voices now so numerous they sounded like dozens of bees buzzing in her ears. Her legs moved without her knowledge, transported by the spirits' energy.

The whispers died, replaced by a deafening silence. River stopped walking, snatched out of her trance.

"Ho-ly-shit," Thomas murmured, as he directed the flashlight's beam to the floor, illuminating the trapdoor.

Though the same visceral dread slithered through River's bones, she didn't waste time and opened the door. The rotten, vicious scent hit them full force like a moist, warm wind. Thomas turned away and gagged. Despite nausea already making her head spin, River descended the steps quickly, eager to do what needed to be done so they could leave this place once and for all. She waited for Thomas's light to reach in front of her, listening to him murmur a series of *fucks* as he followed her.

"Something is different than the last time I was here," she said.

Thomas swallowed, gagging once more. "Did it smell better?"

"No… There were more bodies."

She couldn't explain why it bothered her. The table was bare, cleaned of all the blood. Against the back wall, only one corpse hung from a hook. It could be that the other ones had already been transformed into art or that they'd ended up in the stew upstairs.

But it was that single body that called out to her, made her feel like lead sloshed in her stomach. Without her knowledge, her feet carried her to that corpse.

"Freckles, what are you doing?" Thomas whispered, though he didn't follow her. His voice bounced against the concrete walls and hung in the air in waves.

River couldn't answer. She was transfixed by the shape of the body behind the white cloth, its head leaning against its shoulder. She already knew what she would find, but the need to be sure pushed her to raise a hand and lift the linen covering the corpse's face. Thomas gasped behind her but didn't add another word.

Shelly's milky eyes stared back at River, her mouth open agape. Her forehead had caved in on itself, blood and brains sticking to her dark hair.

A sudden bang made River turn, the cloth still caught between unsteady fingers. Shelly's ghost stood facing the opposite wall, wearing her maid's outfit. She leaned back, gaining momentum, and smashed her head against the wall. A second bang echoed. Blood spattered against the gray concrete. Shelly kept going, crushing and grinding her own skull. When she was done, she turned to River and looked at her with sad eyes, her face painted red by the blood gushing from her broken head.

"River." Thomas gently shook her shoulder.

River blinked the ghost away and looked at him, realizing he had been trying to get her attention.

"It's my fault..." she said, looking back at the decaying body, her eyes moist with tears. "If I had listened to Dorian and left, that wouldn't have happened to her."

Thomas took her hand away from the cloth, which fell back onto Shelly and hid her. "I know... It's awful..." He looked like he wanted to say something else, something compassionate or appropriate for the situation, but ended up squaring his shoulders. "Let's do this fucking thing. For her and everyone else."

River nodded and grabbed the golden rose tucked in her pocket. "Yeah. Let's do this fucking thing."

They headed to the red door. River hadn't taken the time to look the key over but now realized what it truly was: a doorknob. She lowered it and slid it into the thin keyhole. It fit perfectly. She pushed it until it could go no further, the rose tightly pressed against the markings in the wood. Her heart hammering her chest, River turned the doorknob slowly, and a sharp click echoed into the room. She watched the door drift open without moving or breathing. The room was impossibly dark, and when Thomas shone the light inside it, she took half a step back, secretly afraid something would jump at her.

But everything in the small, cold room kept still. A dark, wooden table stood opposite them, running the length of the wall and lined with black candles. Black lace covered it. It wasn't a simple table. It was an altar. Small rectangles were scattered on it, reflecting the light. It took River a moment to understand what she was looking at.

"That's us. That's all of us," Thomas said.

Pictures of the staff stared back at them. They looked like cut out driver's license pictures. But it wasn't all. River squinted at them. They seemed to hover above the altar. She took the flashlight and approached the pictures. They weren't hovering. Each of them had been stuck or glued onto little rag dolls, each picture acting like a face.

River bent over. A strange smell wafted out of the dolls. Seams ran up their legs, arms, and chest. She backed away slightly as a new wave of dizziness made her head spin.

"These are made of skin…"

"What's that?" Thomas said, pointing at one of the doll's chests.

Small pieces of tissues had been sewn into the skin. A brown smudge stained each one of them, bringing River back to the night she'd arrived and cut herself on the handle outside the staff's quarter. Edith sure had been quick to take that tissue out to pat the blood dry, which River had later thrown into the trash bin Edith had shown her.

"Thomas." She cleared her throat, but it refused to loosen. "Did you cut yourself on the handle the first time you got here?"

He nodded without looking back at her. "Roberts asked me to keep the door open for a moment."

"This is how Selene curses us… and kills us."

She dared advance closer to the shrine, shivering at the cold. Their pictures weren't there. Not anymore. Not when they were supposed to be dead. But the rest of the staff was present, along with the people of Stormhedge. But it wasn't all. The alter had three levels. Above the pictures and the dolls, three paintings rested on a higher, round shelf. These were bigger than the photographs, at least ten by fifteen inches. The one to the left represented Richard, his expression as smug as in real life. The picture in the center, which was a bit bigger than the others, was of Selene. Her dark eyes seemed to jump out of the picture. While some people could find her smile ravaging, on the painting it only looked wolfish.

Then, on the right was Dorian. He didn't look at them, re-fusing to acknowledge the person holding the paintbrush dipped in blood. The Blackwells dominated the pitiful pictures at the bottom, holding their lives inside their hands.

And above that shelf, one last layer. A cylinder towered above the paintings, covered in black lace and nothing else. River approached and squinted at the empty space.

"Isn't it odd? Shouldn't there be something up there?"

"Like what?" Thomas asked.

"I don't know…" Dread squeezed her insides the more she looked at the whole setup and at that empty shelf. Something was supposed to be there, she was sure of it.

"What if we burn the dolls and the pictures? You think that would work?" Thomas asked.

"No, it won't." Edith's stern voice made them swivel around.

She and Mack stood in the doorway, unmoving, a knife in her hand, him with an axe.

"The thing you're looking for isn't here," Mack said. "It's too bad, you missed it by only a few minutes. We can take you to it if you want." His eyes shone a malicious light. "It's upstairs. In the ballroom."

CHAPTER THIRTY-NINE

River's heart raced as she and Thomas were forced out of the room and into the passages. Her mind scrambled to find a solution, but nothing came to her. There was no way they could take on both Edith and Mack. Not Mack, at least. Fear squeezed her throat, but it didn't seem to stop Thomas.

"Why do you follow her orders?" he said, glancing back.

Edith made no reply, and when River glanced at her, the woman's expression was as stern as ever, but she thought she noticed a hint of doubt in them.

"Did you see our pictures out there?" Mack answered for her. "No. That's what we get. Safety."

"Quiet, Mack," Edith snapped.

River froze on the spot.

"Walk. *Now,*" Edith said.

River looked over her shoulder. "I saw your picture, Miss Roberts. Mack's wasn't there, but yours is."

Even in the subdued light, she saw Edith's face fall, her tight wrinkles slackening.

"How about that, Miss Roberts?" Thomas sneered. "Mack could have killed you when he bashed Dorian's head with a shovel."

Edith took a sharp step forward, eyes blazing, and shoved him. "Keep moving."

River grabbed Thomas's hand before he stumbled further, and the two of them walked side by side.

That didn't stop him from talking, though. *"Of course* she's not gonna put Mack's picture up there. Who else would cook such fine cuisine for her and feed the town dead bodies once a year? You truly are a catch, Mack."

Mack chuckled, unphased. "How did you survive, Thomas?"

"I'm a lucky bastard."

"Mm-hm. Or someone helped you. Didn't Luke say he'd take care of River, Edith?"

She stayed silent.

"I think he did. Did he help you too, kid?"

Thomas's fingers tightened in River's hand. A second later, he was wrenched away from her grasp as Mack grabbed his collar and yanked him back. He wrapped an arm around him, pressing the axe's blade against his throat.

"Don't hurt him!" River cried out. "Please."

"You want to know something funny?" Mack said in Thomas's ear, ignoring River. "The blood ritual wasn't always the way it is now. To protect themselves, the people of the town agreed to each give some of their blood to Selene, but once upon a time, a yearly sacrifice took place. What do you think we bring it back? Luke would be perfect."

All the wits and sarcasm slid off Thomas's face. "No… Please."

"Then, shut up and walk, asshole." Mack shoved him.

Thomas resumed his walk, head bowed. River gently grabbed his arm and felt him shake slightly. She gave him a gentle squeeze, a quiet way of saying everything would be all right, even if she couldn't promise something like that.

Mack and Edith took them through disorienting paths River had never walked before. They went up and down flights of stairs until they emerged from behind a painting located in the hallway, facing the ballroom. River's hope deflated. She'd thought they would have a chance to run, do something—*anything*—but next thing she knew, they were ushered inside the mansion's biggest room.

A heavy silence swallowed them as they stepped in. No music nor hushed voices floated in the darkened space. The lights had been muted, the day growing increasingly dark outside. The scene happening before River felt surreal.

The townspeople were kneeling on the floor, their heads bowed, forming a large circle. Selene stood in the center, her son a few feet behind her, desperation tightening his features. Richard was there, keeping close, a blood-stained cloth in his hand that he used to pat the gash on his forehead. His other hand was tightly clamped onto Dorian's arm as though wanting to prevent him from interrupting his mother. The Blackwells looked at them as they were ushered inside the room.

"What should we do with them?" Edith asked.

"Kill them," Richard sneered.

Dorian's head snapped up, eyes wild with panic.

"No," Selene snapped. "Watch him. Make sure he doesn't go anywhere," she said, vaguely gesturing toward Thomas before her dark eyes locked on River. She grinned a threatening, wolfish smile that sent shivers crawling down River's spine and raised an arm in her direction. "Come here, child. Step inside the circle."

Quiet murmurs travelled through the circle. Some of the townspeople even glanced over their shoulders to look at her. Selene snapped her fingers, bringing their attention back to her.

"Quiet."

Dorian's jaw worked. He tried to take a step forward, but Richard yanked him back. "Mother, what are you doing?"

"I said *quiet.*"

River glanced at Thomas, who glanced back, slightly shaking his head no. But she had no choice. Balling her fists, she stepped forward, squeezed between two men kneeling, and approached the intimidating woman. It was only then that she noticed the goblet Selene held in her hand. Its deep black reflected the low light. Golden markings ran around the edge, and the piece connecting the foot from the cup was a round, shiny ruby.

"On your knees before me," Selene said, looking impossibly tall perched on her high heels.

Her gaze going back and forth between the woman and her goblet, River slowly kneeled. *This* was the object missing from that room. It looked ancient, and she could almost feel evil energy buzzing from it.

"I know what you are wondering," Selene said, her voice like honey. "Yes, this is what I can only assume you have been looking for. It has been in my family for generations, but not everyone gets to use it."

Mack cleared his throat, getting the stink eye from Selene. "I'm sorry to interrupt, but there is a traitor in the room. Your ritual may be tainted with him in it."

Her heavy stare scanned each person present. They all seemed to shrink into themselves, their heads burrowing further between their shoulders. She stopped on Luke. "I should have known. Remove him."

Mack snatched Luke's collar, dragging him away from the group. River heard Thomas behind her, asking them not to hurt him.

"What are you *doing?*" Dorian said, straining against his uncle's grasp.

"Richard, make sure my son cannot ruin the moment."

Out of the blue, Richard swiveled around and planted his fist in Dorian's midsection, getting a gasp out of him, then shoved him to the floor.

River's eyes watered as she watched him struggle to catch his breath when a cold finger pressed under her chin and tilted her head up.

"I don't know what I'm going to do with you, but I'm sure you will be useful somehow. You are quite special, aren't you?" Selene looked her up and down. "In your own simple, peculiar sort of way. Would you like to know something? I was going to let Dorian have you. I would have allowed him to love you and would have allowed you to stay. To be a part of this family. At least for a while."

River's tongue felt heavy in her mouth.

"You see," Selene continued, "I've always wanted a girl, but after many failures, I was cursed with a boy. Only girls can carry this legacy. The men of our family aren't blessed with the dark magic that has been passed on for generations. It isn't like I haven't tried to teach him, but he is very stubborn, as most men are. I am not asking for the world here, just an heir. A granddaughter. But I need two consenting adults for this. I cannot simply keep one of the town's girls captive in a basement for nine months. Well, I could, but that isn't how it works. There needs to be a marriage for the girl to become a Blackwell. There needs to be compliance." She sighed. "You could have been the one, but you went and ruined it. Tried to go up against me. *Me.*" An amused laugh escaped her lips. "Although I found you and your little tricks irritating, I am willing to give you a second chance."

Dorian shifted on the floor. "River, whatever she says, don't listen to her."

Richard kicked him in the ribs, knocking the wind out of him.

"I'm offering you what you have been wanting, son," Selene said, raising her voice but not turning to look at him. "I could kill her on the spot, but I am willing to let her stay. You can marry her. Spend as much time as you want with her. You should be grateful."

"And then?" River's voice struggled to pass through her throat.

Selene cocked an eyebrow. "Then, what?"

"What happens to me after I give you a granddaughter? What happens to Dorian?"

The grin on the woman's face faded, leaving her dark eyes locked on River, eyes that looked like bottomless pits. She raised her hand and rotated it in a swift motion. A bright red light blinded River. Dark red flames licked the floor, forming a tight circle around her. They inched close, and before River could move or even talk, the flames caught on her dress and burned her legs. She screamed as white-hot pain coursed through her. The unnatural fire kept spreading, enveloping her chest and crawling over her arms. The room went blurry when it reached her neck, strangling her with indescribable pain that left her shrieking and crying.

She collapsed to the floor, her ears filled with the sound of her sobs. The pain was gone. The wood she lay on, though still hot to the touch, wasn't being consumed by blood red flames. She stayed curled up, terrified that Selene would truly burn her alive if she moved. The sounds of the room rose around her as she caught her breath. Dorian went back and forth between calling her name and begging his mother to leave her alone. Thomas was trying to say something as well, only to be shut down by Mack. Frightened sobs and whispers filled the circle of people around her.

"*Silence,*" Selene commanded.

The room went quiet—too quiet—except for River's shaky breaths and Dorian's voice. River opened her eyes and blinked the tears away. Horror sank its claws inside her chest. The men and women surrounding her had no mouths. Their lips had fused together. They looked like overgrown tissues burned and glued together. Fear and panic made them shake, their eyes wide and misty with tears, but none of them moved from their spots. None of them dared.

"For crying out loud, Dorian, be quiet or I'll sew your mouth shut too. Your girlfriend is fine."

Only when River heard those words did she look at her hands, her arms, her chest. There were no burns. Her skin and dress were intact.

Selene took a step forward and crouched gracefully, taking River's hand and pulling her to her feet. River stood on shaky legs.

"What say you, my dear? Burn alive now or stay here with your lover?"

"I—" River cleared her throat. The tears refused to stop coming out of her eyes, though she clenched her teeth to stay as quiet as she could. As quiet as a mouse. "I'll stay."

"Good. Let's begin, then. Daylight is fading fast, and we have a ritual to perform. Richard."

Richard left Dorian's side. He fished a small knife out of his pocket and handed it to Selene. River took a wobbly step back when Selene turned to her with it. She grabbed her forearm before she could go further.

"Let's start with you, dear. You are part of the town now after all. Don't move."

River's body felt suddenly stiff and heavy as though her blood had turned to lead. She helplessly watched the blade inch closer to her forearm and slice through her skin, making a two-inch gash. She clenched her teeth so hard it hurt, still intent on keeping herself quiet.

Selene tilted River's arm, letting the blood drip inside the goblet. As soon as she was released, River's body went limp, and her legs buckled under her. Selene paid no attention to her and turned away. Her red lips moved, whispering words River couldn't hear, as she went around the room, slicing through the skin of each person surrounding her. Some tried to keep quiet. Some let out a muffled, mouthless cry.

Dorian shuffled closer, searching for her. "River." He had pronounced her name so quietly she wouldn't have heard him over the sound of the rain and wind if she hadn't been looking at him.

"I'm here," she murmured back.

As soon as he found her, his arms enclosed her in a tight embrace.

"What are they gonna do to Thomas and Luke?" she whispered, resting her forehead in the crook of his neck.

Dorian's arms tightened around her, but he didn't answer, telling her everything she needed to know. Selene would simply kill them and incorporate them into her sick art. Their skin would be sliced and stuck on portraits, their blood would serve as paint, and their twisted bones would sit on fancy tables to decorate the hallways. Their ghosts would be bound to the Blackwell House forever, condemned to aimlessly walk its halls for centuries.

No.

River glanced at Richard. He was watching Selene go around the circle, his back to them. Selene was several feet away, still mumbling her incantation. River hoped she would be too far and too focused to listen to them. She straightened up and pressed her cheek against Dorian's, bringing her lips as close to his ear as possible.

"The goblet she's filling with blood," she murmured as low as she could. "I think that's it."

Dorian tilted his head to speak in her ear as well. "Even if it is, it will only break her curse on this land. On all of us. But her power is hers, and she won't go down without a fight."

River watched Selene. She made an incision into a woman's arm, who squeezed her eyes shut, her chin quivering under a lipless mouth. "What's going to happen when she's done?"

"I don't really know. I was never allowed to stay for the ritual back when I could see. She will finish reciting her incantation. And then something will happen just as the sun sets, but I could never see what."

Her eyes darted from Selene, the people, Thomas and Luke forced to sit in the back of the room, guarded by Mack and Edith, back to Selene and the goblet in her hands. The goblet was the answer, as well as the blood inside of it.

She could barely move. The spell cast on her still took hold of her legs. She might be able to stand, maybe, but walking or running weren't options just now. But stopping this crazy witch was still within reach.

She turned back to whisper in Dorian's ear. "Will you do something crazy and dangerous if I ask you to?"

He waited a beat before answering. "Yes."

River quickly told him what she wanted him to do. "I'll be your eyes. I'll tell you when."

"Dorian." Selene's voice resonated throughout the room, startling River out of his embrace. "It's time."

She waited for him expectantly, the goblet filled to the brim. Soon, River would either free the land and break the curse or be killed on the spot, burned alive by Selene's red, angry flames.

Or both.

CHAPTER FORTY

Selene raised the goblet high, mumbling. Richard and Dorian stood a step behind her, Richard's hand once again clamped around his nephew's arm. Though Dorian tried to relax his shoulders, River could see how tense his features looked. He was ready.

Selene swirled the blood inside the cup before bringing it back down. "Now, everyone, repeat after me."

After a flick of her hand, gasps of relief filled the room as the people of the town were given their mouths back.

"I give my life to the queen of the land," Selene said. Her voice was deep and bounced against the walls.

Men and women repeated after her, their tone shaky and hushed.

"I pledge my allegiance to the queen of the land."

The wind and the rain, which was starting to turn to hail, slapped the windows outside. The townspeople repeated Selene's words.

"My blood, my body, my mind belong to the queen of the land."

The voices rose once more. The lights flickered, then went out, plunging the ballroom into the darkness. Red flames burst through the floor, forming a circle. River's stomach flipped at the sight of them, but she quickly realized they weren't touching her. Selene stood right in the middle of them, red fire licking the base of her gown. It sent sharp shadows playing over her features, and in that light, she didn't look beautiful but old, incredibly old, her black eyes devoid of emotions. They looked like the empty sockets of a skull.

"In exchange for your loyalty, the queen of the land shall grant you resources in abundance."

She dipped her index inside the cup, swirling some more. When she took it out, her finger was coated with a black, thick liquid. Her glassy eyes closed as she raised the goblet to her lips.

"Dorian, now!" River shouted.

He had been ready for her command. Dorian wrenched his arm out of Richard's grip and pounced away from him. He crashed into his mother hard enough to throw her to the floor. She went sprawling, the goblet flying from her hand and its liquid flying from it. River gave every bit of strength she had to push on her knees and snatch the goblet mid-air, then dropped back to the floor. She expected the black blood to splash all over her and onto the floor, but instead, its consistency changed, thickening into a sickening gunk that bounced right back inside its container as though pulled by an invisible force. It quivered back into its original texture, swirling inside the goblet. After a stunned second of staring at this atrocity, River raised the goblet, ready to smash it to the floor.

Selene snapped her head up and flicked her hand. Red flames burst from the ground, their sizzling heat burning River's skin.

"If you burn me, I'll smash it!" she shouted.

To her surprise, the flames didn't inch closer. Selene glared daggers at her.

"Don't be stupid, little girl. Even if you broke it, I could still kill you and everyone in this room in an instant." She pushed onto her hands to pick herself up but didn't get back to her feet, each movement slow and calculated. "You will break the curses. All of them. But you will also lift the magic keeping this land alive. Everything will die and rot."

River's fingers tightened around the goblet, her arm shaking.

A smirk twisted Selene's lips. "What do you think will happen to Dorian?"

River glanced at him, now restrained by Richard.

"Do you think you can save him?" Selene continued. "You won't. He has died too many times. Once the curse is lifted, his body will go back to the state it was meant to be. *Dead.*"

"I don't care, River. Do it!" Dorian yelled.

"He will die, and then I will kill you and your friends, and I will just do all the rest again. So, think *really* hard about your next move, little girl."

Overwhelming despair filled River. She couldn't let him die. No matter how much she wanted to free him and everyone, the thought that he would drop dead as soon as she smashed that goblet held her back, making her arm as heavy as stone.

"Put it down, and no one will be hurt. I promise."

River slowly brought her shaking hand down.

"River, *please*," Dorian pleaded.

The wolfish smile stretched Selene's lips. "That's it. We still have some time to finish the ritual. Now give it to me." She stretched her arm, fingers splayed open, nails resembling sharp claws. Eagerness distorted her features. Her teeth were bared, and her eyes looked too big for her face.

River glanced one last time at the black liquid swirling in the goblet. She inhaled a sharp breath, brought the cup to her lips, and gulped its acrid content. It slithered down her throat, making her gag.

"No!" Selene roared.

The goblet slipped from River's grasp. The fire around her flared, engulfing her completely. Just as the white-hot pain blasted through her, and she opened her mouth to scream, a surge of energy rippled through her, filling her entirely.

She shut her eyes, swaying for a moment. The pain was gone. Static buzzed in her ears. River opened her eyes and stared through the flames at the goblet in front of her, stuck mid-air.

Not stuck.

It was falling so slowly that she almost couldn't distinguish it. The fire around her receded, crawling back into the earth. Selene reached a hand toward her, her eyes so wide River could see each vein snaking through her eyeballs. She looked frozen in time. Like everyone around River. Like the hail battering the windows outside, creating this deep static sound like a wave crashing in slow motion.

Power coursed through her. After looking around her and seeing the terror on each of the townspeople's face, after gazing at Dorian, who had never backed down despite the atrocities his mother had done to him, after glancing over her shoulder at

Thomas and Luke, who would no doubt be murdered if she didn't act now, River closed her eyes once more and thought about her grandma and everything she had ever loved. About the next world that trusted her enough to reach out to her. About Ireland and Willow's favorite coffee shop.

Warm waves like electricity travelled through her arms and gathered in her hands. She pressed her palms against the floor and opened her eyes. She conjured the tree roots and the damp earth under the house.

Time accelerated, adjusting back to its natural pace. Lights flickered. The wind and hail assaulted the windows. Selene lunged at River.

The floor cracked and crumbled like dirt under River's fingers. A fissure snaked from it and ran the length of the room. Before Selene could touch River, thick roots shot out of the floor and snatched her by the ankles. She slammed against the cracked floor. The roots dragged her back, growing and curling around her body and arms.

The crowd around her screamed and scampered away. Richard let go of Dorian, mesmerized. He took a step back but didn't have time to go anywhere before the floor cracked open under his feet and fresh roots sprouted upward. He struggled as they snaked around him and restricted him. Their thorns snagged against his clothes and scratched his skin.

Dorian fell to his knees, shaken by the earth splitting under his feet. He seemed frightened, not understanding what was happening around him. Through the chaos of people scrambling away and running out of the room, a man went against the current, forcing his way in. Luke. He skidded to a stop next to Dorian and helped him up, then dragged him away.

River's vision blurred. The surge coming out of her had a will of its own, and she let it flow freely. The earth trembled. The lights shattered. The windows exploded, the sound of the storm outside deafening. Rain and ice flooded the space, raindrops splashing River. Roots and ivy snaked over the walls. They strangled and fissured the stone.

The people's screams faded slightly as they ran outside. River glanced over her shoulder in time to see Mack and Edith running out of the ballroom like everyone else, their eyes opened so wide it looked like they were going to pop out of their sockets. River's fingers tightened into the ground. Roots shot out and curled around their legs. The image of Mack bashing Dorian's head with a shovel jumped back at her, and the root wrapped around Mack's ankle lifted him from the floor. It swung him around as he screamed, then threw him to the other side of the room. His body crashed against a wall before falling back like a limp slab of meat.

Her eyes darted to Richard's face. She clenched her teeth. Ivy coiled around his neck. The tiny thorns poked his skin, drops of blood staining them.

Selene twisted and struggled, only allowing the thorns to dig deeper into her skin. The more she moved, the more the rosebush branches became tangled in her dress, refusing to let her go.

"You fucking bitch!" she screamed, though her voice barely rose about the chaos.

Dust rained from the ceiling. The majestic chandelier swung until its chain snapped. It crashed, sinking under the surface of the house as though stuck in quicksand. The remaining floorboards under River shifted. The walls crumbled under the pressure of the nature choking it. Thorned stems slithered through the portraits, tearing them apart.

River knew the roots and ivy and thorns were ravaging the whole house from basement to attic, infesting its hallways and rooms to clean it of all its sins.

Thomas and Luke would get everyone out. She trusted them to alert the staff and make sure Dorian was safe.

Portraits fell off the walls. The floor under the piano moved and cracked as it spit out a huge rosebush. Its branches enveloped the magnificent instrument and strangled it until it snapped in half, letting out its last few, agonizing notes as it crumbled onto itself.

The ground rippled, the house shook. In all the chaos, a hand grabbed her shoulder, fingers digging into her skin and startling her. Arms circled her from behind, and she knew it was him. Why wasn't he outside?

Dorian hung onto her, making her realize how much worse the hail and the wind had become as they fought for dominance. She, on the other hand, was rooted to the floor, the earth keeping her safe and stable.

"River!" He had to shout even as he leaned close to her ear. "Where is the goblet?"

Her eyes darted to the shiny object. It was right there in front of her, stuck between two roots. Dorian only had to stretch his arm to grab it, had he been able to see it.

"You need to destroy it!"

Her hands burrowed further into the earth, fresh dirt sticking to her skin. "You'll die!"

"I don't care!"

"*I* do!"

Roots kept growing and wrapping themselves around everything they touched. Selene twisted furiously still. Red flames kept bursting from the floor, only to be killed by rain and dirt.

Dorian's arms tightened around her waist. His forehead rested against her soaked hair. "River, please. I need this to end."

Through the icy raindrops, a warm tear made her way down her cheek. She pulled a dirty hand from the fresh soil and reached for the goblet. The roots parted as she pulled on it, granting her access.

"It's right here."

Dorian's fingers tickled her arm as they ran down to her hand, gentle and soft. He felt for the goblet and squeezed her hand. "It will be all right."

River's throat closed up, sobs strangling her.

"I love you," he said.

"I love you too."

He took the goblet from her grip, raised it, and smashed it to the ground.

CHAPTER FORTY-ONE

T ime slowed to a crawl like it had earlier. River watched the fissures snake through the goblet in slow motion. It shattered as it connected with the floor, tiny specks flying outward. A sharp edge cut into Dorian's hand. A drop of blood pebbled from the cut.

The loud buzzing sound was silenced when a sudden wave of energy surged from the broken goblet. It rammed into River and Dorian hard enough to knock them down and rippled through the entire house, shaking its walls.

Darkness. Cold. So cold. Shivers shook her. The wind whistled softly through the windows and the cracks, the rain now reduced to a slow drizzle. River remained curled up on the broken floor, feeling weak and empty. It could have been a minute or an hour before she finally opened her eyes. Dorian lay next to her, unmoving. She reached out to him when a coughing noise startled her into a sitting position.

The room was ravaged by nature.

At the back, Mack sat up, his mouth hanging open as he looked around him. Richard coughed some more.

Edith shifted at River's back. "What have you done?" It almost sounded like she was worried about having to clean up the mess, though no one would ever have to clean up this place ever again.

Kicking limp roots and wrenching ivy from her, Selene struggled to her feet, her ponytail not so tight anymore. Black hair hung around her face, the red on her lips was smeared, her gown was in shreds, and her eyes full of hatred looked feral. She straightened up, looking down on River.

"Very impressive," she panted. "But you missed your chance to kill me. You aren't as smart as you think you are."

Mist rolled into the room, making River shudder. It came from the broken windows and the door and from the wrecked ground. Whispers rose from the fog. Quiet voices cackled. Others sobbed.

River rose to her feet, noticing her shoes had fallen off sometime in the process. Her feet made contact with the fresh earth. Mist danced around her ankles. "I'm not a murderer."

Disembodied voices echoed around them, and Selene seemed to notice them this time. Her eyes darted from side to side. Blurry silhouettes floated through the gloom, drawing closer to the witch.

A sad smile stretched River's lips. "Plus, I think *they* want to have a word with you."

A painting scraped against the uneven floor, making them turn. The face portrayed bore a wide, unnatural smile, showing only teeth. A hand pressed against the canvas and shot out of the frame. The face emerged, the skin stretching and splitting as the spirit moaned. The deformed body clawed at the ground with one arm, dragging its canvas. Other paintings emerged from the mist. Some had pushed both arms out, dragging their decayed bodies still attached to the frames. They moaned and groaned as they approached Selene, their mouths opened and drooling at the sight of her, their eyes so wide they looked almost entirely white. They shook their heads in anticipation.

Other spirits gathered around Richard and Mack. River saw Shelly, her head caved in, walk toward Mack, carrying a shovel. Cassie was there, her throat slashed and her fingers gripping a knife. The landscaper tightened the rope around Richard's neck, killing the rising scream in his throat while Cassie compulsively plunged the blade in his chest. Mack shuffled away as Shelly raised the shovel above his head. He didn't make it far before she brought it down, crushing his skull into a pulp.

Edith screamed. River turned in time to see a maid punching Edith's chest so hard her fist tore through it. Her arm rotated both ways until Edith dropped dead. River realized who she was. This was the maid that had died when Selene had given Dorian a heart attack for trying to flee, the one River had met on her very first night in the dormitory.

"No! *No!*"

Selene's cry snapped River's attention back to her. The grotesque paintings had reached her. They clawed at her gown and legs. Selene tried to run away, but the tangled limbs forced her to the ground. They pulled at her hair and body, dirty nails digging into her skin. The rest of the ghosts gathered around. There were so many, River couldn't even count them. They held familiar objects. Objects she had seen in Selene's art room. A scalpel and scissors to cut the skin. A mallet to break the bones. Pliers to pull out teeth. Cutting blades to shape the bones into the desired aspect. One carried a chain, from which a hook dangled.

They pounced on Selene, their dead bodies drowning hers. Her ear-splitting shrieks forced River to look away. She dropped to her knees next to Dorian and leaned over him into the mist, her forehead resting against his chest and her palms pressed to her ears. The screeching went on for so long she thought it would never stop. It churned her stomach and clawed at her chest. She just wanted it to be over with.

The howls of pain turned into weak moans before they finally stopped. River lifted her head carefully, and her heart stopped. A ghost leaned over Dorian's body. She wrapped her arms around him, desperate to protect him even if he was dead.

"Please, not him. It wasn't his fault. He didn't know."

She dared to look at the figure. Benjamin towered over them. He kneeled next to his son and squeezed his shoulder, smiling.

Dorian's eyes fluttered open. He blinked several times, then frowned. "Dad?"

Benjamin's misty form disappeared, billowing away into the atmosphere.

Dorian shot up. "Dad!"

River's mouth fell open. "Dorian?"

He looked at her, and she gasped at the unfamiliar, dark brown eyes staring at her. He blinked a few times, his gaze darting all over the place, a range of emotions crossing his features as he realized only now that he could see. He rose to his feet and slowly turned in a circle, in awe of everything he saw. River stood next to him, both fascinated and anxious. Dorian looked back at her finally, his expression unreadable.

"Are you okay?" she said, wondering what he saw, what he felt, what he thought of her. Was he happy? Relieved? Disappointed by the person that now stood before him?

A smile stretched his lips, illuminating his whole face. The sadness and the worry had vanished. He looked young and careless. He began laughing, his brown eyes misting over. He wrapped his arms around River's waist and held her tighter than he ever had. "You did it." He lifted her off the floor. "You did it!"

The room spun. River hung on to him, letting out a high-pitched squeal. Dorian put her down and gazed at her.

"Well," she said, "technically, it's you who did it."

He cupped her jaw and leaned in for a long kiss. "I could not have done it without you."

The leftover mist slowly died down and revealed the carnage left by the ghosts. Dorian's face fell. River looked in the same direction, at the body lying in a heap of dirt and broken canvases. Dorian took a tentative step, but River caught his hand.

"You don't have to see it."

"I do. I want to make sure."

She let him go. She couldn't bring herself to get closer to Selene's body. Though a few lights had survived the storm, the room stayed relatively dark, and what she could make out from her position was more than enough. The tools the ghosts had used on Selene were scattered around, soaked in blood. The torn frames lay limp. So much blood covered Selene, her eyes, her mouth, her neck, her feet, that River couldn't distinguish where her red gown began and ended. She was reduced to a skinless pulp.

Dorian hovered over her for a moment. Despite all the things his mother had done to him, it couldn't be easy, seeing her like this. He seemed to notice Richard and Mack further away, then searched for Edith in the wreckage. His lips straightened into a tight line when he found her.

"I wish she had made different choices. Better ones. The spirits would have spared her." He let out a ragged breath. "Let's get out of here."

River grabbed her shoes and took his hand. The hallway leading out was as much a disaster as the ballroom. Dirt overflowed onto the floor. The carpet and floorboards had been demolished by roots. None of the paintings remained pinned on the walls, though a few mirrors still hung on for dear life. Ivy clung to every surface, up to the ceiling, little leaves shivering in the breeze.

"Well…" Dorian gazed at the scene. "I like what you've done with the place."

"It was lacking plants."

"Are they gone?" he said, helping her slip under an overflowing rosebush hanging from the staircase. "The spirits."

"Yes." No doubt lingered in her mind about that. The air felt lighter, easier to breathe. No whispers echoed within the walls. "Breaking the goblet freed them from the curse. Getting their revenge helped them move on."

"My dad is in peace, then."

"Yes."

The double doors ahead were wide open. The chandelier in the massive foyer had half sunk through the floor. Leaves, roots, and thorns ran along the staircase, ravaging the banister in some places.

The large dressing room holding all the coats stood open as well, and River grabbed her coat before heading out, a simple gesture that felt out of place. People waited outside, their voices loud as they pointed at the house. River looked up. It looked like the house had shrunk in on itself, strangled by bright green ivy. None of the windows had survived. Large roots had knocked bricks out of their sockets.

The voices ceased as soon as Dorian stepped outside. Everyone turned to him, their mouths agape. The staff was here too. River was grateful they all got out unscathed.

"Freckles!" Thomas ran up the few steps to meet her. "Are you okay?"

"Yes. It's over. They're all…" She cleared her throat. "Gone. Are *you* okay?"

He scoffed, as though the question was stupid. "That shit was wild. I'd go see a doctor if I were you because you drank the blood of, like, dozens of people, so…"

"It's good to see you, Thomas," Dorian said, catching his attention.

Thomas stared at him for a moment. Then, a baffled laugh tumbled out of his mouth. "It's nice to see you too. And to be seen."

"Really, Dorian?" Luke said, joining them. "All you had to do was grab the fucking cup. You could have guessed."

Dorian glared at Luke for a moment before a tight smile lifted his lips. "Call me stupid, I didn't see it."

Luke chuckled, and his expression softened. "I'm glad you're okay."

Dorian pulled him into a hug, patting his back. "You too."

The exchange warmed River's heart. After all they had been through, their friendship could be healed.

Dorian pulled away and scanned the crowd. They all stared at him, terrified or lost or both. He made a point of making eye-contact with everyone. River could feel something bubbling in him. Anger, resentment, sadness. But in the end, he let out a long exhale, giving up on whatever he'd been wanting to say.

"Selene Blackwell is dead. Nothing is keeping you here anymore. This town will slowly die. Go home or anywhere you want." He glanced up at the house one last time. "Feel free to loot the house. I hope we never see each other again."

He took River's hand and climbed down the steps. Thomas and Luke followed. The crowd parted to let them through. River shivered in the wind, drops of water clinging to her still wet clothes. She released a breath of relief, knowing she would never have to come back to the Blackwell House.

EPILOGUE

DORIAN

We had to go back to the house. I hated the idea of it, but River needed to retrieve her things, her car keys and car most of all. She and Thomas insisted I didn't have to go with them, but I couldn't let her out of my sight. Didn't want to. So, we went back. The house was as much of a disaster as when we had left it. It smelled of humidity and rot. It was bizarre, being there. This was the only home I'd ever known. I had walked these halls my whole life. But I felt estranged from it now.

We found River's things in my mother's room. She had kept the crystals and the tarot deck, out of curiosity I'm sure. River's coat was there as well, the car keys tucked inside the pocket. We left, wondering if her small car would survive the rocky forest road, but we made it to Stormhedge and to Luke's place. The town was quiet now. Eerie. Most people had left. Some of them even seemed mad about it.

I sure wasn't. I'd never felt anything like I did the day we drove away, following Luke and Thomas's car. River kept glancing at me while driving, asking me if I was okay. I knew she was concerned about me being so quiet, but the truth was that I couldn't stop looking out the window. I was afraid that if I closed my eyes for too long, I would wake up in the house and see nothing but darkness. Each new road, landscape, and town fascinated me, intimidated me almost.

Now, two years later, I wished I could say that I was as integrated in society as other people were, but I was not. Not really. Luke was right to think I would be pathetically clueless, his words. I realized that my upbringing had severely hindered my social skills. I often didn't understand why people did or said certain things. I didn't know how to react, whether they were nice to me or not. River told me this was called being socially awkward, and there was nothing really wrong about it. I wasn't the only one in this case.

I looked at her now as she gave a customer her tea and a piece of apple crumble cake, one of her bestsellers at Willow's Celtic Cup. The sun flowed through the windows, illuminating her wild, ginger hair. She smiled that genuine smile and wished the customer a great day, and I found myself smiling too. How could you not have a good day after seeing that freckled face and such a brilliant smile?

River had been my rock. So much so that I was afraid to become a burden, to lose her one day when she realized that nothing could fix me. I mostly had good days, and I'd never felt so close to anyone before. We did everything together. She'd dragged me around, showing me as many places as possible. I wanted to visit it all. We had endless conversations. I loved being with her and working with her every day. We went to the movies a lot. Movies had become a consuming passion. I still liked to read, but movies fascinated me. I couldn't get enough of them.

But some nights, I still woke up in a frenzy, thinking I was back at the house, alone and blind. It must be awful, being woken up by a hysterical man shouting your name in the dark. I always felt like an idiot afterwards. But River had a calming effect on me. She simply turned on the light, showing me that I could still see, that she was still there. She wrapped her arms around me and whispered in my ear that everything was fine. It wasn't fair to her. She had her own trauma to process, and I hoped she knew she could lean on me as much as I leaned on her.

I finished cleaning the tables and tidied the bookshelf. I didn't forget to make sure the board game corner was orderly without disturbing the few people playing and laughing together. I quite liked those games. It reminded me of when I played with Luke as a kid. Things like *Connect 4* and *Snakes and Ladders.* They made much more complex games today, and I was again grateful River had the infinite patience to explain to me how to play all of them. The satisfaction of beating Luke the last time he came, all smug and over-confident, was quite sweet.

Luke and Thomas lived close by. After the four of us living together in a two-bedroom apartment for months to share the rent, you would think that we couldn't stand each other anymore. If anything, it brought us closer. The money Thomas and River had earned while working for my family had mysteriously vanished from the bank. As though that money was only real as long as my mother was alive, and as long as it was spent in Stormhedge. It was one of the reasons River wanted to go back and retrieve her car. She couldn't afford a new one. Thomas and Luke didn't hesitate to look for objects to sell inside the house, at least what they could find. The townspeople had already almost emptied it.

We struggled at first. We settled for any job. I tried to find things that wouldn't require me to talk to too many people. We ate cheap fast foods, counted every dime while grocery shopping, and for the first time in my life, I was truly happy. I wasn't even ashamed to admit I gained a bit of weight that first year, which I now lost. I wanted to eat all the sweet and greasy foods I'd been deprived of my whole life. I always got the urge to grab one of River's Guinness chocolate cupcakes before she even put them on display.

Some customers left, and I gathered their cups when the door opened. A man with brown hair walked in. He looked around the place for a moment, then his face lit up when his eyes landed on River.

"Hey," he simply says, a word both trite but charged with something I couldn't quite put my finger on.

She raised her head, her eyebrows shooting up to her hairline. "Zach?"

"The one and only."

"Hi."

He came up to the counter, gazing around the space again. "Wow. When I saw the pics on Insta, I couldn't believe it."

She cocked an eyebrow. "You mean you still follow me?"

"Sure. I sent you messages too, but you never answered."

"Well, I've been busy. A lot has happened in two years."

He smiled a flirty smile that tied my stomach into knots. "I bet. I'd love to grab a cup of coffee sometime. To catch up."

I stared like a psychopath while she talked to him. I had no idea what to do, or if I should even do anything at all. Despite the burning sensation in my chest, I trusted her. Staying away was probably best.

She shook her head. "I'm really busy."

My resolve disintegrated when Zach leaned over the counter. "Come on, for old times' sake. I'll make it worth your while."

My feet carried me there without my knowledge.

"Um…" River said, and I knew she was trying hard not to hurt his feelings because she was good like that. Gentle. I would be happy if she told him to fuck off. "I don't think that's a good idea."

"I won't take no for an answer."

I dropped my tray loudly and stood next to River, hooking an arm around her waist. "You're gonna have to."

Zach's face fell, giving me the sweetest satisfaction. Turned out I was jealous. And petty.

He pushed away from the counter, eyeing me from head to toe. "And you are?"

River spoke before I did. "This is my boyfriend. Dorian. We run this place together."

A warm rush went through me at those words. I hadn't considered myself as a partner in this coffee shop, merely an assistant who did all he could do to help. I tightened my arm and looked at her. She looked up at me with her dark, watery blue eyes, her freckled nose wrinkling as she smiled. A hair clip held the top half of her hair behind her head, but strands of curly, ginger hair had broken free and framed her face. If we were alone, I would kiss her, but I had to resist the urge a little longer.

I turned back to Zach. "Anything you need for the road?"

A bitter smile lifted the corner of his lips. "Sure. Matcha green tea will do. No sugar."

River threw me amused side glances while I made Zach his tea.

I slammed it onto the counter when I was done. "Anything to eat?"

"Nah. I take care of my health."

"Good for you."

He turned to River, cocking his head. A poor attempt at charming her. "On the house? For old times' sake?"

Ah, the old times' sake again.

"Sure," River said.

Zach grabbed the cup, his eyes darting from River to me. "You could be nicer to your customers."

"You're not paying. You're not a customer."

"Right." He gave River a little wave. "Congrats on opening the coffee shop. And good luck with that guy." He exited, the door bouncing shut behind him.

When I looked at River, she was biting back on a smile. "What?" I said, though I knew perfectly well.

"You were jealous."

"Obviously."

She stood in front of me. "You're not even denying it?"

"He's a prick. I have no regrets."

She laughed, which was always music to my ears. "And yet you made him his green tea."

I leaned forward and said in her ear, "I used one of the cheap bags, not the real matcha."

She laughed some more, wrapping her arms around my neck. I held her tight and breathed in the scent of her shampoo.

She pulled away. "Ready for our trip? I can't wait." Her eyes lit up, the way they always did when she talked about Ireland.

"You think Luke and Thomas will be okay running this place on their own?"

"They'll be fine. Luke knows what he's doing."

We'd worked hard to save for that trip, and I couldn't wait. There were so many things she wanted to show me, so many things I wanted to discover. I would never have put so much distance between me and Stormhedge, and I liked the idea. We were already far enough. The landscape here was entirely different. The town we lived in, while fairly small, was still bigger and more dynamic than Stormhedge ever was. It was lush and green, and we couldn't hear the ocean.

But sometimes, dark, intrusive thoughts seeped through the edge of my consciousness. What if I turned into someone I didn't want to be? What if our children were cursed by my mother's power, should we choose to have any? What if she wasn't dead?

No one could survive what the spirits did to her. I saw her dead body with my own eyes. But we hadn't touched it. No one had. Months after the curse was lifted, the word had gotten out about a ghost town called Stormhedge and a mysterious house at the edge of the cliff. The house has been protected by magic for centuries, keeping people away, until now. Quite a few people explored it, putting pictures on the internet or making YouTube videos. The four of us watched those videos. It made me sick, seeing those halls again, but I had to. What had once been my home was now an internet sensation.

No one ever reported anything about a body. Or bodies. No one had ever been able to even *reach* the ballroom. The hallway leading to it and to the staff's quarters collapsed under the weight of the growing vegetation. What River did that day didn't die. It sprouted and flourished and grew, taking more and more space and ravaging the bowels of the house. I knew skeletons were now buried under a mass of rosebushes, moss, and leaves.

A few of those YouTubers reported hearing strange noises and voices. Objects fell while they were exploring. I'd obsessively watched those videos too, trying to figure out if they were fake or if new spirits had taken the place of the dead staff, of my father. River, Thomas, and Luke eventually convinced me—forced me—to stop watching or reading about it. I listened. But if my mother was now haunting the Blackwell House, those explorers had better leave that place alone and never step foot in it again.

"You've got that look again," River said, snapping me out of my thoughts.

I cleared my throat. "Just lost in thought."

She fished one of her crystals from her pocket and placed it in my hand. "It'll make you feel better."

I looked at the pink stone in my hand. These saved her in the past, saving me in return.

"She's gone, Dorian."

She was right, but PTSD was a bitch. I knew that's all it was. Trauma. I didn't think I'd ever forget. Nightmares would never stop plaguing my nights. I didn't tell River, but I was still scared of mirrors. Every time I looked at them, I thought I saw my mother's face, merged with mine. I saw her features in my features, a reminder that I was a Blackwell, and that darkness would always be a part of me.

I looked at River now. The sun streaming through the windows at her back gave her an angelic look. We had been through a lot together, and I was proud of her for accomplishing so much in so little time.

"I love you," I said.

She cocked her head, a bit taken aback, but smiled. "I love you too."

Thomas and Luke arrived to start their shift and let us go. Thomas seemed happy enough to work here for as long as he could, though Luke would probably want to change careers at some point, which wasn't surprising. He'd been doing this job for years after all.

We left the shop, hand in hand, and walked onto the busy street. The sun was warm, and River's hand was soft in mine. She was bubbling with energy, telling me about all the things we'd do in Ireland and how she couldn't wait to get on the plane. I was both excited and terrified to fly, but it'd be all right.

I had my issues, my emotional baggage as Thomas called it, but River was here to keep me stable, rooted to the ground. My past was dark, but as long as her light shone over me and guided my path, the darkness would stay away, allowing me to become the person I wanted to be—Dorian, co-owner of Willow's Celtic Cup with his future wife River, who he intended to propose to during their trip to Ireland.

Made in the USA
Las Vegas, NV
06 July 2024